WAITING FOR THE WORLD TO END

WAITING FOR THE WORLD TO END

❀

Nicole Hunter

iUniverse, Inc.
New York Lincoln Shanghai

Waiting for the World to End

iUniverse, Inc.

For information address:
iUniverse, Inc.
2021 Pine Lake Road, Suite 100
Lincoln, NE 68512
www.iuniverse.com

ISBN: 0-595-32917-9

Printed in the United States of America

Contents

❀

CHAPTER 1

✤

Fog and Light

If you were a fly on the wall, on any given evening you would see Thomas Olsen standing alone at his kitchen sink, looking out his window at the Indiana sky and drinking a bottle of beer. You would see a hot dog in a bun lying on the counter (no plate) in the process of being eaten, or Chinese takeout in little white boxes, fork handles sticking up from the food like funny divers. Depending on the night, you would hear Olsen laugh, maybe say, "Rakowsky!" even though no one else was there, or swear and pound the counter, or most likely stand there silent. You would see him wave out the window to old Mr. McCormick in the back yard next door. You would see him not calling Kristina back. All in all, not what Thomas Olsen would have expected the prime of his life to look like.

Anyone who's ever suffered for love would understand that Olsen had a song for Mary—not the kind that makes two people beam at each other and turn the radio up and say *They're playing our song*, but the kind you keep to yourself.

It's not that Olsen was a big Hendrix fan to start with—but when he heard the song one day, first time in years, he said to himself, **That guy just told my story.**

> *A broom*
> *is drearily sweeping*
> *up the broken pieces*
> *of yesterday's life.*

Somewhere a queen is weeping
Somewhere a king has no wife
And the wind
it cries
Mary

A sportswriter looking for a lively angle on high school basketball coaching would have a hard time working Thomas Olsen's quotes into his story. He'd ask Olsen concrete journalistic questions like, "How did being one of the top college players of your era lead you into high school coaching? What do you like most about coaching kids? What's your #1 piece of advice for boys who want to take basketball to the next level?"

But Thomas Olsen would answer the writer with questions. "What do you love to do?" he would ask. "What are you so confident of within yourself that when they call for volunteers in a crisis, you rush calmly to the front of the crowd and say, Stand aside please, I'll take care of this. What gift do you command so well that you never worry about the competition? You can't wait to get in the ring. And the rush is beyond adrenaline—it's your essence, it's the deepest part of who you are—and the whole point is to share that, to pass it on."

Oh, well—maybe the sportswriter could use the "adrenaline" phrase.

Thomas Olsen would be the first to admit that he didn't have the happiest childhood. That would be the truth. Then he would say it didn't much matter, so nonchalantly anyone would believe him.

He would say he was born in Newport, Rhode Island, and grew up among the bluebloods in Wellesley, Massachusetts, that his father and mother were economists, golf nuts, professors at Northeastern and Wellesley. He would say he went to prep school at Andover, graduated from Ohio State, played Big Ten basketball for them, too, then tacked on a master's in world mythologies for the fun of it. That he dreamed of college coaching but wanted to teach, too—so after some years of circuitous dabblings, he eventually ended up as English department chair and head basketball coach at Indian River High in Indiana. And most people would think he had done pretty well for himself.

That wouldn't be the whole story. Olsen would have left out important parts, like the fact he arrived in the world an only child swaddled in the souls of populist ancestors—a child who knew early on that he was an outsider, kindred in IQ but not in spirit with his patrician parents. He would not mention how he grew up bobbling the aristocratic torch John and Louise Olsen had expected to hand off to him. Or how Olsen's just being himself provoked equal parts disinterest and fury in them—until he finished up at Ohio State, and the three of them buried their bygones in the sensible prudence of getting along.

Two memories Olsen never thought of anymore. As if they had never happened. First, his mother's refrain through his growing-up years that the hospital must have made a mistake and given her the wrong baby to take home (spoken through tight lips or punctuated with her one-syllable laugh). Second, the spring break when John and Louise forgot to pick Olsen up at Andover (they were golfing in Hilton Head) and his English teacher drove him home to Wellesley, and Olsen broke a basement window to get in.

"So what? You got jerks for parents—screw 'em," the jaded, pragmatic types might say. And Olsen would agree: "Right, so what? You grow up, and it just doesn't matter anymore." He made it easy to believe that was exactly how he felt. How could anyone have known that his body and soul had learned to lead separate lives?

Thomas Olsen would never reveal the abortion. Strapped into one of those medieval torture machines or burning at the stake for want of a confession, he would just look up at the sky, his face a blank, and never say a word.

Some choices dog a man's days forever, some choices he knows are utterly wrong even as he is opening his lips and moving his tongue and saying *Yes*, even as the voice inside him is screaming *No, don't do it*, but by then it's too late to reach back into the picture of his life and set things straight.

That's how it was for Olsen when he and Alexandra agreed on the abortion. Back when they were both 23 and occupied, each pursuing a graduate degree at Ohio State. Back when the time wasn't right for them, simple as that. Back when they were engaged, with their wedding date set on the far horizon, and plenty of years ahead to have children.

Olsen wouldn't say how he accompanied Alexandra to the clinic, as all good men did.

Or how after the abortion Alexandra carried on in her focused, cut-and-dried way, but he started to see his life passing before his eyes. Everywhere he looked. Even when he was sleeping: bottomless nights streaming with the jagged edges of a lullaby, tiny footprints like drops of blood across his pillow, a torch lifted high then snuffed in water, the sound of breaking glass, and his own eyes staring back at him.

And when he woke up, there was always Alexandra: brilliant blonde high-speed glacier, smooth and powerful and wearing down everything in her path. To Alexandra, nothing stayed a problem for long. Ah, to be more like her.

He called the wedding off.

If people had told Thomas Olsen that lots of women have abortions, and reminded him that he and Alexandra had not made the decision lightly, so he should get over it and get on with his life like everybody else did—he would have felt like ripping their throats out. How much wiser it was for him to never mention it at all.

Indian River High School parents wanted their children to have Thomas Olsen for English. They made special calls to the guidance counselors when schedules were being drawn up. Because Olsen was the best. Arriving in town at 30, he had resuscitated the high school's gasping English department—and endeared himself to the basketball lovers, because he had also christened a new era of Indian River basketball brilliance. And Olsen had indulged the best of the city's female population with an intimate piece of his body—but that was all the women got. He couldn't explain to them that his soul dwelled in silence somewhere else, somewhere far away. (He was not certain where.) Kristina had once aspired to be Olsen's salvation; but as Indian River years rolled by, she settled for something considerably less.

Student teachers under Olsen's tutelage learned his way of picking poems for senior lit class. He would tell them, "First you have to think about what kids are interested in and find poems about those things. Then you read them. At home. Out loud. It's what you'll do in your classroom. Go out on your porch or your deck and read them out loud. Don't worry about your neighbors."

He would say, "Like this one. By Czeslaw Milosz. You know Milosz, right?" (But he wouldn't hold it against them if they didn't.)

"My parents, my husband, my brother, my sister."
I am listening in a cafeteria at breakfast.
The women's voices rustle, fulfill themselves
In a ritual no doubt necessary.
I glance sidelong at their moving lips
And I delight in being here on earth
For one more moment, with them, here on earth,
To celebrate our tiny, tiny my-ness.

Olsen would say, "Or this one." (He couldn't explain why, but in some strange way this poem felt like his autobiography. He wouldn't say that. He would just say) "Here. This one by Stanley Kunitz. The story of a fatherless city boy in the spring of 1910 who heard that Halley's Comet would destroy the world that night."

> …At supper I felt sad to think
> that it was probably
> the last meal I'd share
> with my mother and my sisters,
> but I felt excited, too,
> and scarcely touched my plate.
> So Mother scolded me
> and sent me early to my room.
> The whole family's asleep now
> except for me. They never heard me steal
> into the stairwell hall and climb
> the ladder to the fresh night air.
>
> Look for me, Father, on the roof
> of the red-brick building
> at the foot of Green Street—
> that's where we live, you know, on the top floor.
> I'm the boy in the white flannel gown
> sprawled on this coarse gravel bed
> searching the starry sky,
> waiting for the world to end.

It was like a prayer, really. Certainly the closest he'd been to a prayer in years. Every time he said it, he could smell the night air, feel the gravel, and see the starry sky.

Olsen knew what to do when he needed to clear his head: get in his silver '72 Corvette and drive north to the Indiana Dunes. He liked the dunes best in winter. Parking alone in the deserted lot, climbing the steep, cold mountain of sand they called Mount Baldy. He liked the sands of ancient seas that flew on those spinning Lake Michigan winds, sand that stung his face and caught in his lungs and reminded him he was still alive. At Mount Baldy's summit, he was

Magellan, Columbus, Vespucci, surveying the sheer blue ice and ice blue sky under the thin white winter light.

❦   ❦   ❦

Olsen couldn't tell anyone about Mary. He couldn't even tell Rakowsky. It was a fragile story…the opposite, for example, of the poems he said out loud on his deck without worrying about the neighbors. If he spoke the story of Mary aloud, she would shatter into a million flecks of crystalline air and never be seen again. That would be his punishment for trying to capture her with words, for thinking he could capture fog and light and beauty in the jar of his words, for believing Mary could happen to him.

Instead Olsen would stand alone at his kitchen sink with a bottle of beer and his thoughts and his view of the sky, and remember the story, silently, for himself.

The very first thing was Ben: "Here's my house…yeah, this one. Thanks for the ride, Coach." Then Ben jumped out of the silver Corvette and started walking up the driveway, bouncing his basketball. Olsen watched him go: long seventeen-year-old legs, neck burned brown on summer courts, his fire unpretentious. **Reminds me of me.**

Ben had played basketball for Olsen two years already, starting as a freshman; now he was a junior and Olsen had him in AP English, too.

Olsen had just turned 41; in years of teaching and coaching he had met thousands of kids, many of them exceptional, but Ben was more than just a good kid: he was a missing piece, a missing person, he was history that had long ago slipped through Olsen's fingers but was now, somehow, restored.

"Hey, I should meet your mom and dad finally—gotta start talking about college! Tell them we should set something up," Olsen called from the car, top down for the warm afternoon.

"Okay," Ben called back, and disappeared behind the house.

It was late September and sunny. It was Indiana, Indian summer, and a few leaves were falling, some withered brown, some crimson and glittering, falling around Olsen's car as he drove away, dreams that had fallen from grace, catching the hope of an updraft briefly, then falling back to earth, drifting, sailing, falling back to earth.

The suburban rush-hour roads were humming with traffic. At some point Olsen glanced over his shoulder to change lanes and saw that Ben had forgotten his book bag behind the seat. **Kid's got basketball on his mind. Nothing**

wrong with that. Slowed down, turned around on a side street. **Hope I can find his house again.** Olsen was in no hurry to get home to dinner for one, quiet hanging in the air, English compositions to grade, phone calls and basketball game tapes to fill the empty spaces.

Olsen pulled back in Ben's driveway, reached around for the book bag: **Whoa, tonnage here.** The bag was half unzipped and Olsen looked inside. Trigonometry, physics, history, the latest *Sports Illustrated*, a smashed bag of potato chips.

Reminds me of me.

Olsen zipped the bag shut and carried it up the stone path to Ben's front door. Big brick house, lots of flowers in the garden. Heard muffled rock and roll coming from inside.

Olsen rang the doorbell but nobody came, then looked through the window in the front door: a big brown dog asleep on a rug, flowers in a vase on a table, pictures in frames dotting a tall bookshelf. Then he backtracked along the stone path and headed up the driveway, book bag slung on his shoulder.

Around back, muffled music, louder, was drifting out from a window upstairs. First Olsen thought about knocking on the screen door. Then he took a few steps backward in the driveway and looked up toward the window.

"Hey, Ben!" he shouted. "Hey, Ben, it's Coach Olsen! You left your book bag in my car—here it is!"

Olsen remembered the first time he heard her voice, voice like rain and sunlight: "I don't think he can hear you," he heard this voice say. He turned around and saw a tree house in a big old oak behind him. The branches waved and rustled, and the tree house swayed.

"Hello?" he said.

Then the voice of rain and sunlight swung down from the tree.

She was dark hair, dark eyes, ponytail, swimsuit top, tiny cutoffs colored like a piece of sky. She said, "I'm Mary. Ben's mom." That was when Olsen understood everything that had ever happened to him and when almost none of it mattered anymore. Forget bad karma, unanswered prayers, a silent waiting room in a stainless steel clinic. Forget solitude, cold winters, empty promises, empty soul. Forget summa cum laude, teacher of the year, state championship trophies, glory.

"I'm Tom Olsen," he said, somehow.

"Thomas," Mary said. She lifted her hand to fiddle with her earring, and a ray of sun lit up her wedding band, bounced off the ring and hit Olsen's heart, lightning—but even then he knew that wouldn't stop him.

❧   ❧   ❧

He hadn't stayed long that afternoon—just long enough for Ben to run downstairs and get his book bag, for Olsen to paint the swirls and sways of Mary's body onto his memory, for the three of them to stand together in the same ray of September sun. Mary's hands fluttered as she spoke: she had been reading Margaret Atwood in the tree house; she loved Indian summer; she was making fettuccine Alfredo for dinner—would Olsen like to stay? Ben stood at Mary's side with an ease that verged on tenderness, book bag slung on his shoulder now, biting a fingernail, looking at something in the sky.

Olsen lingered a little longer (why did it feel like they were father, mother, and son, like he had just stepped back into his own true life), listening more than talking although his mind was working (working on what—wasn't this hopeless?), until Ben went back in the house, and Mary touched Olsen's arm: "Good-bye, Thomas," and left traces of fog and light on his skin.

❧   ❧   ❧

In his mind's eye that September, Mary's image still surged sometimes in fine-pointed clarity, but more often wafted dimly, fading like the hope he would see her again. He had Ben in AP English every day, he had Ben in the gym shooting hoops every afternoon, but that did Olsen no good. After all, he wanted the unthinkable—which was easy enough to bear on the days she didn't cross his mind, harder on days that shook with the feeling she was just around the corner.

Then the story accrued another chapter.

It was a Friday afternoon and Olsen's AP English class was taking an essay test. He tracked the sound effects. Paper rustling. Pens scratching. Sighs heaving. Fluorescent lights buzzing overhead. The absence of gum cracking, as Olsen forbade it in his classes, one of his few absolutes. Olsen watched Ben writing in the back of the room: long torso and big shoulders folded over the little desk, giant in a dollhouse. He scanned the other students. Some wrote with diligence, others with vigor; some looked tired, some out the window; but all could be trusted, and Olsen was restless. It seemed as good a time as any to walk down to the teachers' lounge and check his mail.

The corridors stretched out deserted, except for hall monitors and the stray student en route to the bathroom. Heading toward the lounge, Olsen approached the main office, where a girl had emerged and was heading away from him, sliding papers into a folder, carrying a black leather jacket over her arm. Absent-mindedly he admired her dark hair swinging from side to side over her shoulders, her hips sweeping petitely above legs snugly fitted in snow-blue denim. Then she looked over her shoulder at him. It was Mary.

Olsen could only look at her.

"Thomas?" she said, lifting her eyebrows and smiling as she turned full to face him. "It's me, Mary Wendling—Ben's mom."

He sucked in a breath. "Hi, Mary. What a surprise—I was just going to check my mail—what brings you here today?" Zigzagging in verbiage, he walked straight across the twenty feet between them until he was close enough to breathe in her misty cape of perfume and soap and fresh air.

"I'm running this year's bake sale at 'Art From the Heart,'" Mary said. "You know, that arts and crafts fair the school holds every year? I just dropped off a copy of the flyer I designed so they can get it printed. And picked up some other stuff from the school secretary."

"An arts and crafts show?" Olsen murmured, taking a half-step closer to her. Mary slipped a flyer out of the folder and showed him.

> Eleventh Annual "Art From the Heart"…Indian River High School…Saturday, October 29…Over 100 artists and craftspeople…Do all your Christmas shopping…our famously delicious Bake Sale…proceeds benefit the Mothers Club scholarship fund.

"Oh, yeah," Olsen said. "I remember. I don't usually come to it, though."

Mary laughed and said, "I wouldn't think so!" and swung her hair over her shoulders and swept her fingers across the fabric of Olsen's sleeve, and it felt to him like yesterday instead of a thousand hours ago that she had first and last stood beside him.

"A bake sale sounds like a small thing, doesn't it?" Mary said. "But it makes a lot of money for the scholarship fund."

"It doesn't sound like a small thing to me," said Olsen. **It was not a small thing either when you lay your hand on me to say good-bye that day, when you lay your hand on my skin, the place where I still feel you touch me when I lie in bed at night.**

"Would you hold this for a sec?" Mary asked, and handed Olsen her folder. She slipped her leather jacket on but didn't zip it—held it open, in fact, and looked down at her body; then as Olsen watched, she ran one palm over the curve of her belly to smooth her soft white sweater. She pulled the sweater taut, holding it down over her hips for a second or two, and Olsen glimpsed the ivory shadow of her bra beneath the fabric.

He felt the blood pumping against his eardrums. He heard a trebly blurb broadcasting from the PA speakers in the background, but couldn't make out the words.

"Thank you," Mary said.

She smiled, and the flashes of Ben in her eyes and her face startled Olsen, made his chest ache with aloneness. She reached for him with one of her small hands, and he almost reached for her, but then she said, "My folder."

"Ah," he said, "yes," and gave it back.

"So—a new basketball season! I'm sure it'll be another great one," Mary said.

"I want to win a state championship with Ben," Olsen said. "Been too long since I've taken a team that far. Ben had that taste of Semi-State last year, but there's nothing like winning it all. I'd love to get that feeling back again." He edged closer toward Mary. "I love that boy, you know. Best kid I've ever known."

"Well, then," said Mary. She didn't back away. "We have something very important in common."

"Ben's going to be getting lots of offers," Olsen said. "Basketball scholarship offers from some outstanding colleges."

Mary looked down, started fiddling with the edges of her folder. "I'll be honest with you, Thomas," she said. "I don't want Ben to go to college on a basketball scholarship. I've been doing some investigating. I think that with an athletic scholarship, you're beholden to a college in a way that's in *their* best interests, not yours. I've told Ben he needs to go for an academic scholarship at a college where they also want him to play basketball. I hope you understand."

"I played basketball for Ohio State," said Olsen. "They wouldn't let me pay my own way. Not a bad deal. But I understand what you're saying."

"Are you from Ohio?" she asked.

"No, Boston, by way of Rhode Island, actually. And you?"

"I grew up around Fort Wayne," Mary said. "We moved here when Ben was a baby."

"What brought you to Indian River?"

"Oh, my husband got a job here."

"What does he do?" Olsen asked. **I want to know. I don't want to know.**

"He works for the city," Mary said. "He's the assistant building director."

Olsen folded his arms across his chest. "What's an assistant building director do?"

"Virgil's in charge of new construction, the commercial stuff. Oversees all that."

The intrusion of reality, Mary's husband taking name and form, prickled on Olsen's skin. "I didn't realize there was any new building going on in Indian River," he said dismissively.

"I don't think there's much. But there's at least enough to keep him occupied," Mary replied, and grinned. Her equal dismissiveness shot through Olsen's veins like a burning blur of alcohol; he felt newly bold, lucid.

"How come I've never met you before?" he asked. "This'll be Ben's third year playing for me—and I first saw him in eighth grade at a tournament he played in. But in all this time, all these years, I've never met you. How can that be?"

"I've seen you from afar," Mary said. "I've been to every game, every parents' meeting, every basketball banquet. Guess I just blend into the crowds."

"Impossible—that's impossible." **I have been blind...**

"Not so impossible," said Mary. "You always look like you have a lot on your mind. Preoccupied. Like you're here but also a million miles away."

"I do?"

"And you have quite the fan club—always so many people around you. Lots of parents talking up their sons, I imagine. But that's not my style."

"What is your style?" Olsen asked, but Mary laughed and said, "I don't know! But I don't think you need parents telling you how to do your job. You look like you've got things figured out just fine."

"Well. Maybe the basketball. I've been playing the game a long time."

"You have?" she said, and twirled her hair around a finger.

Can you try and understand what it's been like for me? My body and soul have learned to lead separate lives.

Mary tilted her head and looked at him.

"I've got to check my mail and get back to class," said Olsen. "But can I walk you out first?"

She didn't answer. She kept her eyes on him for a minute, then started walking, slowly, toward the exit, and he fell in step beside her.

When they got to the glass doors, Mary stopped. She smoothed her hair, tucked it behind her ear, played with her earring. "Good-bye, Thomas," she said.

"So," Olsen said, "good luck with your scholarship thing—that fund-raiser—hope you make a lot of money. It's a good cause."

Mary didn't answer, just stood facing him, black leather unzipped over white softness.

Olsen put his hand on the door but didn't open it. He looked back over his shoulder; the hall was empty. "So what do you do in your spare time," he asked, "when you're not leaping from tree houses, and running fundraisers, and raising a great kid?"

She laughed then, and Olsen laughed, too, leaning down toward her face.

"Well, not much else," Mary said. "I read a lot. Work at the Indian River library. Do a little gardening. Help out with Sunday School at our church. Stuff like that."

"Sunday School," said Olsen. "I needed more of that when I was a kid."

"Really?"

"Yeah," said Olsen.

"Why?" Mary asked. "Were you bad?" and the velvet edge in her voice traced its way down through Olsen's body.

Good God. "So," he said, "just think of all the kids you keep on the straight and narrow. You're a good role model."

"That's what they tell me." Mary stroked her earring, looking at some far-away point over Olsen's shoulder. "Can you keep a secret, though?"

"Sure."

"My body behaves itself perfectly," she said, "but my imagination lives a life that would blow people's illusions to smithereens. Do you know what I mean?"

Olsen opened his mouth to answer, but his tongue wouldn't move.

Mary pressed her fingertip against her lips. "Shh," she said. Then she opened the door for herself and walked outside and away into the school parking lot.

Olsen watched her go, his ears buzzing; then he sailed into the teachers' lounge, swept up his mail, and returned to AP English, where even the bored and the sleepy were roused by his high spirits.

In his memory, the chapter ended there. Of course, the real ending was that when school was over that day, he went home to his empty house and stood alone at the kitchen sink, drinking a bottle of beer.

CHAPTER 2

Trances

On a Friday night two weeks later, Olsen was alone in the dark gym of Indian River High, hurling a basketball with such ferocity against the wall that the wrestling mats hanging there trembled in surrender on their hooks.

"Oooh, a little tense, are we? Did your guys look that bad at conditioning tonight?"

Olsen looked over his shoulder and saw Rakowsky walking into the gym. Olsen headed toward the wall. "No, they were all right," he said. He picked up the ball, started lofting shots again. "Didn't think anybody else was still here besides the janitors."

"What's wrong, man?" Rakowsky said.

"Nothing. Just...I don't know. Nothing."

"I know what it is."

"What?"

"We gotta get you a woman."

"Hmm."

"Remember that song?...*We got-ta get you a wooo-man*...that's ancient. Actually, I never liked that song. But how are things going in that department, anyway? Because it seems like Kristina's been out of the picture."

"Oh, I don't know. The ones who want me, I don't want. And the one I want, I can't have."

"Wait, wait, hold the ball!" Rakowsky said. "This is news! Who is she? And why can't you have her?"

"It's complicated. Never mind."

"I've got time."

"Never mind, I said."

"Man, it's me. You can tell *me*."

Olsen dribbled the ball in place for a minute, then turned to face Rakowsky. "Okay." He squeezed the ball between his palms. "I met the woman of my dreams. But it seems she's already spoken for, so I don't know exactly what to do."

"The woman of your dreams? Where did you find her?" Rakowsky asked.

"Here—in Indian River."

"How'd you meet her?"

"Coincidence. Fate."

"Where?"

"Just…in town here."

"When?"

"Oh, maybe a month ago."

"I can't believe you didn't tell me before!"

"There's nothing to tell, really. The whole thing is hopeless. This whole thing—God." Olsen sat down in the front row of bleachers and tossed the ball aside.

"She must be pretty amazing to get an old guy like you worked up," Rakowsky said. He sat down at the end of the row.

"Rick, the first time I laid my eyes on her, it was…like everything else I've ever done in my life has just been killing time."

Rakowsky unzipped his jacket. "So do you have any chance with her? What's the problem?"

"I'm trying to figure out a way—see, I wish I could find out if it's all in my head—but I think she feels something for me, too."

"Ol' Tom's always gotta do things the hard way!" Rakowsky said with a laugh. "Got scores of beautiful women falling at his feet to worship at the house of Olsen—but no, he's gotta want the one he can't have. So what's getting in your way? Is she married or something?"

"Yeah. She is."

Rakowsky looked like he'd been expecting the other answer. Then he asked, "Happily?"

"I don't know. Maybe. I don't think so."

"Well, who is she?"

"Her name is Mary. Mary Wendling."

"*Mary Wendling*?!"

"Yeah—you know her?"

"She goes to my church! Her husband Virgil's on the board of deacons. And Ben! Is that how you met her—because of Ben?"

"Well, yeah, but it's not…"

"Tom! This is a bad idea, man. You could really hurt yourself this way—hurt your career, hurt your*self.* Listen, I've known Virgil and Mary for years. They look happy to me. What makes you think she's not happy? And we're talking Lutherans here. Lutherans don't get divorced."

Olsen got up and stretched. He walked across the gym, picked up the basketball, and started shooting again, first a little jump shot, then backing up toward the 3-point line.

Rakowsky said, "It's not that Lutherans *can't* get divorced, it's that we don't. We invented the stiff upper lip, ya know. Do the right thing even if it kills ya. God's always watching. And what makes you think Mary's unhappy? Did she say something to you?"

Olsen's shot banked in off the backboard. "What's this religious schtick?" he asked Rakowsky. "Like you're so holy. Drowning in your beer holy."

"Hey, beer is also an important part of being Lutheran."

"Okay, Saint Rick," said Olsen, "whatever you say."

"Lutherans don't have saints. Anyway, even if Mary and Virgil are going through a rough time—"

"Jeez! I get your point. Let's just drop it."

"How much time have you spent with her?"

"I don't know. Just a couple of times."

"And what makes you think she likes *you* so much?"

"Nothing." Olsen put up a shot from near half-court; it slipped through the net in silence, then thumped on the floor and bounced away. Olsen jogged after the ball.

Rakowsky stood up. "So…"

"Well, I'm gonna get out of here," Olsen said. "I've got my guys coming back for shoot-around at eight tomorrow morning."

"Hey, don't rush me out of football season. We've got some games left—we got the Stockton game tomorrow night. And you better be here for it, man. Come down and hang out on the sidelines with me."

"Sure. We'll see."

"Wanna come over to the house on Sunday afternoon? Karen's making one of her big Sunday dinners. Buncha people coming."

"Thanks, but I've got too much to do Sunday."

Rakowsky swung his gym bag over his shoulder. "You sure?"

"Yeah."

"Stop by the house if you change your mind," Rakowsky said, "and you better show for my game tomorrow," his voice trailing away as he headed for the door.

Olsen tried once more from half court, but the ball careened off the rim and flew into the bleachers.

Pulling out of the school parking lot after nine, Olsen turned left onto Breezewood, heading home, but traffic around the mall was heavy and he quickly wished he'd gone a different way.

Stopped at a red light, he looked over at the car that pulled up beside him: black Camaro, the driver a big guy, twenty-five, beefy left hand manning the steering wheel, right arm around the girl beside him, who leaned forward, animated, fiddling with something on the dashboard. Olsen could see the bright colors of her makeup. The light turned green. The Camaro shot ahead and turned sharply into the jammed mall parking lot where the chain restaurants conglomerated. Beyond the restaurants, carfuls of couples were backed up in the lane leading into the mall theater complex. Olsen crept past them in the through lane.

I don't miss that at all. The dating game. What a hassle…so contrived. I'm too old for that crap. But you've gotta do it, it's what they want.

Roanoke Road was bright but quiet at that Friday night hour, with streetlights, porch lights, houses glowing. Olsen parked the Corvette in the garage and walked around to the front door, past the little junipers and the big rhododendron. He stuck his key in the lock, then looked next door at Mr. McCormick's house, where the upstairs lights were on. Olsen saw the old man's shadow moving behind the window shade. **Waiting up for me.**

Inside, there were no messages on his answering machine. He turned the radio on, flipped to a college station, and something—the trail of music, the darkening sky outside his kitchen window—something made him think of Mary.

Made him imagine Mary whispering, *Thomas, let's drive up to the dunes and spend the day under the sky together, then we'll buy a pizza and a bottle of wine and take it back to a motel and eat naked and make love, and you can talk to me and tell me whatever's on your mind, or lie around and say nothing at all, till we feel like going home.*

He carried a bottle of beer out to his front stoop and drank it. Mr. McCormick turned his lights out next door. It had been a long day.

❀   ❀   ❀

The next afternoon at quarter to four, Olsen got out of his car at the foot of Mount Baldy, at the Indiana Dunes on the shores of Lake Michigan.

It wasn't a planned trip.

His players had stumbled into the school gym just before eight that morning with bedhead, shoelaces dragging, shivering but without coats, then come to life on the hardwood. His assistant coaches, Kuehn and old Stefanik, led the workout while Olsen took notes: Josh Reiter had bulked up, Matt Pender was quicker than ever, and Ben had mastered his 3-point shot—a nice trick for a big man. The team had depth at every position, and his first-string players were all seniors except for Ben. If they played their cards right, took things seriously, caught a few lucky breaks—they shouldn't have any trouble making it back to State this year.

He was seeing a beautiful season taking shape; it should have made him happy.

After shoot-around Olsen walked out to the parking lot with the boys.

"Man, it's only ten o'clock," Josh Reiter said, "but I feel like I've been up for days."

"Coach, eight o'clock Saturday shoot-arounds are inhuman."

"They're good discipline. A little torture's good for you," said Olsen. "Besides, now you've got the whole day ahead of you. Who's got a big day planned?"

"I'm going back to bed."

"Going out to breakfast."

"Gotta pick up my little brother and take him to football."

"I gotta go to work."

"Me too."

"Where are you guys working these days?" asked Olsen.

"Pets Parade at the mall," Matt Pender said.

"Computer World," said LeVon Powell.

"So, Ben," Olsen asked, "what are you doing this weekend?"

"Uh, let's see. Going out to dinner tonight. It's my mom and dad's anniversary. Plus church and crap tomorrow."

"Wendling, you gonna miss the football game?"

"Naw, I'll just be late."

"Coach, you coming to the game tonight?"

"I don't know," said Olsen.

"But it's the Stockton game!"

"Yeah, I know, I should go. Coach Rakowsky'll be peeved if I don't show."

"Hey, Reiter," somebody said, "can you pick me up for the game tonight?"

"Yeah, Reiter, pick me up, too."

"Me, too."

"We'll see," Josh said. "I ain't no limo service."

"'Ain't no'? Ouch," said Olsen.

"Coach, wanna go out to breakfast with us?"

"Thanks, but no. I gotta get home. Lotta stuff to do."

"Don't miss the game tonight!"

"We'll see if I'm in a football mood."

They drifted apart across the parking lot; Olsen jangled his keys in his pocket, ran a fingertip along the motley pointed edges, watched the boys fade away from him, watched Ben's dark head dip and vanish inside Josh Reiter's car.

He drove back home and the sun shone cold white from the blue sky and the trees around Indian River sang out red and orange in their last days of glory, but he saw only asphalt.

At home he stared into the fridge. He stuck a bagel in the toaster. He read the sports section in silence. The next thing he knew, he was locking up the house and pointing the Corvette northwest three hours to Valparaiso.

❦   ❦   ❦

And as he drove, he thought, **Ben. My boy. Son I wish I had.**

Kid's a great athlete. A natural. Coachable, too: knows he doesn't know it all.

And smart…but a thinker, not a follower. Not afraid to question, argue, be his own man. We don't always see eye to eye—don't have to. Kid's got a mind of his own—like me. Asks my advice but thinks for himself. That's what you want.

A little edge to him. My boy's no goody two shoes. Sure he goes to church but I respect that. Maybe he could teach me a thing or two.

Popular. Plenty of friends but not full of himself. And he takes it easy with the girlfriend thing—there's time for all that—I'd be the first to tell him. Basketball's good for giving a guy some focus.

When I see him staring out the window during English, when I see the light bulb flash over his head if he gets open for a 3, when I see him laughing with his friends—it always hurts—I guess because it feels like he's a part of me but he's not mine.

❦   ❦   ❦

Olsen liked the dunes in cold weather. Today the temperature had peaked around forty and the northwest wind was wicked. Only one other car in the parking lot, a gold Lincoln, its driver nowhere in sight. Olsen pulled his jacket hood up and snapped the flap over his throat.

Mount Baldy was steep and shifting and always looked, in that first second of appraisal, unclimbable. Then as you started upward, and your feet sank down, sliding backward, and you pitched yourself forward and the wind twisted around you, pulling you down and pushing you up, jabbing your face with sharp sandy stings, then it became a matter of principle and you just kept going. The whole point of Mount Baldy was the climbing, not the having climbed.

From the top he jogged down toward the lake, soft footfalls over a cold, wide windplain. He turned his eyes away from the nameless industrial complex to the east, interfering as it did with the feeling he liked of being far away from anywhere. At the water's edge, he looked westward. Two hundred feet down the beach he saw the Lincoln driver he had forgotten about: a man in a black baseball cap and black warmups that were whipping in the wind, and a young girl in a pink hat and parka, probably his daughter. The sun was falling through the sky toward the water.

When the man spied the lone and hooded Olsen, he stopped his pebble tossing, then adjusted his baseball cap, crossed his arms on his chest, and looked out over the lake. The girl turned and saw Olsen. She waved, without guile, then stopped; her father must have said something. Olsen lifted his arm and waved back. The girl looked at him, then took her father's hand and let the water lap the toes of her boots.

Olsen looked out across the lake. Under the hand of the northwest wind, it churned—steely blue, mud brown, ice white.

> Look for me, Father, on the roof
> of the red-brick building
> at the foot of Green Street—

that's where we live, you know, on the top floor.
I'm the boy in the white flannel gown
sprawled on this coarse gravel bed
searching the starry sky,
waiting for the world to end.

He turned around and headed back to his car.

He drove slowly along the dusky roads in the park. On his way back to the highway he saw a Burger King drive-thru and got dinner. He ate in the car, listening to the radio news; nothing had happened. He gathered his trash and walked across the parking lot to dump it in the sticky garbage can, litter skidding around his ankles in the wind. Cars shot by on the five-lane road, neon signs protruded into the air, glowing in every direction, and he didn't know one person in Valparaiso he could pick up the phone and call anymore. He used to have a thousand friends here, a thousand places to go and to stay; now he only had Valpo's basketball coaches during business hours.

Suddenly it seemed like a long way back to Indian River.

"You got a toothbrush, maybe some toothpaste, back there? I'm kind of unprepared," Olsen said to the desk clerk at a motel by the Valpo campus.

No, they were out of their supplies at the front desk, and the maid wouldn't be back till morning, and the clerk didn't have a key to the supply room. Olsen got his room key, then jogged across the five-lane road to the old K-Mart on the other side. He found the toothbrush and toothpaste; he looked at the books and magazines; nothing interested him, but he bought *U.S. News and World Report* and *Sports Illustrated*.

Back at the motel Olsen leaned on the wall, waiting for the elevator, and looked through the glass at the swimming pool. A gray-haired man in Speedos lay on a lounge chair reading *Forbes*. A young woman—wife, mistress?—climbed out of the pool in a very small bikini, her hair slicked back from her pretty face, water streaming off her, and way too much curved skin showing for a man to be able to look away. She looked at Olsen through the glass and smiled. He watched as she walked with a seductive little strut and picked up a towel from the chair next to the gray-haired man, who ignored her. She turned and dried herself facing Olsen, smiling.

Olsen didn't smile back; the elevator door opened and he stepped inside. But the young woman swam through his mind as he rode to the fifth floor and walked down the silent, anonymous hall to his room.

It was still dark when Olsen woke up in the morning, and cold when he set out on the highway for home.

❧   ❧   ❧

The next two days in Indian River simmered with a strange late-October warmth.

When the heat hit Monday, Olsen and his students poached in sweat in his third-floor classroom, even though he ran his industrial-strength fan on high speed until the last bell rang. That night he dreamed about sheets of notebook paper flying up off desks and floating to the floor, of a dull roar he couldn't get out of his head, of faces dissolving in sweat, chalk drawings dissolving in rain.

Tuesday was hotter.

"Can we have class outside?"

"Come on, Mr. Olsen!"

"Please?"

He saw summer on their faces and his chest ached: so fresh yet so far gone, for him, the old feeling that one beautiful day was all you needed, one day with its magic wand of sunlight, all the power of life and the future held in the palm of one perfect day, and you couldn't let it slip away from you.

Outside they went, with their spiral notebooks and little old paperbacks of one-act plays that Olsen unearthed from the bookshelf in the back of his room.

"First we'll do some outdoor theater," he told them. "Let's number off into small groups. One through five."

"Why do we always have to work?" they groaned, but they were laughing.

"Mr. Olsen, come read with us—"

"Be in our play—"

"Mr. Olsen, please, you're the best at it—"

He divided his time between them.

"You should have been an actor," cooed the girls.

I am an actor.

Outside that afternoon with Ben's AP English class, Olsen lay on his back in the grass, watching the rusty leaves rippling on the sky. He rolled on his side, propped himself up on an elbow, scanned the students scattered in the distance. Some were reading; some were writing in their spiral notebooks—their musings on the last gasp of summer; some were talking to each other or strolling in the grass. Ben had walked over to the football field alone, he stood there backlit by afternoon sun, hands in his pockets, staring at the goalpost. Ben turned toward Olsen, as if he felt himself being observed, then headed back Olsen's way.

"Some amazing day, huh?" Ben said, sinking down in the grass.

"Yeah," said Olsen.

"Don't you wish you were anywhere but here?"

"Here, as in school? In this town? In this life?"

Ben tilted his head and looked at Olsen. "In this town, mostly."

Olsen rolled onto his back again. "Ever hear that old saying, Wherever I go, there I am?" he asked.

"No!" Ben said, and laughed. "What's it mean?"

Olsen saw the rusty leaves blur together. "It means running never did me any good."

CHAPTER 3

❀

Oil Change

Olsen's house, its hatches battened, was stuffy upon his return from school Tuesday evening. He opened windows upstairs and down, then lay back in the recliner, drinking a beer in the halo of the living room lamp. The neighborhood was quiet as the breeze drifted in.

Then the phone rang; he heard Kristina's voice broadcasting from the machine in the kitchen; he couldn't make out the words.

When he went to the fridge for another beer, he listened to Kristina's message: "I miss you—do you miss me? I'd love to see you. What are you doing Saturday night?" A few months ago that would have been all the encouragement he needed; tonight he erased the message. But he tested himself to see if he still had her number memorized.

Later Olsen sat at his desk in the dining room, reading and grading poems by his senior lit students. Their melange of savvy and innocence, flair and stumbling, made his ears ring. Two hours flew by; Olsen put the folder of graded poems back in his briefcase, then doodled, sketched a few phrases, ended up with a poem of his own, written in the twilight.

> You, mystery divine
> seeming distant sadly shy
> yet dark eyes aflame
> Your thought surrounds me
> Intimate possession
> of my body and soul

Gently then you slip

back to distant silence

But you linger in me

The calm of his house unsettled him. He decided the Corvette could use an oil change.

Outside in the garage, Olsen flicked on the overhead lights, squeezed between the Corvette and pockmarked wooden work table, stepped over the power mower and around the ten-speed bike he never rode anymore. **Gotta rearrange things in here. What a mess. Put that bike in the back. Where's that case of oil? I know it's here somewhere.** Eventually he found it under a pile of towels and chamois cloths by a can of house paint on the work table.

He backed the Corvette out into the driveway and started draining the old oil. His mind wandered.

An oil change: black slimy remnants of the miles under your belt. Slippery mess made of what had kept you going. Just let it all out, let it flow, let it go. When it's all drained out, put in the brand-new clean stuff—you'll be good for a few months at least. So easy for a car to get sanctified.

Can Virgil Wendling change the oil in his car? Paper-pushing assistant building director probably takes his car to Lube Stop. Probably doesn't like to get his hands dirty.

In the garage, Olsen emptied the oil pan into a tall bucket, filling it close to the rim. When was he ever going to take that to the recycling center? Probably never. At least not before the end of basketball season. Maybe it would mutate into coal and be mined from the ruins of Indian River a million years from now.

Walking back to the car from the garage, he saw a runner lope by out on Roanoke Road. Runners usually blended into the scenery like birds, there were so many, but this one wore light-up shoes. Then Olsen spied Mr. McCormick from next door hobbling along under the streetlights, his infinitesimal squir-rel-dog on its strand of a leash. Quickly Olsen ducked behind the Corvette hood.

The old man stopped and peered up the driveway, drawn by the backyard light. "Tom?" he called.

I hope he doesn't come walking up here. Not tonight. Not with the mood I'm in.

Mr. McCormick hesitated in the silence. Olsen waited; then he looked carefully around the edge of the hood just in time to see his neighbor hobble away.

His face flashed hot. **No time for an old man? You better watch yourself. You don't have five minutes to spare for a lonely old man? He waits up for you.**

Olsen exhaled heavily and looked at his watch: nine-forty. The night air was getting chilly. He poured new oil in the engine, gathered up the empty cans and tossed them in a garbage drum in the garage. He didn't care that the crashing of metal on metal broke the peace of the neighborhood evening. Olsen pulled on the crumpled sweatshirt he found on the work table, picked out a ratchet and a flashlight, went back to the Corvette and folded himself down under the hood to scan the scenery.

An engine was a mute landscape. You could rig up a light to shine on it, you could put on new wires and plugs and hoses and charge the battery and top off the fluids and get everything perfectly tuned, really humming, but after all that, you still had a mute landscape staring back at you.

Mary was a mystery. She looked happy on the outside, but what about the defiance under the smile, what about her startling jibe against Wendling: *there's at least enough to keep him occupied...*

Can you keep a secret?

Blow their illusions to smithereens

Shhh

Olsen tinkered awhile. Plugs, bolts, filters, fluids, wires. Things checked out. Back in the garage, Olsen lay the ratchet and flashlight on the workbench, wiped his hands on a towel, picked up a smudged chamois cloth to rub the car down. Somewhere nearby a neighbor slid a window shut with a slam. The wind was picking up.

He finished rubbing the car down as more snatches of sound flared up in the background. Bass banging from a passing car. Someone's drum practice in the distance. The wind snapping through the trees.

There wasn't a chance Mary might actually be happy, was there?

Olsen put the chamois and tools away and flicked out the garage light.

He backed the Corvette out onto Roanoke Road and headed for the interstate, just a quick spin to clear his head. The warm day was nothing but a memory now. Cold high winds had taken over, shrouding the night sky; traffic lights heaved, crazy tornadoes of leaves cut across the street in front of him; the Corvette shimmied like a Matchbox car as he crossed the Fourth Street bridge. The gale made him think of the dunes. He would take Mary there with him, they would hike on the beaches, they would stay overnight, they would never come back.

Olsen detoured back and swung into Rakowsky's driveway a few minutes later. He rang the doorbell.

"Take a spin?" said Olsen.

"Why not?"

Flying down the vacant interstate, Olsen talked over the classical music on his car radio. "Do you ever wish you and Karen had kids?"

Rakowsky didn't answer right away. Then he said, "Sure, but it wasn't meant to be." He laughed. "That's one great thing about teaching and coaching. We get to have all these kids, all the fun, and don't have to support them."

Olsen said nothing.

"Why?" said Rakowsky. "Are you having a midlife crisis—you wish you had a family? It's not too late for you, ya know. If you'd just settle down. Of course, we all think you've got it made."

"I'd like to have kids," Olsen said. "Especially one like Ben Wendling. Now there's a kid after my own heart."

Rakowsky turned his head toward the passenger window. "Yeah," he said, "but just remember he's not really yours."

"I never told you this," said Olsen. "I almost became a father once. We decided on an abortion." He choked on his saliva; coughed and coughed. "I would have been a father."

Rakowsky cracked his window. "That's rough. Who's 'we'?"

"My old girlfriend from grad school. Fiancée, at the time."

"I take it the wedding never happened?"

"Nope."

"How long ago was all this?" asked Rakowksy.

"Oh, long time. Eighteen years," Olsen said. "You're the first person I've ever told."

"I am?" Rakowsky took a deep breath. "Well, don't beat yourself up over it, man. That's rough, though. An abortion? That's gotta hurt."

"Yeah," said Olsen. He cracked his window, too. Hit all the radio station buttons: commercial, commercial, commercial. He turned the radio off. "So what's this Virgil Wendling like? What's his story?"

"He's all right. I'm not gonna talk him down, if that's what you're looking for. He's a decent guy."

"Yup."

Rakowsky looked out the passenger window again. "I think Wendling's older than us," he said. "He's gotta be mid-fifties. And Mary looks about half that, huh? I don't know how she does it. I wonder how old she is."

"Yup."

"To be honest, I don't really know Wendling that well. Even after all these years. We've been on projects together at Calvary, but I can't say I really know him. He shows up for all the church groups, the committees, all that, but never does the one-on-one stuff. I've never had a beer with him, never really had a personal conversation with him."

"Huh."

"Course that's true of ninety percent of the people I know."

"Yeah."

They drove on in silence. Got off at an exit ramp and drove through McDonald's. Headed home on the interstate, eating.

Half an hour later, Olsen pulled back into Rakowsky's driveway. "See ya tomorrow," said Olsen.

"Look out for yourself," Rakowsky said. "That old stuff weighing on you—it's rough. I'm sorry, man. But don't ruin your life now—midlife crisis, all that crap. You know? Someday they're gonna name a street after you in this town—hell, maybe they'll rename the school. You jerk. Don't blow it."

"I know."

Rakowsky opened the door and squeezed his football coach's bulk out of the Corvette. "Just look out for yourself," he said, and shut the door.

Olsen rolled his window all the way down and drove back to Roanoke Road, his ears freezing. At home he drank a bottle of beer, listened to Jimi Hendrix, and went to bed.

And the wind
it cries
Mary

CHAPTER 4

❀

Empty Cross

Where is she?

At first Olsen didn't see her. He had woven his way past vendors' tables lining the high school halls, through the hunched and crushing blur of coats and faces, the pitched rabble of layers of conversation, the heavy perfumed haze of scented stuff, the jungle of handmade wares; finally he had emerged on the far side of the Art From the Heart craft fair, at the perimeter of the Mothers Club bake sale in the cafeteria.

In the midst of the shifting crowd, Olsen saw Sue Pender, Luanne Kazel, Mrs. Reiter, and some of the basketball cheerleaders working behind the bake sale tables. He took a deep breath, and the air frosted his nose and tongue with sweetness, a rich spread that coated his throat when he swallowed; the air around him glittered.

Then Mary emerged from the cafeteria kitchen in a snowy sugared mist, it seemed, and the taste on his tongue made his head spin. She had a dishtowel over her shoulder, a bucket in one hand, a sponge in the other, her dark hair in a ponytail, gold hoops swinging from her ears. Her *Wildcats Basketball Mom* tee shirt clung to her body. She started wiping tabletops, smiling as she talked to people. She walked to the money table, spoke to the woman sitting behind it, nodded her head, then disappeared back into the kitchen.

Olsen waited.

In a few minutes Mary came out empty-handed and took up her post at the far-flung cake table with Sue Pender, whose son Matt played point guard.

Olsen smoothed his hair, cleared his throat, and checked inside his shirt pocket. Then he headed to the far side of the cafeteria, weaving through clusters of grandmothers wearing teddy bear sweatshirts and women steering baby strollers.

Mary's lips parted into a pink O as he approached, then spread into a smile.

"Hi, Mary," Olsen said. "Hi, Sue."

"I didn't expect to see you," Mary said. "I thought you never came to Art From the Heart! What a nice surprise."

"I want to buy everything you have left," he announced, and swept his arms in circles to include the whole cafeteria, a kaleidoscope of white angel foods and dark chocolates and peppermint pinks and deep red fruits bursting up through pie crusts and muffin tops, and all of it misted in sugar.

"Everything?" Mary said, and laughed, glancing at Sue Pender, who said, "You must be pretty hungry."

"Oh, it's not for me," said Olsen.

"Are you having a party? Feeding the whole basketball team?" Mary asked.

"No, I have another plan. But I especially want to support the Mothers Club scholarship fund," he said.

"You're not kidding?" said Mary.

"No, I want it all. So, what do you think would be a fair price?"

"Well…" she said, a question mark in her voice, "I could try to make an estimate."

She looked at him, tilting her head slightly and smiling. She picked up a pad of paper and a pencil, and came out slowly from behind the swirling chocolate orbs and tiny bouquets of sugar roses and the nut-sprinkled icings.

Olsen pulled a check out of his shirt pocket and handed it to her. "Would this cover it, do you think?" he asked.

Mary lay the pad and pencil on the table and took the check from him. Their fingers touched. The bake sale crowd buzzed around them. She glanced down at the check, then brought it up in front of her eyes and stared at it. "One thousand dollars," she said.

"Well, it's such a worthy cause," said Olsen.

He waited for her reaction, then grew worried when there wasn't one. Mary's body was still. She looked at the check. He stood in limbo. The hum and movement of people around them rose and fell.

Then, Mary turned her face up to Olsen's, with no smile, only an earnestness that spread across her forehead, and in smooth slow motion, she slipped her arms around him, pressing all her softness against him, and lay her cheek on his chest.

She held on just long enough for Olsen to lightly, incredulously, put his hands on her back and press her closer to him. He caught the eye of Sue Pender, whose jaw had dropped, before Mary let go with a sigh, drew back from his chest, and looked up at Olsen again.

"Thank you," said Mary.

"You're very welcome."

"Now what are you really going to do with all this food?" she asked. The snowy mist swirled around her face; when Olsen breathed, he could taste it. Then he said, "Surprise!" and turned back toward the cafeteria entrance, waved a hand above his head, and shouted, "Come on in, men!"

From the crowded hall, the whole boys' basketball team filed in, a tall, short-haired, light-footed group, all carrying large coolers and cardboard cartons. Ben was in the lead, weaving through the cafeteria tables toward Olsen and Mary.

"The guys will pack the food up and load it in the school van," Olsen said. "Then we'll deliver everything to St. Peter's soup kitchen for tonight's meal."

"St. Peter's?" Mary said. "You're donating everything?" She took one of Olsen's hands and held it between hers. "God bless you for this, Thomas."

Ben was grinning as he reached her side. "Hi, Mom! Were you surprised?"

"Yes—very surprised! And I still am—Coach Olsen just told me you're delivering everything to the soup kitchen at St. Peter's."

"Coach, aren't you proud of me for keeping this a secret all week? Every time Mom said, 'I hope we make enough money at the bake sale,' I had to keep my mouth shut."

"Yeah, you were brilliant. You have a future in espionage if the NBA doesn't work out for you," Olsen said, jabbing Ben's tricep as the team bunched together around them.

"What do you think, Thomas—how should we do this?" Mary asked, laying her hand on Olsen's forearm. He looked at her hand, felt her fingertips, her palm, hot on his skin. Then she took her hand away.

"Well," said Olsen, "why not give everyone a last chance to buy something? Then we'll pack up whatever's left."

"Ben, honey, could you get everyone's attention for me?" Mary stood on a chair behind the cake table while Ben whistled through his fingers a few times. "Hello, everyone! Thank you so much for coming today," she said. "Well—here's something exciting—a generous donor has just purchased the rest of the bake sale items to donate to St. Peter's soup kitchen! You're welcome to make a last-minute purchase if you like. Then our boys' basketball team will pack the rest and deliver it to the church."

Olsen started the boys packing: "Divide and conquer," he said; "use your best judgment and don't squish anything; when you fill up a cooler or a carton, load it up outside in the school van, then come back for more. Okay, now go to it."

He drifted to the outskirts of the mix and lingered, watching Mary, watched her moving through the crowd of mostly women, greeting almost everyone, hugging Sue Pender and Luanne Kazel and Mrs. Reiter and some women Olsen didn't recognize. He watched her lifting a plate of muffins from a table and holding it in the air and twirling around on her toes, and setting the plate down again, smiling, the women around her smiling, too.

He watched Mary kneeling down and handing a cookie to a little boy in a stroller, the edges of time dissolving in a blur before him. Mary was a girl, a young mother with Ben, a lover he burned for, the missing piece of his life. Then Mary stood up again, and the toddler's mother strolled the little boy away.

Olsen watched Mary deliver the check to the money table; he observed the astonished reaction of the woman receiving it and read her lips: *Coach Olsen?* He turned away before the woman tried to pick him out of the crowd.

The cafeteria emptied out. Mary started picking tablecloths up and shaking crumbs into a trash can. She folded the tablecloths loosely and stacked them on a chair. Mrs. Reiter had the sponge and bucket now, wiping the bare tables clean, and some of the other women were joining the cleaning effort.

Olsen walked up behind Mary. "Will you come with us to St. Peter's?"

She turned toward him and said, "I wish I could, but I should stay and help clean up."

Mrs. Reiter squeezed her sponge out into the bucket. "Nonsense, Mary! You go with Coach Olsen and Ben and the boys. We'll take care of the cleanup. There are plenty of us here to finish up."

"It'll be easy," Sue Pender added, poking a broom under a table to reach some debris. "You go ahead. You've already done so much."

Mary shrugged. "Okay, then—I guess you've got another passenger, Thomas."

"Great." Olsen saw the look that flew between Sue Pender and Mrs. Reiter. He didn't care. Instead he put his hand on Mary's shoulder, walked her toward the back doors to the parking lot.

Outside, the wet chill soothed him, but Mary shivered in her leather jacket. The sky was the color of bones. Josh Reiter and Ben, LeVon Powell and Michael Cavatelli, Matt Pender and Nate Pytel and the others waited in the parking lot under the clouds, leaning variously on their new and hand-me-down vehicles.

"See you guys at St. Peter's. Remember—the back entrance," Olsen called.

The boys kept their eyes on him as he opened the passenger door of the school van for Mary.

"I said see you there!" Olsen repeated; the boys dispersed. He walked around to the driver's side, got in, pulled the door shut behind him.

Then came the moment Olsen first felt real trouble: alone in the van with Mary, her caramel profile beside him, and her breath, the two of them breathing together in this tiny space, and danger kindling at the base of his spine. He jammed the key into the ignition and twisted it forward, hard.

The van rumbled into gear. He said, "I've gotta warn you, this won't be the smoothest ride," but Mary smiled like she didn't care. He navigated them out of the parking lot, the coolers rattling behind them, and out onto Breezewood Boulevard.

Olsen watched her from the corner of his eye. She slid her ponytail holder off, ran her fingers through her hair. She took a tube of lip gloss from her purse, smoothed it over her lips, then put it away. She took out a brush and pulled it slowly through her hair. She popped something in her mouth.

"Mint?" she offered.

"Sure." He held out his hand and she put a few Tic Tacs in his palm.

"Oops, forgot my seatbelt." Mary unzipped her jacket, pulled the seatbelt down and across her hips. "Thomas, I'll never be able to thank you enough for what you've done today. How did you ever think of doing such a wonderful thing in the first place?"

"Oh, I don't know exactly. Somehow the idea just came to me." No more sideways glances; now Olsen had to keep his eyes on the heavy mall traffic. He turned off Breezewood onto South River, heading into the elbow-to-elbow neighborhood that had withered in the shadows of the mall.

"So, Thomas," she said, "what do you do besides teaching and coaching? Do you have a family?"

"No, actually, I don't," Olsen said. "You don't mind sharing Ben with me, do you?" He cracked his window to get cool air, but kept the heat blowing for Mary.

He kept on talking. "Ben is such a great kid. The world will belong to him when he gets out there. He'll be able to accomplish anything he wants. Fine student, gifted athlete, and funny, too—he always makes me laugh. He's a little stubborn, has that little wild streak, and I can't say I like the tattoo—but that's okay, he doesn't have to do everything my way." Mary's silence indicated that she agreed.

Olsen checked over his left shoulder and merged onto Gary Street, heading for the church. "He's got a mind of his own, and I respect that. In fact, it only makes me like him more. Want to know something else?" He didn't wait for Mary's response, just barreled down Gary Street talking. "You're the only one I'd tell this to. There are times I've said to myself, Ben reminds me of me. Times I've even said, If I had a son, I'd want one just like Ben."

The sound of a sob startled him, and he swung his head to look at Mary for the first time since she'd fastened her seatbelt. Tears were sliding down her face, her shoulders were shaking, and she was pulling a tissue from her purse.

"Are you okay—is something wrong? Did I say something—?" he fumbled in alarm. But she pressed her face into the tissue, and her shoulders shook harder.

"Mary," he said. He reached over and covered her knee with the spread of his fingers.

Mary didn't answer. She didn't ask Olsen to remove his hand. In a minute her tears slowed; she dried her face with small dabs; she breathed in, and out. "Thank you, Thomas—for everything you're doing today—but especially for being so good to Ben. Your kindness to him means a lot to me. More than you could ever really know."

Instead of straightening up, Mary sank deeper into the passenger seat, her leg swaying toward him. Olsen drove steadily with one hand on the wheel all the way into the church parking lot.

❦   ❦   ❦

Olsen stood on the threshold, Mary and the boys behind him, all of them bearing coolers and cartons.

No mystical streams of sun poured before them through St. Peter's basement windows: the dismal fellowship hall's greenish-gray air was lit only by flickering fluorescent lights above a sea of brown linoleum and a motley harbor of tables and chairs, with emanations of clatter off to the side.

Olsen stepped over the threshold. To his left, on the far side of the fellowship hall, he saw green fields of salad and a gleaming river of buttered bread and a scattering of people—teenagers mostly, faces he knew from Indian River High, with a bright and busy kitchen backlighting them.

"Hey, guys, you're here!" and "Let's see whatcha got," and "Bring it on over," the teenagers called, and Olsen and Mary and the boys crossed the fellowship hall and put the coolers and cartons down and they all started talking. Standing behind them, Olsen saw Mary reach her hand up toward Ben's shoulder, holding her palm against his back, as if Ben were grounding her, recharging her, as if the tears had drained some life from her.

Then Olsen heard a voice he recognized, turned and saw Pastor Lieben on the threshold in his dark suit and clerical collar. Olsen walked Mary across the fellowship hall and introduced them.

Lieben was the one Olsen had called when he'd dreamed up this soup kitchen donation. The two men had first met the previous spring when they were both chaperons at Indian River High's after-prom. Lieben had worn minister's garb at the festivities all night long; Olsen had thought that was odd. But from midnight till four a.m., the two of them had talked about life while pouring punch, patrolling the halls, and doing dance-floor duty, and when after-prom was over Olsen had said to himself, **Lieben and I are not so different.**

An observation reproven in that moment at St. Peter's: Lieben was clearly very interested in talking to Mary. And Mary seemed to have recovered from her mystery tears—recovered very well, in fact, thought Olsen.

"Calvary Lutheran," Mary was telling Lieben, her face animated. "Oh, about fifteen years. Very happy there, yes."

"Good," Lieben was saying. "That's good to hear. Good Christian people over at Calvary."

"My husband is a deacon there," Mary was saying. "My son is active in the youth group. Maybe our Calvary kids could help your youth group with this soup kitchen sometimes."

My husband. My son.

"Yes, let's look into that," Lieben was saying.

Mary stood talking to Lieben in the dreary basement air, smiling and shimmering, a shimmer that hurt Olsen's eyes, so he turned and looked back at his players. On the far side of the fellowship hall, he saw the long tables being spread with food, the hubbub of hands and faces, and just then Ben happened to look up, grinned and gave Olsen a thumbs-up across the wide room. Olsen smiled back, nodded. He realized he was barely breathing. He inhaled deeply, breathed out, and in and out. The air tasted musty.

He looked at Mary again. Still talking to the pastor.

Olsen ran a hand over his hair. **Anyway—mission accomplished here. All in all, a good day. A lot of good's been done.**

He looked above Mary's and Lieben's heads to the big wooden cross hanging on the wall. Simple; mysterious; unfamiliar enough to remind him he was only visiting. The cross, he noticed, was spare, bare. Empty.

Where's Jesus? Olsen said, but they didn't hear him.

So he said it again: "Where's Jesus?"

Lieben and Mary stopped talking. They looked at Olsen. He realized his question must have sounded funny, out of context; he pointed then to the cross behind them. Mary and Lieben looked over their shoulders, in tandem, toward the wall, then back toward Olsen.

"We celebrate the Risen Christ, Tom," said Lieben, his Adam's apple bobbing above his black and white collar. "The empty cross is a symbol of Christ's victory over sin and death. A victory He won for you and for me." Lieben put his hands on his hips. "You have a lot of worldly success, Tom. Success in your work, and your coaching. Tremendous popularity in this town. You're very highly regarded. Respected. And for good reason—this project today is an example. But we're saved by faith, not by works. That's why Jesus said, What does it profit a man to gain the whole world but lose his own soul? It's never too late to start learning the Good News, Tom—to find out what Mary and I already know. Why not take a step forward in faith and come to worship service tomorrow morning?"

First there was Mary's face, covered with embarrassment for him. Next there was his own indignation. **Son of a bitch.** "Church tomorrow? No, thanks," said Olsen. **You son of a bitch.** His ears were ringing.

Lieben and Mary were both looking at him. Concerned? Worried? Olsen realized he was barely breathing again.

He looked back toward Ben and the boys. They were laughing with the St. Peter's teenagers, standing beside the tables of food, colorfully spread. He saw Ben and Josh Reiter and Matt Pender walking toward the kitchen.

We're having chili, Olsen heard someone say, stray words hitting his ringing ears.

And just as he took an untimely deep breath, the smell of boiling meat streamed out of the kitchen and flooded the air and gagged him, and as Mary and Lieben stood there, Olsen's stomach went up on tiptoes in his gut, then slammed forward against his ribs, then flopped backwards and lay there, twitching.

"Excuse me," Olsen said, and rushed past Mary's outstretched fingertips.

When he reached the fresh air, he felt better.

*   *   *

Half an hour later, in St. Peter's parking lot, the boys gathered around Olsen, with Mary beside them. The sun was going down, the chill setting in.

"Well, men." Olsen folded his arms and cleared his throat. Time to say something profound. Everyone was watching his tongue tie. "You've done good work today. It's great knowing I can call on you for, uh, this kind of important work." He put his hands in his pockets. "Well done. Now—drive safely, and I'll see you all at school on Monday."

The boys moved toward their cars, opening trunks, tossing coolers in back seats. Olsen and Mary looked at each other. He pointed to the school van and said, "Can I give you and Ben a ride?"

"Oh, Josh Reiter's driving us home," she said. "He lives right down the street from us."

"Your car's not back at the high school?"

"No, Sue Pender picked me up this morning," Mary said. "Anyway, don't you live all the way over by Indian River Park? That's what Ben told me."

"Sure, but I don't mind giving you a ride."

"You're so sweet, Thomas—but you've already done enough for one day. You go ahead and have a fun Saturday night. I'm sure you've got more exciting things to do than give us a ride home."

"Actually—I don't. No plans at all." He laughed.

"Really?"

"Really."

"Wow. Wish I were single," she said.

Ben was across the parking lot, getting into Josh Reiter's car. Mary shrugged and said, "Well, good night."

Olsen walked her to Josh's car. He opened the door for her, his hands slow with reluctance. He watched her slide in, then closed the door and leaned down, smiled at her through the window, desperate for one more image of her face. With the tiniest movement of her lips and two fingers, she blew him a kiss, and the car pulled away.

He got in the van. Drove back to school. Headed for home in the old Corvette. It all felt like slow motion.

Can you keep a secret

Back on Roanoke Road, Mr. McCormick was outside walking his squirrel-dog when Olsen pulled in his driveway. Olsen parked and walked across the lawn to where the old man stood on the sidewalk, waiting and holding his hat against the late October wind, dog leaping at his ankles. "Hullo, Tom," he said, and lifted his hand from his hat, waving once.

"Come in for a beer?" said Olsen.

"Got to take Rocky for his walk. How 'bout after that?"

"Sure."

"Got to have our toast to basketball season."

"Exactly."

"I'll be back," said Mr. McCormick, waving his hand in a weary tick-tock, then pushing his hat down tighter on his head. Olsen watched him shamble into the twilight. Then he walked back across his lawn, past his little junipers and his big rhododendron, and went inside. He flicked on the porch light, turned lights on all over the house.

CHAPTER 5

❀

That's What Friends Are For

Monday at school the story spun bigger, until Olsen's contribution had grown from $1,000 to $5,000 to $10,000 and had garnered him an invitation to the governor's mansion to receive the Indiana Community Leadership medal.

Olsen laughed, and set the record straight over and over, and assigned his classes impromptu essays on the biggest surprise they ever pulled on someone. He liked his students' chatter; besides, it kept Mary present in his day, turned his thoughts away from Lieben and boiling meat and a tied tongue; kept Mary's lips and fingertips in his mind's eye.

Tuesday afternoon, Olsen was standing at the window in his basketball office, looking out at the deserted playing field and the sunny white sky, when Rakowsky came in.

"How ya doin'?" Rakowsky said.

"Good," said Olsen.

"Hey," said Rakowsky, "I heard about the bake sale thing."

"Yeah?"

"Yeah. What was that all about?"

"What do you mean?" said Olsen. "I wanted to support the Mothers Club scholarship fund—and give my players a new experience in community service. What else?"

"Come on, Tom. A thousand bucks?"

"Wish I'd given more. Five thousand or something." Olsen shrugged.

"You know what I think?" said Rakowsky. "I think you're regressing back to your college days—all those myths and crap you studied. Or maybe you just read too damn much poetry. It's like you're writing your own little fairy tale—pardon the expression—with yourself as the hero."

Olsen laughed. "That's actually very perceptive of you. Did you ever read any Jung?"

"Yeah," said Rakowsky, "and forgot it all."

Olsen turned toward the window. "Have you ever felt that compulsion to follow a certain path," he asked, "like it's out of your hands, and you're plummeting into a future you can't change?"

"Not in those words, exactly, but yeah, I guess I have."

"And then other times you feel completely logical? You make a very conscious choice of what to do?"

"Yeah, sure."

Olsen scanned the empty playing field beyond the window, slid his hands in his pockets. "I seesaw between the compulsions and the choices," he said. "I can't even tell the difference anymore."

Rakowsky said, "Hmm."

"The thing is," said Olsen, "I can't believe my life story could end the way it looks right now. Getting old, all alone till the day I die. My parents' curse on me come true: 'Be our guest—ruin your life.' So yeah, I am trying to create a better story for myself. But I don't know exactly what it is yet."

"Well, I hope you don't think it's gonna be happily-ever-after with Mary."

"If only it were that easy," Olsen said.

"Maybe you're like the guy in that myth who has to roll the boulder up the mountain, then it falls down again, then he has to roll it up, and it falls down again—just endless meaningless torture for eternity," Rakowsky said. He came over and slapped Olsen on the back. "Or how about the guy who got his liver pecked out over and over by the vulture? Now there's a story."

"Prometheus," said Olsen. "But no, I'm not that noble." He sighed. "She was crying, you know—on the way to St. Peter's."

"Why?"

"I don't know. But I get the impression things aren't so great in Mary's world as you think they are."

"Well, what do I know?" Rakowsky said. "Hey, have you met Vicky Galliano yet—the new Spanish teacher?"

"Yeah."

"She told a few people she thinks you're hot."

"Really?" Olsen said. "Damn. I still got it."

"So go for it," said Rakowsky.

"You know my rule," Olsen said. "Never date a co-worker unless you want to be out looking for a new job."

CHAPTER 6

❀

Interruptions

That night Olsen lay in bed on Roanoke Road. Thinking about Vicky Galliano. Looking out the window at the streetlights. Looking at Mr. McCormick's dark house next door. Thinking about Mary.

> **pain**
>> **fire**
>>> **compulsion**
>>>> **dream**
>>>>> **escape**

Then he fell asleep.

Vicky Galliano showed up in his dreams, until she morphed into Mary; Olsen woke up. He fell back to sleep, and there was Kristina; a very pleasant dream. In some ways, really, he and Kristina were made for each other.

> **compulsion**
>> **dream**
>>> **escape**

Why bite the hand that feeds you?

He called Kristina the next day, invited her to dinner.

And so Olsen and Kristina picked up briefly where they had left off, as undramatically as if returning to their seats at a play after intermission, they had done it so often.

Lying in bed beside Kristina that Saturday night, he had no small talk. Instead he listened to the stream of songs on the radio, good old classic rock, songs of the good old days, younger days, invincible, when the good life was falling off that silver platter into his lap.

Then somehow he started to pretend that it was Mary, not Kristina, who was lying there next to him, that the bare skin pressed against his bare skin was Mary's—until Kristina said, "Tom?" and he jumped at the strange unexpectedness of her voice.

"What's wrong?" Kristina asked. "Were you sleeping?"

Then the deejay changed the mood of the music, slowed things down, played a song from the long-ago abortion days with Alexandra. Wistful, spare, in a minor key. A song Olsen did not need to hear, because it reminded him the silver platter days did not mean much, that no matter what he did, underneath it all he was only waiting for the world to end.

Blood turned to sadness in his veins, heart pumping that old despair through him. Olsen lay his forearm over his eyes and breathed, tinge of a groan on the exhale; he felt it vibrating in his throat. The sadness simmered, turned molten, turned into anger, anger that had no target but himself.

He got up, shut the radio off with the side of his fist, and returned to bed; he took Kristina in his arms, but it felt like there was nothing there.

        ❧   ❧   ❧

October had become November by then, time for fall conferences. On Wednesday, Olsen found Mary listed on the Thursday night schedule, 6:45 time slot. The two words *Mary Wendling* smoked on the page in his hand like the aftershock of a lightning strike.

Later that day, back on Roanoke Road, Olsen found a letter in his mailbox, addressed to him in an uneven, unfamiliar hand. The return address said *Wendling*, on Dover Drive; the stamp said *Love* with a heart-shaped wreath of flowers. Olsen ripped it open.

On behalf of the Mothers Club, Mary had written. *From the bottom of my heart. I never imagined. Generosity. Gallantry. Quiet hero. I will always remember. With gratitude.*

Mary's handwriting was messy, high energy, a speeding car across the paper. He hadn't predicted this keepsake, this hard copy of her thoughts, the balm of her warm words on his sore eyes. But he felt a vague disturbance at the sight of her disorderly cursive—not the calligraphic hand he had imagined.

He realized he was squeezing the card, crumpling the edges with his fingers. He smoothed it out, put it on the kitchen counter, then carried it to the coffee table in the living room.

That night Olsen went through his closet, leafed through his sport coats, picked out the brown and beige herringbone. The new white button-down shirt. The blue and beige tie. The dress khakis.

If only they hadn't scheduled Mary right in the middle of the evening. 6:45 to 6:55. And those damn ten-minute increments—what could he do with ten minutes?

He went downstairs, picked the card up off the coffee table and reread it.

Olsen bulleted his way through Thursday.

- Freshman English.

- Sophomore English.

- Senior Lit.

- Lunch.

- AP English.

- Creative Writing.

- Basketball practice.

By 5:20 he was back in his classroom: third floor, southwest corner, head of the stairs. Sat at his desk, feet up, looking at the walls. His first conference was set for 5:30.

So. Later that evening, Mary would see his classroom for the first time. She would see his framed Teacher of the Year certificates, his league and district Coach of the Year plaques, his Indiana Coach of the Year trophy—nothing showy, just the facts. She would see his *Odyssey* mural circling the room on the walls above the chalkboards, the gift that some of his artistic students had painted for him.

The mural had happened a few years back. Olsen had driven to school early one spring Saturday to retrieve some ungraded papers. The halls were silent; ascending the stairs he heard only the fall and echo of his own feet. But as he approached the third floor and his classroom, he heard noise, voices, clatter. Entering his room he crossed into a twilight zone, his room that was not his room: instead it was full of kids with paintbrushes, standing on ladders, wading through dropcloths, the smell of paint heavy in the air, with shrieks and shouting and his industrial-strength fan blowing from the back.

His senior lit students.

One by one they saw him in the doorway; paintbrushes stopped midstroke; silence like dominoes ran around the room. Olsen felt a sick flash that they were pulling one over on him, that this was a betrayal he had somehow not foreseen, what were they doing, what were they putting on the walls?

Then he saw a ship painted in a bright blue sea on the stretch of wall above a blackboard.

"Mr. Olsen, we didn't think you'd be here today. We wanted to surprise you."

"What are you doing?" he asked.

"It's like—your own personalized Teacher of the Year award."

"It's going to be the *Odyssey*."

"We don't want you to forget us."

"A bunch of other kids chipped in for the paint and stuff, too."

"We have this card for you. We were going to tape it to the door."

A few days later Olsen gave the class a pizza party during senior lit to thank them. He couldn't eat, though. That day, and now, when Olsen looked at the walls, he recalled his flash of fear, the thought that they were tricking him, before he had realized the truth of their devotion.

When Olsen had first started teaching, he could still recite great swaths of the *Odyssey* by heart. Now those lines lay mostly forgotten under the accumulation of years and the addition of newer favorites, but the story felt even more like his own as time went by: a helpless witness to his own destruction; the years slipping away; holding the hope of a hero's ending; desperate to find his way home from the war—in his case, the war with himself.

   ❄   ❄   ❄

Sometime after 6:45, Mary arrived flying, breathless, landing in front of Olsen at the top of the stairs in a whirl of black velvet and silver jewelry and wild hair, gasping, "Am I late?" And he said, "No, you're right on time—come in, relax, catch your breath."

Sitting before her in his classroom, he could feel the floor trembling under his feet.

"I work at the Indian River Library," she said. "When I do the after-school story hours, I'm a bit more of a performer—that's why I'm dressed this way. The little ones are so adorable. I still remember when Ben was that young." She smiled, breathing softer. "Oh, I have something for you," she said. Olsen watched her lean down and reach into her bag.

"Cookies. When I was baking this morning, I thought of you—the bake sale, you know." She gave him a small foil-wrapped package tied with a white ribbon.

Olsen held it in his hand.

"Nice mural," she said, looking around the walls.

"The *Odyssey*. It was a gift from some of my students a few years ago." He folded his arms on the table and leaned toward her.

"So how is Ben doing in your class?" Mary asked, pulling her hair back from her face and letting it fall on her shoulders.

"Oh. Yeah. He's doing fine," said Olsen. "I remember how he resisted taking AP English when we did schedules last spring—too uncool, he thought. But he's having a good time and doing fairly well. He has a B at the moment. The challenge is good for him. If he'd stayed in regular English, he'd be bored out of his mind."

"I knew AP was the right thing for him, but he doesn't seem to buckle down enough. Right now he's just a funny mix of incredible drive and incredible indolence," Mary said.

"Teenagers. It's not just a study thing, it's everything. My players are struggling to stay focused on their basketball—and it's what they love the most. Adolescence. You know?"

"You're right."

"Which reminds me of Ben's tattoo," Olsen said. "I told him he's got to cover it up for games."

"Oh, definitely. That's fine. I wish he didn't even have it, but he was so determined." Mary looked up at the ceiling; Olsen looked at the long, smooth curve of her throat. "I told him he had to wait till he turned eighteen," she said. "Then one Saturday afternoon, he just showed up at home with it."

"Aha—so he surprised you."

"Yes, he did." Mary's gaze drifted toward the windows. "It was eerie. Without even realizing it, he chose a sun—just like his father."

"Really? Now *I'm* surprised," said Olsen. "From your description, I had a different impression of your husband. I wouldn't have pegged him as the tattoo type."

Mary's eyes darted back to Olsen. She bit her lip. Her glance flashed up to the clock over the chalkboard. "Impressions are funny, aren't they?"

The 6:55 bell rang.

"Already?" Olsen blurted; the doorway darkened, and the 7:00 father lumbered in early.

❧　　　❧　　　❧

It was past nine o'clock when Olsen's last parent finally departed.

As he straightened his room, the fluorescent lights buzzed in the silence like insects, and his irritation festered. Finally he stormed to the wall and snapped the switches off with a swipe of his hand. A bit of light glowed in through the windows from the parking lot. He finished putting the desks in their rows.

Ten minutes. What can you do with ten minutes? Slipped through my fingers and gone.

He put his bag on his shoulder and went out into the hall, scowling. Mary stood at the top of the stairs.

"Turns out I'm still here," she said, tucking her hair behind her ears. "Want to walk out together?"

As they walked down the stairs, he wrapped his hand lightly around her arm, and she stopped and looked up at him.

"Mary," he said.

"Yes?"

"I was worried about you that day—in the van—you were crying."

She looked down the stairs.

"Is everything all right?" he asked.

"Yes," she said, "yes."

He let go of her arm. "Are you sure?" he said. "Because—"

"Thomas, I won't lie to you." Mary was still looking down the stairs as she spoke. "I've got a few things lying heavy on my heart. But I've got to work them out for myself. I can't have you rescue me from everything."

"What do you mean?"

She turned her face to Olsen **the face that is somehow written on my memory of somewhere I have never been but still remember** and smiled at him. "I mean, you were already my knight in shining armor at Art from the Heart. I've got to make that last awhile."

She turned again and started walking the rest of the way downstairs, and he followed, watching her hair swinging around her shoulders and her hand gliding along the railing.

In the main hall downstairs, Olsen and Mary greeted other stragglers—some teachers, some parents—and headed for the front doors.

"What will you do for Thanksgiving, Thomas?"

"What I always do—spend it at Rick and Karen Rakowsky's. He's the phys ed teacher here—football coach, too. Oh, sure you know them—I hear you go to the same church."

"And how did you hear that?" she asked with a lilt of curiosity.

"Oh, I guess Rick must have mentioned it. And of course," Olsen hurried on, "we have basketball practice all through Thanksgiving break. I never stray far from town this time of year. Well, it's the same for you, with Ben."

They kept walking toward the doors.

Mary asked, "What about the rest of your family? Do you have sisters and brothers?"

"Nope. I'm an only child."

"You won't see your parents for Thanksgiving? Do they still live in Boston—or did you say Rhode Island?"

"Well, actually they retired to Hilton Head," Olsen said, "but my father died a few years ago. My mother stayed on down there. She loves it."

"Hilton Head. Is she a golfer?"

"Oh, big time. He was, too."

Outside in the parking lot Olsen followed Mary's crisscross path between the cars.

"And what will you do for Thanksgiving?" he asked.

"My best friend is coming from Fort Wayne for the long weekend," Mary said, the words dangling over her shoulder. "We've been friends since junior high. And she's Ben's godmother, too."

"You should bring her to watch one of our practices when she's here," Olsen said.

"Really? Ben told me your practices are closed. Secret, even."

"Well, spectators are allowed by coach's invitation only," said Olsen, "and now you have my standing invitation."

"That's great. Abby would love to come. She's a big basketball fan...and an especially big Ben fan. Well, here we are." Mary stood beside a black Grand

Cherokee, poking around her bag and pulling out the keys. "I know it's a gas hog," she apologized, "but Virgil bought it for me to share with Ben." She opened the door and climbed in the driver's seat. The dome light shone down on her dark hair.

Olsen leaned toward her, inside the open door, much too close. She didn't flinch, didn't look away, but met his eyes evenly. He felt the heat of her breath on his face.

"Mary," he said.

"Hey, Olsen, is that you?" Rakowsky's shout sailed across the parking lot and grew louder as he approached. "You're still here, too? Some long day, huh? Let's get outta here. Oh, hi, Mary. I didn't realize that was you. How are you tonight?" Rakowsky clapped his hand between Olsen's shoulder blades.

Olsen looked at Rakowsky through narrowed eyes, silent.

"Hi, Rick," Mary said. "I'm good. How are you?"

"Good, good. Well, whaddya say, Tom? Call it a night?"

"Yeah. See you later, man." Olsen chopped his syllables sharply, elbowing Rakowsky's arm away.

"You know what, Tom? I've gotta ask you something. Can I walk you over to your car? Sorry, Mary. It's a football thing. But tell Virgil I said hi. See you at church on Sunday."

"Sure. Well, good night, Thomas. Thank you for everything. And I'll see you soon—I'll bring Abby to one of those Thanksgiving practices."

"Great. And remember," Olsen said, "call me anytime—if you need any-thing—if Ben needs anything." He swung the door shut. Then he turned his back on Rakowsky and walked across the parking lot.

"Tom…"

Olsen kept walking.

"Tom, wait, man…"

But Olsen got into his Corvette and drove away.

CHAPTER 7

❀

The Mother Lode

"All right, men," Olsen yelled over the cacophony of basketballs, "we're done for the day here, but listen up." He stood at center court with his assistant coaches, Kuehn and old Stefanik. One by one the boys fell in around them.

"It's hard to believe that most of you guys played in Semi-State last year," Olsen said. Long silence.

Coach Kuehn said, "You guys are acting like all you have to do is rest on your laurels—and that won't cut it. We have a huge amount of work to do to before the season opener, and I'm telling you right now, I don't know how we're going to be ready."

Coach Stefanik's wild gray eyebrows knotted together.

The boys waited, shifting their feet, eyes on the coaches, arms at their sides. The longer they stood, the more Olsen saw a combination of repentance and worry on their faces. Finally he sighed, and his face softened.

"Look," Olsen said, "use tomorrow as an attitude adjustment day. Have a good Thanksgiving with your families. And for Friday, slight change of plans. Practice will be at six at night, instead of eight in the morning. I decided to fly down to South Carolina to spend Thanksgiving with my mother, and I won't be back till Friday afternoon. So I'll see you all at six on Friday. And you better be ready to play."

Olsen turned and walked across the parquet floor to the bleachers, where his things were piled up: clipboard, notebooks, an Indian River High sweat-shirt. Stefanik and Kuehn presided over the murmuring drift of players moving toward the locker room. Ben lingered behind, picked up a ball and put up a few shots.

"Hey, LeVon," Ben shouted, "come on back. Shoot around with me."

LeVon slowed in his tracks. "I gotta get home," he called. But he turned back through the tide bound for the locker room and picked up a ball. He lofted a shot, muttered as it bounced off the glass and flew into the bleachers, then jogged to retrieve it and kept on shooting.

"Coach, I'm sorry," Ben said. He let go a 3-point bomb; it sailed through the net.

Olsen said, "For what?"

"Letting you down. I'm gonna work harder."

"You're not letting me down. I'm glad to see you sticking around." Olsen pulled his hooded sweatshirt on. "You, too, LeVon."

"Well, see ya Friday," said Ben. "Have a good Thanksgiving with your mom."

"Yeah, Coach," LeVon said.

"The janitor'll be around to kick you out." Olsen stood by the bench, watching them.

"First I wanna make sure," Ben said, "that I've licked this shot." Another long bomb swished through the net.

Reminds me of me.

Back on Roanoke Road, Olsen saw Mr. McCormick out in his front yard in the chilly wind, raking in the garden bed with slow, short strokes, the little pile of brown leaves scattering at his feet.

"What're you doing for Thanksgiving, Tom?" Mr. McCormick called.

"Going to see my mother."

"Have a good time. I'll hold down the fort."

"Hey," Olsen said, "I got your season pass for you. But I left it at school. I'll bring it over when I get back."

"Good enough. It's very kind of you, Tom."

"It wouldn't be a home game without you," said Olsen. Mr. McCormick nodded his head, resumed his slow raking. Olsen stuck his key in the front door, looked back at Mr. McCormick, at the smattering of leaves around his old brown shoes, and went inside.

❦   ❦   ❦

Olsen flew out of Indianapolis on Thanksgiving morning as the thick inland frost was dissolving into glitter and the sky shone clear blue. The plane was crammed with people and discord and carry-on baggage. Considering he booked his ticket last minute, this aisle seat was a stroke of luck; he loosened his tie, pulled Don DeLillo's *White Noise* out of his leather overnight bag, and dove into rereading—fourth or fifth time; he'd lost count—sucked back into the *White Noise* world of Jack and Babette Gladney.

Babette and I have turned our lives for each other's thoughtful regard, turned them in the moonlight in our pale hands, spoken deep into the night about fathers and mothers, childhood, friendships, awakenings, old loves, old fears.

Jack and Babette also shared a great sex life. Their erotic union grounded them in reality and restored their sanity after hair-raising days in the modern world. Nothing—not raising their blended family of multiplicitous children, not maintaining communications with their exes, keeping their household running, surviving an airborne toxic event—nothing could dissolve it.

Even when talk turned heavy in Jack and Babette's bedtime discussions of life and death, Eros was their saving grace: *Her body became the agency of my resolve…Nightly I moved toward her breasts, nuzzling into that designated space like a wounded sub into its repair dock. I drew courage from her breasts, her warm mouth, her browsing hands, from the skimming tips of her fingers on my back.*

❦   ❦   ❦

He changed planes in Charlotte. Emerging from the inching crush of flesh and fabric departing the 727, he bought a bottle of water and a slice of pizza on the concourse and ate while walking to the next gate. Rushes of travelers swelled around and then washed beyond him in ebbs and flows, pulling him with a bit more longing toward the flight to Hilton Head Island. It would be nice to see his mother; it would be good to breathe the salt air; if only tourists hadn't taken most of the place over.

When Olsen emerged from the Hilton Head airport, it was warm and raining lightly. Through the film of drizzle, he saw his mother's white Mercedes pulled up in the dodg'ems array of taxis, cars, and shuttle vans, and he crisscrossed a path toward her, splashing in shallow puddles as he went.

"Hi, Mom. Happy Thanksgiving," Olsen said, as he opened the back passenger door and tossed his bag on the tan leather seat.

"Hello, Tom."

He got in front and they smiled at each other. They had never been a kissing family.

Louise Olsen looked the same as ever: her platinum hair lay chic and short against her head; her golfer's tan was thick and brown. That day she wore a navy blue suit, cut in clean straight lines like a good putt.

Olsen had thought Louise might go downhill after his father's death three years ago—the abrupt end of forty-five years of marriage. But Louise had widowed well. She missed John, she said, but they had promised each other "No tears;" besides, her leadership was needed on Hilton Head town council, and she would always have golf. Time went by, and Olsen saw that Louise did not grow sad, or soft, or introspective; instead, she became even more of everything she had already been.

"Good to see you," Olsen said. Classical music floated in the climate-controlled air.

"You, too," said Louise, squeezing the Mercedes between a shuttle van and a taxi without bothering, Olsen noticed, to check her blind spot. "I thought you might be bringing someone with you," she added.

"Someone?"

"Well, when you called last week about coming down," Louise said, "I wondered if you might have a new young lady you wanted me to meet." She brought up the rear of a short line of traffic waiting for the light at Beach City Road.

"Not this time," he said.

"Just wishful thinking, then."

"I'm not seeing anyone these days." Olsen watched the windshield wipers flip-flop to the tempo of the music.

Louise fiddled with her rearview mirror. "What prompted this sudden visit, then?" she asked.

"I don't know, Mom—I just decided I should spend one Thanksgiving a decade with my own family. And you're it."

The music played on in the cool air.

"So," Olsen said, "what are you up to on town council?"

"Oh, you know," Louise answered. "The usual. Redevelopment strategies. Land management."

Hilton Head's streets were emptier than Olsen had ever seen them. Rain curtained the billboards: Hilton Head Factory Stores 1 & 2. Old Oyster Factory. H20 Sportscenter: Parasailing, Waverunning, Waterskiing. Westin, Crowne Plaza, Marriott Golf Resort.

"You'll run for reelection next year?" Olsen asked.

"Definitely."

"Still golfing?"

"Constantly."

"Days of golf and politics: you've found your nirvana."

Louise laughed. "Don't forget my other vice. I still drive down to Savannah every month for the historical society meetings. Fascinating contrasts between the New England and Southern perspectives..."

Louise kept talking, but Olsen stopped hearing as his thoughts took shape around Mary. What were Mary's vices? Books, of course, and...what else? He didn't know what she loved and craved and hoarded spare time for, what her idea of nirvana would be.

Babette and I have turned our lives for each other's thoughtful regard, turned them in the moonlight in our pale hands...

How would it feel, turning his life over to Mary and her caramel hands in the moonlight...

Louise buzzed down the parkway as Olsen watched the roadside signage. Miniature Golf. Golf. Golf Lessons. Tennis. Time Shares. Waverunning. Parasailing. Charter Fishing. Virtual Roller Coaster. Batting Cages. 4D Theatre. Laser Tag.

"How do you make peace with this tourist crap?" Olsen asked. "No matter how many times I visit, I never get used to it," **to this hollowness that hangs in the air, hollowness that touches too closely to the emptiness in me.**

"I see the things I like," Louise said, "and don't notice the rest."

At last the commercial sector dissolved into Sea Pines Plantation, and they entered the moneyed quietude of Louise's neighborhood. Cruising along Greenwood to North Sea Pines Drive, the blue, brown, and emerald spread of land and water looked impressionistic and misty to Olsen's eyes; it felt like the Indiana Dunes, and he started to relax. The ocean shimmered gray under the light rain.

Louise's impeccable Cape looked over the Atlantic from the end of Peninsula Way. **It's only for twenty-four hours. Enjoy the scenery.**

Inside, Olsen left his shoes and bag in the foyer and walked into the beige living room, home of old familial artifacts: the Oriental rug, landscape of his solitary childhood games; his mother's brown paisley wingback chair; his father's Winslow Homer on the wall.

Olsen sank heavily into the cushions of the new brown leather sofa.

"Can I get you something to drink?" Louise asked. "Planes are so dehydrating."

"Yeah, how about a beer?'

She turned her head toward the grandfather clock and pointed to the time: two-twenty. "If you don't think it's too early."

"I don't," he said, and tipped his head back against the couch, shutting his eyes.

Louise returned in a few minutes and handed him a heavy crystal beer stein foaming up along the edges. She put a coaster on the mahogany coffee table in front of him, then crossed the living room and sat down in her wingback chair, swinging her feet up on the ottoman.

"Nancy Chamberlain will call around three," Louise said, "when she and Bill are heading over to the club. We'll meet them there. The club does a marvelous Thanksgiving feast. We've all said we'll never roast another turkey." She leaned over the arm of her chair toward the stereo. "What classes are you teaching this year?" she asked, as a Chopin Nocturne began to play.

"Freshman and sophomore English, AP English, senior lit, creative writing."

"Why do you have to teach freshman English?" Louise said. "I thought you said you were the department chairman. Don't you have enough people to help you?"

"I teach it because I like it. Every year I take a section or two."

"But why?"

"The freshman are so—fresh," Olsen said. "On the cusp of everything. No college plans to make, no professional goals to figure out, no family pressures to live up to—not yet. Everything is just beginning for them. How could you not want to be a part of that?"

Louise looked at the Winslow Homer on the wall; notes of Chopin drifted through the space between them.

"High school," she said, and gave her one-syllable laugh. "Really, Tom, if only you'd gone for the Ph.D."

Not again. Olsen lifted the beer stein and took a long drink. "Too late now."

"With your talent, your intellect, you could have done anything in the world," Louise said. "I'm still a little embarrassed when I tell people what you do. It always sounds like you took the easy way out, somehow."

"Don't tell them, then," he said.

"Do you remember Molly Chamberlain—Nancy and Bill's daughter?"

"Yeah."

"She just made partner at Bill's firm. Not because she's Bill's daughter. She earned it, of course."

"Of course."

"Molly went to Duke—undergrad and law," Louise said. "She'll take over Bill's Charleston office for him. That way he can semi-retire and still keep things in the family."

"That's nice."

"I take it you're not seeing the TV reporter anymore—what was her name, Kristina?" Louise asked. "She sounded like a good match for you."

Olsen sighed. He tipped the beer stein against his lips again, took a long gulp and swallowed. He wrapped his hands around the glass. "We still get together sometimes. But it's tough. We're both so busy."

"Hmmm. When you told me about her last year, of course I hoped she might be The One," Louise said.

"Nope."

"How do you even *meet* interesting women—women of your caliber—in Indiana? I often wonder."

"I manage."

"But you haven't met anyone since Kristina," said Louise.

"Well," he said.

Louise sipped her iced tea. "Do you think you'll ever settle down and get married?"

"It's too soon to tell."

"It's not going to be basketball and beer for the rest of your life, is it?" she said, with another one-syllable laugh.

Olsen looked at Louise. Then he drank the rest of his beer in one continuous swallow. He placed the stein on the coffee table, not the coaster, and watched the foam slide down onto the wood, spreading into a wet ring.

"Kristina's not the woman I envision spending my life with," Olsen said. "Anyway, in basketball season I have absolutely no personal life. I'm just too busy. It's hard for someone who's never coached a sport to understand how it takes over your life. Every moment of every day and night is booked. Only a woman who really loved basketball could understand."

"Is there such a woman?"

"I hope so." Mary was such a woman. Of course, his mother would never get that. A scene from *White Noise* flashed distractingly into his thoughts:

Babette started taking things out of the refrigerator. I grabbed her by the inside of the thigh as she passed the table. She squirmed deliciously, a package of frozen corn in her hand.

"Somewhere," Olsen said, "there's a woman who will just naturally under-stand me." *She squirmed deliciously.*

"Honestly, Tom. You and your basketball."

"Honestly, Mom. You and your golf."

Louise's lips tightened as she raised an eyebrow, and Olsen felt himself plummeting backward toward a time he had worked hard to forget. So he picked his beer stein up, said, "Time for another," and went into the kitchen.

When he returned, beer in hand, to the living room, Louise asked, "Don't you ever think of leaving Indiana? For somewhere more cosmopolitan?"

God, she is relentless. "I used to. Sometimes I still do. But not for the cul-ture—maybe for more sunshine, or just a new beginning."

"Oh, I just read a new study," said Louise. "This should interest you. They looked at patterns of higher education state by state across the country. Did you know that Indiana is at the bottom of the barrel for statewide percentage of college graduates?"

"No, Mom—I read that study myself. Indiana has made a huge *leap* in per-centage of college graduates because of new incentive programs and other innovations to get kids to college. We used to be way down on the list, but we've come up fifteen or twenty places in the last ten years."

"I think you misread. It was some ungodly low percentage, too—not much better than Mississippi's," said Louise.

"You're wrong, Mom. Anyway—say what you want, but I love Indiana. It feels like home to me. And the majority of my kids do go on to college or com-munity college somewhere. But degrees are not the quintessential defining characteristic of a life. A lot of people without degrees are geniuses and do real good in this world—while a lot of people *with* degrees are idiots."

"Spare me that tired old soapbox," Louise said. "Let's agree to disagree."

Fine. That's all I can do with you anyway.

"What?"

"Nothing."

"Do you ever think of giving up coaching?" Louise said.

"Never." Olsen leaned forward on the sofa and put the stein, purposefully, back on the mahogany.

"Tom," she said, "use the coaster."

Slowly, he lifted the beer stein onto the coaster, then looked at Louise and smiled.

"All right then," Louise said. "Go on up and get settled in the guest room. We have a little time before Nancy calls. I'm going to finish doing a few things down here." She stood up and took her empty glass and Olsen's half-full one into the kitchen. Chopin played on.

Olsen got his bag from the foyer and walked upstairs. He put his bag on the king-size guest room bed and peered out the window toward the ocean: still raining. Across the hall in the bathroom, he brushed his teeth, splashed cold water on his face, combed his hair. A branch of the old cypress tree scratched against the window.

Olsen took a step across the threshold into his mother's study. Above her desk, degrees and accolades adorned the wall in an overwhelming accumulation of curricula vitae.

John Lowell Olsen, Bachelor of Arts, Economics, Swarthmore College.

Master of Arts, Economics, Columbia University.

Doctor of Philosophy, Economics, Columbia.

Carlton R. Murch Chair in Economics, Northeastern University.

The Galbraith Award.

Professor Emeritus of Economics, Northeastern.

Chairman, Massachusetts Economic Council.

Louise Ann Emerson, Bachelor of Arts, Political Science, Swarthmore College.

Louise Ann Olsen, Master of Arts, Economics, Columbia University.

Doctor of Philosophy, Economics, Columbia.

Evelyn M. Bates Chair in Economics, Wellesley College.

The Katherine Copley Church Award.

Professor Emerita of Economics, Wellesley.

Framed photos of John and Louise covered the adjacent wall. Their wedding portrait was a classic 1950's coming-up-the-aisle shot; they looked like contrived black-and-white Hollywood versions of the people they really were. Their fortieth-anniversary picture, hanging beneath it, was truer, a candid shot from the party their Hilton Head friends had thrown for them at the club.

Olsen walked farther into the room, looked closely at a few of the photos. John and Louise had begun their married life looking alike, and grew even more so with time. Both had strong, straight features well-placed on wise, pragmatic faces, with ash blond hair that had whitened through the years.

Olsen's good looks, the vestige of wilder forebears, bore little resemblance to his parents'.

John's and Louise's layers of achievement, their marks on the world, their partnership with each other—those were the only things that had really ever mattered to them. Walls like these only made it official. There were no pictures of Olsen on these walls or anywhere else in the house.

On previous visits to Hilton Head, he had asked his mother about it, but Louise always said she was still decorating. "There weren't any pictures of me up in Wellesley either," he had said once; but Louise appeared not to have heard.

"Hey, Mom!" Olsen shouted downstairs then, "where's our old family portrait?"

"The what?" Louise called back.

"Our family portrait—you know, the old one. From the summer before I went to Andover."

"Oh," she shouted, "it's up in the attic somewhere. I really don't have a place for it. Would you like to have it?"

He wanted to scream, **Are you f—ing kidding?**

Instead he sat down in the chair at Louise's desk and sighed.

A few minutes later, the phone on the desk rang loudly before him. It stopped on the third ring. Olsen went downstairs and heard his mother's voice, animated, on the kitchen extension.

"Yes, he's here...yes, fine...It's supposed to clear up by tomorrow, you know...He flies out first thing...Two o'clock tee-off sounds perfect...Well, are we ready? Meet you there shortly then. Bye-bye." She called from the kitchen, "Tom? Are you ready? Let's head for the club."

❀   ❀   ❀

With great thanksgiving, Olsen flew home the next day.

It felt good to get back to the bare silver-brown trees and the cold Indiana sky. It felt good to get home to his plain, placid street, his quiet house, and Mr. McCormick putzing around in the yard next door. It felt good to walk back into the Indian River gym, to see the boys rededicated, to feel his spirits for the season resurrecting. And to see Mary again.

She and her friend Abby arrived just as practice started. They climbed up to the last row of bleachers and leaned against the back wall, leaning on each other's shoulders and talking, watching the boys run their drills, waving down to Olsen. Abby was a taller, sparer version of Mary; they could pass for sisters with their dark hair and brown eyes and wide-angle smiles. Olsen kept glancing up at them, saw them laughing nose to nose, examining each other's bracelets and earrings, pointing at Ben with pride.

After practice Mary introduced Abby to Olsen, and they stood around making small talk, waiting for Ben to come out of the locker room. Then Mary got thirsty and went to the drinking fountain down the hall.

One on one in the quiet gym, when Olsen realized Abby was scrutinizing him with a curious smile, his body surged with sudden awareness: Mary had told her about him.

CHAPTER 8

❀

Kill Two Birds

Stefanik and Olsen slumped at opposite ends of the couch, beers in hand, and Kuehn sat in the recliner. Scouting reports, scribbled notes, dirty dishes, and Chinese takeout covered Olsen's coffee table; crumpled napkins and wads of paper spilled off the table and onto the carpet. They were as ready as they were going to be for the season opener with arch rival Stockton High.

"I feel a great season coming on," said Kuehn. "I'm pumped. Our guys are back on track. I think we can take it all the way."

"I think you're right," Olsen said.

"After twenty years head coaching in South Bend," said Stefanik, "I thought I was sick of the whole thing. Couldn't wait to get out—so I got out. Then I missed it so much, it drove Rosemary crazy. I used to wake her up nights, kicking in the bed and thrashing and yelling like I was going at it with the refs, she said. All I knew is I'd wake up soaked in sweat. If you love this game, you never get it out of your system. Mark my words, Kuehn, for the day you get old like me. How old are you, anyway?"

"Twenty-five."

"Jeez, I got a grandson your age!"

"Hey, Kuehn," said Olsen, "didn't your wife play basketball at Earlham, too?"

"Yeah, that's how we met."

"You two are gonna have some tall kids someday," said Stefanik.

"Yeah," Kuehn said, and smiled. "Starting around June 15th."

"What?" Stefanik's gray eyebrows flew high and Olsen sat up from his slouch on the sofa.

"Congratulations, man," said Olsen. "This calls for a toast." He brought three cold beers in from the kitchen, and they knocked them together in a tribute to fatherhood.

❦   ❦   ❦

The Wildcats won a barn-burning season opener against Stockton High, then rendered their next opponent hapless for victory number two. Olsen was happy. It was all starting up again.

When he saw Ben at school, Olsen said, "I've seen you shooting around in the gym with LeVon a lot. Before school, after practice. Lotta hours in there."

"Yup."

"He had ten points off the bench in our last game. Whatever you've been showing him is paying off. I'd been starting to think he wasn't going to make it in the big leagues with us."

"I know he was down on himself for his crappy scrimmages," Ben said. "But I needed the extra shooting practice, too. Gotta stick together, right?"

"Always," said Olsen.

The evening before their third game, Olsen stopped in his basketball office at the high school to listen to phone mail.

"Thomas, hi, it's Mary Wendling. I'm calling because I'd like to have a Christmas party for the team in a few weeks, after the home game on December 22nd. I'd like to have the players and cheerleaders, and their parents, and of course you and Coach Stefanik and Coach Kuehn. We'd have the party at our house right after the game. Can you let me know if this would be okay with you? Here's our number…"

Olsen scribbled it down and dialed it immediately, his hand hot around the receiver.

A man's voice answered, "Hello?"

"Hello, may I speak to Mary? It's Coach Olsen from Indian River High School."

"I'm sorry, Coach, Mary's not home right now. This is her husband. May I take a message?"

Olsen hesitated. "I'm…uh, returning her call. Could you ask her to call me? I'll give you my number."

Wendling asked, "Is this about the team party?"

"Yeah."

"Great. Well, what do you think, Coach? Is it all right with you? We'll keep the team curfew in mind—send everybody home nice and early."

"It's certainly fine with me. Absolutely."

"And would you be able to join us? Guest of honor and all," Wendling chuckled.

"Uh—yeah."

"Great. I'll just give Mary the message. I know she wants to get invitations in the mail as soon as possible. Hey, thanks for being in touch."

"Sure…"

"See you the 22nd then. Look forward to meeting you."

"Right." Olsen hung up. He stood up. He kicked his wastebasket over, and it spilled out like a cornucopia. **Son of a bitch.**

❦   ❦   ❦

Stefanik told Olsen he wanted to scout the Tuesday night game at Bristol South to get a look at them and the Valley City team, kill two birds on their scouting schedule, and he wanted Olsen to meet him there.

Just before varsity tip-off that night, they met in the Bristol South lobby in the clammy air that was moist with hot dog and pizza smells and the shoulder-to-shoulder sweat of guys slapping Olsen's back and saying, "Hey, Tom, your guys gonna take it all the way this season?" Stefanik strutted like Bristol South was his old stomping grounds. Next thing Olsen knew, they were climbing the bleachers through the crowd, Stefanik ahead of him waving to someone.

"Got somebody I want you to meet," said Stefanik over his shoulder, puffing as he climbed to the back row.

"Lissa Stevenson," Stefanik said, "I'd like you to meet Tom Olsen. Lissa's an old classmate of my daughter Laura. God, you're looking beautiful, Lissa. Better than the year you were homecoming queen, even."

Lissa smiled at Olsen. "Hi, Tom. It's a pleasure to meet you. I'm a big fan of your basketball team."

Olsen said hello and Stefanik barreled on, "Yup, and now Lissa's living right here in Bristol. Isn't that a coincidence? And Rosemary said to me just the other day, Wouldn't Lissa and Tom Olsen have a lot in common? After all, they both love sports. And I said, Honey, I think you're right."

Lissa was still smiling at Olsen.

Well…why not?

After Bristol South won the game, Stefanik insisted they all drive down the block to a nightspot he knew and have a drink together. They settled into a booth and ordered, then Stefanik said, "Oh, shit. Just remembered I promised Rosemary I'd be home right after the game. You two'll be fine without me, right? Great to see you again, Lissa. See ya, Tom," and slid out of the booth and left.

Olsen and Lissa looked at each other across the table.

"Do you get the feeling he wants us to be alone together?" she said, glass of red wine in her hand.

"No," said Olsen, "I get the feeling he wants us to get married," and Lissa laughed, and Olsen joined in, and Lissa reached over the table and put her hand on top of his and stroked it once, softly. **See how easy life could be? Why do you make it so hard on yourself?**

Mary didn't cross his mind again until he was driving home from the bar.

He took Lissa out to dinner that Saturday night, late, after a buzzer-beating win at home. He took her to a movie, too, the night between two victories the following week.

❋   ❋   ❋

Olsen had seen Mary at all the home games, sitting courtside with the man he presumed to be Wendling, and at the away games, lithely climbing the bleachers, Wendling behind her. Virgil Wendling looked much older than Mary, as Rakowsky had mentioned; he had a close-trimmed gray beard; his face held traces of the better-looking man he used to be. And he was always touching Mary: his hand on her knee as they sat side by side watching the action, his arm around her shoulders as they moved through the post-game crowds.

Home games made it easier: Olsen's own turf, the fervor and favoritism of the home crowd, Mr. McCormick in his honorary seat by the team bench, everything making Olsen feel a part of things, the biggest part, king. Away games were harder, stranger in a strange land, that old familiar unease that no one suspected in him. Home or away, Olsen would look hard at Mary once, then avert his eyes for the night, if he could.

Whenever he tried to be alone with Lissa, Mary inevitably intruded on his thoughts, the arcs of her body drawing themselves in his mind's eye, the kiss from her fingertips coming toward him again and again, the word he savored on her lips repeating in his memory: *Thomas.*

He took Lissa out again the night before Mary's Christmas party. That was a mistake. His body attended dinner, but his soul was far away, finetuning his game plan for the next night, and composing a Christmas toast to share with Mary at the party.

When he dropped Lissa off at home after dinner, she said, "It doesn't seem like your heart is really in this, Tom," and gave him a hug, wished him good luck for the season, and went inside alone, and that was the end of it.

CHAPTER 9

❀

Romeo

On the night of December 22nd, Olsen parked on Dover Drive and climbed out into the snow, hands in parka pockets, his breath wreathed around his head and drifting upward. He started walking toward the Wendlings' house. The clear and frozen December night glittered, not with starlight, but Christmas decorations up and down the street. He saw Kuehn and Stefanik walking toward him from the other direction.

"Are we the last ones here?" Stefanik called out. "Jeez, there's nowhere to park. I'm freezing my ass."

They headed up the front walkway. The Wendlings' house glowed from the inside out: a Christmas tree blanketed with tiny white lights shone through one window, a chandelier through another, and a sea of people floated behind the glass. Olsen rang the bell, and a flash from that September afternoon shot through him—the moment he first stood at this door, ringing the bell, looking through the window with no idea how this house was going to change him.

The door opened and there was Mary in black and gold, the front hall behind her draped in pine garlands and lights, the air draped in laughter and Christmas music and the cinnamon scent of hot cider.

Mary's big brown dog jingled through the crowd and sniffed the men's knees. His collar dangled with silver bells and a red and green plaid Christmas bow.

"Hey, boy," Olsen said, reaching down to stroke the dog's head. "What's his name?" he asked Mary.

"Romeo," she said, and the dog licked Olsen's hand, then lost interest and jingled into the dining room.

❦   ❦   ❦

Ed Pender pumped Olsen's arm, saying, "Hey, Coach, are we going all the way this year?"

"Eight-and-oh—not bad, Olsen!" Mr. Reiter growled with a grin, his plump fingers wrapped around a bottle of beer.

"Yeah, nice job, Tom. You, too, Don, Mike," Howard Pytel said from the swarm of dads around the three coaches.

Ron Powell tried to slap an arm around Olsen's shoulders, but it didn't quite reach. "Hey, how's my kid looking? Pretty good, huh? Quite a difference from last year, wouldn't you say?"

"Yeah," Olsen said, "he's really taken his game to the next level. AAU's been good for him. And he's been taking a lot of extra shooting practice. I like to see that."

"He hit a couple of tough shots tonight," Stefanik said, then harrumphed to clear his throat. Olsen glanced at Stefanik, saw his remaining strands of hair sparkling under Mary's Christmas lights.

"Is LeVon gonna be starting anytime soon?" Ron Powell asked.

"I don't know," Olsen said, "but he'll get some good minutes." Olsen scanned the fathers. Where was Wendling? He wanted to introduce himself and get it over with.

"How about Nate?" asked Howard Pytel.

"Get him to the gym more," Olsen said. "He's got to get serious about lifting."

"Nate's got the quicks and the moves," said Kuehn, "but he's not strong enough out there right now. He's getting pummeled by the big guys."

"My kid's getting pummeled, too," said Michael Cavatelli's father. "I can't believe the size of some of these kids. What the hell are their parents feeding them?"

"Feeding 'em, nothing—some of 'em gotta be on steroids," Ed Pender said. "No normal kid's gonna bulk up as big as some of the guys we've played."

"Yeah," said Mr. Reiter. "Tall and skinny, I can accept. But how about that Pickerton center tonight? A real Sasquatch."

Olsen lifted his beer bottle toward the dads. "All I want to say is this. Our team doesn't need luck, or undue influence, or any artificial means to win. Our guys are gold. Last year, the Final Four. This year, we're going to take it all."

"Here, here!" "I'll drink to that!" "State champs it is!" They clanked cans and bottles together as the 8-0 mood, like a guest at the party, tangoed through the house.

❦   ❦   ❦

Olsen looked across the hall into the living room for Mary. He caught Terese Ciprak's eye instead, and she smiled across the distance between them; Terese was tall and swan-necked and could see over people. She put her hand up next to her cheek and shimmied her fingers at Olsen in a little wave. Her daughter Chloe was Indian River's homecoming queen and captain of the cheerleaders, and Terese loved mentioning how often she was mistaken for Chloe's sister, "sometimes even her *younger* sister!" Olsen didn't see Terese's husband Nick.

In the dining room, Ben, Matt Pender, Nate Pytel, LeVon Powell, and the other players stood shoulder to shoulder around the table, glowing with the power of the undefeated, chugging cans of pop, piling their plates with chicken wings and loaded potato skins and Christmas cookies and pizza, as the cheerleaders clustered and nibbled in their wake.

A man's voice behind him said, "Coach Olsen?"

Olsen turned around.

"I'm Virgil Wendling. Hey, it's great to have you here tonight. Pleasure to finally meet you. Thanks for coming," he said; he was indeed the close-cropped graybeard Olsen had seen touching Mary at the games. Wendling shook Olsen's hand hard, but his skin was soft.

"Good to meet you, too," said Olsen.

Wendling nodded toward Ben and the other players. "Must be great being at the helm with this group. You're a lucky guy. I wouldn't mind having your job."

"I hear that a lot," Olsen said.

"By the way, I heard about your donation," said Wendling, "and I wanted to tell you how great I thought that was."

"Donation?"

"Buying up that bake sale the way you did, and having the boys take the food to St. Peter's."

"Oh, yeah. A couple of months ago. Well, it was a good cause."

"It was such a fine thing to do," Wendling said. "And it really made an impression on Ben. He still talks about it."

"That's good to hear."

"Ben looks up to you, Tom, probably more than you know."

"Thanks. I appreciate that."

"We all read about some of these coaches today," said Wendling, "the terrible example they set, on and off the court—and in high school, no less. I think Indian River is extremely blessed to have you."

"Thanks."

"So," Wendling said, "are you a member over at St. Peter's?"

"No. I'm not a member anywhere." Olsen drank the last of his beer.

"We're over at Calvary Lutheran," Wendling said. "Love to have you join us some Sunday. Every man ought to be in church on Sunday morning," he said, reaching up to clap Olsen's shoulder.

Great. Shades of Lieben.

From across the hall in the living room, Mary announced, "I'd like to propose a toast—well, a prayer, really." She stood in front of the fireplace in her black velvet dress and gold jewelry, lifting her wine glass toward the congregation of partygoers.

Wendling started moving toward the living room. "Coming?" he asked Olsen.

"Right behind you." Instead Olsen turned, walked to the sideboard in the dining room, got another beer. **How about that religious commercial? I'm getting tired of people trying to drag me to church.**

Olsen walked to the outskirts of the living room as Mary started to speak, Wendling at her side.

"God has given us so many gifts," Mary said, "and one of the greatest is the gift of the special people in our lives—and that means all of you! I thank God for everyone here, and I want to read from this Psalm as my hope and prayer for all of us in the new year." She took a black Bible down from the mantel and opened it.

> "Let the morning bring me word
> of your unfailing love,
> for I have put my trust in you.
> Show me the way I should go,
> for to you I lift up my soul.

Rescue me from my enemies, O Lord,
for I hide myself in you.
Teach me to do your will,
for you are my God;
may your good Spirit
lead me on level ground."

She leafed back toward the front of her Bible. "O Lord, let Your beloved rest secure in You, for You shield us all day long, and the ones You love rest between Your shoulders."

Mary looked around the living room, and into the front hall, then let her smile rest on Olsen.

"Forever and ever, Amen," she said, and notes of tinkling glass and a scattering of Amens rose up into the air, and Wendling put his hand on Mary's hair, then kissed her, kissed her for a long time, Olsen thought, watching their lips, and Christmas music played on around him, and people were laughing.

A sick sensation sank through Olsen from his throat to the soles of his feet, burning. **Some fantasy you've been having. Thank God you haven't made a total ass of yourself.**

He drank half the bottle of beer at once. His scalp prickled. **All this religion. God is everything to these people.**

Olsen finished his beer in a final gulp. **So what? Ben is all I care about.**

Stefanik sidled up to Olsen. "Terese *wants* you. Said she'd like to get under some mistletoe with you."

"*Who* does?" asked Olsen.

"Terese Ciprak! Whaddya mean, who? Do you need my Viagra or something? She's divorced now, you know. If it doesn't work out with you and Lissa…"

Olsen squinted in annoyance at Stefanik: "Yeah, there's a great idea—dating the mother of a student. No recipe for disaster cooking there," but he choked as he spoke and started coughing. Across the room, he saw Mary's friend Abby, visiting again from Fort Wayne, and waved to her, still clearing his throat.

Olsen walked over and joined Abby and Ben and Nate Pytel and LeVon Powell for a rehash of that night's basketball victory and predictions for the Wildcats' next game. Abby surprised Olsen with her basketball knowledge. His mind veered onto another course as he nursed a new beer. **I'll call Lissa**

tomorrow and apologize. Explain how basketball had me distracted. Promise her my undivided attention if she'll have me. And I think she'll have me.

Olsen was about to ask Abby what she did for a living back home in Fort Wayne when Mary appeared.

"Thomas, could you help me?" she asked. "I need to bring more drinks up from the basement, and I can't find Virgil."

Her request surprised him, but he excused himself with nonchalance and followed her. Followed her into the kitchen and down the basement stairs, followed her hair swinging darkly across her shoulders, followed her hand skimming lightly down the railing, her nails neatly filed and unpolished. He saw a night-lighted workroom at the bottom of the stairs to the left, but Mary turned right through a doorway into darkness.

With no warning she stopped in her tracks to reach up for a light string overhead, and Olsen walked right into her from behind. Instinctively he reached out to stop her from falling forward: he caught velvet and Mary's breast in his left hand, velvet and the tight curve of her belly in his right. Mary looked over her shoulder and up into Olsen's eyes, and her hair swung as she turned toward him, and in the commotion of touch he reached up and pulled the light on, knowing that light was the only thing that could save him from himself.

They stared at each other; he saw the density of her eyelashes, and the shadows under her eyes, and the gold cross on a fine chain that lay glittering on her skin beneath her throat. Olsen could hear his own breathing. Then Mary slipped away from him. She walked to the far end of the room where a refrigerator stood against the wall. She opened the fridge, slid a twelve-pack of Pepsi out and put it on the table, then a twelve-pack of ginger ale, a six-pack of Heineken, a bottle of white wine.

"Here we go," Mary said. "This ought to do it. Could you carry the twelve-packs up?"

Olsen fumbled in his thoughts for something to say, something to keep her downstairs with him, just to make sure this was definitely not what he wanted.

"Sure," he said, approaching the table. "Hey, thanks for that prayer—the blessing you read upstairs." He slid his hands in his pockets. "I wish I had what you have—that faith. Maybe that's my whole problem. I believe in God—I think I do—no, I'm sure I do—but I don't do anything about it. Don't know where to start. I wish I did."

Mary watched him as he spoke, her lips parted, her hands wrapped around the wine bottle.

"Oh, Thomas," she said.

He shrugged.

"I've thought about you so often since Art From the Heart and the bake sale and St. Peter's," she said. "You're always doing something for others—teaching and coaching and charity work. And I've wondered, who does Thomas turn to when *he* needs someone to care, to listen, to inspire *him*? Maybe you need more of that in your life. Maybe that's why you feel a longing for God."

They turned their heads toward the ringing thumps of someone descending the basement stairs—then Romeo galloped into the room, his Christmas collar jingling. He trotted across the room toward Mary and Olsen, started sniffing the floor near the fridge. Mary twirled the bottle of wine in her hands.

"I never even went to church," she said, "until I met Virgil. Once I started going, it seemed so foreign and like the most natural thing in the world, at the same time. Now I wonder how I survived so long without knowing God—that seems like a miracle in itself."

Olsen pulled a bottle of Heineken out of the six-pack on the table. He twisted the cap off and started drinking. Romeo flopped on the floor at his feet.

"I've never been, you know, the churchgoing type," he said.

"Neither am I," said Mary.

"You sure know the Bible."

"That Psalm I read? Pure poetry, wasn't it? And the part I flipped back to was Moses' blessing on Benjamin; I like to say it for Ben. But it works for everyone."

Olsen took another drink, a long one.

"The Lutherans have this pure, unvarnished doctrine," she said. "I like it, its strict simplicity and all—but it's too spartan for me. I'm a bit of a renegade at heart. A poet and a dreamer—like you." She leaned back against the refrigerator, the wine in her hands.

"How do you know I'm a poet and dreamer?" he asked.

"The way you love Ben. Your *Odyssey* mural. The things you don't say," she answered, and all his previous inner protestations drowned in the well of her words.

"All I know for sure," he said, "is that there's a huge hole in my life, and I don't know how I'm ever going to fill it."

Mary pressed the wine bottle to her chest.

"If only I had your faith," said Olsen.

"Yeah, but it's not like I'm set for life. My faith is strong some days, and weak others. Every time I turn around in this world, there's something just waiting to destroy it. Sometimes I feel like I can't go on another day, even another hour, it hurts so much—pain I can't talk about. Problems I have to resolve on my own. But thank God I have Ben," she said. "How could I look at Ben and not believe there's a God who loves me?" She smiled as she spoke, but her voice caught on *loves*.

"I hope you find what you're looking for," Mary said. "You deserve to be happy."

"So do you."

"Well, we better go up." Mary walked toward the stairway; Romeo scrambled up off the floor and followed her.

Then she turned toward Olsen. "I wasn't much help, was I?" she said.

"Actually, you helped more than you know." He smiled and snapped off the light as they headed upstairs.

Guests still gathered in circles of conversation as Olsen and Mary walked back into the living room. Ben was laughing, his tee shirt sleeve pulled up over his shoulder, showing off his sun tattoo for Abby as Wendling looked on.

"It's fabulous!" Abby exclaimed. "I'm an even prouder godmother than I was before. How did you stand the pain?"

"It was nothing," Ben said.

"Just what he needs, Abby—encouragement!" Wendling laughed. "I like it better when it's covered up." He looked at Olsen. "Like you make him cover it for games, Tom." Wendling stroked his beard.

Olsen knew he was standing too close behind Mary, but he didn't care.

"Oh, Ben knows that's just a formality. Actually I think the sun is pretty cool. How old were you when you got yours?" he asked Wendling. Mary half-turned toward Olsen and brushed the tip of her index finger across her lips; but Olsen didn't know why.

"My what?" Wendling asked.

"Your tattoo."

Wendling laughed. "I don't have one."

"Mary said you had one…" Olsen began, and saw Wendling stiffen; "well, I thought Mary told me that Ben's tattoo is just like yours."

Wendling's eyes flared at Mary. Olsen's mind raced: *what is going on?* He lay his hand protectively on Mary's shoulder and felt the pulse of her defiance as she faced her husband, unmoving.

With the slap of abruptness, Wendling flew out of the living room and vanished up to the second floor, Christmas garlands flapping as he blew by.

The moment reverberated in silence.

"Is something wrong with Virgil?" someone asked, and people began to murmur, and Mary disappeared, too.

Half an hour passed. Long enough for Olsen to decide he'd have to leave without saying good-bye.

But as he headed out the front door, Mary ran down the stairs and put a square box wrapped in gold and white paper in his hand.

He said, "Mary—what happened? What did I say? I'm sorry," but she ignored that.

"This gift is only a token," she said, "but save it for Christmas morning."

Olsen couldn't say any of the things he wanted to say. So instead he smiled, and thanked her, and returned to the world outside her presence, his prison.

❦   ❦   ❦

Roanoke Road was dark that midnight; Mr. McCormick was not waiting up. Olsen parked his Corvette in the garage and went inside.

His house held no lights or decorations, no tree, no indication of the holiday season except for the stack of Christmas cards on his coffee table. It had always been that way for him at Christmastime, and it had always been fine, Christmas being nothing more than a welcome day off during basketball season. But tonight the air hung heavy with the weight of Mary's absence, and the night wrapped him in an echo as he lay her gift on the table by his Christmas cards and went into the kitchen for a beer.

When Olsen saw Ben the next morning at basketball practice, neither of them mentioned the party.

The day after that was Christmas Eve; they did not have practice. In the afternoon, Olsen went next door for his annual gift exchange with Mr. McCormick. He brought the old man a *Wildcats Basketball* hooded sweatshirt, and McCormick gave him a half-mile flashlight. Olsen spent that night before Christmas alone, and did not answer Rakowsky's phone message that night: "We're home from church—come on over—I promise Karen won't make you sing carols this year—and I made a wicked eggnog."

Olsen slept in on Christmas morning, didn't wake up until the sun was a smear of white along the horizon and the temperature matched the time: eight. Downstairs he poured his coffee and turned on the radio.

He opened his mother's card. It held a $100 check and a handwritten note: *Spending Christmas week at Pebble Beach with the Chamberlains and Susan Wilkerson. Have a good holiday. Let's talk in January.*

Then he unwrapped Mary's gift—slowly, handling its gold and white wrapping like a love letter. The white box inside bore a gold label: Pandora's Gallery, Chicago. He opened it and lifted the tissue paper to find a ceramic coffee mug, shining in a glaze of midnight blue, streaked in gold and violet, with a voluptuous handle.

He held the cup between his palms; he stroked the handle's curve; he ran his index fingertip around the rim; he pressed the edge to his lips.

CHAPTER 10

❀

Bit Players

It was a brand-new year, ice-cold January.

Late one afternoon after practice, Olsen returned to his basketball office and picked up the stack of college catalogs he had been accumulating for Ben, then met him outside the locker room.

"Great practice," Olsen said as they walked toward the front doors. "You're definitely ready for the Somerville game tomorrow."

"Really? You didn't seem too happy with us."

"Everybody's gotta stay focused. And remember, I need you to step up and take the lead out on the floor. Your game is getting phenomenal. The other guys are really looking to you."

"This winning streak is cool," Ben said, "but it's a lot of pressure."

"Don't think about the streak. The streak is meaningless. Just focus on the game."

As Olsen pushed the front doors open, the frozen wind slapped their faces; January blackness had descended on the dinner hour.

Olsen said, "I saw you talking to Matt Pender after practice. I know how he's been struggling."

"It wasn't about basketball," said Ben.

"Everything all right? Looked heavy."

"Yeah."

They reached the Corvette and Olsen pulled out his keys. They crammed their stuff and themselves in the car, pulled out of the school parking lot and drove along under the garish glare of streetlights on snow, heading for the Wendlings'.

"Some people want you to be a man," Ben said, "but some don't want you to grow up—and some people want you to do both. What's a guy supposed to do?"

"Is that Matt's problem?"

Ben shrugged.

"You should be a counselor or psychologist or something. Ever thought about that?" Olsen asked.

"Yeah, right!" Ben laughed. His breath frosted the air and his teeth chattered.

"The car warms up pretty fast. Hold on." The condensed trace of Olsen's words drifted in front of him as he turned the heater up.

"No psychology for me. I like history. I'm gonna be an archaeologist," said Ben. "Dig back in time and hold the past in my hands."

"Really? You never mentioned that before."

"I just thought of it this winter." Ben coughed and pulled his knit hat down over his ears.

"History," said Olsen.

"Yeah, and I just finished this book Mr. Whittaker told us about. It's called *Grant*, about Ulysses S. Grant. It's right here—wanna borrow it?" Ben asked, wedging an arm behind the seat and extricating his book bag.

"I'm not much of a Civil War buff."

"But this is a great book. A novel—you know, historical fiction. You'd like it. You can borrow it."

"Well," said Olsen. "Okay. Sure. If you don't need it back right away."

"You're always telling me good books to read. Now I can do the same for you."

"Thanks." Finally the car was warming up. "So we'll be looking at all these college catalogs with your mom. What's your favorite school so far?"

"Tucson State."

"I'd love to see you go there. I went back and counted—I've sent them nine guys since I came to Indian River. Nobody in the past couple of years, though."

"I'd have to do a helluva sell job to convince my mom, even if I get a scholarship."

"She loves you," said Olsen. "She wants to keep you close to her. But we'll talk her into visiting the campus with you so she can meet my buddy Dan Branigan out there. He'd take good care of you, and she'd see that."

"Hey, I'm still only a junior. I've got a year to convince her," Ben said. He bit his fingernail. "I wanna set out on my own. I think she'll understand."

"What does your dad think of your going that far away to college?" Olsen asked.

"He said he'd like to watch me play college basketball, but if I get a good offer from Tucson State, maybe I should take it."

"Hmmm." What did Wendling know? Maybe Tucson State was the best place for Ben, and maybe it wasn't. Olsen decided to oversee Ben's college selection even more closely.

"My dad adopted me," Ben said.

"What?"

Ben looked out the Corvette window. "My real father died before I was born. I love my dad, but I wish I could have known my real father. He died in a motorcycle crash one night when he was coming to see my mom. He was the one with the sun tattoo. That's why my mother told you my tattoo was like my father's. Don't tell anyone, though. Nobody around here knows about it. My dad doesn't like people to know. We moved here from Fort Wayne when I was still a baby." Ben rolled the window down, cleared his throat, and spit with gusto out into the night.

Olsen's heart was sledgehammering his chest. "Your mother was a widow—before you were even born?"

"Well," said Ben, "she wasn't a widow, exactly. She and Daniel didn't have a chance to get married before he died. But I was already on the way. Then her parents threw her out. What a pair of jerks, huh? She was only sixteen. She went to live at my godmother Abby's house. Abby, you know?"

"Sure, yeah."

"Abby and my mom have been best friends their whole life. And Abby's parents took care of my mom, and me, too, when I was first born. That's where my dad met her. He was a friend of Abby's dad. He was a lot older than my mom, but he fell in love with her, and they got married, and he adopted me. I was only, like, one year old or something. I don't remember any of it. I know you won't tell anyone. I just wanted you to know. And anyway, here we are," he said, as Olsen pulled agape into the Wendlings' driveway.

They got out and Ben cleared his throat again and spit into the snow.

They burst in from the cold and found Mary in the kitchen taking bread from the oven while a silver pot steamed on the stove.

"Hi, honey!" Mary said, coming over to squeeze Ben's arm and kiss him. "Hi, Thomas. It's a nice surprise to see you. What have you got there?"

He could feel Mary slipping through his fingers **illusions slipping, slipping away**

"The college stuff we were going to look at together," Olsen said.

"Yeah, Mom, don't you remember?"

Mary looked off into space. "Yes, I guess I do remember now, but honey, you told me last week, before things got crazy at the library." She looked up into Olsen's face. "I've been working extra hours to fill in for someone who just had surgery. I'm sorry I forgot you were coming!" She twisted a pink flowered potholder in her hands.

"Well," Olsen said, "I can just leave the catalogs here, and Ben can show you his favorite schools." He patted the top catalog. "Tucson State's in the pile. It's a great place. Take a look!"

Mary kept twisting the potholder. "Can you stay for dinner?" she asked.

Olsen opened his mouth but nothing came out. Mary and Ben looked at him.

"Well, I guess…well, sure…if you're sure…yes," Olsen said, "I'd like to."

"Wonderful," Mary said. She put the potholder down and stirred the soup a few times. Ben disappeared; Olsen heard his fading voice: "Call me when it's ready," his footsteps pounding away up carpeted stairs.

So. Ben's news had explained more than Wendling's anger. It explained Mary's tears when Olsen had said Ben was like a son to him: too much tenderness on a subject far tenderer than most. It explained the mysterious problems she had said she must resolve on her own—but what were those problems exactly? The spectral ache for a lover long dead?—the gag order imposed by his jealous replacement?—or having to justify it all to Ben?

Olsen managed to smile at Mary; the steam from the soup pot twirled up toward the ceiling fan through the kitchen air between them.

Then Virgil Wendling called home to say he'd be late and they should start eating without him.

At the dining room table, Mary sat between Olsen and Ben and reached a hand to each of them.

"We like to hold hands when we say grace," she said to Olsen.

"O God, we thank Thee for the good things that abound in our world," Mary and Ben prayed together, their heads bowed and their eyes closed as Olsen watched. "Save us from magnifying our sufferings and forgetting our many blessings. Thou hast given us so much, give now but one thing more—a grateful heart. Amen."

"Amen," said Olsen.

As they talked and ate, Olsen realized that this new image of a floundering Mary stirred not sympathy but distaste in him: Mary disowned and desperate, casting her lot and her body with the first taker, a man who stood in as father not only to Ben but also, perversely, to her. He did not know what he had expected, but it wasn't this tired, inelegant story. Olsen had preferred the bittersweet dream of not knowing; if only Ben hadn't trusted him quite so much.

They had just finished eating when the back door slammed. "Hi, everyone!" Wendling called out from the back hall. He came into the dining room. Eyeing Wendling in that first moment of appraisal, Olsen wondered if they would ever mention the Christmas party. Olsen stood up, and they shook hands.

"Hey, Dad," said Ben.

"Hey, son."

"I'm glad you didn't have to work too late," said Mary. "I'll bring you some dinner."

Wendling, Ben, and Olsen sat around the dining room table. Mary brought Wendling soup and bread, then disappeared. Olsen was glad; he had to get his bearings back; he felt a surge of irritation when he heard Wendling slurping soup off his spoon.

So their family was living a lie, basically. But anywhere you went, any day of the year, people were revealing far worse things of themselves. Why wouldn't Wendling and Mary just tell the truth?

Because they knew they would be judged, and they knew Ben would be judged—just as Olsen was judging Mary now, although he had no right.

Living a lie. Living in the shadow of truths that accumulate in the furtive silences of your life, taunting you from dark corners.

Familiar territory.

Olsen and Wendling made small talk about the cold that wouldn't quit, tribulations at Indian River's building department, Ben's jump shot that kept getting better, and the winning streak—now up to fourteen games.

"Want a beer, Olsen?"

"Sure."

"I'll have one, too, Dad."

"Yeah, right. Go do your homework."

Ben tossed a "Whatever you say" over his shoulder on his way upstairs.

From the dining room table, Olsen watched Wendling carry his soup bowl and silverware to the kitchen sink, then take two bottles of beer from the fridge and open them. "Hey, what about these?" Wendling nodded toward the college catalogs on the counter.

"How about another night?" said Olsen. "It's getting a little late for college talk. Maybe I can stop by again next week or something."

Wendling walked back to the dining room table and handed Olsen a bottle of beer. They sat for a minute drinking, then Wendling said, "You've got integrity, Tom."

Olsen leaned back in the chair.

"Let's talk man to man for a minute," said Wendling. "I want to apologize for that thing at the Christmas party. I hope you won't ask me to explain—hope you'll just accept my apology. It's private, you know—kind of a family matter. You have a family, right? So you know what I mean."

"No, I don't."

Wendling's eyebrows went up.

"I don't have a family, that is," said Olsen.

"Oh."

"There's no need to apologize," Olsen said. "I haven't mentioned it to anyone. And I won't. But remember—I wasn't the only one here that night who wondered what was going on. So..."

Wendling stroked his beard. "Fair enough," he said. He took another drink of his beer and said, "You know something? I have only one real regret in life."

"What is it?"

"I didn't go to college."

"Why not?" Olsen asked.

"I started out as a carpenter's apprentice right after I graduated from high school in Fort Wayne. I was good at it, so I stayed with it. Learned a lot about the building trades. And it led to some good opportunities. I've been Indian River's assistant building director more than fifteen years now. So things turned out all right for me. But you know what? Still feel like I don't quite get the respect a guy like you does." Wendling tapped the tabletop with his fingers. "Where'd you go to school, Olsen?"

"Got my bachelor's and master's at Ohio State."

"Oh, a master's. Hmmm," Wendling said.

"Yeah, and in fact, I was summa cum laude."

"Come again?"

"Had a perfect grade-point average. All five years, bachelor's and master's. Played Big Ten basketball for Ohio State, too."

Wendling stroked his beard again; didn't answer.

"I toyed with the idea of coaching college basketball," Olsen said. "But I wanted to teach, too—and of course, you can't do both at the college level."

"No?"

"Not at all. College basketball is all basketball, all the time, all year round. But I really felt the call to teaching. And at Indian River, I can do both."

Wendling reflected, then said, "Oh, yeah, the English, right?"

"Yup."

"Well, it was too late for college for me," said Wendling, "but not for Mary. That's why I put her through college myself, after we moved here from Fort Wayne—the community college, you know. She has her associate's degree. And of course we want the best education for Ben. I know how important it is to get that degree if you want to get ahead in the world."

Olsen had been pegging Wendling as a bit player in this family, but what did he know? Olsen had not been there for all the days of all those years; he was not part of this family that had built itself out of mother love and death; he did not know Wendling's heart. And after all, Wendling had only done exactly what Olsen would have done: scooped up Ben and Mary and made them his own. Olsen had no idea how often Wendling might have said to himself, *If I had a son, I'd want one just like Ben*; how often Wendling might have said, *Reminds me of me.*

Mary never reappeared. When Olsen stood up to leave, Wendling retrieved his coat from the front hall closet.

"I don't know where Mary's run off to. Now drive carefully," Wendling said. "The wind's really whipping the snow around out there."

"Well," said Olsen, "please tell Mary thanks again for dinner."

Wendling opened the front door and a blast of cold air blew in. "'Night, Tom."

"Good night."

Olsen walked away slowly down the Wendlings' stone path. The pain of the frozen wind against his face felt good, like a punishment he wanted. His shoes crunched the salted snow, past Mary's garden that lay ghostly and silent in the black January night. Walked down the driveway, the cold ground and snow draining hope out through his feet, his Corvette a thousand miles away. Once, Mary had inhabited him, a presence he could feel but could not touch **You, mystery divine Your thought surrounds me Intimate possession of my body and soul** but now she was vanishing.

"Thomas, wait!"

Olsen turned, and there was Mary standing on the porch under the light, lifting something out to him: "Here's some soup for you to bring home!" she called, her words echoing across the lawn.

Olsen reached her side quickly, skating over the cold ground through the darkness.

"I'm so glad you came over tonight," Mary said. "Here, you can just bring this container back next time you stop by." Her hands were hot but she was shivering in her coat. "Did Virgil say anything to you—while I was upstairs?"

"Well, he apologized for that Christmas party thing, if that's what you mean."

"Thomas, I'd like to explain someth—"

"No!" Olsen said. He was looking down at his shoes. "You don't owe me any explanation. It's all right." **We have some things in common, Mary…Mothers and fathers who hardened their hearts against us for being who we are…And truths we never speak…And the masks we wear in this world…A world that lies in wait to say we don't measure up.** He was still looking at his shoes.

"See you at the game tomorrow night?" Olsen asked, raising his eyes to hers again.

"See you then," she said. "Good-night."

Olsen felt Mary watching him as he walked back along the stone path and down the driveway to his car. But when he turned around to wave a last good-bye, she was gone.

CHAPTER 11

❀

Slipping

The next night Indian River whipped Somerville, thanks largely to Matt Pender's shower of 3-pointers. The winning streak was up to fifteen games.

As the streak lengthened, Olsen's temper shortened, his patience making only brief appearances at practice.

Not a screamer, he screamed. Not a ranter, he ranted. He apologized to the boys every evening, went home, went to sleep and dreamed about his father, but came back to school the next day and did it all again, before he could stop himself.

Those nights on Roanoke Road, he diligently avoided Mr. McCormick—easy enough to explain away in the cold clutch of an Indiana January—and stayed home alone, drinking Jack Daniel's from Mary's coffee cup on an empty stomach before falling asleep under a rain of snapshot memories from practices: the boys standing at silent and fearful attention as they listened to his diatribes. LeVon collapsing to the floor, Matt Pender toppling backward from the crouch, fatigue from interminable drills taking them out at the knees. Josh Reiter vomiting into the trash can. Michael Cavatelli running a dead-man in tears. Kuehn saying, "It's okay, Tom;" Stefanik saying, "Jesus, Tom, let's get outta here and go get a beer." Ben, wide-eyed, looking at Olsen from across the court, then looking away.

❦   ❦   ❦

It seemed vaguely criminal to contemplate Mary as she must have been back then **younger than Ben is now…just a child really…but far beyond a child's thoughts or a child's life, traveling in that realm of hurricane and fire and blazing fusion and the spinning edges of delusion and dream.** He could not, did not want to, imagine Mary as she was: a girl in the arms of the faceless Daniel, the man who lived on in the life he left behind.

What did it even matter? All that really mattered now was winning State.

Olsen had been reliving his biggest wins: Indian River's state championship six years ago; some of his great college games at Ohio State; but it had all started back in prep school at Andover. What a discovery, what a revelation it had been: winning drove away the pain of parents who eyed you as a disappointment, it drove away your loneliness, because in basketball you won as a team, and because everybody loves a winner, and because the celebrations and the memories filled up the empty spaces in you.

Maybe there were victories, too, that could drive away the ghosts of old illusions, that could make you forget the slow death of a love that could not be spoken.

❦   ❦   ❦

First Saturday night in February, on the barstool next to Rakowsky, Olsen sat staring at the emerald glass of his Heineken bottle. The River's Edge Bar was loud and crowded. A hand clapped his shoulder and he circled around.

"Hey, Coach!" Ed Pender said, a trail of dads behind him. "What a win tonight! There's no stopping us!"

"How long can you keep it going, Tom?"

"Nineteen-and-oh!"

"New Indian River record, did you know?"

The dads' faces and voices blurred in the River's Edge noise and haze.

"Yeah, I know," said Olsen. "The pressure's on. Andy, a few beers for my friends here."

The dads drank their beers and talked to Rakowsky and Olsen for a few minutes, then moved on in a stream of joviality.

Rakowsky shouted down the bar, "Hey, Barnewall! How much did you lose on the Irish today?" and laughed as Barnewall waved him off through the cigarette smoke.

"I can't tell you," said Olsen, "how much I want to win State undefeated."

"Who wouldn't?" Rakowsky said.

"I've been riding the boys pretty hard these days."

"You better!"

"Maybe too hard."

"Hey," said Rakowsky. "Every game, they see those go-for-the-throat looks in the other team's eyes. Not to mention all the dirty crap they've been taking. It's egregious—I've never seen such a bloody basketball season. I don't think you can hurt them any worse than that."

"Every word out of my mouth lately," Olsen said, "I sound like my old man."

"I take it that's not a good thing?"

Olsen didn't answer. He finished his beer, eyes stinging from the long smoky cloud in the air.

"Look," said Rakowsky, "this ain't no rec league. Our boys understand that. You don't have to apologize for being hard on them. Andy? Bring this guy another Heineken."

Olsen drummed the bar with his hand. "Dream On" blared from the bad sound system and the people around them were shouting the chorus together.

"What I'd do for a woman to go home with tonight," Olsen said to Rakowsky; his voice came out louder than he expected.

"Now you're talking. We've all been telling you, you need to get out more! *That's* your number one problem," Rakowsky said. He shook his head.

"I know," said Olsen. He leaned onto the bar with his elbows, folded his hands. "You know what I think?" he said to Rakowsky.

"What?"

"This is God's payback time."

"For what?"

"For all the shit I've ever done."

"What the hell are you talking about?"

"Used to be I could get any woman I wanted," said Olsen, "and I took full advantage of it. After a while I knew I was just using them—trying to fill this empty space in my gut. Of course it didn't work. So I'd move on to the next one. It never really feels like I'm using them—to me." Olsen unfolded his hands. "Then I thought Mary was the answer to everything. Really made myself believe it. Until I came to my senses."

They looked at each other.

"And?" Rakowsky said.

"And it's not going to happen. I don't even want it to happen. Not anymore. That's the sad part. And that's payback time," said Olsen. The bartender gave him his new bottle of beer, and he took a swig.

"You're not the worst guy I've ever known," Rakowsky said. "I don't think God's got you singled out."

"Happy New Year, Tom!" said a woman behind them, and they swung halfway around on their barstools; it was Kristina, a bright figure in the hazy gray air, her eyes and lips and jewelry glittering.

"I know it's already February—but better late than never, don't you think?" Kristina smiled. "So, Happy New Year." She lay her hand on Olsen's face. She drew it down his neck. His shoulder. Arm. Hand. Fingertips. Let it rest there. Music thumped like a pulse around them.

"Well," said Rakowsky, grinning, "on the other hand, God can single a person out in a good way." He got up from his barstool and walked away into the crowd.

Olsen looked in Kristina's eyes: they held the same lure that had kept him coming back to her before. The same promise of an answer that would last. The same anesthesia for the loneliness that wracked him. But he knew there was no antidote for his paradox: for the history that was slipping away from him, for the missing person he had found and already lost, Mary slipping, slipping away.

Later he accepted Kristina's invitation to drive her home, and then her invitation to come inside. His was a tired, inelegant story, too. But it didn't really seem to matter anymore.

❁

Like the Stars

STOCKTON WINS STATE CHAMPIONSHIP

INDIANAPOLIS—The Stockton High School Crusaders avenged their early-season loss to arch rival Indian River by defeating the Wildcats, 65-64, in the boys' Class A state championship game yesterday morning in front of a standing-room-only crowd at Conseco Fieldhouse.

Indian River entered the championship contest with a 26-game winning streak. But they found themselves playing catch-up from the start of this game after senior center Josh Reiter suffered a torn knee ligament early in the first quarter. The Wildcats, hit hard by the flu bug in the last few days, did not look like the formidable opponents they had been in every other game this season...

Junior sharpshooter Ben Wendling was whistled for his fifth foul with 1:47 left in the game and Indian River leading for the first time, 58-57. Wendling had been the Wildcats' go-to man all night, and finished with a game-high 23 points, 11 rebounds, and 6 assists.

After Wendling fouled out of the game, Stockton quickly regained the lead, 59-58, on a jumper by senior Purdue recruit Bob Wanamaker. But Indian River, in a burst of firepower, scored six unanswered points and took a 64-61 into the final ten seconds.

With the clock running out, Stockton's Wanamaker was fouled as he launched a last-ditch 3-point shot. The shot banked in off the glass, tying the game with 2 seconds left, and Wanamaker sank his free throw, giving Stockton the 65-64 lead. Indian River couldn't score on their final possession, and the Stockton Crusaders won their first state boys basketball championship...

In the champions' locker room, Stockton coach Vernon Giles said, "There's nothing better than beating Indian River—and doing it at State is a dream come true. Every single one of my players left it all on the court tonight. This is a historic night for Stockton…"

Speaking to reporters after the game, Indian River coach Tom Olsen said, "These boys are like sons to me. And they're winners no matter what the scoreboard says. We will leave here tonight with our heads held high."

❧   ❧   ❧

Olsen had shepherded the boys through the post-game ceremonies with the autopilot of shock guiding their footsteps, no victory surge to give wings to their exhaustion, the surrealistic wave and roar of thousands of people in Conseco Fieldhouse deluging their eyes and ears. There was no way to really be prepared for this kind of a loss—no way to anticipate the feeling of a battering ram blindsiding your head. But together they survived the motions of runners-up, shoulders straight, eyes upturned, hands clasped behind their backs.

Then Olsen had led them into the locker room.

His heart twisted as he watched the boys file in, mute, dead-eyed, glazed, some crying, slumping against the lockers, sliding weak-kneed onto the floor, or staring at the ceiling, blinking hard, arms crossed over soaked jerseys. Kuehn and Stefanik came in last.

Olsen began a head count. It was hard to roster them: Olsen had to see who had sunk to the ground, who had obscured his hanging head with a towel, who could be heard retching in a stall around the corner. There was LeVon, and Josh Reiter on crutches, and there was Ben in the back of the locker room, his arm around a sobbing Matt Pender, who had fouled Bob Wanamaker on that desperation 3-pointer as time ran out. Ben looked up and across the locker room at Olsen, his eyes full of tears, not allowing one to spill.

Olsen hadn't prepared a speech for this—that would have been bad luck. But he should have known the thing he wanted so much, this state championship with Ben, would never happen. For the past two months, when Olsen had felt the leaden weight of shadow on his shoulders, when he had heard its dark, wordless voice warning him failure was in the air, he had drowned it out with whisky, thinking Mary was the only demise on his hands.

Now he had a locker room full of sinking high school boys who needed the life raft of his words.

So he closed his eyes. He said to them, "You guys have shown heart and spirit and guts and sportsmanship that far exceed the best of my own."

He opened his eyes and looked at the blur of their faces. He said, "You are the guys I admire and love and am proud to call my team. I wish I were more like all of you."

He said, "Coach Kuehn and Coach Stefanik and I are all living proof that you survive even the worst losses, the losses that feel like they'll kill you."

He said, "Your lives all reach into a future far beyond this night, and I won't let any of you forget it."

❧   ❧   ❧

A week later Olsen had to start preparing his remarks for Boys' Basketball Awards Night at Indian River High, but the words weren't coming.

He lay on his bed, the night chill of early April drifting in through the window. Two empty beer bottles stood on his bedside table next to cold Chinese takeout. His window shades were still up; he looked out at the streetlights glowing and the headlights passing on Roanoke Road, at Mr. McCormick's upstairs light next door.

Olsen had been trying to get back in his routine—schoolwork, yard work, reading, drinking with Rakowsky. He hadn't talked at length to any of the boys; instead he waved to them from his classroom doorway, or spoke a word or two of support in the cafeteria, or lay a hand on their shoulders when they passed each other in the halls. He felt their sadness mix with his own, pumping through his veins. The whole horrible ending of the season was too crushing, cruel, a shock, but you couldn't say so; you had to be a man. Had to show it didn't bother you a bit, even though the clues seeped out around the edges of your stoicism. Like with Ben: jaw tight, feet heavy, no smiles, no tears. **Reminds me of me.**

That afternoon had seemed better, though. Olsen had seen Josh Reiter grinning as he swung through the hall on crutches, talking to Chloe Ciprak. In the cafeteria Olsen had heard familiar laughter, turned and seen it was LeVon Powell, eating lunch with his friends. Olsen even thought he had seen the spring returning to Ben's step as he walked into AP English.

And all of it, the shock, the pain, the pinning of hope on small signs of healing—all of it was because of the big win that wasn't. What did the big wins matter, anyway—what could they really do for you?

Olsen lay his forearm over his eyes and sighed.

He had returned to a hero's welcome in Indian River, his local popularity deepened by what the city esteemed as a valiant loss. Woven through the last seven days were the calls and letters he received from parents, fans, and colleagues, lauding his leadership.

> *you have made us all proud*
> *your courage and character are an inspiration*
> *we hope our boys turn out like you*
> *now I know I have seen a real champion*

It was all part of his tall tale: role model, rock of Gibraltar, man for all seasons; he imagined the reply he would send to all of them.

> *This Thomas Olsen, this hero you wrote to, is a figment of your imagination. I know, because he was once a figment of mine.*

Olsen swung his legs around and sat up at the edge of the bed. It was his own fault that his life had gone this far this wrong, this silently; it was his own fault that his public self was divorced from his soul, that his life was an act from morning till night, that his pain was his shame, that he had no one to tell his truth to, even if he had known what it was.

Atop his dresser he spied the spine of *Grant: A Novel*, the book Ben had loaned him back in January. It peered out at him from under old receipts and clean socks and miscellany he had tossed there during the basketball- and Jack Daniel's-induced haze of the past few months. **By Max Byrd**, he saw along the spine, with the thumbnail portrait of Ulysses S. Grant.

Olsen got up and extracted the book from the bottom of the pile. He lay back down on his bed, started reading; didn't get far before he went back to the dresser and dug around for pen and paper.

Afterwards Olsen threw the Chinese takeout and beer bottles away. Then he put the words he had copied from *Grant*'s prologue on his bedside table.

> *Put your face close to the picture. Under the shell of a mute, determined reserve do you hear a sad and sensitive little boy crying?*
> *A child's feelings are like the stars, they never burn out. They have to be buried or drowned.*
> *Thus great generals are born.*

✿   ✿   ✿

The next day, Olsen saw Josh Reiter and Ben eating lunch in the cafeteria. Josh's crutches leaned against an empty chair beside him.

"Hey, how're you guys doing?" Olsen said, sitting down next to Ben and reaching over to grab one of his chocolate chip cookies.

"My mom made those," Ben said, and slid the bag toward Olsen.

"Hanging in there, Coach. What about you?" Josh asked.

"Oh, I'm doing good. Great. Moving forward." But Olsen stopped, turned his chair at an angle toward the boys. "You know what? Actually, I'm not doing so well. I'm still really hurting. How are you guys getting through?"

Ben and Josh looked at each other across the cafeteria table.

"Well—we're not doing beers and girls and shit to get over it—if that's what you mean," said Josh, and stuffed the last of a sandwich in his mouth and scratched the side of his neck and chewed. Ben bit a nail.

"Of course that's not what I mean. You guys are too smart for that kind of stuff. Right? You stay on the straight and narrow where you belong. And watch your mouth."

Josh mumbled, "Right. Sorry, Coach," while he was still chewing and Ben said quickly, "My mom hasn't baked these cookies for like a year, and suddenly she's sliding 'em out of the oven like there's no tomorrow. That's how I'm getting by."

"Ah, yes," said Olsen, "the healing power of cookies," and laughed. Ben and Josh looked across the table at each other again.

"My pastor's helping me, too," Josh said. His voice was louder now, loud and clear. "I told him about everything. He gave me a Bible verse to focus on and stuff."

"Me, too," Ben said to Josh. "What verse did he give you?"

"You guys go to the same church?" Olsen asked them.

"Yeah. Since like kindergarten," Josh said. "Mine's from Jeremiah. Uh, it's pretty long," he said, pulling his wallet from his back pocket and extracting a slip of paper.

> *This is what the Lord says:*
> *"Let not the wise man boast of his wisdom*
> *or the strong man boast of his strength*
> *or the rich man boast of his riches,*

but let him who boasts boast about this:
that he understands and knows me,
that I am the Lord..."

"Wow." Too heavy for Olsen. "What's yours?" he asked Ben.
"I memorized it." Ben looked up at the cafeteria ceiling.

"*Forget the former things;*
do not dwell on the past.
See, I am doing a new thing!
Now it springs up; do you not perceive it?"

"I like that line: *See, I am doing a new thing!*" said Ben. "Sounds like Dr. Seuss or something."

"That's about your speed," said Josh.

Olsen looked at the boys, at the traces of laughter and pain on their faces as they spoke, at the whiskers poking through the last of their peach fuzz.

The boys finished eating and wadded up their trash while Olsen ate another one of Mary's cookies. The chocolate chips melted on his tongue. "I wish I had what you have," Olsen said, "that faith," but then the bell rang.

Ben pushed his chair back and stood up. Josh got up, too, and slipped the crutches under his arms.

"You know what else, Coach?" Ben said to Olsen. "My mom's been praying for you. She told me."

"Praying for me?" Olsen said. "I don't think anybody's ever done that before."

"Well, see ya later," said Ben.

"Take it easy, Coach," Josh said, and swung away on his crutches, Ben walking slowly behind him.

Olsen stayed at the table. Mary prays for me. He tried to imagine it. **Does she fall down on her knees for me? Does she lie in bed at night, next to Wendling, her hands clasped against her breasts, and whisper my name to God?**

❦   ❦   ❦

As Awards Night approached, Olsen's thoughts kept turning back toward the past, sinking deeper into layers of memory.

Sinking back into a June evening, summer vacation from Andover, into his father's office in the Econ department at Northeastern in Boston, Tiffany lamp on the credenza backlighting John Olsen as he worked at his desk.

John's eyes narrowed, looking up toward the doorway. "Tom. What are you doing here? I thought you were in Newport with your mother."

"I've gotta talk to you, Dad." Olsen saw his father holding his hands above the typewriter keys, waiting, wanting to get back to work. His stomach clenched into a fist as he said, "Jennifer thinks she's pregnant."

"Who's Jennifer?"

"Jennifer! My girlfriend. You met her when you came to Andover, remember? What do you mean, who?"

"Pregnant? You're seventeen years old, for Christ's sake! So that's what you're doing at boarding school?"

Sinking back into the brawl of verbiage—

"Abbott Academy, eh?" said John Olsen. "In my day, we used to call them the Abbott Rabbits."

"I don't give a damn what you say, Dad. Why should I? You don't give a damn about me!"

"Keep your voice down! I don't want anyone else to know my son is an idiot!"

"Yeah, we wouldn't want to spoil your perfect image!"

"Stupid goddam kid…this is how you show your gratitude?"

"Gratitude for what?"

Sinking back into the tussle of decrees—

"Both your lives would be ruined…essential to be practical…these things can be arranged."

"I love Jennifer. I couldn't ask her to do that…"

"How do you know her parents haven't already…"

And sinking back into the rage that spilled over the edges of their lips—

"I thought I could turn to you for help, Dad. *That's* what makes me an idiot!"

"I've given you everything—yet this is how you waste your life? I won't let it happen!"

Then three weeks closer to fall, back in his father's office, Tiffany lamp lighting a darker darkness. John Olsen looked up at the sound of footsteps.

"Tom?" he said to his son, who stood briefly in the office doorway.

"She's not pregnant after all," Olsen said, and walked away.

❦   ❦   ❦

Olsen's Aunt Jane, his mother's sister, visited them in Newport every August. The summer Olsen turned seven, he was a barefoot Indian brave practicing his silent tracking. He tiptoed behind Louise and Aunt Jane as they sipped iced tea on chaises longues under the waving green trees. He lay in the grass, unheard, unseen, behind them.

"Have you ever heard stories about babies being switched at birth? You know—when the hospital makes a mistake?" he heard his mother say.

"Yes, I suppose I have," Aunt Jane replied.

"Sometimes I wonder if that happened to John and me," said Louise.

"That's a strange thing to say."

"I don't know," said Louise. "Somehow it doesn't seem right. I don't know if it's ever seemed right. Tommy's just so different from John and me. Sometimes it all seems like a big mistake."

Aunt Jane sipped her iced tea and didn't answer.

I'm invisible now. They can't see me.

❦   ❦   ❦

Summer vacation in Newport.

Four years old.

His summer pajamas dotted with motorcycles.

The scent of breakfast bacon luring him.

Walking into the kitchen.

Unnoticed, but seeing Louise sipping coffee, stirring something on stove.

John reading the newspaper.

Climbing onto a chair by the counter to get a better look at the bacon, maybe snatch a piece.

Leaning toward the electric griddle.

Sizzle of skin, bite of burning flesh, cry of pain.

Louise sipping coffee. John reading paper. Not noticing. Not hearing.

Slipping down from chair, slipping out door.

Hiding underneath sweep of branches in pine tree clubhouse, squeezing arm, squeezing back tears.

No one calling his name.

❦   ❦   ❦

When second grade let out, he would walk home through Wellesley with his friends, and in good weather play outside with them, until their mothers called them in.

"Tommy, come inside and have a snack with us."

"No, thank you, Mrs. Sturgis…No, thank you, Mrs. Quinn…No, thank you, Mrs. Hamilton…"

You'd be imposing, Tom, and that's not acceptable. You just come home and get settled in here. Make yourself something to eat. You're a young man now, not a baby anymore. Your father and I both have important jobs, and so do you. Your job is to be responsible for yourself after school until we get home.

Walking home to aloneness in the days when no one's mother worked except his.

The emptiness compressed around him as he came inside through the back door of the big house in Wellesley. Blood pounded in his ears. He listened for footsteps, ghosts, murderers. He turned on the radio. His parents' classical music was peaceful. Nothing bad ever happened to the sounds of classical music.

He kept his favorite books inside the piano bench in the living room—not upstairs, because the upstairs might devour him. He lay on the Oriental rug, his books spread open to the tales of his heroes: Odysseus, Hercules, Prometheus. He liked when anyone outwitted Zeus and Hera, though he noticed it never lasted.

He poured Rice Krispies and milk in a bowl and ate it under the kitchen light. Afterwards his chest hurt, a fist clenched beneath his throat. He turned on more lights. Sharp pains pinched him from the inside.

He perched on the couch and watched out the wide picture window for Louise's car; she usually got home before John. When he saw her sedan cruising down the street, he ducked down behind the seat so she couldn't see him waiting.

She came in through the back door and found him reading his mythology books in the living room.

"Hello, Tom," she said with a smile.

"Hi, Mom," he said. He smiled back.

They had never been a kissing family.

CHAPTER 13

❀

I Learned This, At Least, By My Experiment

"Welcome to Boys' Basketball Awards Night," Olsen said. He stood on the stage in front of the podium, a microphone clipped to his lapel. The boys sat with him in a line of folding chairs across the stage.

Olsen looked out over the hundred faces in the high school auditorium: family faces, parents and loved ones wanting consolation. Mary was out there somewhere. The weight on his shoulders seemed crushing—then out of the blue he felt the weight transform into a lightness like wings, just as in the bitterest of winters his hands, verging on frostbite, began to feel deliciously warm.

Olsen walked across the stage, behind the line of folding chairs. Put his hands on a couple of the boys' shoulders. Looked out at the crowd and started to talk.

He had intended his prepared remarks to inspire, to revive. But as he spoke, Olsen's words hit his own ears as glib, bantamweight. He stopped short. He scanned the audience's faces, kept his hands on the boys' shoulders. **If only you knew These are hard-fought words Hard-won These are driving all night to the Indiana Dunes and back again without sleep words And these are the best I can do.**

Looking out on that ocean of people, impossibly he saw Mary, and the crowd around her blurred. He saw, in perfect focus, the shadow of her dark hair curving around her face, and her eyes like rain looking right into his, as if there were no distance between them. Then her face dissolved back in the crowd.

He continued speaking; finished, and took a deep breath; walked back to the podium.

One by one Olsen called his players across the stage as he recited their stats and awards, then loaded them with trophies, plaques, varsity letters. When it was time to introduce Ben, last man in the team alphabet, Olsen made a surprise announcement: Ben had just been named to the Tri-State Showcase team—the best of the best 11th-grade players from Indiana, Illinois, and Ohio. Ben would be a starter in the Tri-State game at Valparaiso at the end of April. For a high school junior in Indiana, it was one of the highest basketball honors.

Olsen tried to pick Mary out of the applauding crowd again, to see her reaction, but he couldn't find her.

The clapping crescendoed and Olsen looked over at Ben, who was still sitting in his folding chair, his jaw dropped, as the boys beside him thumped his back with enthusiasm, and the applause rolled on.

Then Ben stood up.

Olsen watched him cross the stage. Ben was smiling, smiling, as he drew closer to the podium—then Olsen saw his eyes were filled with tears.

Ben reached him, and clung to him, and Olsen clung back.

In the background Olsen heard clapping and cheering, the embrace of the crowd, but what meant the most were those tears that had fallen on his shoulders.

❦   ❦   ❦

Olsen went directly to his basketball office when the awards were over and shut the door; locked it from the inside.

A half-hour later, when he emerged into the corridor, he saw Mary at a distance. She stood by the front doors talking to Ben, who was grinning, and Josh Reiter, leaning on his crutches and laughing, and Mr. and Mrs. Reiter. He saw Mary hug Mrs. Reiter. Then Ben and Josh and the Reiters went out the front doors, and Mary stood alone in the hall. Was she waiting for Virgil? Olsen didn't recall seeing Wendling that night, but the faces had all melted together for him.

Mary pulled a tissue from her purse, pressed it to her face. She was crying. She was crying and transporting Olsen back to the day before that basketball season had ever started, that bake sale day, in the school van with him, on the way to St. Peter's.

"Mary!" he called.

❁   ❁   ❁

"Buy you a drink?" Olsen asked as they passed the school vending machines.

"Sure. How about a bottle of water?"

"One for you and one for me," said Olsen, sliding the dollar bills in.

"I could use a Twix, too," Mary said. Olsen got her the candy bar and himself a bag of pretzels.

Down the corridor, he unlocked his basketball office and held the door open. "Please," he said, "take the good chair," pointing to the cushioned swivel seat behind his desk.

"Where's Virgil tonight?" Olsen asked, sitting down in one of the hard plastic chairs near the door. "I'm surprised he's not here."

"He's not feeling well," Mary said. She sat down and swiveled back and forth, turned toward Olsen's bookcase. "He started having chest pains last Sunday during Easter dinner. It may be an ulcer. They're not sure."

For Easter dinner, Olsen had eaten at the Rakowskys' with Rick and Karen and all their relatives—smiling on the outside, odd man out on the inside.

"Hmm," said Olsen. "Well, I hope he's better."

"Yeah. I hope so, too." Mary opened the bottle of water and took a drink. Olsen watched the curves of her profile, her hair falling back over her shoulders, her throat in a rhythm of swallows. Her lips glistened as she screwed the cap back on.

"Want to turn on some music?" Olsen asked. "CD player's right behind you."

Mary looked through the little stack of CDs: Hendrix, Mozart, an old, old Allman Brothers. "Maybe in a minute," she said; "I want to tell you something first," and swiveled in the chair.

"Thank you for everything you did tonight," she said. "When Ben started crying up there—when he reached out to you that way—"

She drank some more water. "I realize how much Ben's held inside, how much he's held back from me—and how much he trusts you." She picked up the Allman Brothers CD; put it down again. "You carry a lot on your shoulders. For these boys, for all the kids who must turn to you. I don't know how you do it."

"Well." Olsen said. He wished he could trace her profile with one fingertip, start where her dark silk hair met her forehead and run his finger down, slowly, over her caramel brow, the arc of her nose, the rise of her lips, the small upsweep of her chin, and down her long, caramel neck, down, and down.

"Sometimes," said Mary, in a voice Olsen had to lean forward to hear, "I think about the Christmas party. How you and I talked in the basement. How I asked who you turn to when you need someone to care about you? I don't think you ever really answered me. So I still wonder." She picked up a pencil and doodled on a notepad. Olsen couldn't see what she was drawing.

"Nothing fazes you," said Mary. "You're the one everyone comes to for strength. What's your secret?"

"It's all an act," Olsen said. "Inside I'm dying. At least I think I'm dying. I've been doing this iron man act for so long, I'm not even sure."

Mary stopped drawing and looked up at him, her pencil in midair.

Olsen opened his water and drank some, put the bottle on the desk, but held the cap to fidget with. Mary put the pencil down, and they looked at each other. Olsen leaned back on two legs of the chair.

"The aftermath of that state championship game—well, my own private aftermath," he said, "reminded me how long I've been pretending nothing hurts." He took another drink and screwed the cap back on the bottle.

Mary leaned on the desk toward Olsen, her forearms framing her breasts as she looked at his face. He made himself look at the ceiling.

"When Ben broke down that way tonight," Olsen said, staring upward, "well, he might feel embarrassed, but it was the best thing that could have happened. There are plenty of guys on the team who can take physical pain like you wouldn't believe, but don't want to face that inner pain. And that's partly my fault—it's what I've always taught them, though not always in words."

Olsen looked at Mary again. She had leaned back in the chair.

"When you've done it long enough," he said, "the pretending starts to feel like who you really are. I wish I could go back, or forward, or something. But I think it might be too late for me."

Mary didn't try to stop him, so Olsen just kept talking.

"Guys always tell me they envy my life—basketball and freedom and fully-paid summer vacations. And why should I tell them any different? I used to believe it myself. But the real story? The boys I love like sons go home to their real families after the game. I go home to a empty house.

"I look at old Mike Stefanik," Olsen went on, easing his chair forward onto all four legs again. "Even with all his grump and grizzle, he got it right; he got life right. Has a wife who adores him—forty years or something of marriage, all those kids and grandkids. He goes home to a lot of love. But he says he's jealous of me—all this freedom he thinks is so great."

Olsen took his tie off, rolled it up and tossed it on his desk. "Even Don Kuehn—he's much smarter than I was at 24 or 25, whatever he is, just a kid, really, but he has his priorities straight. He and his wife are really happy; you can see it when they're together. They're having a baby this summer. Life is just beginning for them. But Kuehn says he looks up to *me*. Aspires to be like me."

Olsen couldn't believe he was telling Mary these things, but the confessions kept coming. "So, I've got all these guys envying me," he said, "but do you know who I remind myself of? Not Stefanik, not Kuehn, but old Joe McCormick. Old Joe McCormick who lives next door to me. Eighty-some years old. All alone. Never married. No children. No one to go home to. No one to talk to. No one but me who notices if he's dead or alive…

"But, hey—it's great being Tom Olsen!" he said, tipping his chair backward, then forward again. "I wouldn't want to burst anyone's bubble—especially my own."

He was still staring down at the gray linoleum when he felt Mary coming around the desk toward him, sitting down beside him and taking one of his hands in both of hers, her small hands pressing warm and smooth against his calluses and the ridge of his knuckles.

"I know what you mean—feeling like an actor in your own life," Mary said. "Like your own life isn't even your autobiography, but the story of somebody else."

Olsen felt Mary's eyes on him, but he couldn't look at her.

"Ben told me that he told you," Mary said. "Told you the truth. The real story of our lives, the way he came into this world. About his real father. I'm glad he told you, glad he feels that close to you. You're the only one who knows. Well, the only one in Indian River."

Olsen looked at her then, but Mary let go of his hand and picked up a pen from the edge of the desk. She drew geometric shapes on the pad of paper in front of her, little triangles and cubes, as she said, "Virgil just wanted us to be a nice, normal, happy family. So he's always been private about the way things really happened. Secretive, really. He wanted to erase the past. I know he didn't want me to be sad—and I was so sad when I met him—terrified, really. I had this precious baby boy and wondered what possible hope his future could hold with me for a mother.

"Virgil wanted me. He wanted Ben. He loved us both," Mary said. "But he didn't like the way Ben came into the world. He didn't want me to have the past I had. And he sure as hell didn't want anyone else to know about it. God, how I learned to hate the word *illegitimate*. The kind of word that makes me want to rip a person's throat out."

Olsen looked at her, surprised, her lips flaring red to his eyes.

"Nobody cared that Daniel was my one and only, the only one I loved," Mary said. "I was still the slut, the outcast, the untouchable—even to my parents. To this day, Ben has no idea how hard things really were for me. I don't ever want him to know, either. I don't want him to know that my own parents would have killed him."

"They were violent?"

"They tried to make me get an abortion. When they did that, they crossed a line no parent should ever cross, and there was no going back, no way to reconcile that. Not for me. It didn't matter anyway—they threw me out."

"They never tried to see you again, or Ben?"

"They tried, but after what they did, they had no right. And Virgil wanted nothing to do with them. I don't know what ever happened to them and I don't care."

Olsen's face burned. He pretended steadiness as he leaned back in the chair.

"Can you imagine, Thomas? If I'd listened to my parents, Ben would never have been born. He would be dead. That's enough to fuel my anger for a lifetime. I don't know if you can really understand, but I know you love Ben enough to try."

Olsen was almost certain he spoke the word, "Yes."

"Think of it," Mary said. "Think of how empty our lives would be. Who would I be, who would you be, without Ben?"

"I don't know," Olsen said. "I don't want to think about it—I can't." He feared his face was beet red, betraying him, but there was nowhere to go.

Mary coughed, then took another drink. Her bottle was almost empty. She started coloring one of her triangles in with the pen. "So what do you think of my parents?" Mary asked.

Olsen said, "Unforgivable," as the jagged edges of a lullaby were streaming through his head.

Then Mary put the pen down. She picked up Olsen's pretzels and opened the bag, nibbled on a pretzel until it was gone. "Virgil wanted to keep the past a secret—he felt like it humiliated him, made him look like my second choice. He figured if we just presented ourselves to the world as a regular family, everything would go a lot better for us. And it was easy enough to do back then—Virgil used to look really young for his age, and we moved down here where nobody knew us." She took another pretzel out of the bag. "He said, just act like this is how we've been from the beginning. Don't get too close to people, don't give them room to ask a lot of questions. And it seemed like a good idea."

She put the pretzel down. Olsen waited.

"And who am I to argue with Virgil?" she said. "Because where would Ben and I be without him?"

"What about Daniel? What was he like?" Olsen asked.

"He worked at a gas station near my high school. He was cool, and wild—he rode a motorcycle. But he read a lot, too. He had a bunch of paperbacks. He didn't have any money so he was always waiting for the paperback editions to come out. He had a lot of friends, but no family. He was alone in the world. He died wanting Ben. And you know what? I can't even remember the sound of his voice."

Mary looked toward the window opposite them, and Olsen followed her eyes: in the outside dark and inside light, the window glass reflected them side by side. Mary looked down at her hands. "Why did I agree to treat the truth like a dirty little secret? And you know what the worst thing is? That it hurt Ben. I love Virgil, though, I love him," she said, and twirled her wedding ring around her finger. Then she tore the triangled page off the pad, crushed it into a wad and threw it across the office toward the wastebasket. It bounced off the rim onto the linoleum.

Mary crossed the office, picked up the wad of paper and dropped it in the wastebasket.

"I love Virgil for everything he's done for Ben and me," Mary said. "And I hate him for everything he's done for Ben and me."

Olsen's temples pounded; he looked at Mary as she sat down beside him.

Mary pulled her hair back, twirled it up on her head. "I know what kind of life Ben and I would have had if Virgil hadn't swept in and saved us. There is no way I can ever say I have repaid that debt." She let her hair fall on her shoulders. "Virgil and I both know it. Of course we never say it. But I can always see it—I feel it—I hear it," she said, then picked her water bottle up and swallowed the last drop. "It's okay, though, because I really do love him—he's a wonderful man, and a great father to Ben," she said, the last words falling smoothly from her lips.

Olsen reached for her hand, wrapped it in his callused one.

Mary didn't look at him, didn't pull her hand away. "I found a poem once," she said. "I learned it by heart so I'd never lose it. I've probably said it to myself a thousand times."

"What's the poem?"

"'Wild Geese,'" she said. "By Mary Oliver."

"How does it go?"

Mary leaned back in the chair and closed her eyes, with Olsen still holding her hand, and she said,

> You do not have to be good.
> You do not have to walk on your knees
> for a hundred miles through the desert, repenting.
> You only have to let the soft animal of your body
>   love what it loves.
> Tell me about despair, yours, and I will tell you mine.
> Meanwhile the world goes on.
> Meanwhile the sun and the clear pebbles of the rain
> are moving across the landscapes,
> over the prairies and the deep trees,
> the mountains and the rivers.
> Meanwhile the wild geese, high in the clean blue air,
> are heading home again.
> Whoever you are, no matter how lonely,
> the world offers itself to your imagination,
> calls to you like the wild geese, harsh and exciting—
> over and over announcing your place
> in the family of things.

All the questions Olsen wanted to ask spun up inside him, pressing to get out. But he had far too much to hide to risk having Mary ask him anything in return.

He leaned back in his chair, closed his eyes, still holding her hand. They sat side by side, in the silence, for a long time.

✤   ✤   ✤

Arriving home later, Olsen found a flat, gift-wrapped package inside his front storm door, with a card addressed to "Tom" in Mr. McCormick's hobbling old handwriting.

Olsen flicked on a lamp in the living room and sat down. Inside the envelope was a note.

∾

Dear Tom,

My mother gave this to me a long time ago, and now I want you to have it. Whether you boys won or lost that game didn't matter, because you are the best basketball team Indiana has ever seen. And I'm proud to be able to call you my friend.

Sincerely,

Joseph McCormick

Inside the yellowed paper was a plaque framed in scuffed, gilded wood, its words obscured behind the hazy old glass, but readable:

> I learned this, at least, by my experiment:
> that if one advances confidently
> in the direction of his dreams,
> and endeavors to live the life
> he has imagined,
> he will meet with a success
> unexpected in common hours.
>
> —Henry David Thoreau

All night Olsen tossed and turned and dreamed of words: words on walls, words on paper, words on the wind, words…

I learned this at least by my experiment. I can't even remember the sound of his voice. So what do you think of my parents? Tell me about despair, yours, and I will tell you mine. Meanwhile the world goes on. Meanwhile the world goes on.

CHAPTER 14

❀

A Shrine For Her

O Lord, I know I'm just another in a long line of people who come to You unschooled, unworthy, and needing Your favor.

I believe in You, but I have no idea how to know You.

Have You forgiven me yet, for everything that happened with Alexandra?

Just give me a sign, some sign to show me You're there—or here—or somewhere nearby.

And don't give up on me.

❀   ❀   ❀

The telephone rang. Olsen didn't know if he was dreaming, or how long he had been sleeping.

"Hello?"

"Thomas, it's Mary."

He struggled through the haze of sleep, swung his bare feet around to the floor, sat up in slow motion.

"Mary," he said.

"Virgil can't come to Tri-State this weekend."

"What?" Olsen said.

"Thomas, did I wake you up?"

"No. What time is it?"

"It's about ten," she said. "Virgil just got home. The building department's being audited, starting Monday, and I guess there could be some problems. It's going to take Virgil all weekend to get organized for it."

"Let's drive up to Valparaiso together then," he said, "you and Ben and I."

"Oh, good," said Mary, "that's just what I was hoping we could do. Ben and I can pick you up. Abby's going to meet us at the hotel in Valparaiso, same time and all. I just talked to her to make sure."

"Great."

"So Abby and I will share a room," Mary said. "Do you want me to call the Creston Plaza and cancel the third room?"

"No, that's okay, I'll take care of it."

"Virgil said to tell you that he's glad you'll be along—to look out for us."

"Yes," said Olsen, "I promise to take good care of you."

"We'll stick to the same time frame, then? Should Ben and I pick you up around five?"

"Perfect."

"What's your address?"

"5735 Roanoke Road," he said.

"Great," Mary said. "See you tomorrow."

"Tomorrow, then."

After Olsen hung the phone up, he sat on the bed for a few minutes. Then he pulled a pair of socks from the drawer and went downstairs. He put on his basketball shoes, flipped on the backyard light, and went outside and starting shooting hoops. 3-pointers. Little jumpers. Fast-break lay-ups. Stopping to catch his breath at one point, he saw Mr. McCormick's upstairs light come on, and the old man's shadow behind the window shade, and the light go off again.

After a while he went inside and drank a beer in the dark as he stood at the kitchen sink. He took a long shower, and drank another beer, and went to bed, and could not sleep.

🍁   🍁   🍁

Olsen was ready the next evening when Mary and Ben swung through the dusk into his driveway. He put his overnight bag in the back of the Jeep. "I'll drive if you want," Olsen told them; the three of them were standing together under the five o'clock sky.

"Great," said Mary, "but first I need to know where your neighbor Mr. McCormick lives."

Olsen pointed to the white house next door. He and Ben stood side by side in the driveway and watched Mary walk across the lawn, her legs in pale blue denim, hair merging into the afternoon shadows; she carried a plastic container, tied with a white ribbon.

"How does my mom know your neighbor?" Ben asked Olsen.

"She doesn't. But I told her about him. Lonely old guy. Good friend of mine." Olsen clapped a hand on Ben's shoulder. "You excited?"

"Hell, yeah."

Olsen laughed. "I still remember the first time I saw you play—skinny 8th grader in that AAU tournament. I thought, what can that lightweight do? Then you muscled the ball away from some giant kid and sank a 3 to win the game."

"You have a good memory."

"I have a whole scrapbook in my head of times you've made me proud." Olsen put his hands in his jacket pockets. "It's not just times like this, either. It's the tough times, too, that you've made me proud."

"Times I'd probably rather forget, right?"

"I'll always remember in the locker room after State—poor Matt was falling apart and you stood by him, took care of him, talked him through it. You had your own pain but you looked out for him. I don't know where you found that strength at your age. You're a helluva good friend."

Ben looked off into space. "I don't even remember that. Wait, maybe I do." He leaned on the hood of the Jeep. "What else? When I cried at the basketball awards? Proud moment, huh?" He spat into the grass.

"You showed you have heart. That's not such a bad thing. And I *was* proud of you for that. Because you were man enough to show your feelings."

"Man enough or an idiot? I definitely want to forget that."

Mary came back across the lawn through the shadows and stood beside Ben in the driveway. "I gave Mr. McCormick some chocolate chip cookies," she said.

"Does he think you're a psycho? He doesn't even know you," Ben said.

"I told him I'm a friend of Thomas'. Told him you're my son. He said to speed up your footwork on defense and keep up the good rebounding."

Olsen burst out laughing. "Everybody wants to tell me how to play," said Ben, and got in the front passenger seat. Mary climbed in back and picked up her book; Olsen got behind the wheel.

He captained the Jeep calmly, traversing the streets of Indian River en route to the highway, but he felt like he was piloting an airplane. Flying. Soaring along the interstate, with Mary reading in the back seat, Ben in charge of the music, playing Pearl Jam, flipping through his CD case. Olsen leaned back. Smiled. Sighed. When he looked over at Ben, the weight of his affection lay wistful on his heart.

The early days of Ben had been all fun and ego: **Reminds me of me.** Then time had sobered Olsen, brought him nose to nose with his own helplessness: you cannot save Ben from life; you cannot stop yourself from loving him; and you have to set him free, time and time again.

"I have plenty of snacks and things if we get hungry," Mary said behind them.

"I'm hungry," said Ben.

Olsen asked, "What do we have?"

"Chocolate chip cookies, fruit bars, bananas, little boxes of raisins, a big bag of walnuts. Bottles of water. Gum. TicTacs."

"I'll take some cookies," Ben said.

"Me, too," said Olsen, and Mary handed each of them a ziploc bag.

Later on down the highway, Olsen glanced over his shoulder and noticed Mary had a tiny clip-on light fastened to her book. "That's a clever gadget."

"Yeah," she said. "It's great for the car. Or if you want to read in bed but the other person can't sleep with the light on."

"So what are you reading?" Olsen asked.

"*Lady Oracle* by Margaret Atwood."

"Ah, yes—also of *Blind Assassin* fame." **The one you were reading the day you leaped down from the tree.**

"Have you ever read her short stories?" Mary asked.

"Probably some along the way."

Looking in the rearview mirror, Olsen saw Mary was looking out the side window. "Margaret Atwood is a master of everything," she said. "Every kind of writing. The first time I read her short story, 'Hair Jewellery,' I wanted to build a shrine for her."

Olsen looked out at the highway, studded with red and white lights, coming and going.

"Come on, Mom. A shrine?" Ben laughed.

"After you read that story," Mary said, tapping Ben's shoulder from the back seat, "you'll want to design the shrine blueprints."

"Why would I want to read a story called 'Hair Jewellery'?" he groaned.

"Ben," Mary said. "Don't judge a book by its cover."

They flew along.

How would it feel being married to Mary—what would it be like to rest in the knowledge that she was his, to fly and dive and rest with her, to spin on the edge of hurricane and fire with her, to feel the danger and not have to suffocate it, to know he was not the same man he once had been—now sadder, wiser, his body and soul learning to live one life?

They arrived at the Creston Plaza in Valparaiso about eight. Tri-State Weekend was a huge enterprise. The parking lot was packed, and the Creston Plaza lobby surged with a buzzing ocean of tall males, an army of leviathans with the cool confidence of men and boys in possession of impossibly long and skilled extremities.

"Tom! Olsen!" A rosy, balding big man with a hairy arm and hand waved to them from the edge of the lobby crowd, and in a second Olsen recognized him.

"Hey, Wally!" Olsen and Ben and Mary moved into the current of men, women, and teenage boys creeping across the lobby. When they reached Wally Bruner, Olsen made the introductions; then Olsen put one arm around Ben's shoulder, with his other hand touching Mary's waist, and she didn't move away.

"I coach at Greendale High in Columbus—Ohio, that is—your coach's old stomping grounds in college," Wally Bruner said to Ben. "Mrs. Wendling, you have a very talented son here. Tom's told me all about him."

"Thank you," Mary said. She leaned into Olsen; her hair smelled like flowers.

"What schools are you looking at, Ben?" Wally Bruner asked.

"Coupla big schools—Purdue, Ohio State—but I like Tucson State the best. It's gonna be hard to pick."

"You got time," said Bruner. "Dan Branigan still out there at Tucson?" he asked Olsen.

"Yup. And he keeps trying to recruit *me*—or plant the seed, anyway, in case a spot opens up on the coaching staff. But I'm happy where I am," said Olsen, his arm still around Ben's shoulder as he spoke.

"Have it your way," Wally Bruner said, "but that Tucson sunshine would get me out there in a heartbeat. Give him my name!" He scanned the teeming lobby. "This is the greatest. I like Tri-State even better than the state championships. Now listen, Ben, you have a great time this weekend."

"Sure—thanks."

"Well, I better get back to my rounds. Catch me later, Tom, we'll talk some more. Nice meeting you both. Good luck, Ben," Bruner said, and reabsorbed into the crowd.

"So," said Olsen. The lobby swam around them, humming at a bass pitch. He took his hand from Mary's waist, slowly, and clapped Ben's shoulder. "How do you want to do this?"

"I'm going to let you two do your Tri-State thing—all this registration and stuff," Mary said. "I'll see you upstairs later, Thomas." She swung her overnight bag forward and back, lightly, and smiled at him, tucking her hair behind her ear.

"Upstairs?" said Olsen, swallowing.

"Yeah, Abby's probably checked in already. So stop by our room when Ben's all set and you're settled in. The three of us'll watch a movie or order a pizza or something."

"Right. Sure," said Olsen. "I might be awhile, though. Ben and I have a lot of schmoozing to do down here." He looked at Ben, at the color of excitement spreading across his face, the face in which Olsen saw himself. **My boy.**

"I'm pretty proud right now," Olsen said, "proud to be here with you," and Ben smiled, first at Olsen, then Mary.

Ben and Mary put their bags down and hugged each other. "I love you, honey," she said, her face pressed against his tee shirt. Ben kissed the top of her head; the tenderness scorched Olsen's eyes; he looked away and heard Ben say, "Love you, too, Mom."

Then Olsen put his arm around Ben's shoulder again. "I'll take good care of him."

"I know you will," said Mary.

❋   ❋   ❋

A couple of hours later, Olsen climbed the stairs to the third floor of the Creston Plaza. He let himself into 311, flipped on the light switch. He tossed his suitcase on the low-slung dresser. Extracted toothbrush and toothpaste. In the bathroom he washed his hands, splashed cold water on his face, smoothed his hair, brushed his teeth. Then he went next door and knocked on 313.

"Who is it?"

"It's me—Tom."

Mary opened the door and the blaze shot up inside him, flared up dangerously, for there was so little separating them, only a foot or two of space and the pastel fabric of her robe and pajamas.

"Come in!" Mary said. "Are you hungry? We have pizza."

"Hi, Tom," said Abby. She was sitting on the bed closer to the door, in turquoise pajamas, painting her toenails. "Good to see you again."

"You, too, Abby."

"We're watching *Enchanted April*," Abby said, dabbing the brush into the bottle of polish. "The British film?"

"Haven't seen it," said Olsen.

"About the two women on vacation at the mystical castle in Italy? Mary loves this movie." Abby stroked the polish over a toenail. "How many times have you seen it?"

"Oh, five, ten," said Mary. "A hundred. I lost track. But it's almost over, Thomas."

Olsen glanced at the television absently and returned his gaze to Mary. Her robe was loosely tied around her waist, the pale pink fabric dotted with little flowers. She was wearing her gold cross; she was playing with the chain; it was catching the light; now her ring was catching the light. Her face and hands and bare feet glittered like butterscotch sauce. He could hear his own breathing.

"Want some pizza?" Mary asked. She went to the round table and opened both pizza boxes. "We have pepperoni and veggie."

"I'll wait till the movie's over."

Mary lay down on her stomach on the bed, propping her face in her hands. "Come sit by me, Thomas. Pull one of those cushy chairs over," and he did as she suggested.

She was waving her brown bare feet in the air languidly. Her toenails were painted pink. The sways and crescents of her body, so close at hand, made his midsection tighten. "Here's my very favorite part!" she said.

Departing the mystical castle, the formerly crippled old woman plunges her walking stick into the earth and strides with a new and lively lilt down the hill. The walking stick transforms into a blossoming acacia tree. A young woman's voiceover, soft British accent, says, *That last week, the whole country seemed to dress itself in white. There were white lilacs, white stocks, white roses, and the fragrance of the acacias. Even after we'd gotten to the bottom of the hill and passed through the iron gates and out into the village, we could still smell the acacias. We could still smell them even when we reached London…but that's another story.*

The final scene faded. The credits started scrolling up the screen. Mary rolled onto her back and closed her eyes.

"I love that ending," she said.

Olsen tried to focus on something else—Abby in her turquoise pajamas, the cloying hit of nail polish, the clatter of the room fan, the fire on his skin.

"It is a great ending," Abby said, standing up. "Just when you think every story's the same old moldy rehash, you get surprised."

Abby and Olsen locked eyes. Then she grinned at him. She picked up the remote and clicked to the weather channel.

"See what it's going to do tomorrow," she said.

"Thomas, have some pizza. And tell us about Ben," said Mary. She lay on her back, hands folded behind her head now, looking at the ceiling. "What's his roommate like? Did you meet any of his teammates? Who's coaching them? Do you remember his room number?"

Olsen answered all Mary's questions, and all of Abby's. Yes, Ben was already having fun; the next day the boys would practice in the gyms over at Valparaiso University; they were already inundated with freebies—basketball shoes and shirts and gym bags; Ben's Tri-State coach was a teacher from Chicago, a good guy, Olsen had met him a couple of times before.

He heard his own voice from a distance as he talked; it sounded deep and steady; it sounded as if a ventriloquist were speaking for him.

Eventually Olsen found himself standing at the door of the room with Mary. She was saying, "Let's meet for breakfast in the morning. See you down in the bistro around nine?"

"Yes. Good. See you then," Olsen said.

Walking out into the hall, he heard her voice trailing him: "Sweet dreams, Thomas."

He turned around, expecting to see her smiling, but she was biting her lip, her head tilted against the door, looking at him.

Back in 311, he stood in the shower for a long time. Then he ordered *Enchanted April* on the hotel movie channel.

❧   ❧   ❧

Olsen awoke unrefreshed and prickly. An image flashed in his mind: *Grant: A Novel* by Max Byrd lying on the coffee table in his living room in Indian River. He cursed out loud that he had forgotten to pack it.

It was only 6:45. He didn't want to horn in on Ben and the Tri-State breakfast buffet in Ballroom C, although he had an open invitation from Wally Bruner to join in all the weekend activities. And he didn't want to appear unattractively eager to Mary by arriving too prompt and fresh-scrubbed for breakfast at nine. So he yanked on shorts and running shoes and a tee shirt, and proceeded down the unpeopled halls and stairs to work out at the hotel gym.

Of course there had to be an overly made-up, tanning-bedded, platinum-topped woman wearing fuschia spandex—"Hi, I'm Judi! With an i!"—ensconced in the gym, and of course she had to be talkative. Olsen's mood darkened further. Judi seemed more like the residue of a bad dream than a real person, and he growled in response to her chirp and cheer, though she was hardly thwarted. Eventually she left, and he ran on the treadmill in peace for half an hour, Tri-State pushed to the back of his mind and Mary pulled to the front. He twirled her around in his thoughts. His agitation began to melt away.

Back upstairs and showering in 311, Olsen had a talk with himself. Abby was a roadblock but also a built-in conscience, and in any case there was nothing he could do about her presence; Olsen liked her; and he shouldn't forget that Wendling would have ruined everything if not for the stroke of good fortune that had kept him at home.

So what did Olsen want this weekend? To be close to Ben. To emboss Mary's fingerprints on his skin. To trace it all in the landscape of his memory.

Who was he kidding? He wanted much, much more than that. But for this weekend, it would have to be enough.

❦   ❦   ❦

He glimpsed Mary and Abby across the lobby, two dark and shining heads in the breakfast bistro, in a half-circle booth by the window.

The Tri-State boys had long since finished breakfast in Ballroom C. Only a few stragglers still loped through the lobby, gym bags slung over their shoulders, en route to the waiting buses to Valpo.

Olsen slid into the booth beside Mary. "Good morning," he said, coming to rest against her shoulder.

"Good morning," Mary smiled; Abby said, "Hi, Tom." Mary picked up her knife, dipped it in some red jelly, raspberry or strawberry, spread it back and forth across half of an English muffin. Abby nibbled a bagel, poured cream in her coffee, then sugar, and stirred.

"Did you sleep well?" Mary asked Olsen. Her coffee was black.

"No, I was restless all night," he said. "And you?"

"I was, too! That's funny," she said. "If only we'd known, we could have watched the midnight movie or taken a walk together or something."

"I slept like a baby," said Abby. She bit into her bagel and grinned around it, her eyes crinkling.

"So, we've got the whole day. Ben's game doesn't tip off till 7:30. What would you like to do?" Olsen said.

"What do you suggest?" Mary spread jelly on the other half of her English muffin. She licked the edge of the knife, her eyes on Olsen. He felt his body tighten and he looked at Abby, who was watching him pleasantly, leaning back against the cushioned booth.

"Mary, Tom looks hungry. Let him get something to eat." Abby sipped her coffee. "I'd love to go to the dunes today, Tom. It's not far from here, and I haven't been there in years."

"The dunes," said Olsen. "Perfect."

"It's a glorious day, just like the weather channel promised." Abby turned her face toward the window, and Olsen noticed the Valparaiso morning sky, draped in aqua light and white sun.

❦   ❦   ❦

In days and years and times gone by, Olsen had taken other women with him to the dunes.

He had taken Alexandra once, long ago and before the abortion, when they were still engaged and doing their graduate work in Columbus. Alexandra had just decided to pursue the Ph.D. in mathematics.

They had sat side by side on the dunes. Olsen had talked about the ancient mariners who had evaporated along with the seas. Then Alexandra had talked about TOE—the mathematical Theory Of Everything, and its unfathomable ten dimensions, including one of time. Alexandra had already, unknowingly, lost Olsen's heart, but he loved her theory: if there was indeed another dimension of time, then he couldn't be trapped in this one. It would be the quintessential freedom.

People were always fooled by Alexandra's blonde prettiness, her cheerleading-captain façade; they were never ready for the way she wielded her brains. Olsen admired her, wanted her lush, lithe body for himself, even believed once that he loved her. But something in Alexandra was iced over, frosty, even in Olsen's arms, even before the stainless steel clinic, a chill he eventually realized he would have to escape.

❋   ❋   ❋

Olsen, Mary, and Abby stood at the base of Mount Baldy, looking up. They had left their jackets in the Jeep; the April air that day was a surprise breath of summer, and the parking lot was getting crowded.

"You're sure Lake Michigan's on the other side?" Mary said, surveying the swirls of Baldy's shifting incline. Two boys in cutoffs and tee shirts started grappling with the sandy climb. "I wonder how Ben's doing this morning," she said.

"I'm sure he's having a great time." Olsen checked his watch. "They're practicing now. I'm sure he's in his glory on that big college floor. Probably the most fun he's ever had."

"Enough procrastinating!" Abby said, and hit Mount Baldy running. "Whoo-eee!" she called. "Here I go! Last one to the top's a rotten egg!" Her feet sank and twisted in the sand as she ran, and her hips twisted in rhythm, a comic, jerking dance. Olsen held his hand out to Mary.

"Let's do it," he said, and they started to climb.

Just over Baldy's crest, Abby was waiting for them, the wind lifting her hair in a dark flutter. She was looking out at the water. Then she started the long run down and across the plain of sand to the water's edge toward the colorful sprinkles of people on the beach below.

Olsen and Mary lingered on the summit. He looked out to where lake met sky in a blur of aquamarine.

"It's like a desert," she said, "and an oasis."

Olsen looked at Mary, at her smooth brown profile, lips parted in a white flash as she gazed north across the lake, hair spinning in a wild updraft.

"Moses discovered God in the desert," she said, "and I can see why. I can imagine the desert sky open wide, and the light unchained, and the wind sweeping everything clear." She twirled her hair up on her head and held it there. "Things were so much easier in Moses' day, when God just boomed His instructions down from heaven, clear and intact. Wouldn't that be great? But nowadays we have to really listen, and try to feel the knowing in our hearts. And that's so much harder to be sure of."

Olsen was still watching her profile.

"This sand and water and sky—such beauty," she said. She let her hair down, tilted her head against his arm. "I've been landlocked too long—but I know paradise when I see it." Then she started jogging down toward the water, across the plain of sand, and Olsen followed.

Later, on their way back down Mount Baldy, he made a decision. It was time to stop spectating while his life story passed before his eyes; after Ben's game that night, after dinner, after settling Ben in for the night, there would be no more chaperoning.

CHAPTER 15

❁

Come Back For Me

It seemed almost graceful when it happened, until the chill of impending grotesquerie froze Olsen's spine. It was one of those slow-motion moments you want to reach into with your bare hands, to stop it from happening, to pull everyone back to safety, especially the ones you love.

Olsen, Mary, and Abby were sitting courtside watching Ben's Tri-State game in the loudly crammed Valpo gym. It had been a typical high school all-star contest: point guards at both ends of the court hogging the ball and sinking most of their shots.

So when one point guard's shot finally hit the rim instead and spun up toward the rafters for the taking, the forwards converged, all elbows and knees poised to leap for the rebound—and the ball twirled, and hovered, then plummeted down like a bomb, bounced up off the rim again, almost as high, then sank down toward the leaping mass of 4- and 5-men—and Ben rose up above them all, the ball spinning atop his fingertips.

Then the unsuccessful shooter burst wildly into the mix, bent on reclaiming the ball from the big men, and somehow in the leaping and landing, the twisting and tangling, Ben, high in the air, his eyes at the rim, got his legs upswept out from under him—

and as Ben flipped upside down, Olsen saw a miscellaneous flying elbow uppercutting into his mouth, and Ben's front tooth, torn from his gums, sailing out into the air, a comet with a trail of blood—

then Ben crashing through a scattering of knees and elbows, plunging toward the ground like a falling guillotine—

Ben slamming on the crown of his skull into the hardwood—blood spurting out of the hole in his mouth—his neck folding forward—

then Olsen saw the rest of Ben splattering down in a jumble, tailbone, arms, torso, legs, in no particular order—

and the whole of Ben being stampeded beneath the stomping feet and twisting ankles and crumpling knees that crashed on top of him—

and Ben's head coming up off the hardwood once, then falling down, and staying there.

Olsen flew from the stands to Ben's side on a catapult of light, outside of time, to where Ben lay fluorescent, glowing silvery blue. The other players yelled, moaned, rolled off each other, found their feet, stood up. But as Olsen called his name, Ben did not open his eyes; he lay crumpled and unmoving; then a convulsion seemed to electrocute him—the shock pushed Olsen backward—and Ben fell, lifelessly, back to the floor.

Olsen saw the blue veil that already covered Ben's skin; his swelling lips were parted; blood was pouring from the side of his mouth. Olsen felt a groan hitting his ears, a groaning chorus from somewhere around him; then realized it was sprawling up out of his own throat. He pressed his ear against Ben's chest; the heart still pulsed dully; but he was not breathing.

Head roaring, world in front of him spinning, Olsen pulled his own shirt off, wiped the blood from Ben's face and lips and gums, swabbed the inside of Ben's mouth with his fingers, cleared the airway, pinched Ben's nose closed, lay his lips over Ben's and exhaled.

But Ben's chest lay flat and still. His face was still silvery blue; he lay unmoving. Again Olsen breathed into him, and again; and again; but nothing happened.

No

No

No

No

Come back   Come back to me   Come back for me

He breathed into Ben again; again; again, in a steady rhythm lined with panic; the groaning roar took on color now, red and rust and orange hurtling around him, screaming red in his ears—

then everything went silent, a muffled, pulsing silence cushioning Olsen's ears, an underwater dive.

In silence now, Olsen saw the hardwood floor with excruciating clarity, glossy brown and spreading all around them like a sea of gleaming mud and he saw the other boys, motionless in a half-circle, caught in a game of freeze tag

and he saw the crowd, like painted scenery in the stands, flat and unmoving.

He looked down; Ben's face lay blue beneath him; Olsen leaned toward him.

Breathe into him   Look   Nothing
Breathe into him   Look   Nothing
Breathe into him   Look   Nothing
Nothing

Child of my heart   My boy   You must come back to me

A shadow passed over Olsen in the silence. He looked across Ben's body and saw Mary facing him on her knees, her eyes stretched white with terror, the backdrop of freeze-tag and painted scenery behind her. Her face looked coated with silver ashes. He saw her lips say *Thomas.*

Olsen looked down again at Ben's face, at the blue skin fading into gray.

O God, listen to me   Without this boy I was only waiting for the world to end

The groan inside Olsen lurched up into a roar, the silence broken, and Mary leaned toward him, and the freeze-tag players started moving again, the crowd began swaying, and the roar kept coming.

And then Ben's body heaved colossally, and he gagged, strangling on wet, choking coughs, and Olsen turned Ben's head to the side, gingerly; Ben vomited a blood-soaked flood that spread across the hardwood floor. His eyes were still closed. He began to breathe again. But he did not wake up.

🍁   🍁   🍁

Olsen ran across the parking lot toward Porter Hospital's emergency room, toward its façade of serenity, toward the peace glowing in the white building lights. Shirtless, blood-smeared, and far ahead of Abby, who ran behind him, he flung himself through the automatic doors into the ER, into the buzzing gray-green glare and air heavy with sweat and tears, the waiting area almost vacant, eerie, a mausoleum.

"How's Ben?" he panted.

"Thomas—thank God! Nurse, can you give him a shirt—scrubs—something to put on? He used his shirt to get the blood off Ben."

"Are you the trainer, sir? Sir?"

"No, he's not," said Mary, "the trainers were out in the Valpo parking lot, someone's grandmother had fallen, broken her hip—Thomas saved Ben—got him breathing again—but I don't know how, with all that blood."

"How's Ben? Where is he?" **My boy flying falling falling hold on** "Breathing, is he still breathing on his own?"

"Yes, but he's still unconscious," Mary said. "They're trying to find out how bad his head injury is, and if his neck and spine are hurt."

"Mary," said Abby, "have you called Virgil?"

"No, could you call him? These are his cell and office numbers," she said, scribbling. "Tell him what happened. Tell him Thomas is with us. Then call my pastor—here's his number—ask him to send this out on all the prayer chains."

Get me to Ben

Get me through this gray green fluorescent buzzing maze to Ben

Ben

oh Ben

boy in the white flannel gown

sprawled on this coarse gravel bed

waiting for the world to end

please open your eyes

"Are you Ben's parents?"

"I'm his mother. What can you tell us?"

Checking neck spine brain internal injuries EEG X-rays CAT scan

"All right. Thank you, Doctor. Could you leave us alone for a few minutes?" said Mary.

they have to be buried or drowned

thus great generals are born

"Thomas, it's time to pray," Mary said.

"I can't—I don't know how."

It always sounds like you took the easy way out, somehow

"You don't have to know how. Hold my hand, hold Ben's hand. We like to hold hands when we pray."

You do not have to be good.

You do not have to walk on your knees

for a hundred miles through the desert, repenting.

You only have to let the soft animal of your body love what it loves.

"Let the beloved of the Lord rest secure in Him," said Mary, "for He shields him all day long, and the one the Lord loves rests between His shoulders. O

Lord, Ben is Your beloved, let him rest secure in You, let him rest between Your shoulders," Mary said.

"Amen," said Olsen.

Come back for me, Ben

You know our story cannot end this way

"Tom," said Abby, "your friend Wally Bruner called the main desk when I was out there. Mary, I can't reach Virgil. The answering machine at your house keeps picking up, and his cell rolls right into voice mail. But I didn't leave messages."

"It's almost eleven," said Mary. "Maybe the building department records are in even worse shape than he thought. Did you try him at the office?"

"No answer there either."

"Thank God Thomas is with us."

"Wasn't Virgil having that heart trouble—chest pains or something?" Abby said.

"Yeah, but his heart checked out."

Forget the former things, don't dwell on the past

See, I am doing a new thing

"Lord, Ben is Your beloved, let him rest secure in You, let him rest between Your shoulders," Mary said.

"Amen," said Olsen, and touched her hand.

If only I could reach back into time past

no twisting, tangling, falling, flailing, slamming, smashing, bursting, breaking, no final snap splatter on hardwood, guillotine and guillotined, but reaching into time past

"Let him rest secure in You," said Mary.

1:09 a.m.

Meanwhile the world goes on

"Here, Mary, have a water. Abby, here's one for you," said Olsen.

"Thanks, Tom."

"Thank you, Thomas."

2:31 a.m.

Mary did you know that when we lost at State, our boy did not shed a tear

he was too stoic then

thank God he learned to cry

cried right on my shoulder that was good

let's not let him grow up to be like me

"Thomas, did you say something?" Mary asked.

No, but I learned this, at least, by my experiment
meanwhile the world goes on
and I cannot go on without Ben's breath breathing in this world
4 a.m.
4:02
4:06
4:13
4:20
4:22
4:24
4:24
I wouldn't want to burst anyone's bubble
but time is soaked in blood now
without you I was only waiting for the world to end
"Thomas, come sit by us. I'm starting to feel more peaceful," said Mary.
"Peaceful?" Olsen said.
4:44 a.m.
4:47
Can you try and understand what it's been like for me?
put your face close to the picture
it always sounds like I took the easy way out
"Yes, see, I feel very peaceful now. I think everything is going to be all right,"
Mary said.
"Yes, I think so, too—" said Olsen.
Oh, I know that feeling, Mary—when the crushing weight on my shoul-
ders transforms into lightness like wings, just as in the bitterest of winters
my hands, verging on frostbite, begin to feel deliciously warm
4:59 a.m.
5:00
5:00
5:01
Dozing
Don't you wish you were anywhere but here?
Here as in school in this town in this life?
Wherever I go, there I am
"Oh, my God—Thomas, get help! Go get help—Abby!"
"Ladies, sir—you'll have to go to the waiting area—now!"
"Sir, please go out to the waiting area! Your son needs our help *now*."

Not my son but the child of my heart
and I will not leave him
there is nothing worse than being all alone in this world
left all alone and no one can hear you call for help
or maybe you have no voice
or maybe you cannot find the words

"Sir, please—you need to get out of the way and let us do what we need to do."

"I want to stay with him—I don't want to leave him," Olsen said.

You need to bring him back
back to me back for me

"Thomas," said Mary.

"Come on, Tom," Abby said. "We have to get out of the way."

"You two go to the waiting room. I'm staying here to make sure what they're doing," said Olsen, on the outskirts.

5:37 a.m.
5:40
5:41
5:41
5:41

Come on Mom a shrine?
Wherever I go, there I am

"Sir, are you Ben Wendling's father? You need to sign some papers."

"No—" said Olsen.

"Are you family?"

"No—let me find his mother for you," he said.

Look for me Father
they never heard me steal into the stairwell hall
and climb the ladder to the fresh night air

"Mary, there are papers for you to sign," he told her.

7:31 a.m.

"It's getting light out," Abby said.

Olsen walked to the window.

7:34 a.m.

"I'm going back to the hotel for a bit," Abby said.

"That's good. Get a little rest," said Olsen. "Mary, do you want to go, too?"

"No, I'll stay."

"Can I bring you two anything when I come back?" Abby asked. "Something to eat?"

"No," Mary said.

why would I want to read a story called Hair Jewellery

"No, thanks," said Olsen.

8:33 a.m.

"Thomas," Mary said. But he was dozing again.

Look for me, Father, on the roof
of the red brick building
at the foot of Green Street—
that's where we live, you know, on the top floor.
I'm the boy in the white flannel gown,
sprawled on this coarse gravel bed
under the starry sky
8:34 a.m.

"Thomas, listen to me," Mary said. "He's awake."

one kiss for the boy in the white flannel gown
one small kiss to celebrate your tiny, tiny my-ness
did you know that, without you, I was only waiting for the world to end
I could not go on without your breath breathing in this world
O God please
Let him rest secure in You

❦   ❦   ❦

Rumpled in the glaze of obliteration, Olsen stepped out into the new day, taking Mary's hand. They crossed the parking lot together.

As he drove them back to the hotel, Olsen could only stare north at the empty road. The early Sunday morning traffic passed by him like flickers of thought. He left the car stereo off. Looking over at Mary, he saw her blink slowly, but her lips curved up sweetly at the corners, her expression smooth, a mask's veneer.

Approaching the Creston Plaza, Olsen pulled up to a stoplight and looked into the car at his left. The man at the wheel was shaving with an electric razor. Across the intersection, a car and a couple of vans lined up southbound. The light turned green. No one moved. Then a horn ripped blaringly through the Sunday morning air, and Olsen and Mary jumped reflexively up off their seats.

Olsen didn't know who had honked; it was all part of the same blur of nothingness that had no meaning. He stepped on the gas and moved forward.

They reached the Creston Plaza.

Their passage across the lobby streamed like an airport's moving walkway; he couldn't feel his legs, his feet, the ground.

They moved past the open doors of Ballroom C. Olsen spotted people setting tables. A piece of awareness floated through his thoughts.

"Excuse me," Olsen said. "This is for the Tri-State awards, right?"

"Yes, sir, the brunch starts at 11:30," said a set-up man.

"I need to leave a message for Wally Bruner or one of the guys in charge of Tri-State, as soon as somebody get here."

"What's the message?"

"Tell them Ben Wendling is okay. He's okay."

Mary remained silent at Olsen's side. Her lips still curved up slightly. She stared beyond the set-up man's head.

"Ben Wendling?" said the man. "Sure. I'll tell someone. What, was he hurt or something?" But Olsen and Mary had already turned around.

Upstairs in Mary and Abby's room, the curtains were still closed. Abby was back at the hospital with Ben. Her suitcase lay on the bed where she had painted her toenails the night before during *Enchanted April*.

Mary sat down on the edge of the bed by the window.

"We should try and sleep for an hour or two," Olsen said. He didn't want to leave Mary, didn't want to lie in the tomb of his empty hotel room alone. "I'll stay with you till you fall asleep."

Mary stood up, swaying. "Let me brush my teeth," she said, disappearing into the bathroom. The sound of water, streaming and muffled, soothed him. He pulled a chair to her bedside and sat down.

When Mary came out, her hair was brushed and shining and her cheeks were pink, still damp from washcloth and water. She crossed the room and pulled the curtains open. "I'd rather sleep in the light," she said.

She lay down on top of the bedspread, her hair dark on the white pillow, staring at the ceiling. "Stay with me, Thomas," she said. Reached out and wrapped her hand around Olsen's index finger; closed her eyes; held on.

Slumped in the chair, Olsen heard birds singing right outside the window, just before he fell asleep.

CHAPTER 16

❀

World Goes On

The nightmares began as soon as Olsen returned to Indian River.

They left Valparaiso late Tuesday, pulled into Olsen's driveway on Roanoke Road that night. Olsen got his bag, kissed Ben's sleeping forehead, and hugged Mary. Then he waved good-bye as she backed the Jeep down the driveway and drove off. He saw the upstairs lights on at Mr. McCormick's, a vision of normalcy that seemed far away.

Inside, Olsen's house was dim and throbbing; the windows had been closed for three days. As he stepped farther into the interior, with shadows pounding around him, he started flicking lights on, flinging windows open, cranking the stereo, everything he could think of to escape the sound of blood hammering his ears and the black thickness of being alone.

His answering machine overflowed with messages: the Indian River High School principal, the athletic director, Rakowsky, Wally Bruner, Rakowsky again, Kuehn, Stefanik, Kristina.

Olsen erased them. Conversation had not yet returned to the realm of the possible.

Later in the evening he lingered over his review of lesson plans. Contemplating the next day's return to school soothed him, along with the beer in his veins. He avoided going to bed until fatigue slurred his thoughts, then he trudged upstairs, where he opened more windows. He brushed his teeth, stripped off his clothes, and fell onto the bed, too hot to get under the covers. He didn't remember falling asleep.

In the first dream, Olsen was leaning over his own bed, where Ben was lying with his eyes frosted shut, his face, lips, skin, all ice blue. Olsen lifted Ben's hand, and the shock of its lifelessness froze him, and Mary materialized by the headboard, not speaking or moving, her face lined in gray.

Olsen woke up stone cold, flat on his back on the mattress, his arms spread out to the sides. He stared at the ceiling,. He turned toward the alarm clock, where the time glowed red in the silence: **1:24.** Fell back to sleep.

In his next dream, Olsen was walking down the Indian River High School hallway, and Ben came around the corner toward him, dead boy on foot, and Olsen turned to flee, and Mary stood at the other end of the corridor; Olsen's legs were concrete; Mary vanished; Ben kept coming toward him, his lips moving but no sound coming out.

When Olsen woke up, he was standing next to his bed, his chest thundering and wet, his knees bent as if ready to run. He sank down onto the bed. **2:34.**

When he woke up again, or thought he had, he felt someone in bed beside him. He turned his head on the pillow, and there was Ben, dead and blue, lying cold beside him, and the telephone rang; he answered and it was Mary asking, "Is Ben there? May I speak to Ben?"

Finally Olsen fought his way out of the hood of sleep. Cold blew in through the window. He staggered across the carpet and slammed it shut. **3:44.**

Olsen took some sweats out of a dresser drawer and pulled them on. He sat on the edge of the bed. Then he lay back down and pulled the bedspread around himself. He stared at the ceiling again.

He kicked the bedspread off, got up and picked his keys up off the dresser.

The quiet muffle of night padded Olsen's ears as he walked outside across his driveway. The clatter of his garage door jackhammered the silence.

A few miles later, Olsen turned off the main road onto Dover Drive. He shut his headlights off, parked the Corvette just east of the Wendlings'. Their house stood dark and silent. **See, if something was wrong, there would be a commotion, ambulances, neighbors.** But tragedies kept spinning up from his exhaustion. He tried to stay awake.

Olsen awoke half an hour later, cramped up behind the wheel. His dashboard clock said 4:41 and a car flew past him, heading for the main road.

Remnants of Olsen's nightmares hung thick and sticky in his head. Should he go to the Wendlings' door, pound on it, ring the bell? Then he saw something: a light came on upstairs. Wasn't that Ben's bedroom? Yes—front bedroom over the porch.

Olsen climbed stiffly out of the Corvette and stood on the pavement in his clammy clothes. He looked up at the light in Ben's room.

He saw a shadow pass behind the shade.

Then he saw a light come on, one window over: the bathroom.

Olsen felt lines of sweat drawing themselves down the cold sides of his face. In a minute or two, he saw the bathroom light go out.

He saw the shadow pass behind the shade in Ben's bedroom window again. The light in Ben's room snapped out. Olsen's shoulders heaved. He pulled his forearm across the sweat on his face.

He got in the Corvette and drove back across Indian River to Roanoke Road, where he brewed a pot of coffee and got in the shower. It was almost time for school.

❦   ❦   ❦

The principal and athletic director sought Olsen out together before first period. Olsen followed them to the A.D.'s office and told them the story tonelessly, hearing his own voice from that distance he was growing accustomed to.

"What a great thing you did, Olsen." "You're a hero, Tom." "Thank God you were there." "Thank God you knew your stuff."

"Yes, thank God."

In every class, his students bounced in their seats, spilling questions, starving to hear exactly what had happened, but Olsen could only tell the story in that distant, colorless way, subduing them.

"How is Ben?"

"I haven't talked to him since yesterday, but I'll call him during lunch to check and see."

"When will he be back at school?"

"Not sure yet."

"What about his tooth?"

"His own tooth couldn't be saved. He'll get a fake one, an implant."

Rakowsky was waiting for him outside his classroom after Senior Lit. "How ya holding up?"

"Fine."

"Are you sure you're okay? You look a little…tired. Have you gotten any sleep?"

"Not much. I'm gonna go call Ben right now."

"Try and get some sleep tonight. I'll talk to you," Rakowsky said, and turned down the hall toward the cafeteria.

Olsen walked the opposite way to his basketball office, and the crowd in the hallway separated into two waves, pressing against the lockers, a zipper of people unzipping. Stray phrases roared in his ears and faded away, jets taking off in the sky of his mind, a boy saying: "Coach Olsen! We heard about what happened!" and a girl's voice: "Mr. Olsen can give me mouth-to-mouth anytime."

He went in his office and shut the door, but shrieks from gym class on the playing fields outside his window penetrated the panes.

Mary answered the phone on the second ring.

"Mary, it's me," he said. "How are you? How's Ben?"

"Hi, Thomas. He's doing a little better today. He's right here eating a bowl of cereal. Want to talk to him?"

Ben came on the line crunching. "Hi, Coach."

"How're you feeling?"

"Like a bunch of guys stomped on my head. Hey, my mom said you did the mouth-to-mouth on me, got me breathing again—how can I ever thank you for that? I hate to think what would have happened if you weren't there."

"Let's not think about that. Let's just get you better."

"I know I'm gonna get bored staying home. I never just sit around like this."

"How about if I bring you some stuff from your locker? I'll drop some books off after school, so they'll be around if you want them."

"On second thought, I'd rather be bored."

"What's your locker com?"

"18-36-10."

"Okay. You take it easy. And listen to your mother."

"I will. See you later then."

"Let me say good-bye to your mom."

❧   ❧   ❧

Lifesavers come in many guises—the rumpled stranger; the angelic envoy; the man who cries **child of my heart your story cannot end this way O God listen to me.**

And when the lifesaving is complete, what then? A modest shrug; a departure into the sunset; an unspoken vow to keep guarding the treasure?

*   *   *

The spring trees lined Dover Drive in greens and pinks and shades of white, impressionistic. Olsen had been coming here for three seasons now—first in the fall, as yellow leaves had sailed on the winds of Indian summer; then in the biting sting of white December; and now, in this freshly painted hope of spring.

The front door was open. Olsen carried a couple of Ben's school books in one hand and called through the screen, "Hello, Ben? Mary?" and Romeo ran into the hall, barking.

"Come on in, Coach—it's open," Ben called from the living room.

Olsen stepped inside and Romeo licked his hand. Olsen turned toward the living room where Ben lay on the couch, propped up on a few pillows and grinning, the raw hole in his gum a gruesome souvenir.

"When do you go to the dentist?" Olsen asked from the hallway.

"Why? Don't ya like my new look?"

"Oh, yeah, it's gorgeous."

"Hi, Thomas!" He heard Mary's voice, turned his head and saw her on the landing. She came down the stairs and Olsen asked her, "Is that a long process—that tooth implant?"

"Yeah. First they'll just give him a temporary cap, because they can't do the implant for a few months—the whole thing—it's complicated. It takes awhile." She stood beside Olsen and put her hand on the small of his back, only for a second.

"You slept well last night?" Olsen asked Ben, putting the school books down on the table.

"I guess so. I don't remember," Ben said. "Took a bunch of pain pills for my headache."

"Want something to drink?" Mary asked. "Some iced tea or pop or something?"

"Nah," said Ben.

"I'd like something," Olsen said. "I'll help you." He followed Mary into the kitchen.

"So how are you holding up?" he asked.

"Pretty well." Mary stood in front of some cupboards and opened them, resting her hands on the knobs, but took nothing out. Her back was toward Olsen. "It's good to be home, isn't it? Thank God we all made it home," she said. Her hair was in a tangle. Olsen wanted to step across the kitchen and smooth it; he wanted to comb it and spread it out on a pillow, the pillow where she would lay her head next to his.

He said, "I missed you and Ben last night—I worried about you both."

"I missed you, too," she said, her back still to him.

"Mary…"

She turned around then. Her face was smooth, her eyes red; she bit her lip, and lifted her arms toward him. Olsen crossed the floor and they wrapped around each other and held on. Then Ben appeared in the kitchen, wobbly, fragile, and Olsen and Mary each opened an arm to bring him in, and the three of them stayed secure in that safety for a while.

That night back on Roanoke Road, Olsen dreamed of a stainless steel hospital, and a baby lying on the cold mirrored floor; he could see the baby was blue, needed help, but Olsen couldn't bring himself to move; instead he stood on the far side of the room, knowing he should do something, and doing nothing.

When Olsen woke up, he found himself teetering at the top of his stairway. Quick—reached through the fog for the railing. Sank down onto the top step. Sighed. Went back to bed.

❦   ❦   ❦

Olsen stood on the sidewalk at the bottom of the wide granite stairway leading up, up to the entrance doors of Calvary Lutheran Church. He heard waves of music; the service was underway. He climbed the stairs.

Inside, the narthex spread out wide and deserted except for an usher with his hand full of church bulletins, and Olsen heard a loud chorus of voices, must be the whole congregation singing, from beyond the sanctuary doors, and electric guitar and bass and percussion and trumpet. The usher said, "They're just finishing the first song," and handed Olsen a bulletin. The music wound down, the usher said, "Now's a good time," and opened the sanctuary door.

Olsen went in and hovered for a moment, surprised by the multitudes jamming the pews. He couldn't see Rakowsky and Karen, or the Reiters, or the Wendlings. A line of people scooted over for him, and he sat beside them in the back row.

The minister read church announcements into a cordless microphone, and Olsen, skimming the church bulletin, heard the scattered phrases: "Vacation

Bible school...new roof...Altar Guild...fundraiser...business as usual...one of our own...praise be to God...his story...Ben Wendling."

Olsen looked up and looked around, people clapped, the guitarist played a few bars, and Ben appeared at the front of the sanctuary.

"Some of you may have heard," Ben said into the microphone the minister handed him, "I had a little accident last week. I was playing basketball up in Valparaiso, took a bad fall, got my front tooth knocked out—got myself knocked out, too. I don't even remember it—but I went unconscious and had convulsions and stopped breathing. It was totally God's miracle that I didn't break my neck when I hit the floor headfirst and everybody fell on top of me. The athletic trainers weren't even there—they were outside in the parking lot with somebody's grandmother—but thank God, my coach was in the gym, Coach Tom Olsen from Indian River High School. Who knows what could have happened if someone didn't get me breathing again—but Coach Olsen ran down from the stands and did rescue breathing on me, and it wasn't easy either, because my mouth was gushing blood and I was throwing up blood and stuff. But none of that stopped my coach—he did everything it took to save me.

"So then I started breathing again on my own, but I was unconscious for like twelve hours. I know a lot of people here at Calvary were praying for me to come through, and God answered those prayers, and today I want to thank God for the awesome ways He saved me, because it's only by His grace that I'm okay. And I want to thank everyone who prayed for me, and I was hoping we could say a special prayer of thanks for Coach Olsen," Ben said to the minister, handing the microphone back.

The field of hands applauded and the minister said, "Almighty God, our Loving Father, we come before you in thanksgiving and praise for Your unfailing goodness, and for Your servant, Tom Olsen, through whom You gave breath and life to our brother Ben in his time of need..."

Olsen hoped no one would recognize him, because he had only slipped into Calvary to find out how it felt to be here, to sit in church, alone and unnoticed.

The minister wrapped up his prayer and the drummer tapped out a new tempo for the band, and they dove into a couple of rolling songs with everyone around Olsen clapping, and he even got swept up in the musical spirit a bit himself. The bulletin called them "Rock of Ages" and "Days of Elijah"—weighty titles but soaring songs, new songs, not hoary hymns like Olsen had mouthed in the occasional Episcopal service of his childhood...singing, singing...then Olsen saw Mary—the crowd shifted and he saw the half-moon of her profile, her hair swinging as she clapped to the music, her lips wrapping around the words, tipping her head against Ben's shoulder, Wendling on her other side.

❦   ❦   ❦

After Ben returned to school, Olsen stayed in the habit of calling Mary from his office at lunch. They always talked about Ben, and she usually had other things to tell him, too: questions, and little funny stories about the library, ideas that had dawned on her while she dug in the garden, snatches of poetry she thought he'd like, and sometimes a recollection from the dunes or Tri-State, mementos of their shared life.

She never mentioned Wendling.

Olsen told Mary he had gone to Calvary, sat in the back pew and listened during that Sunday service, heard the things Ben said, and the pastor's prayer. That surprised her. "Why didn't you stay to say hello?" she asked. "I would have loved to see you there. Ben and I would have introduced you around."

"I haven't been to church in decades," he said. "I've been trying to pray. I don't know if it's going to work out."

Olsen lay in bed nights on Roanoke Road, spring breezes blowing in through the window, and wondered if that breath of life he had given to Ben had come from his own human body, or if God had commandeered him. Wondered whether Ben would have survived so well if Mary and the others had not prayed. Lurking in the shadows of his gratitude was the fear of what might have been; his *Thank You, God*'s trembled.

God, I remember that drive to Valparaiso with Mary and Ben, and our first night at Tri-State—the peace I felt, that real happiness—it was the closest I ever felt to being family. Let that be enough for me.

God, I feel like life is always slipping away from me, I don't know why, I don't know what to do.

God, this empty house is killing me.

God, just let me sleep tonight.

❦   ❦   ❦

"Have you been praying?" Mary asked Olsen on the phone one day. "You said you were going to try."

"A few times, yeah—but it's hard for me. I don't know what to say."

"Just have a conversation with God," said Mary. "Whatever's in your heart."

"That's hard for me to put into words."

"Well, you could pray in bed," she said. "That's a good time—a peaceful time. Quiet. What do you think about when you lie in bed at night before you fall asleep?"

He closed his eyes. **Oh, Mary, let's see: some intermingled imagery of you and your son, both of whom I love. Your butterscotch skin glittering. A comet trailing blood, leaving a crater behind. The rises and falls of pale pink fabric. A tattoo of the sun. A wedding band around your finger. Your voice whispering, Stay with me, Thomas.**

He finally answered, "It depends."

❧   ❧   ❧

"So, let's see that new tooth," Olsen said when Ben walked into AP English.

Ben put his books on Olsen's desk. "It's just the temporary cap, remember? The real one will look better." He bared his teeth in a clenched grin, showing off the dentist's handiwork.

Olsen reached up and held Ben's chin in his fingers, surveying the tooth. "Are you getting taller?" he asked, surprise in his voice.

"Ah hink sho," said Ben through his teeth.

Olsen let go of Ben's chin and clapped him on the shoulder. "Almost good as new," he said. "Hey, got something for you." Olsen dug around his bag and pulled out *Grant: A Novel* by Max Byrd. "You weren't kidding. This was a good book. I even copied a part to keep."

"Which part?" Ben asked.

Olsen hesitated. "I'll have to show you sometime."

❧   ❧   ❧

Summer softball league started in the middle of May. It was good to hang out with Rakowsky and the guys again, pull on his new lime green "All-Pro Insurance of Indian River" tee shirt and hit the diamond a few nights a week.

Olsen announced he would bequeath the high school summer basketball league to Dave Kuehn. Give Kuehn some independence and experience, and give himself a break.

Olsen took it as a clue, a hope, a sign, a quandary, that Mary still never mentioned Wendling—although Wendling dogged Olsen's thoughts anyway, as a thankless, lusterless, humorless parson of a character whose place in Mary's life grew increasingly undeserved.

"I was wondering," Olsen said to Mary on the phone, "what did Virgil ever say about everything that happened at Tri-State?"

"Didn't he ever call you?" Mary said.

"No."

"He told me he wanted to thank you personally," Mary said. "He asked me for your phone number and address so he could get in touch with you."

"I never heard from him."

"Hmm."

"Well, what did he ever say to you about it all?" Olsen said. "I'm just curious."

"He didn't say much. I think he's really been preoccupied with his own health. He's been having that terrible heartburn and chest pain again," Mary said. "But I'm surprised he didn't call you."

That was the last time Olsen asked.

❧   ❧   ❧

"Did you work yesterday? I called, but there was no answer."

"Yes—I did story hours all day—the tiny tots in the morning, my kindergarteners in the afternoon, and first graders after that."

"Did you wear your black dress—the velvet one—and all your silver jewelry?"

"Thomas, how do you remember stuff like that?" she laughed. "No, it's too hot for velvet."

❧   ❧   ❧

Olsen's nightmares still hounded his sleep. He mentioned it to Mary; she told him she still had bad dreams, too; neither of them volunteered the contents.

But Olsen always slept well on softball nights in June—after the sweat- and shout-soaked innings on breezeless muggy evenings, playing for the good guys in the lime-green All-Pro Insurance tee shirts, Olsen in his starring role as first base gatekeeper and cleanup king, pounding, poking, flying, diving, slamming; scents of leather, dusty grass, and hot and waterlogged air commingling in his nose; his eyes stinging from downpours of salt and upswipes of dust, his ears gauging thunks and smacks and thuds and grunts; the sky pale, the stands speckled with wives, and bordered by small and aimless children drawing in the dirt or squinting toward the field; enclaves of coolers poised and dripping.

Kristina came to watch a game one night, with Terese Ciprak tagging along. Olsen didn't know how they'd found out the schedule; he suspected Rakowsky.

After All-Pro won the game, Kristina and Terese came down from the stands and talked to Olsen for a few minutes in their suntanned splendor and snug shorts and halter tops. Part of him felt the flare of interest, but another part recalled Mary in her cutoffs leaping down from the tree house. He declined Kristina's offer to meet at the bar for victory drinks, though he watched the two women walk away, their hips tight and swingy, their legs bare and golden in the evening light.

Olsen decided his back yard looked barren. One hot afternoon he was standing at his kitchen sink drinking a bottle of beer, looking out at the back yard, and the thought struck him: the front yard's fine, with the little junipers and that big rhododendron, but back there it's just an empty rectangle.

The next morning while it was still cool outside, he dug a garden bed. Then he borrowed a neighbor's rototiller and wrestled it into service. He asked around and heard about a good tree nursery in Springwater, where he went and picked out a blue spruce, almost as tall as he was; planted it in the thick of June's heat wave; it stood alone in the wide bed he had created.

Later that week, Olsen and Mr. McCormick were watering in their back yards. Mr. McCormick was tending his patch of yellow flowers; his squirrel-dog was jumping in the grass.

"Nice tree, Tom," said the old man. "But it looks a little lonely. Think you might plant something around it?"

That weekend Olsen returned to the nursery and bought two more blue spruces, smaller ones, to plant when a cool day came.

❦   ❦   ❦

It was the first week in July, and Olsen was at the Wendlings' house again.

"Thomas, come sit with us out back and have some lemonade. Ben can tell you about our trip to Arizona—we're leaving Tuesday morning."

Olsen and Ben walked to the far corner of the Wendlings' back yard and sat at the round wooden table, tall trees shading them from the sun.

"So you'll get to Tucson when?" Olsen asked.

"Tuesday afternoon," said Ben. "Spend a couple days at Tucson State, do some sightseeing, and get home Sunday night."

"It's gonna be hot there. Wow—Tucson in July. I try to make my goodwill visits to the Tucson State campus in the dead of winter."

"Yeah. Oh, well."

"So you got your basketball meeting all confirmed with Coach Branigan?"

"Yeah, it's Wednesday morning."

"He'll take good care of you. I talked to him again this week, and he said he's going to drive you around Tucson, show you the sights."

"Cool."

"And you've got your Admissions interview set up?"

"Yeah. They have a few different scholarships I'm going for. Gotta write an essay for one of them. But I've got plenty of time."

"Don't procrastinate!"

Mary walked barefoot over the grass with lemonade and glasses on a tray, and Ben and Olsen pulled their chairs up to the table. The ice chimed as Mary poured, one for Olsen, one for Ben, one for her.

"And what kind of sightseeing?" Olsen asked.

"Some ruins, some caverns," Ben said.

"I don't do caverns," Mary said, sitting down beside Olsen. "I'll sit outside and read a book instead."

They heard the muffled rumble of a car in the driveway and turned around. It was Josh Reiter in his rickety brown Taurus, waving a hand high out of the window.

"We're gonna shoot around at Indian River Park," Ben said, then gulped his lemonade. "I'll be home for dinner, Mom. See ya later, Coach."

"We're eating around six," Mary said. "Grilled fish and a big Caesar salad. Josh can join us—I have plenty."

"Okay, I'll ask him. 'Bye."

Ben jogged away over the grass and Olsen said to Mary, "Dinner sounds good. Is there enough for me?"

Mary smiled, but only with her lips, not her eyes.

"Do you still remember that Mary Oliver poem, 'Wild Geese'?" she asked.

"Sure."

"I've been thinking about the last three lines," Mary said:

the world calls out to your imagination,
over and over announcing your place
in the family of things.

She put her glass, half full, on the table, and said, "Ben is so young and fresh in this world—he hears that call, he senses his place. There are no blocks, no impossibles for him. And after this trip to Tucson State, if he really wants to go there, I'm going to say yes—no matter how much it scares me to let him go—and to let him go so far away."

Olsen relaxed in his chair, drinking his lemonade, but then Mary startled him.

"Have you found your place in the family of things in Indian River?" she asked. "Or do you feel like there's something more for you? Is the world calling to your imagination, calling you somewhere else?"

In a year, after all, Ben would be gone, and then she would have only Wendling to while away the hours of a life with.

"I used to think there was something else for me," Olsen said. "But that was a long time ago. I'm happy here. I like my work. My favorite people in the world are all right here in Indian River. And you?" he said. "I could ask you the same question."

"I used to have a huge wanderlust," she said. "But I wanted roots for Ben." She shifted in her chair and drummed her fingers on the tabletop, her hand shadowed under the canopy of leaves.

Wendling pulled in the driveway then, in his midnight blue LeSabre. He got out of the car and stood on the concrete. He stared across the yard into the deep corner where Olsen and Mary sat drinking lemonade from wet, slippery glasses under the shade of tall trees.

Mary raised her right hand and waved to him. "Hi, Virgil—come have some lemonade with us!" she called.

Olsen lifted a hand in requisite greeting. Finally the bum would have to thank him.

But Wendling stood on the driveway staring at them, then went into the house, letting the screen door slam shut behind him.

CHAPTER 17

❁

The One Good Thing

During the Wendling family week in Arizona, the hours in Indiana circled slowly on Olsen's clock, days turning like sluggards. He found himself missing the boys and basketball, drove out to Leavittown High and watched a couple of summer league games from the Indian River bench, getting the update from Kuehn, seeing the boys in action again, a jolt, refreshment, a return to regular life.

When Olsen got up Monday morning, the air hung hot in his house, traces of Sunday.

Late Monday afternoon he had a taste for Chinese and picked up takeout at the strip mall. The biting mists of soy and Szechwan cheered him briefly; then summer traffic snarled the streets, disquiet jammed his ears again, and his knuckles whitened around the Corvette steering wheel.

When he pulled back in the driveway, Mr. McCormick was watering his garden next door. "Your friend was here," he called across the shrubbery to Olsen.

"Who—Rakowsky?"

"No. Your pretty friend," said the old man. Water spray glittered around him in the sunlight. "The one who brought me the cookies."

"Mary was here?"

"Yes—Mary. Said she'd stop by another time."

🍁   🍁   🍁

Ben answered the phone at the Wendlings'.

"Ben, hi, it's Coach Olsen. I'm not interrupting dinner, am I?"

"Nope."

"Hey, how was the trip to Arizona?"

"It was great. Tucson State's awesome. It's definitely where I want to go. The desert's cool. We went to these ruins from the 1300's."

"Yeah? Which ones, Casa Grande?"

"Yeah, then the ruins of an old fort…"

"Hmmm."

"And these caverns—Kartchner Caverns—man, those were cool. My dad and I liked those. My mom wouldn't even go in."

"Hey," said Olsen, "I want to hear more about everything, especially Tucson State, but my neighbor told me your mom stopped by—guess I just missed her. Can I talk to her for a sec?"

"Really? Are you sure? Mom? It's Coach Olsen for you."

Olsen heard muffled shuffling, Ben and Mary talking, the phone handoff. The Chinese takeout steamed, silver-handled boxes on his counter.

Then Mary said, "Hello," her voice blank and far away.

"Mary?" he said.

"Yes."

"It's me."

Silence. Then: "I know."

"Uh…" said Olsen. "Mr. McCormick said you stopped by."

"Yeah."

"I'm sorry I missed you. Wish I'd known you were coming."

"Oh, it was spur of the moment. I have something for you," she said, but the space after her words rang empty.

"Is everything all right?" he asked.

"Can I come back?" she said. "Are you going to be there?"

"Sure, come on over," said Olsen.

He hung up the phone, put the silver-handled boxes in the fridge, pulled out a Heineken instead.

❦   ❦   ❦

Mary arrived at Olsen's door with a gift in her hands, which she did not offer him, and a cramp in her smile.

"Come in," Olsen said. He could not read her face. "Want to sit on the deck? Or is it too hot?"

"No, the deck's good." She was wearing cut-offs. She followed him through the house without small talk and out onto the deck, where they sat under the hot evening sun.

Mary slid her gift across the tabletop to him. "For you."

"Thanks." Olsen pulled the ribbon loose and tore off the gift wrap, uncovering a framed, smiling photograph of him with Ben.

"I took it last October, at the pre-season parents' meeting," she said. "A few days before Art From the Heart. Doesn't that seem another lifetime ago? Such a happy time—almost innocent, really—just pure fun, excitement, camaraderie, everybody healthy, the future stretching out so brightly. That's what you and Ben are all about. That's what I want you to feel."

Olsen looked at the picture. He stood it up on the table.

"Thomas," Mary said, "I realize there's no way I'll ever be able to thank you for what you did to save Ben." She toyed with the untied ribbon on the table, curling it into a pile, then around her fingers. "But you deserve to be set free."

"What do you mean?"

"Free from the weight of Ben's life on your shoulders—weight I see you carrying still."

Mary, you don't understand—that weight is where I finally found my freedom.

She said, "I've prayed so much these last few months. And some things are very clear to me now."

"Such as?"

"Well," Mary said. She shifted in her chair. "Such as, it's so clear God put you at Tri-State to save Ben's life. And He spared Ben from a broken neck, brain damage—I can't bear to contemplate it, really—this is hard for me to explain—but I know this much: I have to change."

Olsen shivered in the sun. "What does that mean, exactly?"

Mary wrapped the ribbon around her fingers. She unwrapped it and pulled it taut.

"I have a good life," she said. "Virgil has given Ben and me a good life. What does the rest of it matter anymore? I've been holding all of it against Virgil like a ransom. But he's been a good father. A good husband," she said, and Olsen's stomach lurched.

"I have to do the right thing for Ben's sake," Mary said. "I want Ben to have faith in me, be proud of me. What else really matters?"

"Ben's proud of you already!"

Mary reached for Olsen across the table, but before he could move, she pulled her hands back, pressed them down into her lap.

"Promise me we'll always be friends, Thomas," she said, "even if it's only in our hearts. I couldn't go on without that—but I've depended on you too much, and that isn't fair to you. You're not responsible for me."

Mary got up, swaying as she stood, steadied herself on the deck railing, and Olsen stood up, too, gripped her slim arms in his hands.

"It hasn't been unfair," he said, and tears filled her eyes.

"I want you to depend on me," Olsen said, louder, and her face, her body, softened. "Shouldn't you be set free, too, Mary?"

"Thomas, I can never say the things I really want to tell you—I promised myself I never would."

"Why, Mary? God, please! Why can't you and I tell each other how we really feel? In between the words we say out loud, we both hear the truth we leave unspoken!"

"I have my reason," she said.

"I'll talk you out of it!" he shouted, and he was squeezing her arms with pleading in his fingers.

"My son is my reason," she said.

My son.

Mary's face stayed serene—incongruous under two silver paths of tears. "What do I really want to stand for in this life?" she said. "Ben is the one good thing that I have ever done."

She slipped out of Olsen's grasp, went out through the deck gate and disappeared, leaving everything behind in the invisible dust of her footsteps.

Olsen sat back down at the deck table. He heard the Jeep start up, and its engine fade away down Roanoke Road.

The sun pierced his skin, and he sweated. The two spruce trees stood patiently in the yard, waiting to be planted. The watercolor-blue sky stretched out over his head.

Olsen looked down at the torn wrapping paper and untied ribbon on the table, at the picture of Ben and him—a picture Mary had taken, so that he would always be looking through her eyes when he saw it.

> Look for me, Father, on the roof
> of the red-brick building
> at the foot of Green Street—
> that's where we live, you know, on the top floor.

I'm the boy in the white flannel gown
sprawled on this coarse gravel bed
searching the starry sky,
waiting for the world to end.

An hour and a half and a sunset later, he sat there still.

CHAPTER 18

❀

The Things He Carried

August stagnated in the slow waters of Olsen's solitude. The men's summer softball league ended, and those other summer traditions he and Rakowsky kept—friendly contests in the weight room, wee-hours barhopping, their annual interstate race to the Indiana Dunes—none seemed worth doing anymore. Anyway, Olsen didn't want to talk about Mary, didn't want to see the I-told-you-so look flash in Rakowsky's eyes.

Night after night Olsen had trouble falling asleep, trouble staying asleep. Instead of nightmares he now dreamed only of gray, awaking capped and draped in grayness, garments he couldn't shed even in the long days of Indiana sun.

He planted the two new spruce trees in his backyard. He tinkered with the Corvette. He waved to Mr. McCormick across the lawn, watched Mr. McCormick's little squirrel-dog leap around the grass as the old man walked slowly behind.

Going After Cacciato, The Sportswriter, The Snows of Kilimanjaro all lay in limbo around Olsen's house—rereadings begun, then forgotten, on coffee table, bedside table, kitchen counter. He didn't answer Kristina's phone messages. He felt Mary in the rooms of his house sometimes, saw her in trails of light that penetrated the windows on sunny afternoons.

He kept the picture of Ben and himself on his dresser.

He worried about Ben, what Ben thought of his vanishing, but he couldn't call the Wendlings' house, couldn't take the chance of hearing in Mary's voice that she didn't want to hear his.

Olsen's 42nd birthday came on August twentieth. He didn't think he had
ever told Mary the date. His mailbox held birthday cards from Kristina, the
PTA Sunshine Committee, the Wildcats basketball cheerleaders, his All-Pro
Insurance agent, his investment broker. Nothing arrived from his mother who,
being unsentimental, had forgotten his birthday more often than not in his
adult years. "I even forget my own!" Louise liked to say.

Olsen realized he hadn't called Louise, nor she him, since before Tri-State
four months ago, although she had sent him a postcard from somewhere,
some golf resort, in May.

Around five o'clock he went online and found an e-mail from Rakowsky:
*Happy Birthday, you old fart. From your friend who will always be younger than
you.*

Leave it to Rakowsky to be the one to remember…

E-mail!

ᦔ

Ben, these days have been busy. Call me when you get a minute. 555-4327.

Still want to hear all about AZ. Coach Olsen.

Olsen's phone rang around seven.

"Wondered what happened to you," Ben said. "Figured you got busy."

"Sorry. Yeah. I dropped off the face of the earth for a few weeks. Hey, guess
what?"

"What?"

"It's my birthday," Olsen said.

"No joke? What are ya doing to celebrate?"

"Nothing."

"Wanna do something?" Ben asked. "Get something to eat? Nobody should
do nothing on his birthday."

"Well—sure. That's so thoughtful of you, I won't correct your English."

"Can you pick me up? There's no cars here—my mom and dad are both
out."

"Living it up, are they?"

"Not really—Mom's at a church meeting, Dad's working."

"Sure, I'll come and get you," said Olsen. "Suddenly I'm starving."

"Okay—it'll be Dairy Queen, on me."

Instead Olsen suggested the steak house by Breezewood Mall, his treat. They ate shrimp cocktails, cheese-soaked potato skins, loud mounds of house salad, slabs of butter on hunks of bread, New York strip steaks, and brownies floating in bowls of hot fudge. Then Olsen drank black coffee while Ben kept talking about Tucson State.

"I knew it as soon as I stepped off the plane in Tucson. It's where I wanna be. I just need to get enough money together," Ben said.

"I'll write you the greatest recommendation letter of your life," said Olsen. "And apply for all the financial aid you can get—the loans, grants, all the scholarships, everything."

"There's an English scholarship I'm gonna go for. The Turbin Award. I had my interview for it when I was there. I still gotta write the essay."

"On what?"

"'A topic of great personal significance.'"

"How long?"

"Supposed to be five hundred words. But I don't think I can get that verbose."

Olsen laughed. "Well, what's of great personal significance to you?"

"I've got some ideas. But I'll only show you the essay after I win."

"I like your confidence." Olsen sipped his coffee. "And you're still liking the basketball program there?"

"Yeah," Ben said, "and I know they want me." But his voice trailed off.

"Of course they do. Everybody does," said Olsen. "Tucson State just happens to be one of the few schools good enough for you."

"But I can see what they expect," Ben said. "I mean, you devote yourself to the team, way more than in high school. Reminds me of what my mom says—she thinks college basketball is more a business than a sport."

"Speaking of your mom," Olsen said, "how's she doing?" but he swallowed too fast as he spoke, and his question cut off midway through, and after coughing and clearing his throat, he had to start again and repeat himself.

"She's good," Ben said.

❦   ❦   ❦

Olsen pulled the Corvette in the Wendlings' driveway. Lights glowed behind their living room curtains.

"Coach, thanks for taking me out to dinner. That was awesome."

"Hey, thanks for celebrating my birthday with me."

"Woulda been a bummer for you to spend it alone," Ben said.

"Yeah."

"I'da thought you'd be having a big party or something," said Ben, "because it seems like you have a ton of friends."

"Well…" Olsen said. "Forty-two isn't a big milestone or anything."

"Plus you don't have a girlfriend or anything to celebrate with," Ben said, "but I'd think you could get any woman you want."

"Well, it's more than just wanting them," said Olsen. "A guy's gotta have something worthwhile to offer. And they've gotta want you, too." He leaned back on the headrest, looked at the light in the window. "And it's more than that. It's finding the missing piece of yourself. The missing person in the story of your life. Anything less than that, any woman less than that, is just killing time."

At first Ben didn't answer. Then he said, "Just hope you're not lonely or anything."

Olsen shrugged. "Sometimes."

"Yeah."

"I gotta tell you, Ben, part of what gets me through is that you're like a son to me. It's been like that since long before Tri-State. Not that I'd play favorites with you. In fact, I'm probably harder on you because of it. But, listen—you've got a friend in me—a friend for life. No matter what."

"Hey, same here."

"Yeah?"

"Yeah." Ben tried to stretch, but his hands hit the dashboard. He burped. ""Scuse me. Well, I better let ya go. Thanks again. Man, I'm stuffed."

"All right—see you next week at school. BMOC. Senior year."

"BMOC?" said Ben.

"All you gotta know," said Olsen, "is it's gonna be great."

❧   ❧   ❧

Olsen let September sweep him up in its dailiness. He flung himself back into the saving grace of his students and players, arriving early at Indian River High School, staying late, his presence on the premises a stand-in for his true attentions—attentions that now lived in trails of white light, and the breath of Mary's memory, and the edge of betrayal that cut a little deeper each time he turned and saw the emptiness behind him.

Olsen volunteered to run the writing lab Tuesdays after school until basketball practices started in November. He initiated the English department curriculum review a year early. He fine-tuned the basketball schedule. He agreed to pinch-hit as faculty rep on the Indian River school board. Wherever Olsen went, he knew what to say and how to say it; he knew what to do, and did it well—shouldn't he, after all these years? He noticed the embrace of admiration encircling him from the school community—noticed it, but couldn't feel it. He kept scraping for something to inject life into the staleness that curtained his days.

❦   ❦   ❦

The Friday before Halloween, Olsen set out for Ohio State and the regional English teachers' consortium.

Boarding the plane to Columbus, he overheard other teachers introducing themselves to each other, launching conversations; he reached in his carry-on and pulled out *White Noise*: still the greatest story ever told.

Last Thanksgiving he'd reread parts of the book on his trip to Hilton Head; he had been envying DeLillo's brainchildren Jack and Babette Gladney, coveting their erotic marriage, looking for pointers; but Eros had since wilted around him. This year Olsen felt a different theme from the book looming center stage: the airborne toxic event that blew into Blacksmith, the town where the Gladneys lived.

> "They want us to evacuate…It was a fire captain's car with a loudspeaker…It said something like, 'Evacuate all places of residence. Cloud of deadly chemicals, cloud of deadly chemicals.'"
>
> We sat there over sponge cake and canned peaches.
>
> "I'm sure there's plenty of time," Babette said, "or they would have made a point of telling us to hurry. How fast do air masses move, I wonder."…
>
> Twenty minutes later we were in the car…As we waited our turn to edge onto the four-lane road we heard the amplified voice above and behind us calling out to darkened homes in a street of sycamores and tall hedges.
>
> "Abandon all domiciles. Now, now. Toxic event, chemical cloud."
>
> The voice grew louder, faded, grew loud again as the vehicle moved in and out of local streets. Toxic event, chemical cloud. When the words became faint, the cadence itself was still discernible…

At Friday night's meeting, a pretty teacher with long auburn hair sat beside him. Her smile felt like a kiss but Olsen stayed distant, nodding pleasantly, keeping to himself. On the shuttle from Ohio State back to the Hyatt, the joviality of all those teachers on the loose swelled up around him, and when they congregated in the hotel lobby making plans to paint the town en masse, he went up to his room, took a shower, and watched ESPN. He chafed for beer but didn't want to go out for it. Eventually he fell asleep.

Saturday morning in the hotel restaurant, the pretty teacher approached his table, where he sat alone reading *The New York Times.*

"Mind if I join you?" she said. "I'm Erin O'Meara—I'm with the English teachers group, too."

Olsen looked up at her: green eyes, white smile, butter pecan skin. He decided to give in.

They drank coffee and ate bagels together. Erin said, "Do you enjoy these seminars, consortiums, whatever?"

"They're a good escape," said Olsen.

"Really? What are you escaping from?" she asked.

Olsen laughed. "So where did you fly in from?" he said, instead of answering.

"Indianapolis. I saw you on the plane. What were you reading?"

"*White Noise.*"

"Ah," she said, "Don DeLillo."

"You like him?"

"He makes me laugh. He makes me think. I like that combination," she said.

"So where do you teach?" Olsen asked.

"Stockton High School."

His stomach contorted, but his face stayed a casual mask. "You had a pretty good basketball player last season," he said. "Wanamaker, I think his name was."

"You had a pretty good player, too—Ben Wendling," Erin said.

Olsen's mask fell.

"I recognized you right away, on the plane," Erin said. "I'm a basketball fan from way back. I'm an Indiana girl, after all." She stirred cream into her coffee, her spoon tinking in rhythm inside the cup. "Your boys showed such heart in that state championship game against us. You had a great team. I'm glad Stockton won, but I'm sorry you had to lose."

"Yeah, that one hurt," Olsen said.

Erin tilted her head, smiling at him with sad eyes, the way Mary used to do.

❦   ❦   ❦

After Saturday's wrap-up meeting, the teachers discussed recreation for their waning afternoon, and made plans for last-chance carousing before their orderly lives called them home on Sunday.

Erin asked Olsen where he was going.

"The Book Loft," he said. "It's an old brick house in German Village. Thirty-two rooms of books. A hike down Third Street, but it's perfect fall weather. You're welcome to join me."

On the walk to German Village they dissected the weekend's meetings, then split up at the bookstore to peruse. Later they strolled to Schiller Park, swinging their bottom-heavy Book Loft bags, talking about basketball, high school kids today, their own college years. They walked back through the brick streets of German Village and ended up at Lindy's restaurant, which Erin said was too expensive, but Olsen insisted it was his treat. There they drank too much, ate dinner, and took a cab back to the Hyatt, where Erin led Olsen up into her room, "just to talk," as they agreed in serious, fuzzy voices.

Inside her room, Erin took her shoes off and said, "Just going to freshen up."

Olsen sat in a chair, Book Loft bag toppled at his feet. He heard water running in the bathroom.

His thoughts meandered back to the last hotel room he had been in with a woman. Creston Plaza, at Tri-State. He had sat beside Mary as she lay on her bed, after they'd returned at dawn from the ER. Mary had said, *Stay with me, Thomas.* She had wrapped her hand around his index finger and held on tightly. He had heard birds singing outside the window.

So he took the Hyatt notepad and pen from the table.

"Had to go—feel sick—sorry," he wrote, and left the note on Erin's bed.

In the morning, Olsen took a cab solo to the airport. Erin inquired about his health as she boarded the plane, then sat far away, leaving him to *White Noise.*

> Through the stark trees we saw it, the immense toxic cloud, lighted now by eighteen choppers—immense almost beyond comprehension, beyond legend and rumor, a roiling bloated slug-shaped mass...We sat in the car, in the snowy woods, saying nothing... I recalled with a shock that I was technically dead...There was nothing to do but try to get the family to safety.

❦   ❦   ❦

When the schedule for parent-teacher conferences appeared in Olsen's mailbox one day in November, he didn't look it over, just stuck it in his planner, walked out of the teachers' lounge and headed for lunch.

He ate rubber cafeteria pizza while listening to Rakowsky describe his newly enflamed season of rapture with his wife. "And they say marriage kills your sex life! Bullshit," Rakowsky leered. Olsen's stomach balled up into a cheese sponge and he said, "Catch ya later," seeking asylum in his basketball office.

Olsen looked out the window. The baseball diamond lay emasculated, forlorn, its offseason grasses frozen brown. Two bundled, hatted runners plodded around the track beyond.

He sat down, pulled out the conference schedule, scanned the list of names…and saw *Mary Wendling*—not saw, really, but heard *Mary Wendling* reverberating up from the page.

❦   ❦   ❦

Mary was last on Thursday night's conference schedule. She must have asked for the last time slot, because some of the earlier ones weren't filled.

On Thursday morning he listened to the weather forecast: an unusually frigid prediction, high of fifteen. From his closet Olsen selected what he had worn on Awards Night—the white button-down shirt, the brown and beige print tie, dress khakis—and pulled on his brown wool sport coat.

Thursday evening, Olsen tried to focus on the parents who preceded Mary. His eyes met theirs as they spoke. He nodded, smiled, and knit his eyebrows at appropriate moments. All the parents said they wished for more time to talk because Olsen was so helpful, and he invited them all to come back sometime, as he moved them toward the door.

Finally it was time for Mary. Olsen went out and stood in the hallway, leaning against the wall.

He would smile. He would extend a hand. He would wait and see what she was going to say.

It was late, and the upstairs hall was empty. Olsen listened: one pair of footfalls approaching the stairs. His throat clamped closed. One pair of feet now ascended, with the drag and scuff of heavy shoes, not Mary's. Olsen waited.

It was Virgil Wendling.

Wendling in black wool dress coat, black gloves, scarf around his neck, wearing what looked like a smirk.

Heat spread across Olsen's face. Wendling was alone. Olsen knew his face had betrayed him, but he stayed leaning on the wall. "I was expecting Mary," he said.

"Of course you were." Wendling strolled toward Olsen. He pulled off his gloves, put them in his pockets. Neither man extended a hand.

Olsen narrowed his eyes. "Won't you come in?" he said, going into his classroom, then stopped around the corner inside the door and turned to face Wendling, planting his feet in a roadblock.

Wendling stopped short. His face twitched. "Look, Tom," he said, "I wanted to come alone tonight—it's already taken me much too long—I want to thank you for what you did for Ben—at that Tri-State thing."

"Tri-State was months ago."

"I'm sorry I waited this long to do it. I was going to get in touch with you before," Wendling said. "Really." He lifted his left hand to smooth his hair; Olsen looked at him.

"Better late than never," Olsen said. "Is that all?" He turned, walked to his desk, began packing up to leave.

After a moment of silence, Wendling started lashing out in snippets: "Appalling rudeness—I don't have to take this—came here to thank you—been very busy—the least you could do—your attitude—" Then Wendling was gone.

Olsen stood at his desk, his hands shaking. Stretched his arms above his head. Tightened the muscles. His armpits were cold and damp. It took a few minutes to finish packing his bag for the night.

Then, from the corner of his eye, he saw Wendling's shadow.

Wendling stepped back inside the room and shut the door. He pulled his black gloves out of his coat pockets, held them between his hands.

"I kept telling myself I should have been there," Wendling said. "Kept telling myself if I had been at Tri-State with all of you, I could have been the one who saved Ben. Then it hit me: I don't know first aid, CPR, none of it. So I wouldn't have done any good anyway. You still would have been the one to save him, Olsen. Can you understand how that's made me feel?"

Olsen zipped his bag closed. He hated Wendling's poor-me subtext. He hated the too-late gratitude. Mostly he hated the wedding ring. So he turned toward Wendling and crossed his arms over his chest.

"Sounds like you need to take a first aid course," Olsen said.

Wendling stared.

"You wanna know something?" said Olsen. "I love Ben like my own son. Like my very own flesh and blood," he said, drawing out the last three words. "I'm in it for the long haul with that boy. I'm looking forward to seeing him through his college years. Being in his wedding. Watching his children grow up. Running him ragged in one-on-one games till I'm too old to hit the courts. So you better get used to having me around." Then he picked up his bag and flicked the lights off as he walked out, leaving Wendling in the dark.

Olsen worked hard to get angry at Mary that night, and succeeded. He felt stronger in fury, didn't want to let the feeling go. But he knew it was just a disguise; and his rage turned, eventually, to nausea, then a cross of sadness pressing down on him. He tried to forget the invisible dust of Mary's disappearing footsteps, and the way she had twisted the ribbon around her fingers, and the sound of her voice when she said, *Ben is the one good thing that I have ever done.*

❦   ❦   ❦

It was early December, four months since Mary had walked away from him.

At the basketball home opener, he spotted her during pre-game warmups. He had prepared for this moment, but still the blood hammered in his stomach.

She sat in the last row of the stands, her back against the wall, although she used to sit courtside. Wendling was not with her. Her hair curved around her face, a dark frame, like the shadow of Olsen's longing, the ache he could not conquer. Olsen looked away quickly, turned around and started glad-handing all his well-wishers, clinging to his defenses with every handshake.

But the warm-up drills lulled him, the crowd's buzz and the basketballs thumping on hardwood soothed him, and his assistant Kuehn was making him laugh. Eventually Olsen forgot himself and his armor, and looked up over the sea of heads to Mary in the stands. He smiled at her as if it were the old days instead of the new.

Mary was looking at Olsen, too. She did not smile, but lifted her hand and waved to him. Even from that distance, he could see the heavy gray circles under her eyes.

He waved back; put his hands in his pockets; turned around to shout directions to the boys on the court.

❦   ❦   ❦

The Wildcats were pegged as underdogs that year, instead of the team to beat—Olsen's first string from the year before had all graduated, except for Ben, now a senior. But it turned out to be a season of surprises.

Occasionally they overpowered an opponent in victory, but more often that winter, Indian River stayed in the game through sheer stubbornness or the luck of the hapless. Since they had nothing to lose, they often won—with the buzzer beaters, the fortunate rolls, the fingertip put-backs, the hands perfectly aimed and timed to blocks shots, the sweet executions of plays unburied from Olsen's Ohio State memories. It was a different kind of heyday. Laughter bounced off their locker room walls all winter long for the winning balls that rolled crazily their way, and they finished the regular season third in the conference.

In tournament season, good fortune kept grinning at them. Balls that careened off rims and out of bounds for their opponents banked in neatly off the glass through the net for Indian River. Off-kilter foul shots righted them-selves in flight, roads opened for their fast breaks, rebounds took surprise routes into their upstretched hands, and they kept laughing all the way to the regionals in March, where they played and lost, then traveled home in high spirits, happy for a season that had surprised them with its kindnesses.

CHAPTER 19

❀

Straw into Gold

Where is God—is He in my greatest moments, and days of serendipity, and dreams that bear fruit? Is God in the shame of my secrets, in terror that hits like a sniper, and all the tears I'm too old and numb to cry? Is God the Life that gives me life, or is He just a beautiful story?

🍁   🍁   🍁

In April of Ben's senior year, the soon-to-be graduates started announcing college plans. Ben had indeed chosen Tucson State, thanks in part to the Prescott L. Turbin Award for excellence and interest in the field of English. But he added an unforeseen postscript to his decision: he would not play college basketball after all. He was ready to move on to new things, he said; basketball was not his life anymore.

A minor community uproar followed. Diehard Indian River fans assumed familial rights where college careers were concerned, and they counted on Olsen to change his protégé's mind. But Olsen agreed with Ben. "You have to let a man decide for himself," Olsen told them, "and anyway, now basketball won't become for Ben what it tends to be at college...a job. He'll just keep high school basketball forever—and we all know that's basketball in its most unsullied hour."

During those April days, Olsen would watch Ben's gait down the school corridor, springy and dawdling, his shoulders no longer tight and taut, with an expression residing in his face that Olsen could only describe as peace.

❦   ❦   ❦

How do you get faith? Not the fleeting kind, the bargains with God, but faith that becomes a part of you. What if I have longed for it, prayed for it, looked for it, but nothing changes inside me? How do you spin faith out of thin air, spin straw into gold?

He asked Ben once, one day after school when they were cleaning out the basketball equipment room together. And Ben said, "Church is like a cafeteria, the Bible is, too, and God is the food. See, I can bring you to the cafeteria with me, but I can't eat for you. That's something you can only do for yourself." Olsen said, "Fine, but how about giving me some utensils?" Ben thought for a minute. Then he said, "Yeah, I can do that. But give me a chance to think about what they could be." Later, when they were locking the equipment room up, Ben said, "See, you start with God, but eventually you gotta get to Jesus." Olsen said, "Okay."

The next day Ben told Olsen, "I asked my mom about what you said. You know, how does a person get started when they want to have faith but don't yet? I didn't tell her it was you. And she said, 'Let me think about it, because that used to be me.' Then she gave me these. She said there are so many choices, but you have to just start somewhere. She once read a saying: *Begin; the rest is easy.* So you could start with these. Remember, it's between you and God. He doesn't want you to be lost. But you gotta keep trying."

And Olsen said, "That's fair enough."

❦   ❦   ❦

Mary had copied the passages almost neatly, taming her hell-bent handwriting for the unknown recipient who wanted faith, onto sheets of bright white paper.

> Where can I go from your Spirit? Where can I flee from your presence? If I go up to the heavens, you are there; if I make my bed in the depths, you are there...All the days ordained for me were written in your book before one of them came to be.

> And when he was still speaking, there came from the ruler's house some who said, "Your daughter is dead. Why trouble the Teacher any further?" But ignoring what they said, Jesus said to the ruler of the synagogue, "Do

not fear, only believe." And he allowed no one to follow him except Peter and James and John the brother of James.

When they came to the house of the ruler of the synagogue, he saw a tumult, and people weeping and wailing loudly. And when he had entered, he said to them, "Why do you make a tumult and weep? The child is not dead but sleeping." And they laughed at him.

But he put them all outside, and took the child's father and mother and those who were with him, and went in where the child was. Taking her by the hand he said to her, "*Tal'itha cu'mi*," which means, "Little girl, I say to you, arise." And immediately the girl got up and walked; for she was twelve years old.

And immediately they were overcome with amazement. And he strictly charged them that no one should know this, and told them to give her something to eat.

❦   ❦   ❦

Sunday noon Olsen was pruning his shrubbery out front on Roanoke Road when Mr. McCormick pulled into his driveway next door.

Olsen stopped, waved a hand, called, "Getting home from church?"

"Yup," said Mr. McCormick. He stepped slowly across the lawn toward Olsen. He wore a black tie, wide and faded, and a Sunday hat.

"Where do you go?" Olsen asked.

"Oh—here, there, and everywhere."

"You're not Lutheran?"

"Nope."

"I thought everybody in this town was Lutheran," said Olsen. "Well, except me."

"Surprise," the old man said.

"Where do you go, then?"

Mr. McCormick straightened his hat. "Let's see. Bristol Presbyterian. A holy roller place. A Christian Science church up in Indianapolis. A Byzantine church up there, too—but I just sit in the back and listen."

"You get around."

"Yup." Mr. McCormick glanced at Olsen's rhododendron, held out his hand. "Lemme have those shears," he said. He took over the pruning as Olsen looked on.

"Don't you feel like a stranger, going alone to church that way? I hate that feeling," Olsen said.

"I don't mind being an outsider. You get too comfortable on the inside. You stop thinking for yourself." The old man clipped a few branches of the rhododendron and they dropped in the dirt. "God and I haven't always been on good terms," he said. "Lots of times, we're not even speaking."

"But you still go to church?"

"Sure. Just in case. Maybe force of habit. Oh, I believe and all—that's not the problem."

Olsen picked the branches up from the dirt. "Problem?"

"Life didn't turn out how I planned. I didn't get some things I really wanted—things I really prayed for, thought I couldn't live without. Well, I lived. Obviously. But part of me is still mad at God." He clipped one more branch, then handed the shears back to Olsen. "I'll keep going to church, though. Just in case God and I can work it out before I die. Well, see you later. Got to go see my dog." He waved one hand and made his way slowly back across the lawn, step by step.

❦   ❦   ❦

Olsen decided it was time to read *White Noise* again. Security blanket, ironic comfort, strange and endless eye-opener.

> I said to my nun, "What does the Church say about heaven today? Is it still the old heaven, like that, in the sky?"
>
> She turned to glance at the picture.
>
> "Do you think we are stupid?" she said.
>
> I was surprised by the force of her reply... "You don't believe in heaven? A nun?"
>
> "If you don't, why should I?"
>
> "If you did, maybe I would."
>
> "If I did, you would not have to."
>
> "All the old muddles and quirks," I said. "Faith, religion, life everlasting. The great old human gullibilities. Are you saying you don't take them seriously? Your dedication is a pretense?"
>
> "Our pretense is a dedication. Someone must appear to believe...As belief shrinks from the world, people find it more necessary than ever that *someone* believe...Those who have abandoned belief must still believe in us. They are sure that they are right not to believe but they know belief must not fade completely. Hell is when no one believes."

Olsen had reread this conversation in its entirety a hundred times through the years, he had found it brilliant and uproarious, he had entertained people by reading it at dinner parties, he had even incorporated it in his master's thesis. But that day in Indian River, the words fell off the pages and into his hands sadly and simply, unvarnished and still too true: the light they shed only illuminated his confusion.

CHAPTER 20

❀

Three Fathers

"Hey, you keep forgetting, I wanna see your essay!" Olsen said. He and Ben were shooting around in the gym after school, the gym doors opened outward for the May breeze that wasn't blowing in, and sweat was flying.

"I know," Ben puffed, "I'm gonna make a copy for you," and he slammed a basket in over Olsen's head.

"Don't forget…" Olsen dribbled around half court. "You keep forgetting…" He put up a jumper. "But I want to read it!" he said after his shot fell lightly through the net.

When they were done outdoing each other, Ben pulled the outside doors closed and latched them. They wiped their faces on their tee shirts, picked their gear up from the sidelines, and Ben said, "When I go to Tucson State, you know what's gonna be as hard as leaving my mom and dad?"

"What?" Olsen said, swinging his gym bag over his shoulder.

"Leaving you."

Olsen looked at Ben, then closed his eyes for a second. He took the bag off his shoulder and set it on the floor.

"Remember what I told you last summer—before your senior year even started? Friends for life."

"I remember."

"Well, I wasn't just saying that. It's a promise. I'll be out to Arizona to visit you, you've got my number, my e-mail, and I'll see you whenever you're home on vacation. Hey, you should help me out at practices on your Christmas break."

"But you know how it goes, Coach," Ben said. "You'll be busy. We both know basketball takes everything over. My mom and dad can't forget me—I mean, they're my parents. But I'm afraid you will."

Olsen's eyes burned. He picked up his bag again. Then he reached up and put his hand on Ben's shoulder.

"I'm afraid you'll forget *me*," Olsen said.

They looked at each other, and Ben laughed but a tear fell out of the corner of his eye. "I don't know where that came from," he said, wiping it away, and they walked out of the gym together.

❧   ❧   ❧

A week later, Olsen found an envelope from Ben in his mail on Roanoke Road. He tore it open. "Here's the essay, Coach," Ben had jotted on a post-it note.

The cover sheet read:

Prescott L. Turbin Award Competition
"Three Fathers"
by Benjamin Wendling

Underneath was the essay.

A father is the one who helped to give you life, the one who lives in you even after he dies. He is the deepness in your voice, the strength in your arms, the one you sometimes see looking back at you from the mirror. He is the memories you have but don't remember making, he is the places you've never been that somehow feel familiar, and the things you know how to do that no one ever taught you. He is one of the reasons your mother smiles with tears in her eyes sometimes when she looks at you.

A father is the one who devotes his life to you. A father takes the time, even when he doesn't have the time, and gives his all for you, even if it means there is nothing left for him. He is the one looking out for you without your realizing it, the one who loves you without your really appreciating how much that means. A father is the yeoman, the shepherd, the laborer in the vineyard, the one who logs the long, late hours so that you can follow your dreams, because his dream is that yours will come true.

A father is the friend who loves you for who you are and sometimes in spite of who you are. He is the one you don't have to explain yourself to, because somehow he just knows. He is your lifesaver, your master teacher, your wise big brother; and when he says that you'll be friends for life, you hope to God he's right.

A father is a leader and a loner, a sinner and a saint, a man and a boy. He is blood, he is soul, and he is heart. A father walks with you to the door of the future, and knows he can't go with you, and sets you free.

❧   ❧   ❧

Olsen carried Ben's essay out onto the deck. The sun had set; the air that night was cold.

He read Ben's words for the third time.

Later that night as Olsen lay in bed, he said to himself, **I am not alone in this world.** And even though he knew it was true, his eyes burned.

> Look for me, Father, on the roof
> of the red-brick building
> at the foot of Green Street—
> that's where we live, you know, on the top floor.

He got up and went downstairs and drank a bottle of beer at the kitchen sink.

Later he brushed his teeth and lay back down in bed. His window shades were still up; he looked out at the streetlights on Roanoke Road, at Mr. McCormick's dark house next door.

❧   ❧   ❧

Even by the time Ben graduated in June, Olsen still could not inhabit thoughts of Mary, although he sometimes tested it, just to see, crossing the threshold of memory and dwelling there briefly with her; but the sadness was still too deep.

CHAPTER 21

❀

Go West, Old Man

The call came unobtrusively near the end of June, not heralded by any premonition or hinted at by an inkling, no fanfare, no sun rays streaming down from heaven, just a simple, out-of-the-blue telephone call from Dan Branigan at Tucson State, telling Olsen they wanted him for the JV coach's job.

"We'd like to have you out here to talk about particulars," Branigan told him. "Can you get away for a few days?"

And that's how Olsen ended up on his way to Tucson two weeks after Ben graduated from Indian River High.

The books Olsen brought along on the plane lay forgotten in his carry-on bag as he looked out at the field of clouds beneath him and the white-blue sky that felt like they were flying too close to the sun. The night before, he had dreamed—finally a good one—of standing atop the Tucson State bell tower and seeing the taupe and clay-red campus below, the slate blue mountains beyond, everything clear and white under the canopy of never-ending sun; and Olsen leaped from the tower, and flew.

Branigan was waiting for him at baggage claim in Tucson. "It's gonna be great," said Branigan, pumping Olsen's arm. They watched the river of luggage flow. Branigan said, "When Vasquez retired, I told everybody I'm getting Tom Olsen, period. Gotta inject some new blood in our program. You've sent us some great players through the years, Tom—that speaks for itself. And your guys are always crème de la crème, not just in basketball but everything. Just really good kids. Pretty nice ambassadors for your school."

"Thanks. I've been very lucky—blessed, really. Hey, remember Jesse Birnhoffer? Very first player I sent your way? What a character. Wonder whatever happened to him."

"He was working in Chicago, last I heard," said Branigan. "Stockbroking or something."

"Good job for him."

"I'm still bummed that Ben Wendling decided not to play for us," Branigan said.

"Yeah," said Olsen, "but he'll make Tucson State proud in some other way. I guarantee you that."

"It'll be great for Ben to have you out here."

"And vice versa," Olsen said, grabbing his suitcase and swinging it off the conveyor belt. "You know, it's been years since I thought about getting into college coaching. But this is a great opportunity for me. And I'm ready to make a change."

"Then we have good timing. That's a good sign. Hey, it's about a hundred degrees here today," Branigan said. "Run-of-the-mill summer temperature for us. Think you can stand it?"

"I can get used to anything," said Olsen.

They hit the highway flying in Branigan's Jimmy, Branigan chewing on an unlit cigar and high-powering the air conditioning. Olsen would need a new vehicle out here. Time for something monstrous and indestructible. A Suburban. A Hummer. He would sell the Corvette. Rakowsky had always said he wanted it.

Tucson was a highway town and Olsen didn't love that, but he liked his destination: the Tucson State campus north of the city, over the river and flirting with the mountains, its narrow and leisurely main road sketched lightly around two hundred acres, low buildings camouflaged in the landscape, punctuated by the bell tower, walkways and pathways weaving through unremitting Arizona sun and the shadowy awnings of the foothills. Tucson State was far enough out of town to feel wild, but close enough to civilization for students to take part-time jobs at the resort down the road. Olsen felt at home in this desert corner; he liked the massiveness of the quietude, the silence of the air: not a lonely silence, but vibrating.

Branigan parked outside the Skyhawk athletic complex. The summer campus was almost empty. They walked inside and Branigan said, "Let me tell you about the players coming into the basketball program—show you what you'd be getting into." In a conference room that had windows for walls, they leafed through everything and everybody: the scholarship picks, the walk-ons, the likely JVs; the head shots of boys whose uncertain eyes and nervous mouths belied their efforts to look like men; the scouting reports, written in a lingo of excruciating fine points that affirmed college basketball was serious business.

"I give you a lot of credit, Tom," Branigan said, "coaching a successful big-school basketball program, playing a tough schedule every year, and your trips to the state finals—wasn't it three altogether? Plus your English department—the chair and the teaching. Shows your drive, focus—your versatility—shows you can more than handle what you'll be doing here. I think you'll find out that all basketball, all year round, will be easier than splitting yourself in two."

"All basketball, all year round," said Olsen. He folded his hands behind his head and tilted his chair back.

Later Branigan drove Olsen along the narrow main road through the dusk, to a gravel road beyond the dorms that led to a cluster of adobe guesthouses. Olsen got his suitcase, then crunched across the gravel under the lavender sky, following Branigan inside.

"You got your food and beer stocked in the fridge," Branigan said, touring Olsen through the circle of rooms, "your big screen TV, DVDs, CDs. Have some fun. Make yourself at home. Gamboa and I'll pick you up for breakfast tomorrow around ten, ten-thirty."

"Gamboa?"

"Our new shooting coach. Just recruited him from the university—he was a TA in their phys ed department. New blood, remember? I'm on a mission."

Branigan left and Olsen sampled a few things from the fridge: a cube or two of cheese, a shot of gazpacho, a few bites of spicy pasta salad. He drank two bottles of beer, didn't turn on any music or the TV. He stood outside under the lavender sky, then got undressed, cleaned up, and lay down in bed.

Way back on Mount Baldy, Mary had said something that Olsen now remembered: it was so much easier in Moses' day when God just boomed His instructions down from heaven. Clear and intact, she had said.

I don't need God to tell me it's time for a change…but what would I be giving up, if I do take this job?

Teaching high school English. It's an excuse to read constantly—and so much of what I can't explain about myself, I uncover in what I read…in that endless succession of the acclaimed and the amateur where I occasionally uncover the grail I can never get enough of: the perfect words.

But I don't have to be an English teacher for that.

I also teach because I love the kids. Love them for themselves, and because they remind me of who I might have been, and because teaching's given me the chance to redo my adolescence from afar—and in the process I've gotten the last laugh on the old sadness. But it's starting to feel like the same old song and dance, like I'm just repeating myself day after month after year.

Of course I also teach because the kids like, even love me in return. But that's a bottomless pit. I'll never be done dying for that feeling...

He thought about his heralded arrival almost thirteen years ago at Indian River High, with its skidding English department and a basketball program gone to seed under the blotchy red nose of a coach who needed rehab.

...Back then I was at the top of my game, wearing all the power of youth—but how many new offers am I going to get now? I'm a midcareer public high school teacher with midlife malaise and a great basketball record.

This Tucson State job is a sign, a definite sign that Ben and I share a link of fate, history—like family. It's the greatest offer I could hope for, because of Ben...

And because of Mary.

It was only a matter of time before she would realize what a mistake she had made; and when she finally came to her senses, she would know exactly where to find Olsen: in Tucson with the child they both loved.

Olsen had never done this until now: imagined Ben's response to the words "I'm in love with your mother." Not a fairy-tale imagining, but an honest one. "I love your mother."

He could imagine the look on Ben's face.

He could see Ben's eyes saying *You used me.*

Then he could hear himself protesting **No, no, child of my heart—you are the missing piece, the missing person, the history that slipped through my fingers and has somehow been restored—how could I not love her for bringing you to life?**

Ben's eyes

All right, it's true, she is also more than that to me. She is more than your mother, and the day she leaped down from the tree house, that was the day I understood everything that ever happened to me and when almost none of it mattered anymore. Can you try and understand what it was like for me? My body and soul had learned to lead separate lives

You used me

No, Ben—you are when and where and why my life began again
He closed his eyes.

Dozing, he saw an image of Mary hearing the news of his job at Tucson State: her face darkened, and she turned away without comment, silent at his refusal to extricate himself from her life. Olsen's eyes flew open.

With his thoughts in a knot, he fell into a deeper layer of sleep where Mary lay on the living room couch of the little adobe guest house, watching *Enchanted April* on the big screen TV, beckoning Olsen to her, and when he got close enough, he kneeled down beside her, and she smiled and whispered, "I love that ending," and he jerked awake at the moist warmth of her breath in his ear.

It took him a minute to remember where he was.

❧   ❧   ❧

On Saturday morning, Branigan and Gamboa picked Olsen up for breakfast when it was still only eighty-one degrees. Olsen squinted with fervor: here the sun bounced off the ground and the buildings and sailed through the clean dry air; when the sun shone in Indian River, the trees trapped it and the haze dulled it. He put his new sunglasses on.

They drove into the city for breakfast and Branigan talked about coming to Tucson State from Boston fifteen years ago, and how much he liked the people, the weather, the feel of the place right away; how neither his wife nor their two teenage daughters had shared his lust for the desert or his desire to relocate; how they had humored him nevertheless, and had grown to love Tucson in spite of their best efforts, although their family vacations always led to the seaside.

Gamboa, the new shooting coach, had been born and raised right in the city, a University of Arizona grad with a native's self-assurance. "It's a great place to grow up, and to raise a family," Gamboa said. "You have a family?"

"Not yet," said Olsen, "but who knows?"

After breakfast they drove out of the city and into Tucson Mountain Park, talking about the basketball season ahead, listening to sports radio, Branigan chewing on his cigar and then pulling off the scenic road along a rocky, empty stretch. He put the Jimmy in park, but left the AC running. The temperature was already breaking ninety.

"There's been a lot of development in Pima County," Branigan said. "Some say too much. But I think we have the best of both worlds. All the benefits of a city—the arts, the culture, the amenities. And then we have the opposite: the desert. There's no getaway like the desert. Guy wants to be alone, clear his head—here it is."

"Yeah," Gamboa said from the back seat.

"I'm gonna get out for a minute," said Olsen.

"Help yourself." Branigan chewed his cigar.

Olsen opened the door and jumped down, walked a hundred feet across the sand, temperature rising with each step he took. He pulled his arm over his forehead to wipe the streams of sweat. Felt his feet and head and bones melting. He stopped, looked out over the wide rocky fields of Arizona sand and took a deep breath. Remembered Mary with him on Mount Baldy: *I can see why Moses found God in the desert: the sky open wide, and the light unchained...*

He walked back to the Jimmy.

They dropped Gamboa off in the new development on Tucson's east side, where he and his wife had just built a house, then Branigan and Olsen headed back to the campus, soaring over the river, flying along the canyon road, and Olsen realized he would have to accelerate his driving habits even further when he moved there.

The summer campus and Skyhawk athletic complex were almost empty of students as Olsen finalized the generous particulars of his new job with Herb Motts, the college athletic director, and Branigan, who had left his cigar in the Jimmy's ashtray. Olsen could barely believe his good fortune as details of the deal fell into place; he kept waiting for Branigan to yell, "Sucker!"

But after Olsen signed, they all smiled and shook hands and reclined in the window-walled conference room; then a man in a white shirt and black bow tie rolled dinner in on a cart: grilled steaks, and something made of rice and onions and cheese, and a fresh pitcher of ice water.

Eventually the conversation steered away from the business at hand toward Indiana.

Olsen said, "In Indian River, a guy has to fit a certain mold: basketball, God, and family. Preferably all three, although you can get by with only basketball if you're good enough at it. But out here, being your own man is more the benchmark. I think that's why I've always felt at home in Tucson. Haven't been out here for a couple of years, but it still feels like home."

"Tom, you're going to be very happy here," said Herb Motts. "And we're lucky to get you."

They talked about the leanness of Olsen's possessions and the relative ease of his imminent move. Branigan made some notes for the relocation service.

"When I moved out here from Boston," he said, "it was like the procession of the Taj Mahal, hauling my wife and daughters' stuff—furniture, clothes out the wazoo. But the sum total of my own personal crap took up one little corner of one of the moving vans. Know what I mean? You ever been married, Tom?"

"Nah."

"Ever been close?"

Olsen shrugged. "Who hasn't?"

"Your time might be coming. You'll meet some great women out here."

"Are you leaving a girl behind in Indiana?" asked Motts.

"Too late. She already left *me*," Olsen said, and they all laughed.

❦   ❦   ❦

That night, Priscilla and Dan Branigan hosted a dinner party in Olsen's honor, with Herb Motts and six assorted coaches and their wives, plus a few extra women who seemed unattached to basketball or to any man at the party, everyone celebrating Olsen, gliding over the ceramic tile floors with tinkling drinks in hand and the Boston Pops serenading them from hidden speakers vibrating under the high ceilings. He didn't want to, but Olsen saw Mary in the butterscotch glow of the Tucson women who surrounded him. The coaches smiled in the background, sipping Cokes and club sodas and scotches, as Olsen drank beers and heard himself bullet-pointing his life story.

"Ohio State basketball

"Master's in English

"World mythologies

"New England born and bred—now an honorary Midwesterner

"No children

"Never married—right, no girl has been lucky enough yet

"Indian River High in Indiana

"English department chair, head basketball coach

"Three trips to the finals

"State champs once, runners-up twice

"The secret to my success? Be true to myself and the kids. And never go corporate."

Olsen noticed that the eyes of his listeners didn't wander as he spoke, that the other coaches grinned, and nodded, and laughed, and raised their glasses with "I'll drink to that!" and "Here, here" at Olsen's words, and that some of the women touched his arm, leaned into him, when he answered their questions; and it started to feel like a reunion.

Around the dinner table, Priscilla Branigan said, "Tom, we all just loved your Ben Wendling when he visited the campus with his parents. He is a wonderful young man. And he certainly thinks the world of you."

"He was one of your best references," Branigan laughed.

"Yeah," said Sandoval, "everything he said was Coach Olsen this, Coach Olsen that."

Gamboa said, "He told us how you saved his life, resuscitated him when he got knocked out at that all-star game," and the women said, "What happened?" and Gamboa told the story, and the women ooohed in a hush.

"It's a mutual admiration society," Olsen said; "I love that boy like my own son." He looked around the table. He felt as if he were looking back on these people from some future day when they had all been his friends for a long time, and this was just the whisper of a memory, the imprint of their first night together.

Later Olsen lay in bed in the guesthouse, thinking of all the times he'd been to Tucson. Never with the thought of staying, but always with the thought of coming back. It had taken him a long time to figure out that it was home.

CHAPTER 22

❀

Linger In Me

But it wasn't until Olsen arrived back in Indian River on Sunday afternoon that he realized how much he needed to move. Indian River's sameness hung grimly before his returning eyes: same road home, same old rows of same old houses, same old people who never left, same old dreams that didn't come true.

Back on Roanoke Road, he waved across the lawn to Mr. McCormick, who sat on his front stoop watching his squirrel-dog leap in the grass. Olsen pulled bills and flyers from the mailbox, went inside and skimmed the messages on his answering machine: his new contact lenses were in at the optical center; a telemarketing computer voice intoned that he may have won a trip for two to Florida; his All-Pro of Indian River agent wanted to review his insurance needs and would call back to set up an appointment. Olsen erased them all.

"God," he said.

He slouched around through the first floor and came to rest on the living room recliner. Tucson had painted itself on his imagination: a new life. But no one to share it with. "Sweetheart, I have great news," he said to the wall. "I took the job at Tucson State! We're moving to Arizona! You're proud of me? You're happy that an exciting new chapter in my life is beginning? Thank you, sweetheart. You know, all this glory, all this happiness, wouldn't mean a thing if I didn't have you, the one I love, to share it with. That's what makes it all worthwhile."

Olsen kicked the recliner upright and went into the dining room.

He logged onto his computer, pulled his address book out of the desk drawer. He typed himself a list of names and phone numbers for tomorrow's phone calls: the Indian River High School principal; the athletic director; Kuehn and Stefanik; Grant Groman and Ruth LoPiro and the other English teachers. He typed "RAKOWSKY" at the top of the list, and printed the page.

Then he e-mailed Ben. *Great news. Too good for e-mail. Give me a call as soon as you can. Coach Olsen.*

❧   ❧   ❧

Ben was already waiting by the school doors, his basketball in hand, when Olsen pulled into the parking lot at ten o'clock that night.

"So what's the big news?" Ben called out as Olsen walked toward him.

"Let's go inside first," Olsen said, and unlocked the front entrance.

They walked side by side down the unlit corridor to the gym, and Olsen unlocked the doors. "Turn on the lights, wouldja?" he said, and Ben dribbled across the floor to the bank of switches. The lights came on overhead, too bright at first. Ben dribbled as he walked across the gym and propped the outside doors open.

Olsen picked a ball up from the floor and took a few shots—a jogging lay-up, a little jumper, and a 3.

"Guess who's going to Tucson State?" Olsen said.

"Besides me? I don't know," said Ben. "Who?"

"See if you can guess," said Olsen, watching his shot bounce high off the rim and fly toward the bleachers.

Ben put up a long 3; it spun around the inside of the rim and dropped through. "Girl or guy?"

"Guy."

"For basketball or not?"

"Yeah, for basketball."

Ben jogged toward the basket, picked up the ball, and held it under his arm. He looked at Olsen. "I have no idea."

Olsen smiled. "It's me."

"You?"

"They just hired me as their JV coach. So I'm going to Tucson State with you."

Ben's mouth opened into the same O that Olsen used to see on Mary's lips. Finally he said, "No joke?"

"No joke," said Olsen. "So I definitely won't be able to forget you."

Ben said, "Did this just happen?"

"Yeah, actually, just this past week. Branigan called and offered me the job. I flew out to Tucson and took care of the details. So it's a done deal."

"Because I've been praying for you," Ben said, "praying that something really great would happen in your life, something as great as you deserve, so you could really be happy," and as he spoke, Olsen saw the outline of Ben's body dissolve into a silvery haze; Olsen blinked, and the silver faded back into a clean edge.

"Your mother used to pray for me," Olsen said. "Remember you once told me?" But Ben didn't answer, didn't seem to have heard.

"Think you can put up with me for four more years?" Olsen said.

"This isn't a joke, right?" said Ben. "Are you just messing with me?"

"No joke," said Olsen. "Now give me a hard time here, help me stay sharp," heading for Ben, who faked left, then spun right and beat Olsen to the basket for 2.

Early Monday morning Olsen stopped by Rakowsky's house, breaking in on his summer vacation slumber to surprise him with the news and coffee and donuts. They toasted his success with a vow that Tucson would become Rakowsky's home away from home and a pledge to squeeze in as many bar nights as possible before Olsen's bon voyage.

Later Olsen drove home to Roanoke Road. He called the Indian River principal, who said, "Tucson State! What a great opportunity! Congratulations," and Olsen said, "I know it's very late notice. I'm sorry to leave you in the lurch like this," but the principal said, "Don't worry—we'll get it covered. I think Ruth would make an excellent department chairman, don't you?"

Next Olsen called the athletic director, who said, "Way to go, Tom! Moving up in the world," and Olsen said, "What'll we do about the season?" and the A.D. said, "Kuehn's ready for this, just like you're ready for Tucson State."

Next, Kuehn and Stefanik were both happy for him; then Groman and Ruth LoPiro and the rest of the English teachers were happy for him; all their voices were ripe with felicitations for his departure. When he was done calling everyone on his list, Olsen realized that Indian River needed him to leave as much as he needed to leave Indian River. He had received streams of congratulations—and not one "It won't be the same without you." Not one "Is it too late to make you change your mind?" Not one "Don't go."

As the days ticked by, there was no word at all from Mary, although Olsen was certain Ben had told her by now. She couldn't call, write a note, send a card? She wouldn't even talk to him? But eventually her congratulations did arrive. On the day Olsen found her card in his mailbox on Roanoke Road, he ignored everything else that had been delivered and brought her envelope into his dining room, opened it at his desk, pulled the card out.

It was a formal design with short preprinted best wishes, signed "Virgil, Mary, and Ben" in her handwritten scrawl.

The card shook in Olsen's hand: a historian going through the rubble of his life would dismiss this greeting as a social grace. It held no trace of their story. No trace of Olsen and Mary's truth that there was a boy they both loved, who had almost died before their eyes, the boy who was the reason they had been together and the reason they would never be together.

Olsen turned the card over to see if Mary had written any note, any word on the back. And in fact, she had written *Dear Thomas*—then scribbled it out and never finished the message.

&

Dear Thomas,

Good luck and all the best to you in your future endeavors.

&

Dear Thomas,

I can't imagine Indian River without you.

&

Dear Thomas,

I love you and I can't live without you.

Dear Thomas,

Don't go.

He put the card into the wastebasket by his desk. But from there it seemed to be watching him. He extracted it and stuffed it in the kitchen garbage under the sink.

*   *   *

Tucson State hired the relocation service to move Olsen, so all he had to do was throw away what he didn't want to bring, and pack his luggage for the plane trip. People started stopping by Roanoke Road unannounced to wish him well: colleagues from the high school, students, players, the neighbors, his softball teammates, and an old girlfriend or two.

Kristina surprised him the most.

Olsen had plugged in an old fan and turned it on high to break up the hot, heavy air in the garage while he tossed all the junk off his workbench into a garbage can. He saw Kristina walking up his driveway, wearing shorts and sandals and a tight sleeveless tee shirt under the muggy late afternoon sun. As usual, she modeled perfection: no sweat, smooth tan, hair shining neat and blonde, bright pink polished fingernails. She had a small purse over her shoulder and held a present.

"Kristina!"

She smiled. "Weren't you even going to tell me that you're moving?"

"It's good to see you," he said. "How did you hear?"

"Terese Ciprak told me," said Kristina. "She seems to keep good track of you." She touched Olsen's hand. "This Tucson move is very exciting—a big step up for you. Of course I wanted to congratulate you in person. Maybe you'll even invite me out west to visit you sometime." Kristina stroked his arm. "I've missed you, Tom."

Her obviousness struck him as a pleasant diversion, and for a few minutes they made the chitchat of old lovers, discussing Olsen's new job and Kristina's promotion from reporter to weekend anchor on the Indianapolis station where she worked; Olsen's aspirations to coach college varsity and her goal to anchor in Chicago, hopefully as a springboard to a job in LA.

"I have a going-away present for you—a picture of me." Kristina handed him the package. She stroked his arm again, looked into his eyes. "We're two such hard-driving, independent people," she said. "Who knows what might have happened if even one of us could have eased up a little?"

Olsen sighed, because he didn't know how to answer her. "Do you want to come in and have something to drink?" he asked.

But when Olsen stood facing Kristina in his kitchen, handing her the glass of wine she asked for, he realized how far behind him the old days and old ways were. So he told her instead how much she had meant to him, and that with her beauty and talent, she would succeed in everything she did, and that he would be jealous of whatever lucky guy would marry her someday.

Kristina looked disappointed. Then she reclaimed her happy face, thanked Olsen for his good wishes, and drank her wine quickly.

     ❦   ❦   ❦

Why don't you just get over it; why does it even matter anymore? But Mary wasn't something to be explained or reasoned with. She simply was: like rain and sunlight, like despair, like a child who is not dead but sleeping, and like all the days ordained for him, written in God's book before one of them came to be.

Sometimes Olsen was sure he felt Mary behind him—but he would turn around and see only a shadow. Sometimes he saw his front window shimmering with the brilliant remnants of a reflection, but he could never be certain it had been her. He even heard Mary's voice once, he was certain, singing sadly in his backyard after he had gone to bed, as if she were drifting among the three blue spruces; but he knew it was no use; he lay in bed and waited for her voice to fade away.

     ❦   ❦   ❦

The dining room would be the worst room to pack because of his desk: crowned with the computer, piled with mounds of notebooks and papers, drawers jammed with basketball notebooks, coaches' conference notes, newspaper clippings, recruiting materials, English department notes, reading lists, wish lists, syllabi. He went into the kitchen and got his new roll of 30-gallon trash bags and the first of several beers to christen the afternoon.

Then he found that cleaning through this stuff wasn't so bad. Many more of his ideas had borne fruit than he remembered: combining the literature and speech comm classes into one freshman English course; adding a playwriting elective to the curriculum, and tying it in to the Drama Club; retooling senior lit to better captivate the seventeen-year-old imagination.

All had been Olsen's brainchildren. All had redefined English at Indian River High. These days, seniors like Ben were winning English scholarships to college—unheard of in the years before Olsen arrived. And he was giving it up.

"Well, I was never going to get a job as an English professor," he said, out loud.

Olsen went through each desk drawer, paper by paper, and stacked the basketball stuff: Offenses. Defenses. Great plays. Shooting techniques. Inspirational/motivational. Ohio State. Indian River scrapbook. Miscellaneous.

Olsen pulled a notebook up from the bottom drawer, and a loose page, in his handwriting, fluttered out of it into his lap.

> You, mystery divine
> seeming distant sadly shy
> yet dark eyes aflame
> Your thought surrounds me
> Intimate possession
> of my body and soul
> Gently then you slip
> back to distant silence
> But you linger in me

Written for Mary. Written for Mary when he had believed that she would be his, because living, for him, had meant believing that. And in a way she had become his, after all: in reflections in the window, in flickering shadows, sad songs in the night, and in the presence that so often stood behind him, heavy with regret, but lighter than the blink of an eye.

❧   ❧   ❧

The next day Olsen was cleaning his bedroom closet, throwing holey old tee shirts in a 30-gallon trash bag, when the phone rang. "Hello?" he said.

"Tom?"

Olsen hesitated for a few seconds. "Hi, Mom."

"How are you?" Louise said.

"I'm good. And you?"

"Fine. What have you been up to?"

"Well, I'm packing. I'm moving to Tucson."

"What?" said Louise.

"Well, Tucson State College offered me a coaching job, and I accepted. I've been packing up the house. Be heading out west in a week."

"Were you going to tell me? Or were you just going to move?"

"Honestly, Mom, I forgot. This all came up in the last few weeks, literally. It was late notice for the high school, and I've been helping them get things in order. And the packing and cleaning—all these years here—what a mess."

Louise said nothing.

Olsen said, "So what have you been up to?"

"Not much. The usual. But something told me to call you, and I'm glad I did. Otherwise I wouldn't even know where you were."

"I'm sorry, Mom. It just drives home what a crazy time this has been, that I didn't even think to call you. I'm really sorry. Hold on, let me get you my new phone number and stuff—I'll be staying on campus till I buy a place."

By the time they said good-bye, Olsen's stomach was clenched in a fist. Why did he and Louise even bother anymore? He stood in front of his dresser, the garbage bag at his feet, and doodled on a piece of scrap paper.

A little later he knocked on Mr. McCormick's front door, and the old man opened it almost instantly, his little squirrel-dog in his arm.

"Hullo, Tom. I saw you coming there," he said, and his dog wriggled.

"Hey," Olsen said, "I just stopped by to tell you a little news."

"Well, come in." Mr. McCormick shuffled across the old carpet into the living room. "Sit down," he said, and sank into a green plaid easy chair. His face sagged with a bluish-gray tinge but his eyes glittered, young man peering through an old-man mask.

"You'll be seeing a lot of activity over at my place in the next few weeks," said Olsen. "I'm moving to Tucson. Just wanted to let you know."

"Tucson, eh? Well, well. What will you be doing there?"

"Coaching basketball at Tucson State College."

Mr. McCormick raised his eyebrows. "Giving up the English?"

"Yeah. Well, giving up the teaching, anyway." In twelve years, Olsen had never been inside here; now he noticed Mr. McCormick had more books than

Olsen himself did, mostly old ones, jammed into bookshelves, stacked on the matted carpet, stacked on end tables.

There wasn't much other than books, though, just the old furniture, a few sun-dulled prints on the walls, and some potted plants on an old desk by the clean windows. No family pictures, no cards or letters on a table, no touch of another human being.

"Well," said Mr. McCormick. "I'm going to miss you, Tom." He got up from his green plaid chair and walked to the desk, pulled a piece of yellowed paper from the top drawer. "Give me a call sometime, let me know how you're doing out there," he said, writing slowly, then handing the paper to Olsen.

"Sure. I will. I'll miss you, too."

"Now how about a beer—a toast to your success?" McCormick said.

"Sure."

Olsen followed the old man into the kitchen, where the house's original avocado-colored appliances stood watch over the past. McCormick pulled the refrigerator door open.

Olsen stood behind him. The back of Mr. McCormick's scalp, crisscrossed with veins and white wisps of hair, looked ancient.

"Here we go," McCormick said. He handed Olsen a Miller and said, "Need a bottle opener?"

"Nah." Olsen twisted Mr. McCormick's beer open, then his own, and they tapped their bottles together.

"To Tucson," McCormick said, smiling at Olsen, but his young-man's eyes were focused somewhere far away.

❦   ❦   ❦

"Not one person has tried to talk me out of leaving," Olsen said to Rakowsky. They were packing up Olsen's classroom, taking down his Teacher of the Year awards, his Coach of the Year plaques and trophy, his Seniors' Choice Graduation Speaker certificates, his basketball photos, his class photos, and putting them carefully in cardboard cartons.

"You'd already taken the job," Rakowsky said. "You never gave us a chance to talk you out of it!"

"Well, how about a little regret? A little mourning at my departure? Instead, they're all set to go with Ruth chairing the department and Kuehn coaching the team—instantly. Like they've just been waiting for me to leave! The congratulations are great, but a little 'You'll be missed' tacked on at the end wouldn't hurt, a little begging me not to go."

"We're just jealous," Rakowsky said. "You were handpicked for a college spot and we weren't. So we can't get you out of town fast enough to assuage our aching egos."

"Just make sure no one ever paints over my *Odyssey* mural," Olsen said, and took a last look at his fading tribute on the wall.

❧   ❧   ❧

Rakowsky had said, "Karen wants to have you over for dinner the Sunday before you leave," so on that night Olsen pulled his old silver Corvette, soon to be titled over to Rakowsky, into their driveway. A hot July downpour had driven the kids and the dog walkers and the joggers indoors. Rakowsky's street was deserted, utterly depressing to Olsen's eyes under the gray showers and the sky's shadow. "So what?" he said aloud. Soon he would be luxuriating under three hundred days of sunshine a year.

Inside Rakowsky's house, the air conditioning cooled him and lights were on everywhere, replacing the sun; Rakowsky was blasting good music and Karen was chopping vegetables on the counter. She said, loudly, "Tom, I'm making this soup you like, the southwestern soup, and a little burrito smorgasbord—plus that pitcher of margaritas." She pointed to the far counter. "It's your southwest sendoff. Is that too corny?"

"No," said Olsen, "it's great." He walked across the kitchen and poured himself and Rakowsky drinks.

Karen dropped handfuls of chopped onion and tomato into the pot of soup, then started crumbling tortilla shells into it. "It's still going to be half an hour before everything's ready," she said. "So, Rick, do you think you and Tom could haul Gram's old freezer up from the basement and put it out on the tree lawn? Tomorrow's garbage day."

"Aha," Olsen said, "so you had an ulterior motive for having me over!"

"Caught me!" Karen said.

Olsen and Rakowsky drank long gulps from their slippery glasses and headed for the basement door. Rakowsky flicked the light on and Olsen followed him down the stairs.

"This old freezer finally went kaput," Rakowsky said. "Karen's grandmother bought it a million years ago, then gave it to Karen's mother, then she gave it to us. Our fridge upstairs? Our third one in thirteen years. The new ones keep crapping out. Lemons."

"Yeah," said Olsen. They were heading into the utility room. "My neighbor Joe McCormick still has his appliances from forty years ago—they're still humming away. You should see the color..."

"SURPRISE!" screamed a utility-roomful of people as Rakowsky flipped on the lights and Olsen leaped backwards in raw shock, the rolling melange of voices and laughter sweeping around him, the faces at first merging together like a stadium crowd, but then Olsen made out Mike and Rosemary Stefanik, and Dave and Julie Kuehn, Matt Pender and his parents, and the Cavatellis with Michael, and the Reiters with Josh, and the Pytels and the Powells and more of his basketball players past and present, and the principal and his wife, the athletic director, and Grant and Hayley Groman and Ruth LoPiro and everyone else from the English department, and a crowd of his English students; and Olsen saw Ben, and Wendling, and Mary.

Above all their heads on the back wall hung a banner that said, "TOM—DON'T GO!"

The surge of handshakes, hugs, and backslaps lifted Olsen higher on the wave of his surprise. He thanked each person who reached his side, thanked them for coming, his eyes darting to keep Mary in view on the other side of the utility room. He had seen her two months ago, just a glimpse from afar, at Ben's graduation; during Ben's senior basketball season Olsen had seen her many times in the distance; they had waved to each other at the home opener; but he had not spoken to her for almost one year.

Presents were thrust into his hands, and he piled them atop the ancient freezer, star of the ruse that led him to the basement. The unwrappings revealed mostly Indiana memorabilia: *Hoosiers* on DVD, John Cougar Mellencamp on CD, a couple of Indy 500 caps, a set of Indianapolis Colts nylon warm-ups, a coffee table book about the Amish, a framed print of Mount Baldy in the summer. The good-bye cards were funny, and he read them out loud to the crowd; laughter seemed to be the evening's theme song, and it finally sank into Olsen that they weren't happy to see him go, they were just happy for him.

Then Karen called down to the basement and said the food was ready, and everyone flooded the stairway, except for Olsen who stood at the bottom of the stairs thanking people again as they went up. The basement emptied until no one was left with Olsen but Wendling and Mary; Ben had already gone upstairs with his friends.

Wendling approached Olsen first, smiling. Olsen glanced over at Mary; she was standing on the far side of the room, with her back to them, apparently rereading the "TOM—DON'T GO!" banner hanging on the wall.

"Tom," said Wendling, "all the best to you. I'm really happy you'll be out in Tucson to watch out for Ben." They shook hands and looked at each other. Then Wendling said, "Ben is blessed to have you in his life. I wanted to be sure to tell you that before you left."

"Thanks," said Olsen.

"Friends?" Wendling asked, his eyes round. "I was thinking we could put the rest behind us."

"Sure—friends," Olsen said. Wendling's eyes misted over and he looked like he was considering a hug, so Olsen stuck his hand out for another handshake.

Wendling looked over his shoulder for Mary; she was still turned toward the banner. "Mary," he said, "I'll see you upstairs," but she didn't answer. "See you up there, too, Tom," Wendling said to Olsen, hesitating. He looked back over his shoulder once more. Then he clapped Olsen on the back and disappeared, his footsteps on the stairs fading into the party hubbub. And Olsen walked across the cool basement floor toward Mary.

He steeled himself for her cheery send-off, or perhaps her formal one, setting his jaw in a half-smile as he got closer to her. When Mary turned to face him, though, tears were slipping through her black lashes, and all that she had done and undone was passing in waves of shadow across her face. Olsen translated her despair: it was still over between them, and always would be. But she opened her arms to him anyway, as she once did in the brief days of their shared life.

Olsen held her until her body stopped shaking, with one hand on the small of her back, and the other on her hair. He wanted to tell her it was not too late, that it would never be too late, but his voice had been swallowed up in the pit of his stomach. The only word Mary said to him was *Thomas*.

Then he dried the path of her tears, gently, with the edges of his tee shirt. He saw that the clasp of her necklace had come around to the front; it was stuck at the cross, beneath her throat. Olsen lifted the cross in his fingers; then slowly, with his other hand, he pulled the clasp back around to the nape of her neck, under her hair, and let it go. He could not look in her eyes.

Then they went upstairs together.

❦   ❦   ❦

Olsen recopied the poem on a clean sheet of paper and addressed the envelope to Mary at the Indian River Public Library. He didn't need to sign his name.

A few days later, on a clear morning, Rakowsky picked Olsen up on Roanoke Road. They put his bags in the back of Rakowsky's old Blazer and headed for the airport.

On the way out of Indian River, Olsen said, "Can you swing by the post office? I have to mail something before I go." When they got there, he said, "Just give me a second," got out and walked across the pavement, stood in front of the mailbox, then slipped the envelope into its wide and silent mouth.

CHAPTER 23

❀

Long Way Home

September in Tucson, Arizona, two years later.

Olsen stood behind Cara as she slipped her key into the lock and opened her front door. He followed her inside, put her cat carriers down in the ceramic tile foyer and opened the little doors. Antony and Cleopatra slunk out simultaneously in their smooth Siamese coats, restaking their lair together.

Cara put her suitcase down. She slipped her arms around Olsen's waist and pressed her face against his chest. "I love you so much," she said, "and I had such a wonderful time."

Olsen stroked her hair. He lifted her off the floor; "I love you, too;" kissed her.

In the kitchen at her gleaming terra cotta counter, Cara opened a bottle of Shiraz with a corkscrew. She liked doing it herself, and Olsen liked to see the little muscles in her arms flexing. He listened to the climactic thwunk of the cork popping; the peaceful glug-glug of the Shiraz filling their wine glasses; and the song of the cats, mewing in a duet for something to eat.

"Let's have another toast to your fabulous promotion," said Cara; they clinked their glasses together, entwined their arms like bride and groom, and drank to the new varsity assistant coach.

Later, back at his own house, Olsen unpacked his suitcase, came across the card Cara had just given him on their Hilton Head vacation with Louise. Skimmed it, put it down. Picked it back up and reread it word for word, everything she had written, in her pretty handwriting.

I love you for challenging my mind, captivating my body, and caressing my soul. I love you because your face is music to my eyes; because you are brilliant and thirsting, a poet in the body of a superhero, and vulnerable and sad and tender. I love you because you are proud of me, and because you make me feel heard and respected and adored.

He loved Cara; he did. She was a Ph.D. in psychology, a Tucson State assistant professor and director of the student counseling center. And she was beautiful, sexually unabashed, fifteen years younger than he was, and would have killed a lesser man; a decade or two had melted off Olsen into the heat of her skin. And Cara loved him. Lusted for him. Looked up to him. Priscilla Branigan had introduced the two of them as soon as Olsen had moved to Tucson two years ago, and they had dated ever since.

Cara was his unadulterated queen; she was Helen of Troy without the war, she was Penelope without the long way home. Funny how, when you finally give up on something—love, for instance—it suddenly shows up in your life, blithe, lithe, and nonchalant, as if to say *What were you worried about? I was on the way.*

Olsen kept three souvenirs of Mary: the coffee cup; the framed picture she had taken of him with Ben; and the words she had copied from the Bible onto bright white paper. Those things were enough, for Olsen had learned in the course of time to prefer Cara, who had no despair, Cara who was warmth he could touch and sweetness he could taste, Cara who could make him forget.

Olsen opened his top dresser drawer and took out the black velvet box with the diamond ring. He had been saving this surprise for Cara's birthday in September.

But why wait?

Forty-five minutes later, he was engaged.

❋   ❋   ❋

Olsen woke up the next morning in Cara's bed, kissed her good-bye, drove home. He showered, dressed, read the paper. In the sports section he saw a high school football column and thought of Rakowsky. **I'll have to call and tell him the good news.** Eventually he headed for the campus to help with the first day of freshman orientation.

Hard to believe that only two years earlier he had arrived at Tucson State pale-faced and emotionally haggard, walking the fine line between has-been and just-about-to-be, clinging for dear life to the threads of Ben and new hope.

Now he was varsity assistant coach, Branigan's right hand, and engaged to a beautiful woman he loved, and Ben was an archaeology major coming back that afternoon to start his junior year.

Traffic thickened near Hernandez Student Center, mostly SUVs and minivans skippered by fathers and mothers, some pulling U-Hauls, with a few Tucson airport shuttles peppered in. Olsen drove to the far end of campus and parked in one of the dormitory lots, then walked back across the grounds toward the student center, soaking up all ninety-nine degrees Fahrenheit as he went. Olsen made it a rule not to criticize the Arizona sun, that ever-burning, ever-present light that had burned away the fungus of his depression.

On the sidewalks approaching Hernandez, Olsen saw the swells of freshmen and their parents, dressed up and dressed down, heard the buzz and scale of many voices, all moving in a tide toward the student center doors, toward the upperclassmen greeters in their blue and white Skyhawks tee shirts and baseball caps, smiling and waving the newcomers in.

Inside the lobby, Olsen turned right and headed for Dean Acuri's office. There he said a group hello to everyone: a few coaches, a few professors, some of Cara's students from the Psych department, Olsen's varsity players, all on call to help with freshman orientation.

Olsen picked up his silver-chained nametag and hung it around his neck, poked through the pile and saw Ben's nametag was still there with a few others. Then Olsen went and stationed himself on the lobby outskirts, a supply of campus maps in hand, pointing students and parents in the right directions through the organized chaos.

Long after lunch, Olsen saw Ben come through the front doors of Hernandez, blurring into the crowd.

"Hey, Ben!" Olsen shouted, but his voice must have gotten lost in the dull roar, because Ben didn't look in his direction; he headed instead down the hall toward Dean Acuri's office.

Olsen snaked his way through the crowd.

He saw Ben, shoulders slumped forward as he ruffled through the nametags left on the table.

"Ben!" said Olsen. "Welcome back. Good to see you!"

Ben turned toward him. Olsen saw two heavy gray circles, so much like Mary's, under his eyes. He felt discord rising off Ben's skin. "Man," Olsen said. "Are you okay?"

"Sure," said Ben. He cleared his throat. "Good to see you, Tom. How was your summer?"

"What's wrong?" Olsen said. He put his hand on Ben's shoulder. "Are you sick?" He didn't get an answer. "Are you all right?"

"Tom," Ben said, "I've gotta talk to you later."

"Sure, yeah. I'm doing Tucson Tours tonight, but I'll be home around ten."

"I don't know when I'm going to be done tonight, though," Ben said. "I'm an RA. I'm responsible for like twenty freshmen in my dorm. This is going to be a long day."

"Wanna talk now? You don't look so good." **Is it Mary? Wendling? Jasmine? What is it?**

"I can't," Ben said. "They're waiting for me. How about if I stop by your house tomorrow morning. Early. Like eight?"

"Sure, but call me later tonight if you're free."

"Okay," Ben said. He walked quickly toward the crowded lobby without saying good-bye.

"Doesn't matter how late!" Olsen called after him.

❦   ❦   ❦

That evening, Olsen stood at the front of the dining hall in Hernandez Student Center and whistled through his fingers to quiet the crowd. "How many are going on Tucson Tours tonight?"

Freshman hands shot up, crept up, waved, fluttered.

"Okay," said Olsen, "listen up. You are looking at the actual Tucson Tours creator here! I'm Coach Tom Olsen from your Skyhawks men's basketball team, and here's our itinerary for tonight. First we'll head south into the city and cruise around. You'll see the malls, sports arenas, concert halls—all the important stuff. Then we'll drive around the University of Arizona campus, in case you end up at grad school there. Hey, it's never too early to plan your future. Then we'll take a scenic route west of the city in Tucson Mountain Park, maybe get out and stroll around a little. Then we'll head north for home—our own beautiful campus here in the foothills of the Catalina Mountains. So everybody clear your trays and meet by the vans out front."

Before setting off from Hernandez, Olsen asked everyone in his van where they were from. They each had a different home state: Arizona, California, Oregon, New Mexico, Florida, Ohio.

"Ohio?" Olsen said. "I used to live in Columbus," but the freshman girl was from Toledo, and sick of Great Lakes weather, the gloom and gray and rain and snow; she had come in search of the sun and independence.

"You'll find them here," Olsen told her; "the sun and yourself are two things you can't hide from in the desert," and they set off.

Two hours later, Olsen dropped his vanload of freshmen off at their dorms and parked the van back at Hernandez. He crossed the campus on foot to Ben's dorm, Turbin Hall, where every light was blazing, every stereo cranking, the lobby reeked of pizzas and wings, and Olsen couldn't find Ben anywhere, although everybody kept saying they had just seen him. Eventually Olsen gave up, accepting he would have to wait until morning.

At home, he called Cara.

"Hello?" she said; her voice consoled him.

"How's my beautiful fiancée tonight?" he said.

"Wonderful," she said, "and how is *my* fiancé?"

"Better, now that I hear your voice."

"Just walked in a little while ago," Cara said. "I'm exhausted. I think most of the new kids are settled in—no crises today. That's a nice change." Olsen imagined her spread across her bed, green eyes closed, her summer nightgown translucent.

"Will you be able to sleep tonight," he said, "without me and my magic touch?"

"Barely. I'll have to gaze at this glorious ring you slipped on my finger and dream of tomorrow. How about your day—did you see Ben?"

"Yeah, but just for a minute. He's stopping by here first thing in the morning."

"Okay."

"I love you," he said.

"I love you, too," she said, "more than you know. I can't wait to be married to the love of my life."

"Sweet dreams, Cara."

"You, too," she said. "Dream about me."

He sat on the sofa and worried about Ben for a few minutes. He thought about how much he loved Cara. How blessed he was to have her. How much he liked her unencumbered life. Then he put *Are You Experienced* on the CD player, drank a bottle of beer, and fell asleep in the recliner.

❈   ❈   ❈

Two years ago, when they first arrived at Tucson State, Ben and Olsen had spent a lot of time together, finding steady ground in each other's familiar eyes and voices and shared memories. Gradually they also took up with new friends and pursuits, still in e-touch with old friends far away—Josh Reiter and Matt Pender for Ben, Rakowsky for Olsen. In those early days, Olsen sometimes thought of Mr. McCormick, remembered making the promise to call; but he never got around to it.

Right away Ben and Olsen started a tradition: they met religiously for Sunday breakfast at the campus coffee shop. One Sunday—it was October of his freshman year—Ben told Olsen, "My mom says hi."

"Really? When did you talk to her?"

"Last night."

"Well, tell her I said hello back." **Tell her I said it's not too late…that it will never be too late…Tell her I still read the words she copied from the Bible…Tell her she left traces of fog and light on my skin the first time she touched me and they have never faded away**

"Sure," said Ben, "I'll tell her."

After Sunday breakfasts they would leave the Skyhawk Café and drive off in Olsen's Blazer, sometimes picking up a few of Olsen's basketball players on the way, rent dirt bikes or go hiking or just drive around, until Ben had to hit the books and Olsen and his players had to hit the gym for conditioning or practice. When the season officially kicked in, Ben and Olsen saw each other less—familiar rhythm, strange twist—but didn't sacrifice their Sunday morning ritual if Olsen and the Skyhawks were in town.

Sometimes Cara joined them at the Skyhawk Café for breakfast. She seasoned their conversations with laughter and complaints and funny stories, insider notes on the college, questions and praise and encouragement. And sometimes Ben brought a young woman with him, a Tucson State student named Jasmine he'd been dating since shortly after his arrival in Arizona. Why should Olsen be so surprised when he saw Ben and Jasmine together, smiling the way they did, nose-to-nose, and slouching intimately against each other in the booth? Well, he had never seen that side of Ben; or maybe Ben had never shown it to him.

All is as it should be…he's growing up, growing away
Child of my heart   come back for me

It occurred to Olsen, in one of those epiphanies suggesting a ton of bricks, that Ben had always been just tattooed enough, just quiet enough, and just good enough to get away with anything. How much had Olsen missed through the years; how much had Ben hidden? From the beginning, Olsen had put him on a pedestal and trapped him atop it in a freeze-frame, pedestal built of love and sorrow and history that had slipped through his fingers.

How much of Ben have I not seen? As much as people do not see of me?
My boy
Don't be like me

One Sunday when it was just the two of them, Ben said to Olsen, "Know what? This place is really good for you. You're already so much happier than you were in Indian River."

"I am?" Olsen said.

Ben tilted his head in that way he and Mary had. "Definitely. You're more relaxed. You laugh more. You have more fun. We're always jumping in your Blazer and going somewhere. And you have Cara." He paused. "It's not just her, though. It's that you followed your dream to come here—you didn't stay stuck in Indian River for the rest of your life. You made your dream happen."

"But I didn't make it happen," said Olsen. "One day Branigan just called me out of the blue. If not for that, I *would* still be stuck in Indian River. I have to give God the credit for a miracle on this one."

"Remember back when I was still a senior," said Ben, "when you and I were talking about God, and I said church is the cafeteria and God is the food, that I can bring you with me to the cafeteria but I can't eat for you?"

"Sure I remember. A great analogy. Profound, really."

"I feel like I should have helped you more," Ben said, "like I kinda left you in the lurch spiritually. And now I don't even go to church. I don't know what I think about any of it. Maybe I just believed because my mom and dad did. Now that I'm on my own, I haven't set foot in a church. Maybe I never will again."

"But do you remember something else you said that day? 'In the end, it's between you and God.' And you were right. I don't think God tallies your church attendance. And if He does, I'm going straight to hell."

Ben stretched his arms above his head in the booth and tapped his knuckles on the window glass behind him. "Remember those things my mom wrote down? The Psalm thing, and Jesus resurrecting the little girl?"

"I still have them. Still look at them from time to time."

"Really?" Ben said. "Wow."

Olsen picked up his coffee cup, held it with two hands. Now the sun was glaring through the tall windows behind Ben, obscuring Ben's face in shadow.

Olsen thought about dreams—how it could look like you made your dream happen, when it was all just a lucky twist of fate. He thought about going straight to hell. About things that had stayed between him and God because he didn't know how to say them aloud.

Across the table Ben was still just a shadow in the sun. Olsen said, "I could never find the words for what I really wanted to say to your mother…It was probably better that way…*Gently then you slip/back to distant silence/But you linger in me.*"

Then a cloud blocked the sun, and Olsen could see Ben's face again: he was staring at Olsen, steady, serene.

"Anyway," Olsen said, and took a quick sip of coffee. "Your mother is very important to me. That's why I appreciate those Bible quotes she gave me—even though she didn't know they were for me. Parts of them I know by heart. You know what my favorite line is?"

"What?"

"*The child is not dead but sleeping.*"

Ben looked at him with such surprise, then love, that Olsen couldn't help it: his eyes filled with tears, some of the tears he thought he was too old and numb to cry, and a few spilled down into his coffee; he pulled a paper napkin across his face brusquely.

"Do you ever wonder," said Ben, "what's ahead for us? It's been a wild ride so far, hasn't it?"

Olsen did often wonder what was ahead for Ben, his future ordained and shining in mystery before him; but didn't want to think about the day Ben would be gone.

That afternoon Olsen finally leafed through his address book, through the paper scraps with phone numbers scribbled on them, looking for the one with Mr. McCormick's number, jotted down that day last summer when they had said good-bye and toasted Olsen's move with Miller beers.

But when Olsen tried to call him, there was no answer.

A month later he tried again, but a recording said the number had been disconnected. Olsen slipped the paper scrap into the back of his address book, his fingers shaking slightly as he put the book back in the drawer.

❦   ❦   ❦

From the time he first moved to Tucson, Olsen would drive into the desert alone on Sunday mornings before breakfast, park in some unpeopled, off-road spot, and think.

Different Sunday mornings brought different things to mind, and as Ben's freshman year had rolled on, Olsen lay far less of Mary on the altar of his thoughts, far more of Cara. He knew that he would marry Cara someday. He wanted to thank God for her, wanted to ask God to help him be worthy of her, to believe that God might listen. But Cara was an agnostic, so Olsen wasn't sure praying would work; and in any case, he worried it was too late for God to take him in.

Sometimes Olsen thought about Mary, hoped that she was happy; sometimes, he just prayed he could forget. When he thought about Mary, he closed his eyes; and when he closed his eyes, he felt her softness pressing against him again, envisioned his hand stroking the gold cross on the chain as it lay softly on her skin beneath her throat—and he would have to stop thinking and get back on the road and turn the radio on, loud.

One Sunday, Olsen decided not to think in the desert; his mind had been wandering too far toward Mary again. Instead he drove into town to the first church he could find, slipped in the back pew at the end of the confession, when the people were saying, "Be gracious and merciful to me, a poor sinful being," and the pastor was saying, "As a called and ordained servant of the Word, I announce the grace of God unto all of you, and in the stead and by the command of my Lord Jesus Christ, I forgive you all your sins…"

If Olsen had heard words like that at Calvary Lutheran years earlier, he didn't remember. They seemed as clear and intact as the voice of God from heaven. After church, he shook the pastor's hand with gratitude.

Baptized into a fresh start: that's how he saw it, that's how it felt. Cara was part of his new life; so was Arizona; and so was Ben. Mary was his old life; let it rest in peace.

Ben's freshman year was almost over by then. At Sunday breakfast, Ben told Olsen, "Guess what? My parents are coming for a visit."

Olsen sipped his coffee, then coughed when he swallowed too fast. "That's great," he said. "When?"

"Saturday."

"Wow. Short notice."

"Oh, they told me a long time ago. I just forgot to tell you. They're spending a couple of days here, then going up to Phoenix."

"Hmmm."

"Anyway, my mom called yesterday and said she and my dad want to take us all out to dinner Saturday. I told her that I'd ask you, but that you usually go out with Cara on Saturday nights—then my mom said to bring Cara, she'd love to meet her."

Olsen stared out the window over Ben's head.

"My roommate's coming, too," Ben said. "You know, to dinner with us."

Olsen sipped his coffee again, and swallowed carefully. "Where are they staying?"

"My parents? The resort down the road. Some of my friends are probably working in the restaurant there on Saturday night."

Olsen stretched. "Sure, sounds great. I'd love to see your mom and dad. Cara and I don't have any special plans Saturday."

He drove into Tucson the next day, went to the best jewelry stores, but didn't find what he was looking for.

Tuesday he drove to Phoenix. The shopping gave him a throbbing headache, but he came home with what he wanted.

Wednesday night he called Cara. "I have a surprise for you. Can I come over later?" When he arrived at her house at midnight, she opened the door in her white velour bathrobe, and they went in the living room. Cara unwrapped the package he gave her, and Antony and Cleopatra played on the living room rug with the ribbons. She opened the velvet box and found a diamond choker, a tiara for her throat, the throat he loved to kiss. She looked up at Olsen, blushing with surprise.

"Do you want to try it on?" he asked. Cara held the box out to him, and he lifted the necklace from its velvet bed. She untied her bathrobe, let it fall to the floor, stood before Olsen for a minute, with a cat smile like Cleopatra's. Then she turned for him, and lifted her hair up off her neck.

The shopping had been worth it.

On Saturday night, they dressed for dinner. Cara wore her new necklace. They stopped at Turbin Hall to get Ben and Brian, both dressed in ties and sport coats, then drove to the resort to meet Wendling and Mary.

Olsen was aiming for a spirit of insouciance, found it easier than he thought. His first glimpse of Mary was the only one that stung. She smiled at Olsen across the restaurant lobby with no trace of their history on her face, and he felt sucker-punched—then in the next moment realized it didn't matter: he had Cara now, and he had Ben. Mary was over. He felt giddy, confident, ready to party; he grabbed Cara around the waist and kissed her. Then they crossed the lobby and he introduced Cara to Mary and Wendling, who cranked Olsen's arm robustly but kept Mary fastened to him with a grip around her waist.

The restaurant was jammed and noisy with Saturday night revelers and live music, a pianist and a jazz singer. In the confusion, their group of six was seated at a table for eight by the windows. Their waiter swept the extra settings away. Cara ended up in between Mary and Wendling, opposite Olsen and Ben and his roommate Brian.

Ben and Brian, flanking Olsen, leaned behind his chair to talk, laughing loudly with their Tucson State friends who were working that night; and there was Wendling across the table from him, yacking and yukking it up, and Olsen not listening to him but nodding his head.

Mary and Cara, sitting side by side, seemed to have struck up an instantaneous friendship, something Olsen had not expected. Mary's red dress swept low in the front, her gold cross on its fine chain catching the light; Olsen watched her lips moving as she talked to Cara; he couldn't hear her over the currents of song and conversation. Occasionally Mary glanced at him and smiled, and once when she sipped her wine, she looked at Olsen and licked her lips, but he thought she must not have realized.

He directed his attentions to Cara, too; she looked at him while fingering her new necklace, mouthing words to him that looked sweet but which he couldn't make out over the noise.

Olsen had never imagined Cara and Mary as friends. However, something very strange was happening: Cara and Mary were becoming bosom buddies, and fast, and there was nothing Olsen could do except watch them through the sheen of the evening. It seemed to Olsen that Cara and Mary were sitting very close to each other, looking in each other's eyes, talking, smiling; then he realized they were also looking around the restaurant, laughing with Wendling and Ben and Brian, listening to the music, not as intent on each other as he was in watching them.

They ate dinner, and drank more as they ate, and Olsen had at least two too many beers. Olsen thought he saw Wendling peering into the shadow at Cara's neckline as he sat beside her.

Then Cara turned toward Mary, leaning into her as they talked, apparently so Mary could hear her through all the restaurant noise; Mary nodding as she listened.

Then Olsen saw Mary's eyes on Cara's necklace; she was admiring it, asking about it. Cara lifted the necklace up from her throat toward Mary, and Mary took it in her fingers and looked at the diamonds as Olsen watched.

Then Mary let the necklace down, softly, on Cara's skin. She turned and leaned closer to Cara, and whispered something in her ear. Olsen could hear

Ben's voice, and Brian's, behind him. His heart was pounding in his ears, he could feel the pounding racing through him, spinning in his head—then his eyes darted toward Wendling, who seemed to have been watching him. Wendling jolted Olsen with a wink, and Olsen couldn't quite interpret his expression—a "we're two lucky bastards" leer? Olsen fought an undertow of vertigo, focusing on Ben, diving into conversation with him—classes, basketball, summer plans, anything.

Eventually the beer began evaporating and the mists in Olsen's mind lifted, leaving his scalp damp. Then they drank coffee and the beer wore off completely and Olsen's ears stopped ringing. He knew that he and Mary talked a little across the white linens that stretched between them, although he didn't remember what they said. Eventually it was time to go; they made their way into the restaurant lobby, but Olsen never even got close to Mary; Wendling had attached his arm around her waist again.

After all their good-byes, Olsen turned to follow Cara to the door, then he heard Mary's voice behind him, just barely:

You linger in me.

When Olsen whirled around, Mary was there, smiling at him, Wendling was in the background shaking hands with Ben, and somewhere behind Olsen, Cara called out, "Goodnight, Mary—let's keep in touch!" and Mary called back, "Yes, let's."

After they dropped Ben and Brian off at Turbin Hall, Olsen was going to say, "I used to be in love with her, you know," and tell Cara the whole story. But Cara would lay some neat, tidy, Ph.D. in psychology analysis on it; and he knew it was not so black and white, not so simple, although he wished it were.

Olsen drove them back to his house. They went inside, and Olsen carried Cara into the darkness of his bedroom, but he did not whisper to her when he lay down beside her; he did not say her name as he ran one fingertip along the diamond necklace, or when he closed his eyes and began to stroke her skin.

*   *   *

Back in the breakfasts of his freshman year, Ben had still worn the soft edges of boyhood on his face; he had argued against the validity of core curriculum requirements; wondered if he should take advantage of the many credit-card offers in his campus mail; complained about his campus job—the Admissions counselor wanted Ben to call prospective students three nights a week, but often didn't show up to unlock the Admissions office door.

Olsen had told Ben that core requirements made some sense, that it behooved a person to be as broadly educated as possible, that specialists paint themselves into corners. He had advised Ben to lay off the credit cards till he got rich after graduation (and even then to pay off the balance every month); he had promised he would check into the Admissions problem. After that, Ben had said, the door was always open when he showed up for work.

Then somewhere along the way, Ben started calling Olsen Tom instead of Coach. And as he walked the path of time, the gait of Ben's youth, springy and freeform, slowed to a pace of casual power, his torso and shoulders and arms filling out from adolescent muscle to the brawn of maturity, surprising Olsen after semester breaks and summer vacations. Ben began to argue larger questions with a contemplative inner eye: the rights of indigenous peoples; the ethics of his intended major, archaeology. Olsen watched as Ben talked, noticed how Ben's jaw had squared and broadened, how his voice rang deep and steady, the malleable boyish undertone gone.

The biggest change in Ben, the one that unsettled Olsen, was his spiritual metamorphosis. Churchgoing was all over, certainty had ended; Ben was solely one-on-one with God, and everything had become a question. Olsen missed the old Ben of Indian River days, the tattooed kid who went to church with his school buddies, who taught Olsen that church is the cafeteria and God is the food, who once said, "My mom's praying for you," and trusted it would make a difference.

Or had it all been a figment of the pedestal?

That was when Olsen stopped trying to spin faith out of thin air, straw into gold. He was too old, he decided; too jaded for real faith to get through to him; that was why it had never worked. But he did keep thinking about it, and wondering; and at odd times—he could be running a basketball practice, lying beside Cara, driving at night along Tucson highways—words flashed through Olsen's mind in Mary's handwriting.

If I make my bed in the depths, you are there

Do not fear, only believe

🍁   🍁   🍁

He woke up in his recliner, looked at the living room clock through the haze of sleep: six fifty-six. **Cara and I are engaged,** he remembered. **And there's**

something wrong with Ben. He got up slowly, pushing the recliner in, went to the kitchen and put on a pot of coffee.

An hour later, Ben was sitting in Olsen's living room with a mug in his hand and darker circles than the day before under his eyes.

"Ben," said Olsen.

Ben took a long sip of coffee. He tipped his head against the back of the couch and looked up at the ceiling.

"My parents just got divorced," he said.

CHAPTER 24

❀

Tell Me

Ben sat on the couch with his coffee and told Olsen the story.

He had gone home for summer vacation in May and arrived to a changed world: his father had initiated divorce proceedings and moved out of their house on Dover Drive. By early August, his parents' marriage was officially over.

"What happened?" Olsen asked. He feared the worst: Mary in love with another man. But that wasn't the case.

"My father had a girlfriend. She's young—only eight years older than me. She worked with my dad at the building department. Turns out they were having an affair since my junior year at Indian River. And now they're already married, even though my parents' divorce was only final a few weeks ago.

"My father's life for the last four years has been totally built on lies. All those nights and weekends he claimed to be slaving for the city, he was actually at his girlfriend's apartment—including the weekend you and my mom and I went to Tri-State and you saved my life, remember?

"My father says he has nothing to apologize for. He says my mother never really loved him, that he doesn't hold it against her, but now he deserves some real happiness after all these years and everything he's done for her and me. He said he's sorry for hurting me, but I should be mature enough to handle real life. He said I should forgive him and try to understand.

"My mother said he should have told her a long time ago how he felt, so they could have worked the problems out, or ended everything before all these lies got going. She said he always seemed so happy and devoted, a real family man. My father said if she had been paying attention, she would have known something was wrong, that he had always felt like an outsider in his own supposed family. He said his new wife is going to change all that for him.

"One night when I was at home, I heard them arguing in the living room. My mom said, I don't care what you do to me, but how could you do this to Ben? And my dad said if she was going to harp on his behavior, he would go ahead and spread the truth about my illegitimate arrival in the world. That's what he called it—can you believe it? But my mom said she would spare him the trouble and just tell everyone the real story herself, like she wished she'd done a long time ago. Then she went upstairs to her bedroom and closed the door.

"I was so mad, I was furious, and I stormed in the living room ready to fight him—but he was sitting in the chair, crying into his hands. I didn't know what to do. But when he looked up at me, I walked away. Walked right out the front door and all the way across town to Indian River Park. Didn't come home till the middle of the night.

"Another day I asked him how he could face God, call himself a Christian, call himself a father. At first he didn't say anything. Then he said Lutherans were a sorry bunch of tight-assed holier-than-thou's determined not to enjoy life, and he was glad to get away from them and start fresh.

"I said, Forget about the Lutherans, what about God? But he just shrugged. He said he'd always been on the outside looking in, but now he was the center of attention. With his new wife, he meant. I told him, Dad, you were never an outsider, you're my father, and I love you, always have. But he didn't say anything, just looked sad and turned away.

"My dad said it was all my mom's fault because she never really loved him, so her life had been just as much a lie as his.

"My mom said it wasn't true that she never loved him. She said she did love him, and still does, and even though she wasn't perfect she had been a good wife to him. But he didn't care.

"I was so mad the last time I saw him, I said, Dad, when I look back on the last four years of my life, you are the lie that casts a darkness over every happy memory. And my dad said, I don't blame you, and I'm sorry. Then he and his new wife moved to the other side of Indianapolis, where they already have new jobs. My dad says that when my mom sells our house on Dover Drive, she can keep half the money. He didn't take much of our furniture. He wants to start fresh—that's what he keeps saying.

"My mom's been working full-time at the library since I started college, but now she wants to change jobs. She wants to work at a pregnancy center in Indianapolis or something. She keeps apologizing to me for what happened, even though it's not her fault. She gave me a poem. She printed it and put it in a silver frame. 'Wild Geese,' it's called. But it's not a nature poem—it's about life. I'll show you sometime."

Ben finished his coffee; lay down on the sofa. And Olsen felt himself plunged back into Indian River, even as he sat there in Tucson in the old recliner—the same chair in which, two thousand miles ago, he lounged and listened to Jimi Hendrix and drank a million bottles of beer and plotted ways to get closer to Mary; the same chair where he had mourned the emptiness of a life without her, and then moved on.

"Jesus, Ben," said Olsen.

"I know." Ben's broad forearm rested over his eyes.

"Why didn't you call me from home, tell me what was going on this summer?"

"Guess I hoped my dad would change his mind."

"I want to help you," said Olsen. "First things first: how are you for money? Do you need any? Just name it. How about your bill with the college?"

"I'm fine," Ben said. "My scholarship's full tuition, and I get free room and board now because I'm an RA."

"What about pocket money? Books?"

"I'm good, I think. Earned enough at the rec department this summer."

"How about your mother? Does she need anything? Is anybody helping her out, helping her keep up the house and yard and bills and all?"

"Oh, yeah. Mr. and Mrs. Rakowsky stopped over a lot this summer. Abby came from Fort Wayne for a week, too. My mom's going to sell our house and get something smaller for us."

"I never imagined your father pulling something like this," Olsen said. "He doesn't seem the type."

"That's how he fooled everyone."

Olsen was sipping coffee from his favorite mug, the one Mary had given him.

"I wish my mom weren't all alone back in Indian River," Ben said. "She says she doesn't mind. But I hate the thought of what she's going through."

"I don't like it either," said Olsen. "But remember, your mother is very strong." He wrapped both hands around the mug. "I'll call her later, say hello, see if I can do anything to help out."

Then Olsen made more coffee and a couple of omelets for them. Ben turned the stereo to a hard rock station and turned the volume up: it was Metallica Weekend, raw noise, the perfect jarring soundtrack for the day. They ate together at the kitchen table. Olsen looked at the gray shadows under Ben's eyes, wedges like bruises from an assailant he couldn't outdo; and his throat swelled with the bulk of his rage at Wendling.

Later Olsen said, "I'll drive you back to Turbin—we'll just throw your bike in the Blazer." On the road back to campus, he told Ben, "I'm gonna hang tough with you on this. I can't fix it, but I can promise you that you won't have to go through it alone. And I'm old enough to know that makes a difference."

Olsen glanced over at Ben, saw the edges of boyhood on his face again. When Ben said, "Thanks, Tom," his voice shook.

That night Olsen called Rakowsky, who said he prided himself on his bullshit detector, which had totally failed him in Wendling's case, so he was disgusted not only with Wendling but with himself for being fooled; he said the Calvary people had rallied around Mary and Ben with one hundred percent support, and that Mary would come through this and be better off without Wendling.

Before they hung up, Olsen said, "Why didn't you tell me about this when I talked to you over the summer?"

"It was their business," Rakowsky said. "Not for me to be telling. And I almost didn't believe it myself. Guess I kept thinking Wendling would come to his senses."

"Yeah," said Olsen. He looked out the window at the Tucson afternoon. "Nobody in Indian River keeps in touch with me anymore. I never hear from people at the high school except you. I don't even know what happened to Mr. McCormick, the little old man who lived next door to me on Roanoke Road."

"Well, you are a couple thousand miles away. But I'll try to keep you on the grapevine better."

"By the way," said Olsen, "Cara and I just got engaged."

"Finally!" Rakowsky laughed. "Congratulations. When's the wedding?"

"I don't know yet—we haven't set a date."

After Olsen clicked off with Rakowsky, he dialed Mary. He didn't have to look the number up in his book. One ring…Two rings…

"Hello?" Mary answered, and all the months and miles fell away.

"Mary," he said, "it's Thomas. Tom Olsen."

He could feel her fingers holding tightly to her receiver, before she said, "You've talked to Ben."

"Mary," he said. "I can't believe what's happened…" His tongue froze; all his carefully planned words of support and comfort disappeared from his mind, and he thought he could hear her crying. She was defenseless; he was helpless; and Wendling was to blame.

Then the words fired from his lips before he could stop them: "That son of a bitch—I can't believe what he's done—the way he's hurt you and Ben—he needs to answer for this—selfish lying goddam son of a bitch! Mary, he never deserved you."

"Oh, Thomas," she said, "we did have problems, but I love Virgil—he's a good man—he was, I don't know what happened to him—I thought he loved me, too, and especially Ben. How could he throw our family away like this, as if we didn't matter?"

"I don't know, but I know he's a fool. He should be ashamed of what he's done, how he's treated you and Ben."

"My heart was so far away from him sometimes, and that's my fault—but I love him, I really do."

"He doesn't deserve your love!" Olsen said. His voice reverberated into the receiver, vibrated against his face. "Maybe he did rescue you and Ben, in some ways—but then he made you both live a lie all those years, as you had something to be ashamed of! And yet look what *he* was doing!"

"I know," said Mary, "but still, if not for Virgil, who knows what would have happened to Ben and me! Then—this bombshell—the lies—God help me. I'm afraid—I…"

"Mary, what can I do?" said Olsen. "Let me help you."

"I don't care what happens to me," she said, "but when I think about yesterday—when I took Ben to the airport—the look on his face: a sad boy looking at me through a man's eyes, and the past pushing him into a future he can't see. Thomas, I could barely let him go."

They talked for a while, about Ben, and selling the house on Dover Drive, about Tucson, and basketball, and Olsen's promotion; then Mary asked about Cara. It seemed a graceless time to mention the engagement, so Olsen just said she was fine.

After he hung up with Mary, Olsen called Cara and said, "Sorry I'm running so late—here I come," and drove to her house.

Later that night, he lay under the covers beside Cara; Antony and Cleopatra lounged at the foot of the bed. Olsen said, "Remember Ben's parents, Mary and Virgil? We had dinner with them at the resort a couple of years ago?"

"Sure," Cara said.

"They got divorced this summer."

"What happened?"

"Turns out Virgil Wendling had a secret girlfriend for years, and decided to marry her."

"Wow." Cara twirled a blonde strand of hair in her fingers, her diamond ring flashing in the light of the bedside lamp. "How's Ben taking it?"

"Taking it very hard—Virgil had been lying to him and Mary for years! Virgil was very active in his church, too—a deacon. Pretended to be Mr. Upstanding Citizen. Ben and Mary are devastated."

"This is so typical," said Cara.

"What do you mean?"

"Using a Christian façade to conceal his illicit sexual activity. It's textbook behavior. I could have written a dissertation on it. In fact, one of my colleagues at UA did."

Olsen stopped. Wendling could go to hell, but Ben and Mary were not dissertation data.

At the foot of the bed, Antony licked a paw; Cleopatra flicked her tail.

Olsen turned the light out.

Cara said, "Now that I look back on that night we had dinner, I can see some of the signs were there. Virgil spent a good portion of the evening looking at my cleavage, for one thing." She laughed, and twirled another strand of hair. "Couple that," she said, "with all his possessiveness of Mary, all that touching and fawning—please! And Mary didn't seem to return the feeling. I should have known something was afoot. But I didn't think we'd ever see them again. I really didn't give it another thought."

"Anyway," said Olsen, "I don't want to get into analyzing it. The thing is, I'm worried about Ben."

"Would you like me to talk with him? He could stop by the counseling center and set up a time to meet with me."

"Well, I don't know." That wasn't what Olsen had meant. He had only wanted Cara's sympathetic ear, not her clinical intervention, but that was too blunt to say with the diamond so fresh on her finger. "I don't know about your Christian angle," he said instead. "Nobody wants to think about their parents' sex lives, either. So what do you think you'd say to him?"

"I'd let him give voice to his feelings—he needs to face that grief, that sadness, and not let it intimidate him into denial or some kind of emotional shutdown. I wouldn't get into analyzing his parents. Look," said Cara, "Ben's an upbeat, savvy, loving kid. He'll come out of this just fine, but some guidance would help anyone in a time like this."

"I'll tell him he can call you," Olsen said. "But if he does, just, you know, be careful with him." Mary's words ran through his mind: *sad boy looking through a man's eyes…how could Virgil throw our family away?* "I could kill Wendling for hurting Ben like this." He surprised himself with the snarl in his voice.

There was scurried shuffling at his feet, and the bed felt suddenly lighter; Antony and Cleopatra had fled.

Cara didn't answer Olsen immediately, but she did stop twirling her hair. "That's a lot of emotion," she said. "Are you sure you're okay?"

Olsen closed his eyes.

"Lies," he said. "Lies, and truth that's never spoken, and things that don't matter hogging the conversation for a lifetime—is it any wonder the world is falling apart?"

Cara lay beside him, not moving.

A minute or two ticked past. Then Cara rolled toward Olsen and lay her head on his chest. "Tom," she whispered, "I know how much you love Ben. I'm positive he'll come through this fine."

Olsen didn't answer, but opened his eyes and lay awake for a long time, staring through the darkness at the ceiling. He felt better in the morning.

He never mentioned the counseling idea to Ben.

The fall of Ben's junior year rolled on and immersed Olsen into varsity preseason—Branigan's promise of all basketball, all year round, had come true—but he always found time for phone conversations with Mary. They called each other often. And he soon stopped worrying that he was neglecting Cara, because she was busier than he was. She was teaching two courses, advising five Psych majors, counseling on campus Tuesday and Thursdays and in Tucson on Saturdays. Cara was also drafting a research project and a book proposal, tentatively titled "Why Love Dies," on the subject of failed romantic relationships, plotting the course of her clinical study with an old friend and colleague from UA's graduate psych program.

Cara found endless real-life fodder for her new field of inquiry in the students she counseled and her clients in Tucson. Many nights, she regaled Olsen with anonymous details of love gone down the tubes—death by unmet expectations, diverging goals, decaying bliss, the lure of greener pastures. This accumulation of unhappy endings disturbed him.

Cara was unperturbed, even enthusiastic, as her body of work took shape; it was, after all, her profession to research such things. Olsen asked if her book would propose solutions, and Cara said it might, in the last chapter. Olsen told her she might be violating some kind of confidentiality rule by telling him those gory details night after night, but Cara said no, not as long as she didn't tell him anybody's name.

He wished she had picked a different topic.

That was also the fall when Ben gave Jasmine the ring, a small square-cut sapphire, set in a band of silver; a piece of sky for her, Ben said. They had been dating for two years, like Olsen and Cara.

Jasmine was an English major, a junior like Ben, an RA in O'Keefe House. When she joined them for Sunday breakfast, the ongoing tradition, she and Ben still laughed and teased and started each other's sentences; she impressed Olsen with her mind and her kindness; she curled up under the shelter of Ben's arm and gazed at the piece of sky on her finger.

One autumn afternoon at the Skyhawk athletic complex, Olsen sat with his feet up on the desk, reading a scouting report in his basketball office. He heard a girl's voice: "Coach Olsen?" and looked up.

"Jasmine," he said. "Hi." He swung his feet down off the desk and swiveled his chair toward the open door.

"May I come in for a minute?" she asked.

"Sure, come on in. What can I do for you? Is everything all right?"

Jasmine sat down. A stream of Skyhawk basketball players passed by Olsen's door heading toward the weight room, talking loudly, laughing with each other. Then they vanished, and the hall was silent.

"Ben told me how you once saved his life," Jasmine said.

Olsen leaned back in his chair. "Yes, I guess I did."

"He told me not to say anything to you about it because you'd be too embarrassed—but I had to thank you."

"I don't deserve the credit—I always feel like God commandeered me that night and did the saving through me."

Jasmine took a deep breath. She held her backpack in her lap, her hands clasped around it. "The first time Ben and I met, in our freshman year here, it was like we recognized each other. We both felt it. It was like before we were even born, we knew each other, and it was only a matter of time and God and destiny until we found each other here. Here on earth, you know—in this life." She looked at Olsen, her eyes wide. "Do you know what I mean?"

He swiveled his chair, put his feet back up on the desk. "Yes," he said. "I do know."

"Then when Ben told me how you saved him, I thought, what if Coach Olsen hadn't been there—what if he hadn't been that courageous, or known what to do? And I realized that if it weren't for you, I would have gone through my whole life searching for something I had already lost! A life without Ben would have been the worst, most endless torture—like eternal purgatory, or Dante's *Inferno*, or something. I know that some people would say I wouldn't have even known anything was missing—that I would have just met and fallen in love with someone else. But they're wrong. So I had to thank you."

"There would have been a huge hole in my life, too, without Ben," Olsen said. "He's the son I never had. Child of my heart, I call him sometimes—to myself, that is—don't tell him I said that," he added quickly. "I don't think I ever said that out loud!" He felt the heat spreading across his face.

Jasmine said, "You should say it out loud to Ben sometime. He always tells me he doesn't know what he'd do without you, especially with everything that's going on with his dad. He told me you're like a father to him."

"Yeah?"

"He said you like poetry," Jasmine said, shifting her backpack in her lap.

"I do, yeah—but don't tell Coach Branigan. Poetry isn't good for my basketball image."

"We're doing contemporary American poetry in one of my lit courses. When I first read this poem, I cried. It's by Donald T. Sanders; did you ever hear of him?" She unzipped the backpack, pulled out a piece of folded paper, handed it to Olsen. "I read it and thought, this is exactly what I have with Ben. And it never would have happened if not for you. I'll never really be able to thank you enough."

Olsen unfolded the sheet of paper, curious, and skimmed the photocopy.

Love Tells Us Who We Are
…We are No one
Before Love
A missing clue looking
For a Person
A Star looking for
A sky
An "I am" waiting for
An I…
Before You I was Nothing But

When You Gave me Your Hand
I took My Hand
For Love Tells Us Who
We Are So
When I asked the
Answer "Who?"
Love Answered
You.

He looked up, but Jasmine was gone. Read the whole poem, slipped it in his center desk drawer. Stood up and sighed. Then he walked down the hall to the weight room.

❦   ❦   ❦

Olsen told Cara about his phone conversations with Mary, because he had nothing to hide, and because Cara said she liked to hear what they had talked about, since the vagaries of suburban Indiana constituted another planet to her. One evening in October, when Cara was at Olsen's house, the telephone rang, and it was Mary.

After Olsen had talked to her for a few minutes, he felt Cara's irritation and said, "Hey, I bet Cara would love to say hi," and gave the phone to her, then went into the dining room and pretended to transcribe basketball scouting notes at the table as he listened: first some pleasantries and chitchat, then Cara said, "Did Tom tell you the wonderful news?...We're engaged...Since August...No, we haven't set the date yet...Thank you so much, that's very kind...Yes, I hope you can make it out here...We'll keep you posted. 'Bye now."

Cara came into the dining room and stood beside his chair. She said, "You didn't tell her?"

Olsen shrugged. "I was going to. It just never seemed like the right time, after all the pain she's been through—pain she doesn't deserve."

Cara said, "If I didn't know better, I'd think you were in love with her," and laughed.

"We're friends. We've known each other for years," Olsen said.

"And it doesn't hurt that she's so beautiful, does it?"

The old fire shot up, burning and unbidden, through Olsen's body, fire for Mary, so he quickly said, "She is—but not as beautiful as you," and pulled Cara into his lap, and kissed her.

"You need to stop feeling sorry for her…You'll hold her back with all that sympathy and coddling…Let her get on with her life," Cara said, between his kisses, but he didn't answer; instead he swept her up in his arms and into the bedroom.

Later Olsen told her, "Don't be jealous of Mary," and Cara said, "Jealousy is a useless emotion." He said, "Don't be so hard on her. It hasn't been easy for Mary, but she's one of the best people I've ever known—and the greatest mother." Cara said, "I'll be right back. I'm thirsty;" got out of bed; went into the kitchen.

A week later, Cara called Olsen to say Mary had sent a lovely card and an engagement gift to Cara's house: a gorgeous handblown glass vase from a gallery in Chicago.

"Pandora's Gallery?" Olsen asked.

"Yes."

"That's where Mary got my coffee mug—the one I always use," he said; "the big one, glazed in gold, with that cool handle."

Cara said, "She's so determined to inject herself into our lives."

His grip on the cordless phone tightened. "What do you mean?"

"Come on, Tom."

"You come on. What are you talking about, *inject herself*? What does that mean?"

"You and I have talked about this behavior pattern in some of my cases. The relationship fails, but one person can't let go. Of course, you and Mary didn't have a romantic relationship, but you and she are very close because of Ben. It's a funny situation. Unique."

Olsen's knuckles turned white around the receiver. He walked into his bedroom with the phone. "What is your problem?" he said. "Mary and I are friends. She doesn't have to 'let go.' Why can't you understand that?"

"She depends on you too much," Cara said, her tone calm. "She's clinging to the past, something she imagined she had with you. She needs to move forward."

"How do you know what Mary needs?" Olsen said.

"She needs to let Ben go, and let you go, too," Cara said. "She needs build a new life for herself. Way back there in Indiana. Two thousand miles away."

"You know what?" Olsen said. "I'm late for practice. Talk to you tomorrow." He hung up the phone, lay down on the bed, and closed his eyes.

❦   ❦   ❦

One Saturday night in November, the last weekend before the floodgates of basketball season officially opened, Branigan and Priscilla had Olsen and Cara over for dinner.

"I'm so excited about your wedding!" Priscilla said as the four of them sat in the solarium, drinks in hand, watching the sun drop through the sky behind the mountains. She reached for Cara's hand and looked at the ring again. "Still gorgeous. And of course, I still take full matchmaking credit for having introduced you two! Have you set the date?"

"No," said Cara, "we just haven't had the chance." Olsen felt Cara looking at him, so he added, "No, not yet," smiling but preoccupied; he had been wondering how Mary was, and planning to call her the next day.

The solarium sat silent.

"You know how it is at the start of basketball season," said Cara. "I'm sure we'll have time to plan everything once things settle down a bit. It's crazy right now."

"Crazy, sure," said Branigan. He chewed his cold cigar. "You'll probably wait till May or June. That's when all basketball coaches get married."

Olsen sipped his beer. "Yeah," he said.

"When's your anniversary?" Cara asked.

"June 1st," said Priscilla. "And this time it'll be twenty-five years."

"Wow! Sounds like Hawaiian vacation time," Cara said, and she and Priscilla clinked glasses.

"Ben Wendling's parents had been married twenty years," said Olsen, staring out the windows. "They just got divorced this summer. Can you imagine? Half a lifetime with someone—gone up in flames. The dad had a secret mistress for years—and married her two weeks after the divorce from Ben's mother. Ben is devastated. And poor Mary. She's an incredible person—and the world's greatest mother. Ben is certainly a testament to that."

The room returned to silence.

"Well, that's very sad," Priscilla said. "I'm so glad Ben has you to look after him out here. I trust his mother will pull through. But it sounds like a terrible shock."

"Secret mistress," Branigan said. He laid his cigar in the ashtray and took a long drink of his scotch, the ice clinking as he swallowed. He looked at Priscilla. "I confess, dear, that I have a secret mistress, too. Her name...is Bee Ball." Branigan guffawed and stuck the cigar back in his mouth, and Priscilla shook her head, laughing.

"Mary had to have known, on some level, that her husband had a mistress," Cara said. "She was either in denial, or didn't care, or hoped the affair would end on its own so she wouldn't have to confront the situation. Ben needs to realize that. It wouldn't be healthy for him to cast his father unequivocally as the devil and his mother as the saint. In a case like this, both spouses share some of the responsibility."

Olsen looked at Cara, narrowing his eyes. "Mary is not a case," he said. "Ben and Mary are family to me." He put his beer down quietly on the coffee table. "Just because someone's in a bad situation doesn't make them responsible for it."

The timer beeped in the kitchen.

"Oh, good," said Priscilla, "dinner's ready."

When Olsen drove Cara home later, he said nothing; his thoughts, breath, body still smoldered. He pulled into her driveway and sat, silent, with the engine running; he was irked to see Antony and Cleopatra watching them from the living room window.

"Why do I still get the feeling that I'm competing with Mary for your affections?" Cara asked.

"I don't know," said Olsen. "Maybe you should psychoanalyze yourself the way you do to everybody else."

Cara sighed. "I don't know why you've been treating me this way," she said. "I think it's some kind of subconscious fear you're experiencing—a fear of commitment, fear that our love won't stand the test of time—so you're trying to drive me away—subconsciously testing—"

"See, this is part of the problem," Olsen said. "You've gotten so damn clinical—everyone has become a *case* to you—even me." He laughed—one sardonic syllable. "If you really knew me, really knew everything about me, and everything that goes on inside my head—you'd find out I'm the worst case you've ever known. You think I'm as perfect as *you*?" He laughed again, another lone syllable, then his voice rose along with his anger. "You think you know all the reasons people do the things they do? You've got it down to such a science? That kind of arrogance—it's dangerous, Cara. What about God, and destiny, and the mysteries of the human spirit? Is there any room for them in your philosophy?"

Cara stared at him, her eyebrows high with surprise on her forehead.

"Listen," said Olsen, "you can stop trying to tear Mary down. Here's something your textbooks won't tell you: there is nothing you can say about Mary that would turn me against her. You don't know what her life has been like. And no matter how many studies you perform and books you write, you will never understand what it's been like for her."

Olsen stared straight ahead toward the garage at the end of Cara's driveway. Then he said, "Mary is Ben's mother. The two of them will be part of my life forever. But I love *you*, Cara. We're getting married. I've pledged the rest of my days to you. Isn't that enough?"

He leaned back against the headrest and closed his eyes, not caring how she reacted. He expected she would pronounce some diagnosis on his anger, or dissect his verbiage to illustrate his neuroses, or storm out of the Blazer and slam the door behind her.

Instead, Cara sat quietly beside him.

Then she said, "Tom, I'm sorry;" but he didn't reply.

"I always say jealousy is a useless emotion," Cara went on, "but I'm jealous of Mary. Simple as that. And I took advantage of another chance to make her look bad in your eyes—and in Dan and Priscilla's eyes. I'm sorry. There's something in the way you talk about her that makes me feel like I could lose you. And it terrifies me."

Olsen opened his eyes and reached across the seat and took her hand. "You will never lose me," he said.

She looked at him, her eyes uncertain. "And you're right," she said, "Maybe I have gotten too clinical. I haven't been fair to Mary, or to you, or to your friendship," she said, looking like she might cry. "I'm sorry."

Olsen squeezed her hand. "It's all right."

"I love you, Tom."

"I love you, too."

Olsen did not lean over to kiss her, just stroked her hand, his thoughts distant. Cara slid across the seat, and touched him in a way that began to bring him back to her, and the harshness of the evening dissolved away.

They decided that Olsen would not spend the night; when Cara reached her front door, she turned to him and waved; Antony and Cleopatra disappeared from the living room window. Olsen drove away. Eventually he found himself over the rivers and west of the city in Tucson Mountain Park. He drove for miles, parked far off the road, got out and started walking through the cold, following the path of moonlight.

He loved Cara. He had been resurrected by her love and friendship, her lust and brains, into peace he never thought he'd have.

And he loved Mary.

If he wanted a sign, a lightning bolt, he had it: he had planned to propose to Cara on her birthday, September 30th, then suddenly decided to give her the diamond ring on that August night when they returned to Tucson from their Hilton Head vacation with Louise—so that hours later, when he found out about Mary, his honor was already sealed.

If I knew then what I know now...

It was a question he could not ask, and could not answer.

The irony weighed on him as he walked under the moon. Mary had brought Ben into the world, into Olsen's world. She had done the right thing by ending it with Olsen before it began, for Ben's sake—while Wendling had been secretly doing the wrong thing and turning the family into a time bomb. And now Ben was with Olsen, Olsen was with Cara, Wendling was with his new bride—and Mary was alone.

And there was nothing he could do.

He waited to see if the moonlight or the irony would change his mind. But after a while, he walked back across the rocky sand and drove home.

CHAPTER 25

❊

It's Whatever You Want It To Be

As the winds blew colder, time began to sand the rough edges off of Olsen's distress, and the days resumed their steady pace; no more wandering through grim interior plains in his dreams, awakening to vague discontent, walking through miles of his life with his feet beneath him but his mind far away. The fall had been surreal; but he was waking back up to the landscape of his real life: Cara, Tucson, basketball, and Ben.

Skyhawk basketball travels became the map of his weeks as November unfurled. Flung on the road with kindred athletes, with the team mostly winning and Branigan mostly happy, with days and nights stringing into one long conversation about basketball, Olsen relaxed back into the embrace of his old and faithful friend, the season.

Ben was better, too; apparently he had already moved beyond the shock phase of Mary and Wendling's divorce. He seemed strangely, to Olsen, peaceful; he seemed to have wrestled his anguish into submission, and quickly. Denial, Olsen presumed. That false sense of serenity—like when those frozen fingers suddenly feel toasty warm right before they drop off your hands from frostbite. Ben's self-possession seemed authentic; Olsen didn't detect the distracted, edgy undertone he knew so well in himself. But he was certain he sensed Ben's fatigue, and decided it was time for a pep talk.

Olsen told him, "Life is like a story, you know, and all my life I've been asking, what do I want my story to be? We can't control the catastrophes, the bad luck and bitter pills—but it's all about taking a stand for yourself, reaching inside for that inner strength, rallying your inner warrior into battle. Refusing to take the bad lying down but staying one step ahead of it, believing you deserve the best and fighting for it—making the decision every day that you're gonna fight against anything that tries to tear you down. Don't be like me—I spent most of my life just waiting for the world to end—then when I found some things I really wanted to live for, I didn't know how to fight to make them mine."

"It doesn't matter what happened before," Ben said, "and it doesn't matter what happens later. God gave us free will. Whatever happens, you don't have to fight it—you can just keep writing your own story, your own way, no matter what's going on around you. And it's never too late; you just make your life exactly what you want it to be, starting today. Like my mom says—Begin; the rest is easy."

"I don't think it's that simple," said Olsen.

"It's whatever you want it to be. And now that I know that, everything is different."

❧   ❧   ❧

It was December and Ben had gone home to spend Christmas vacation with Mary in Indian River. The Skyhawks stayed in town for the Tucson Holiday Classic the week between Christmas and New Year's.

The morning of December 28 was cool and sunny. Olsen changed the oil in the Blazer. At lunchtime, he brought his mail inside, leafed through the envelopes as he walked to the dining room table.

Alexandra?

A letter from Alexandra.

Her name was still Alexandra Muro, according to the return label, but the address was in San Diego.

The white envelope felt as if it held several pages.

She had written Olsen's name and address in her distantly familiar, neat, square, all-caps printing.

She had used a Madonna and Child Christmas stamp.

What did she want?

For God's sake.

How many years?

Twenty-two years.

Olsen put that envelope on the dining room table; opened the rest of his mail; stood at his kitchen sink and drank two bottles of beer quickly.

When he looked back over his shoulder toward the dining room, Alexandra's letter was still there.

What the hell did she want?

Couldn't be anything good.

What was there to say after a baby they had called off together and a wedding he had called off all on his own? Alexandra had said everything to him twenty-two years ago. He did not need to hear it again.

He drank another bottle of beer.

Then a thought hit his head as he gripped the edge of the sink and looked out the window where everything, sky, earth, the house next door, was the color of sand. Had Alexandra had the baby after all, secretly? And hidden it from him for twenty-two years? My God, maybe he had a child! That stamp she used. My God.

No. Idiot. He had driven her to the stainless steel clinic. He had sat in silence with other men in the waiting room. He had taken her home. He had slept beside her, but not with her, after that. Four months later, he had moved out.

Olsen walked to the dining room table, his head swirling, and looked down at the envelope. Her neat, squared printing. Her address in San Diego.

Couldn't be anything good.

Three beers at lunch. And now he had to get over to the Skyhawk gym to help run afternoon practice. **Shit.**

It seemed dangerous to leave Alexandra's letter lying around. What if Cara came over and let herself in? She didn't usually do that, but you never know. There's always a first time. You wouldn't think Alexandra would write him a letter after twenty-two years, either, but see—you never know. So he folded the envelope in thirds and put it in his back pocket behind his wallet, where it bulged uncomfortably.

Olsen brushed his teeth, popped three Breath Assures and drank a glass of water, started on a pack of gum.

On campus for practice, Olsen kept his distance so Branigan would be none the wiser. His back pocket burned.

Olsen couldn't get his head in the drills, told Branigan he must have eaten some bad chicken at lunch. Branigan said, "You do look a little green around the gills," and sent him home.

Olsen sat on his living room recliner, furious. He sucked down a fresh beer, furious. He took the letter out of his pocket again, and hurled it on the coffee table, furious, and realized he was going to vomit, and made it to the toilet just in time.

❦   ❦   ❦

Olsen found himself dozing facedown in bed when the phone rang later. His house was dark, his mouth rancid.

"Are you coming over?" asked Cara. "I thought we said six."

"Sorry. I'll be there soon."

Couldn't find the letter. **What did I do with it? Shit, shit, shit.**

He found it on the kitchen counter; didn't remember putting it there; but he had not opened it. Stuck it in his back pocket again.

Olsen went to the taco drive-thru, ordered a big burrito, on his way to Cara's. He parked in the lot and ate the thing from the top down while the bottom oozed out like slop into the paper wrapping in his lap. Then he took Alexandra's envelope from his pocket, left it folded in thirds, and pushed it down into the burrito remains. Crumpled everything up inside the paper wrapping, stuffed it in the bag, stuffed the dirty napkins in on top. Got out of his car and walked across the parking lot and dropped it all in the garbage can.

❦   ❦   ❦

"I'm sorry," Olsen began. "I've been a real jerk. Please forgive me. Let's set a date. Let's get married in June." He put his arm around Cara's shoulders.

"Have you been drinking?" Cara asked. They were sitting on her couch.

"No," he said, "that's the burrito I ate."

"Oh," said Cara.

"So let's set the date. Let's look at the calendar. We can pick the date tonight—right now."

Antony and Cleopatra strolled into the living room. Cleopatra walked across the rug and jumped up into Cara's lap, but Antony sat on the far side of the room, looking at Olsen.

"Tom," said Cara, stroking Cleopatra's head, "I don't want this to be coming from a place of guilt, or obligation. It has to come from your heart."

"It's not guilt or obligation—it is from my heart. I just see things clearly all of a sudden, and I realize I've been unfair. Thank God you've put up with me." He reached over to pat Cleopatra, too, but she jumped off Cara's lap and ran out of the room.

"I don't know, Tom," Cara said. "You once told me that if I knew everything there is to know about you, I'd find out you're the worst case I've ever known. Maybe I should pay attention to your ominous warning."

The digesting food in his stomach lurched upward in a twist. He couldn't answer. He saw Antony eyeing him from the other side of the living room.

"You should see the look on your face!" said Cara. "I'm kidding around! What, you think I'm serious?" She laughed, and so did Olsen.

"We have the rest of our lives together," Cara said. "I can't plan a wedding in six months—especially at this critical juncture in my research and with the book proposal. Let's set our date for a year from June instead."

"If you don't think that's too far off," said Olsen.

"I think it's perfect," Cara said, and kissed him on the lips.

❧   ❧   ❧

The next morning at dawn, Olsen stood over a dying dog on the shoulder of Canyon Road.

Blood flowed from the dog's nose and mouth as it lay on its side on the asphalt, its dark eye open, staring. Guts hung down from the rip in its skinny stomach.

Olsen's hands hung at his sides, reverberating with the crash of flying steel into helplessly soft flesh trying to make it across the road in time. Olsen had seen the blur flying from the side of the road too late. The sound and feel of the hit, hateful, hateful, replayed in his body, especially his hands, like a phonograph needle hacking over and over in the groove of an scratched record.

A semi roared past on the road and Olsen shivered in the wake of its giant freezing whoosh. He was cold in the dawn air; the dog must be cold, too; it blinked slowly, in silence. It was brown, with spindly legs, and no collar. Olsen got his blue and white Skyhawks stadium blanket from the Blazer, laid it over the dog's bleeding body.

"911, what is your emergency?"

"I just hit a dog—where's an emergency clinic I can take it to? I'm on a cell phone on Canyon Road, near the Tucson State campus. We're on the shoulder right now, but I can't leave the dog here."

❦   ❦   ❦

The vet was smoking a cigarette out front, his face to the cold December sunrise, as Olsen crossed the parking lot with the dog dying in his arms, wrapped in the Skyhawks blanket.

"What happened?" the vet asked.

"He ran out in front of me on Canyon Road."

"Ouch," said the vet. "Let's go in and have a look." He held the glass door open for Olsen, pointed across the narrow lobby to a dim hallway.

The dog looked so small, to Olsen, lying on the exam table. Its eye was still open. Its nose and mouth and gut seeped blood.

The vet washed his hands, examined the dog. "He's been on his own a long time. Half-starved."

"I figured that, from the looks of him."

"He won't survive these injuries," the vet said. "I'd put him to sleep. Otherwise it could take him awhile to die."

"I was hoping he'd make it," Olsen said. "I was going to take him home with me."

"Nope," said the vet.

"I don't want him to suffer."

"You want to pay? Or is this one on me?"

"I'll pay," Olsen said.

"I'll go get what I need. Back in a sec."

Olsen crouched beside the table and looked at the dog's face, stroked its head.

"God, I'm sorry," he said. "Good boy."

The vet came back and said, "He might give a death gasp, but I doubt it." Olsen kept his hand on the dog's head, watching its shallow breathing as the vet gave the injection. The dog died quietly, with its eye open.

"Jesus," said Olsen.

"How do you want to dispose of the body? Cheapest way's the mass grave. Nothing to feel bad about." The vet closed the dog's eye, lifted its lifeless head and closed the other.

"I guess so. What else is there?"

"Mass cremation. Or cremation and you get the ashes. You probably don't want that."

"You know what?" said Olsen. "You decide. Just put it all on my bill when we square up."

"Do you want your blanket back? The disposal place only wants the bodies. They charge by weight."

"No. Could you just throw it away?"

"Do you want a few minutes with the dog?" the vet asked. "I'll go out front and write this up."

"Yes," said Olsen. "I'll be right there. Thanks." Olsen stroked the dog's head again; he realized it was dissolving the feeling of the hit from his hands.

"What was your name?" Olsen said. "Everyone should have a name."

In the parking lot, he got his cell out of the Blazer and called Branigan.

"Where the hell are you? You forget team breakfast?" Branigan shouted.

"I hit a dog on Canyon Road on the way—brought it to this emergency clinic—but it died."

"What? Just now?"

"Yeah," said Olsen.

"All right. Well, get here when you can."

"I will. I'll be there," Olsen said. He got in the Blazer, slowly, and shut the door. He looked over to where the dog had been. There was blood on the passenger seat.

❧   ❧   ❧

I did what I did.
It is what it is.
And it's over.
It has been over for twenty-two years.
Call it acceptance.
Call it release, letting go, serenity, call it whatever psychological lingo makes you happy, but I did what I did, and it's over.

It was a new lightness, it was a stripping off of the garments of guilt that had hung heavy from his shoulders for so long. It was new citizenship in a country where he had never traveled; and it made him wonder who he might have been if he had arrived there a long time ago: how differently he would have seen the world, who he would have been, and who he and Mary might have been together.

At least he had Ben; he had fought for Ben; made it up as he went along, sure; but it wasn't true that he didn't know how to fight for some of the things he really wanted.

❀   ❀   ❀

On a Sunday night in February, just back from a three-day basketball road trip, Olsen started a load of laundry, and the phone rang; it was Rakowsky.

"Hey, what rich people do you know?" Rakowsky asked.

"Why—do you need a loan?" Olsen said, walking around with the cordless phone and going to the fridge for a beer.

"No, this is about you," said Rakowsky. "So tell me. What rich people?"

"None," said Olsen. "Well, my mother, I guess. That's about it. Why?"

"Because," said Rakowsky, "our esteemed principal has given me the honor of delivering to you some very cool and mysterious news."

Olsen walked into the living room and sat down in the recliner. "What is it?"

Rakowsky cleared his throat. "A pair of anonymous donors," he said, "has just given a large amount of money in your name to Indian River High School. They ask that you personally establish criteria for The Thomas Olsen Scholarships, which you are to begin awarding this May on an annual basis until, based on the size of their donation, the end of time."

"Come on!" Olsen said, and took a long swig of beer.

"No, this is for real. Don't ya love it? It's the biggest excitement we've had in this town for ages."

"You're not kidding?"

"Nope. You've got some admirers—some rich admirers."

"Who are they?"

"Nobody knows—only the attorney who represents them, and he's sworn to secrecy."

"An attorney from Indian River?"

"No, from a big firm in Indianapolis. Lourdes, Schwartz and Bickman."

Olsen stopped and thought his way backward. Then he said, "I have no idea who these people could be. My mother's loaded, but she's only one person. And she's not a big fan of mine." Olsen didn't want to explain about Alexandra, didn't want to mention his worry that this was somehow connected to her unopened letter in a vengeful way that he couldn't figure out on the fly.

"Anyway, this is a couple," said Rakowsky. "That much we do know."

Was Alexandra married? Kept her own name? Her husband in on the game? "Why me?" Olsen asked.

"You must have had a great influence on someone's kid, and now the parents are repaying you—honoring you."

"And I design the scholarships? Set up the criteria? Anything I want?"

"Yup. It's all up to you."

❦   ❦   ❦

Once Olsen had some time to think, he didn't believe Alexandra was behind it after all. Indian River had some well-to-do families and, like many places, it surely had some families who were richer than they looked. Or maybe a kid had made it big after graduation and wanted to give something back to the community where it all started. A lot could have happened that Olsen didn't know about; he had taught and coached there for twelve years, had been gone for almost three.

The secret engaged him, amused him, confused him. But he didn't tell a soul in Tucson, partly because of his nagging paranoia about Alexandra; partly because it was one thing to ask, *Why me?* and quite another to hear, *Why you?*

By early March, Olsen had drawn up the scholarship guidelines and submitted them as required to Mr. Bickman at Lourdes, Schwartz and Bickman in Indianapolis. Nothing fancy. A high GPA, a varsity sport, an essay about your family or your faith; and for the finalists, a good old-fashioned, in-person conversation with Olsen that would, he hoped, make his choices of four winners clear. That hope began to dim, however, as the scholarship applications arrived to him in Tucson and he spent hours, days, nights, weekends, holding the youthful dreams in his hands, trying to weigh what could not be fairly measured.

There was no poetry in his head those days; no Biblical flashes in Mary's handwriting across his field of vision; no wrestling with angels; no prayers. There was Cara, of course, and basketball, and Ben; always Ben.

❦   ❦   ❦

The first Monday in May, Olsen told Cara, "I'm going to Indian River. I'm awarding four scholarships at my old high school."

"When are you leaving?" she asked.

"Tomorrow morning."

"When will you be back?"

"Sunday."

"Long trip."

"I guess so," said Olsen.

"Why did you wait till the last minute to tell me?" asked Cara. "Never mind. Don't answer that."

"I'll only be seeing Mary one day. The rest of the days will be work."

Cara said, "Don't forget to come home again."

CHAPTER 26

❀

In the Time of the Prodigal

The afternoon Olsen returned to Indiana was spring's most glorious day. He emerged from the Indianapolis airport and saw the old silver Corvette pulled up to the curb. Rakowsky got out and came around to the passenger side, grinning. Olsen dropped his bag to the ground, and they stood together briefly, backslapping, shoulder-clapping, laughing.

"It's a beautiful day," said Olsen.

He was shocked at how Rakowsky had aged in three years, dusted with snow, it seemed, wisping hair, crinkled eyes.

Talking all the way, they took the interstate back into Indian River, Olsen sailing on a wave of nostalgia for the town he had once called his refuge and his home, with places that inhabited him: Indian River High, Roanoke Road, the River's Edge bar, the softball fields, Rakowsky's house, Dover Drive; this town where history had slipped through his fingers.

Rakowsky parked the Corvette in his driveway, slapped the keys in Olsen's hand. "No hot rodding, son," Rakowsky said. "Are you going to see Mary this week?"

"Sure."

"Well, don't do anything I wouldn't do."

After drinks and dinner and dusk on the deck, after more drinks and music inside, Rakowsky and Karen went to bed. Olsen took a shower, drank another beer. Then he went upstairs to the guest room, lay down on the bed, and called Mary.

At the sound of her sleep-tinged "Hello?" he realized how late it was. "Did I wake you? It's Tom."

"Thomas," she said. He heard her covers rustling. "No, I was just going to bed. Are you here?"

"I'm here," he said. Olsen had told Mary about the scholarships when he was planning this trip, but nothing, of course, about Alexandra. They talked for a few minutes, then Olsen asked, "What time should I come on Saturday?" and she said noon, for lunch, and gave him directions to her new house.

They said good-night, and Olsen hung up the phone, stared up at the guest room ceiling through the dark.

If he could do anything he wanted right now, what would it be?

He would forget Cara.

Forget her. Erase her from the story because the true story was this: Olsen and Mary, rain and sunlight, despair and resurrection, and all the days ordained for them, written in God's book before one of them came to be.

❦   ❦   ❦

Olsen's first scholarship interview was scheduled for ten the next morning. On his way to Indian River High, he steered the Corvette toward Roanoke Road, for old times' sake.

His block had changed in three years: the plain, placid street of white houses was now multi-colored in trendy shades and lined with elaborate new landscapings. A few children too young for school played outside in fresh air that was still warm from the night before. A galloping dog herded the children away from the edge of road, as mothers hovered.

Olsen parked on the street and got out. His old white house was now blue, with newly dug garden beds flowering around the perimeter; the little junipers and the big rhododendron were gone. Next door, Mr. McCormick's white house was now yellow, and on its front lawn, a tiny bicycle with training wheels lay toppled next to a bright red ball. It didn't look like an old man's house anymore.

At the brick house on the far side of Mr. McCormick's, Olsen saw a little boy dash across the grass toward a young woman who sat on the front steps.

Olsen straightened his tie and called across the grass to her. "I used to live there!" he said, pointing to his old house.

"Really?"

"Does Mr. McCormick still live there?" Olsen asked, nodding toward the yellow house. "It looks so different."

"He died a couple of years ago, right after we moved in," the woman said. "The Frankens live there now."

Olsen had expected this explanation, but not how much it would hurt. He reached up and loosened his tie, stared down at his shoes, then up at the yellow house. The young woman walked across the lawn, letting her son leap up into her arms as she approached Olsen.

"I'm sorry," she said. "Was Mr. McCormick a friend of yours?"

"Yes," he said. "But I moved out to Tucson a few years ago and didn't do a good job of keeping in touch with him." Olsen folded his arms on his chest. "What happened to him?"

"Just old age, I guess. We met him when we first moved in, then didn't see him again for a few weeks. He didn't answer the door when my husband went over to check on him—so John called the police. They got in the house and found him—well, found him passed away."

Olsen's scalp prickled. "Where is he buried?"

"I honestly don't know. He told me he didn't have any family. I don't know what happened after they found him. So sad being all alone like that." She pressed her cheek against her son's, who wrapped one arm around her neck, then wriggled down to the ground.

"He had a dog," Olsen said. "A little one. I forget his name."

"I never saw a dog," said the woman. She shook her head.

Olsen stared at Mr. McCormick's house. "Well, thanks," he said.

"You're welcome. I'm sorry I didn't have better news. He seemed like a sweet little old man. I'm sorry you never got to say good-bye." Her son ran in a wide circle around the front lawn, his arms spread like wings, and a few doors down the galloping dog barked, and Olsen said, "Yeah," got back in the Corvette and set out for the high school.

*   *   *

Ten interviews later, on Wednesday night, Olsen holed up in Rakowsky's guest room with the finalists' files in hand, fresh imprints of the students' faces, voices, and aspirations in his mind.

He was used to the tumultuous idealism of adolescent lives, used to making difficult choices philosophically. So why did it now seem utterly cold to laud four kids and send the other six packing? There, in the night, on the spot, on his own, the burden seemed too much.

He walked across the guest room and stood at the window. Looked out at the twilight, the lights in the neighboring houses. Recalled afresh how it had felt at that age to be unchosen, in his case by his own parents: too busy to come to Andover for his games, too importantly occupied to feign gusto for his dreams, too in love with their image of themselves to love him.

In the morning Olsen dialed Lourdes, Schwarz and Bickman and asked for Mr. Bickman.

"I'm having a hard time choosing my final four," said Olsen, "and I know I have to decide by tonight. Listen, is there any way, any way at all, that you could put me in touch with the donors? I feel like I need their input, someone to bounce my ideas off of."

"Hmmm," said Mr. Bickman.

"I want to be true to the donors' purposes," Olsen said, "to hear it from them—what do they have in mind—and why me? Maybe if they could explain why they singled me out for their honor, it would help me. See, it's very difficult for me to say yes to four students and no to the rest. Tougher than I thought it would be."

"Hmmm," said Mr. Bickman.

"It's not Alexandra Muro, is it? The donor? Because if it is, let me tell you, she's up to no good. And the ones who'll get hurt are these kids."

Mr. Bickman did not say anything.

"Here I am halfway to 50," Olsen said, "but I can still remember some rejections from my teenage years—and the pain still as fresh as yesterday. Crazy, sure—but it's such a raw, unvarnished time of life—all your dreams laid bare to the world—and so many ways for them to get trampled on."

Silence on Mr. Bickman's end.

"So if I could just talk to the donors," said Olsen, "even just on the phone—they won't even have to tell me who they are—just so it's not all up to me."

"Tom," said Mr. Bickman, in a grandfather's voice.

Olsen waited, catching his breath.

"The donors picked you for a reason," Mr. Bickman said. "They trust your judgment. Maybe part of what they have in mind is for you to believe in yourself as much as they do."

Olsen sighed. "I don't know," he said.

"I remember back in March," said Mr. Bickman, "when I first read your criteria for the scholarships—that mix of mind, body, and spirit, as it were. Of course I didn't know you at the time, but it gave me a tremendous picture of you, of the kind of person you are. I could understand right away why the donors feel as they do."

Olsen ran his free hand over his hair. He leaned back in Rakowsky's guest room chair. "Thanks."

"And it's not only mind, body, and spirit. I see you add quite a lot of heart to the mix as well."

"Without the heart," said Olsen, "what else matters?"

Quiet on the line.

"Guess I'm ready to get back to work," said Olsen. "I'll call you later."

"Good luck, Tom," Bickman said, and they hung up.

❧   ❧   ❧

That night Olsen called the runners-up first.

He talked them through the silent spaces of their disappointment, through their high-pitched concessions that collapsed into sobs. He spoke to all their parents. By the time he was done, his stomach was on fire, and he emerged from the guest room, drank a glass of baking-soda water in Rakowsky's kitchen, and walked around the block to clear his head in the evening air.

Calling the winners was much easier. He announced his good news, and their screams and cheers and tears of happiness cooled the flames in his stomach, and he reminded them to bring their parents and meet him the next morning in the principal's conference room. Finally, he called Mr. Bickman, gave him the names for the scholarship checks.

At the small ceremony Friday, Olsen extended simple congratulations to the winners. Mr. Bickman praised Olsen in a brief history of the newborn scholarships. The principal lavished praise on the prize pupils, and on their parents for raising them, and on Olsen for honoring them, and Bickman for administrating the scholarship program. Then Olsen walked around the table to distribute the checks, there were hugs and handshakes all around, a bit of conversation, and then the students went back to class as their parents went off to make bank deposits.

Olsen shut his briefcase, said good-bye to the principal, then headed for the school parking lot with Mr. Bickman. It was almost lunch time. The May sky was clear blue.

As they approached the Corvette, Mr. Bickman said, "Tom, I have something to tell you."

"Yeah?" said Olsen, reaching in his pocket for the car keys.

"Now that you've awarded the first annual scholarships," said Mr. Bickman, "that is, now that you've established and inaugurated the program successfully—I'm permitted to tell you the identities of the anonymous donors."

"Wait a minute!" Olsen said. "I thought I was never allowed to know! In fact, as recently as *yesterday*, I was never allowed to know."

"I simply wasn't permitted to say anything until now," said Mr. Bickman.

"So who are they? This is great. I'd thought I'd never find out."

"Would you care to hazard a guess?"

"Honestly," said Olsen, "I have absolutely no idea," although Alexandra still lurked in his mind. He unlocked the Corvette, tossed his briefcase on the passenger seat, and turned to face Mr. Bickman.

"Well, then," said Mr. Bickman. "The anonymous donors—who thought so highly of you that they wished for your legacy to continue through the Thomas Olsen Scholarships—" He paused. "The donors are Joseph McCormick…and Rocky."

Mr. McCormick? And Rocky…Who is Rocky?

Mr. Bickman's face was clear and serious. Olsen realized that some strange error must be at work. "Mr. McCormick died two years ago," Olsen said. "I just found out this morning. I went back to Roanoke Road."

"Yes," said Mr. Bickman, "but he arranged everything to happen after his passing. As executor of his estate, I'm fulfilling everything just as he requested. He wanted to surprise you. He had it all planned before he died."

"Rocky, though—who is Rocky?" Olsen thought for a minute, then looked at Mr. Bickman.

Together they said, "His dog."

Olsen began to laugh. He laughed so hard he began to cry. He cried so hard, his shoulders shook, and Mr. Bickman went to his car and came back with a white cotton handkerchief.

Olsen wiped his face as students started streaming into the parking lot for the first lunch period. "I'll be in touch, Mr. Bickman," Olsen said. "I'll call you when I get back to Tucson."

"Good-bye, Tom. I know this is—well, I knew Joe McCormick well. He would have been happy today. And very proud."

Olsen and Bickman shook hands, and Bickman disappeared between the cars, and Olsen got in the Corvette and lay his head on the steering wheel.

❦   ❦   ❦

The next day, Saturday, at noon, Olsen drove slowly down River Lane under another sky of unabridged sunlight, looking for 223. He found it and parked the Corvette, top down, in the driveway, and followed the path that led to Mary's door, but she was already stepping onto the little porch, and running down onto the grass.

Olsen had not counted on this fresh impact of Mary in the flesh: the butter-scotch of her skin, shadow of her hair, her body swirling in the curves he had catalogued in his memory.

They stood before each other on the lawn, and she looked up into his eyes—then Olsen lifted her up off the ground and swung her around, and as she laughed and held onto him, all his thoughts ran together, and she said, "Come in! Let me show you around," and just inside the front door, Romeo shuffled with happiness in his old age and licked Olsen's hands.

Olsen followed Mary as she led him through the first floor rooms, recalling nothing of what she said, smiling at what seemed the proper moments, until she said, "Are you hungry?" in the kitchen.

He didn't think he answered.

"Are you all right?" Mary asked him.

Olsen looked at her and said, "It's just so good to see you."

"And how is Cara?" said Mary.

She had made their lunches, a salad for herself, a towering club sandwich for Olsen, a pitcher of iced tea for them to share. They carried everything into the dining room and sat down.

"So how did it go with the scholarships? Who won? Anyone I might know?" she said, her ringless fingers catching his eye.

Olsen took a drink of iced tea. "I found out who the anonymous donors were."

"Who? How did you find out?" she said.

"The attorney told me."

"Who are they?"

"Remember my old next-door neighbor, Mr. McCormick?"

"Yeah."

"Did you ever meet his little dog?" Olsen asked. "It looked like a squirrel. Mr. McCormick could hold it in one hand."

"No, I don't think so," Mary said. "Wait, yes, I did see it—the night I brought him the cookies. The night we went to Tri-State," she said, then coughed. She picked her iced tea up, took a long drink, put her glass down.

"Well, it was them," said Olsen.

"What do you mean, it was them?"

"Mr. McCormick and his dog were the anonymous donors. He died two years ago. I don't know what happened to the little dog," said Olsen. He watched drops of condensation slide down the side of his glass and soak into the yellow cloth placemat. "The attorney said it was all in his will. He worked out this whole plan and put it in his will to surprise me. What a guy, huh? Sweet guy and a real schemer—had me fooled. He lived so simply. Who would have guessed he had all that money? Sweet old lonely guy—God, I used to count on him, on seeing him there in his yard, playing with that dog, watering his garden—I counted on that. On seeing his light on at night. I used to lie in bed and see his light on next door and it just made me feel better. I moved to Tucson and you know what? I missed seeing that light. Then I forgot about it. Just forgot. Like he didn't matter anymore. He didn't forget *me*, though!" Olsen said, and laughed abruptly—one sad, staccato note. He put his elbows on the table, folded his hands and leaned his forehead against them, so Mary couldn't see his face.

When he looked up, her eyes were glimmering and began to overflow. She picked her yellow napkin up off her lap, pressed it to her eyes in silence.

She said, "I have an idea. Let's drive to the dunes," and the next thing Olsen knew, they were in the Corvette, the top down, heading north.

❊   ❊   ❊

They drove past some churches en route to the interstate, and Olsen asked, "Do you still go to Calvary?"

"Oh, yeah. I wouldn't have survived the last year without my friends there. The Rakowskys, the Reiters, everybody."

They got on the highway. Mary's hair blew straight out behind her; she took her sunglasses out of her purse and put them on, her arm brushing Olsen's as she moved beside him.

"Ben quit going to church in Tucson," Olsen said over the wind.

"Yes, that's what he told me."

"I can relate," Olsen said. "I've never been the churchgoing type. Well, you knew that."

"How's your spiritual life, though? How's it going with you and God?" Mary asked. She tucked her left foot up underneath her, turned her body and leaned toward him; Olsen gripped the wheel and the car seemed to accelerate, the highway flying past his head at a thousand miles an hour.

"Oh, I don't know," he said. "I think it's just too late for me."

"There's no such thing as too late."

"Really?"

"Not for God," she said. She poked through her purse, pulled a ponytail holder out and put her hair up. "Do you ever think about the things we once talked about that night in my basement? Way back when?" she asked. "You had that longing for God—but you didn't know where to start. And after Tri-State, we talked about it even more. Whatever happened after that?"

The wind roared in his ears. "I've done a lot of soul searching—a little Bible reading—some praying," he said. The sky was creamy blue, an oil painting, a sea that was going to soak them up into itself. "I keep trying to pray, and I always wonder: are the answers from God or are they just my own thoughts? My own agenda? I can never tell for certain. I always think of you when I wonder about that."

"Why?"

"Because you talked about it the day we climbed Mount Baldy. About how much easier it was when God just boomed His instruction down from heaven."

They drove along. Then Mary said, "Does Cara believe in God?"

"Well, she's more of a scientist. A social scientist, you know."

"So—she doesn't believe?"

"I don't think so. No. No, she doesn't," Olsen said. "She's got her psychology. Cara analyzes, dissects stuff down into psychological detail, bytes of information. She can take pain, anger, any emotion, you name it, and transmute it into logic, make it nice and neat so it makes perfect psychological sense. By then it doesn't even hurt anymore—that's the goal anyway. But that doesn't work for me."

Mary didn't answer. They drove along with the sun shining down on them from the blue-cream sky and Olsen said, "You've got that faith, faith that carries you through the toughest times—I'd give anything to have that. But it's just not in me. God, I wish it were. So I live in this no-man's land: not enough logic, and not enough faith."

"What do you do then," Mary asked, "when something hurts you? When you have a question you can't answer?"

"Drink a few bottles of beer. Run myself ragged on the court. Read something. Hang out with Ben," Olsen said.

Mary straightened her sunglasses, her lips curving up at the corners. Olsen thought she was going to say something, but she just let her ponytail sail out behind her, and turned the radio on.

❦   ❦   ❦

Everyone with cabin fever had flocked to the dunes that afternoon. Olsen and Mary climbed Mount Baldy side by side, walked west through the brush to a place apart. They sat and looked out at Lake Michigan, at the waders, the children splashing, the teenagers barreling across the sand and shoving each other in the water and shrieking, at the lovers hand in hand, meandering.

"Tell me about Tucson," she said.

Olsen thought about Arizona sunlight, wind, sky, as he looked out over the sands that skirted the water. "It feels like home there," he said. He scooped up a handful of sand and let it fall through his fingers. "I never feel lonely out in the desert," he said. "But I used to feel lonely here at the dunes. I kept coming back here because I felt drawn to this place—it has a wistfulness I can't shake—it feels like a part of me. But it always felt lonely to me here."

"Even that time we came here together—you and Abby and I?" Mary asked. "Even today?"

He lifted another handful of sand. "No," he said. "Never with you." He sifted the sand through his fingers, and watched it fall, glittering.

They walked down to the water's edge at the rocky western end of the beach, where few so far were venturing. Olsen scoured the carpet of sandy stones and picked up a few flat ones, then saw Mary had beaten him to the draw: she skipped a stone with a quick snap of her wrist, and it skittered far out over the smooth blue water.

"What are the people like in Tucson?" she asked, and skipped another stone.

"They do their own thing, and they let you do yours. None of that petty judging, that midwestern need to conform." Olsen cocked his elbow, flicked his wrist, and his stone catapulted nicely over the water before sinking. "They'll help you out, introduce you around, show you the ropes, drink you under the table—but they know when to leave you in peace, too," he said. He and Mary faced each other in their dark glasses.

"They don't take offense. They shrug off the unimportant stuff. But if they believe in something? What fire," he said, kneeling down, picking up a stone, and skipping it toward Canada. "They're loyal, too. If they call themselves your friend, you can bank on their being there. And all that sunlight—maybe that's what makes them a little wild. That's my favorite thing about them," Olsen said. "They have a wanderlust that never goes away. No matter how successful they are, they still have a faraway look in their eyes."

He stared out over the water, then turned back toward Mary. Her ponytail rippled behind her like a dark flag.

"Know what?" she said, tilting her head. "You just described yourself."

Olsen laughed. He picked up one last stone and whipped it so it bounced like a water-skier off into the distant blue. "Hey," he said, "are you still thinking of changing jobs? Ben told me you want to work at a pregnancy center."

"Yeah, but not till he graduates. It'll be a big pay cut after all my years at the library. It's what I want to do, though."

"School's practically free for him now, with the RA thing and his scholarship. Do you really have to wait?"

"I want to keep a cushion in case Ben needs me," Mary said. "When I'm on my own, it'll be fine. I don't need a lot of money."

"Don't you ever long to get out of Indiana?" Olsen asked. "To go somewhere, anywhere, see the world, move away?"

"Sure I do," she said.

"And what about Abby? Last Ben told me, she was still in Fort Wayne, still single. Did she ever get married?"

"Nope."

"See—you two could move out to Tucson," Olsen said. "Ben's talking about staying there for grad school, and maybe longer. Wouldn't that be great, with Ben there, and Jasmine, all of us out there together?"

"And Cara," Mary added.

She picked up a skipping stone and snapped it across the water; it careened over the still blue surface, thwack, thwack, thwack, far beyond where Olsen's farthest stone had sunk, until it disappeared into a pool of sunlight on the water.

❋   ❋   ❋

They had dinner at a coffee shop near the campus in Valparaiso.

Olsen asked Mary, "Did you know that Virgil was having an affair all those years?"

"Does it matter?" she said. She was leaning back in the cushioned booth, looking at Olsen evenly, her voice quiet.

"No. I just—I just wondered."

"It's funny," Mary said. She picked her coffee up and sipped it. "If I didn't know about Virgil's affair, then I'm gullible, blind. If I did know but didn't confront him about it, then I'm a weakling, a pushover. If I did know and just didn't care, then I got what I deserved. And in every case, I'm a failure. So I lose no matter what." She put the cup down on the tabletop and turned it, slowly, between her hands. "I'll tell you this, though," she said. Smoothed her hair, opened her purse and extracted lip gloss, ran it over her lips. Olsen waited.

She said, "I am so happy without Virgil. Life is all mine now—to fly or fall—it's all up to me."

Mary, can you give me back my days lost, nights lost, hopes lost, life lost...All lost for nothing now that you sit before me and say you are so happy without Virgil...Can you hurl that clock back through time...Hurl time backward to the day you said "Ben is the one good thing that I have ever done"...And say instead "To fly or fall, it's all up to me, I am so happy without Virgil"...Then everything would change...Instead it is long past too late

Olsen said, "That's good, Mary. You deserve to be happy."

Then he said, "Are you ready to go?"

❦   ❦   ❦

On the night road home, with the top up on the Corvette, Mary said, "I was thinking about Mr. McCormick again."

The inside of the car was shadowed and warm. The radio murmured at a low volume.

"Isn't it amazing," Mary said, "what can be going on in someone's mind and heart that they never put into words?" She sat so close and spoke so softly, it felt like she was whispering in his ear.

"We leave so much unsaid to the people we love," said Mary, "and for what? Because we're afraid, or shy—because we just don't know how to put it into words—and then it's too late. Boom. Your chance is over. Then you tell yourself it didn't matter anyway, and move on to the next thing. But some things you can't forget—the if-onlys that would have changed your life. Years later you still ask yourself, *What if?* When all you had to do was be true to yourself in the first place."

Mary, what are you trying to tell me? We both know it's too late now isn't it

"Do you ever think about stuff like that?" Mary asked.

"Are you kidding?" said Olsen. "That's mostly what I think about."

"Well, now you have Tucson State, and Cara, and a new life," Mary said, "and you don't need your if-onlys anymore."

Mary, when I eat drink sleep wake up, it's all "If only"…My life and love slipped through my fingers

"But what if I told you I've always loved you?" Mary said. "What if I told you I've dreamed for years about a moment like this with you? What if I asked you to leave Cara right now—to never go back—and you said you've always loved me, too, and we created a whole new life together?"

"God," said Olsen. "Am I dreaming? What are you saying?"

"I'm saying—I'm saying," and she sighed. "If we did all that, what would make us any different than Virgil and his new wife, and what they did to me? Would you want to do that to Ben?"

Knife in the heart was what that felt like.

"Do you see what I mean?" Mary said. "A rock and a hard place."

"I think," Olsen managed to say, "a lot of things would be different about us."

"If only," said Mary.

And so they sped toward Saturday's end. Mary lifted her fingers to smooth her hair again, and fiddle with her earring; she folded her hands in her lap; and they kept heading back to Indian River.

❦   ❦   ❦

Olsen parked the Corvette in Mary's driveway on River Lane; they got out and walked through the dark toward her front door; the warm air had a cool night edge. He asked her, "How long have we known each other?" although he had already counted.

"Let's see," Mary said. "Since the beginning of Ben's junior year at Indian River. Almost five years."

"Feels like longer," Olsen said. "It's hard for me to remember the time before I knew you."

"That's the same way I feel about you," said Mary. "I think it's because we're so much alike."

They stood and faced each other at the bottom of her front steps.

"We are a lot alike, aren't we?" said Olsen. He took a half-step closer to her.

"Well, I better let you go," she said, "since it's so late. Rick and Karen will be waiting for you."

"What about before—what we were saying in the car?"

"About how much we love Ben?" Mary said. "About doing the right thing for his sake? And how we'll always put his good before our own?"

Olsen stood there speechless, hands at his sides, but only for a moment. He looked at her through the twilight. "Will you ever come visit us in Tucson?" he asked.

"Sure. Will there be a wedding sometime soon?"

"Ben and Jasmine?" said Olsen. "Not yet, I hope. They still have another year of school."

"No," Mary said. She laughed. "You and Cara."

Olsen caught his breath, slid his hands in his pockets. He considered some of the things he could say in reply; but they were all either too late, too little, or too true. Instead, he said, "I guess that's the next step, isn't it?"

What do I really want to stand for in this life?

They looked at each other.

Truth…And courage to face it…The right thing…And courage to do it…Whatever will make Ben proud of me…Because he is the one good thing that I have ever done

"Well," Mary said, "please tell Cara I'm look forward to seeing her again—sometime—at your wedding, I guess."

"I will. Yes."

"And give Ben a big hug and kiss for me when you get back to Tucson tomorrow."

"Well, maybe the hug," Olsen said, and they both laughed, voices tinged in blue. "So then…" he said, "good-bye, Mary." He thought he would be able to walk away, until he saw the sadness in her eyes.

He wrapped her up into his arms, sank his lips into his hair, touched his lips to her forehead, before he let her go.

Then Mary said, "Good-bye."

When he reached his car, Olsen turned around to wave to her. She stood by the door, lifted her hand and waved back, then slipped away from the grasp of his eyes.

❈   ❈   ❈

The next day Olsen returned to Tucson, and Cara, and Ben, and life in the desert.

He did not call Mary again, and she did not call him, though from time to time they still conveyed greetings to each other through Ben. Olsen knew this was the only way his life, and hers, could go on; and the silence from Indian River, silence that stretched through the fall across a long, cold winter and beyond, and beyond, told Olsen she must have agreed.

CHAPTER 27

❀

Our Story Cannot End This Way

July in Indian River, Indiana, three years later.

Olsen turned slowly in front of the full-length mirror, checking his tuxedo from a few vantage points. Then he faced the mirror head on, adjusted his bow tie, and smiled. "Not bad," he said. His hair showed signs of aging—shoots of white poking through, some thinning acreage—but his eyes still pierced blue and strong, no glasses needed; he could still out-benchpress most of his players, and he could still hit a shot from half court.

"Are you ready, Tom?" Rakowsky called through the guest room door. "Gotta get you to the church on time," then Olsen heard Rakowsky's footsteps drumming down the stairs.

He walked across the guest room to the window and looked out at Rakowsky's back yard, at the lush deciduous tangle of trees, the stroke of blue sky.

Three years—has it been that long? So, what have you been up to for the last three years? How time slips away.

Then he took a deep breath, checked his pockets, and jogged downstairs to head for Calvary Church.

Rakowsky drove. On the way there he said, "Awfully good of old Virgil to kick the bucket last year—in plenty of time for today, that is."

Olsen looked over and saw Rakowsky grinning or grimacing, he wasn't sure which. "I didn't like the guy either, but come on," Olsen said. "Let's not speak ill of the dead—no matter how much they may deserve it."

"I know. Sorry."

When Olsen and Rakowsky got to Calvary, they went in the back entrance and headed for the Luther Room, where the groomsmen and ushers and moral supports were gathering. Ben was already there with Josh Reiter and Matt Pender, and Olsen stopped in his tracks at the time warp: he hadn't seen Josh and Matt since his going-away-to-Tucson party six years ago, when they were still gangling and horseplaying and edging toward the solid planting of adulthood. But he had no time for nostalgia: the smattering of tuxedoed and suited arrivals mushroomed, a crescendoing horde of male jocularity in ties, circling the table and crowding in the corner pockets of the room—friends from the old days in Indian River resurfacing, friends from the new days in Tucson flown in for the weekend. There came Mike Stefanik, and Dave Kuehn, Nate Pytel, and LeVon Powell, and Michael Cavatelli, the good old basketball days revisited. Great scents floated out from the church kitchen, where the caterers were whipping up dinner: salty wafts of ham and roast beef, Italianate breezes of tomatoes and basil, interweavings of the robust and the sweet. The promise of a good meal invigorated them. Olsen and Ben and a couple of the others were keeping track of the time, until at five-thirty Olsen said, "All right, gentlemen—gentlemen," and the buzz wound down.

"The groom and his best man," said Olsen, "need to have a few minutes alone here before embarking on this life-altering experience—so if you'll kindly vacate the Luther Room…" After a few old-ball-and-chain commemorations, the stream of suits and black tuxedos funneled out the door, and Olsen and Ben sat down next to each other at the table.

"So did you ever think you'd be back here at Calvary?" asked Olsen.

"Figured I'd be married and buried here, at least," Ben said; clasped his hands behind his head. "And it was so important to my mom that we have the wedding in Indian River. I think it's the first thing she ever really demanded of me. It was cool with Jasmine, so here we are. And you know what? It feels good to be back. That good old days feeling." He unclasped his hands, lay them palms up in his lap.

"There *were* good old days, weren't there?" Ben asked.

"Sure. What do you mean?"

"Lotta shit to look back through to get there—back to the good times." Ben looked up at the ceiling. "Like basketball. Man, we ruled the world, remember?"

"We did rule our own little universe for a while. Fun while it lasted."

"Things were simple then. God and basketball. And look at me now—I lost them both."

"You didn't lose them. You moved on. We all move on. And they're still there if you want to go back. Besides," said Olsen, "what are you talking about? You're getting married in church. You haven't lost God."

"It's not the same," Ben said. "But it still feels good to be here."

Olsen tilted his chair back onto two legs. "I've thought of you as my own son for such a long time now. I wish I could take away some of the pain you've had. But it's made you stronger—it's part of what's made you the man Jasmine fell in love with." He tilted the chair forward again; folded his hands loosely on the table.

"Anyway," he said, "just remember you can always come to me for anything you need, you and Jasmine both. I know I have my failings—I'm certainly not the greatest example in the romantic relationships department. But I would do anything for you. That's a promise."

Ben said, "Remember my old essay from high school, 'Three Fathers'?"

"Are you kidding? I memorized it."

"So did I," said Ben. Across the room from where they sat side by side, a faded portrait of Martin Luther stared back at them, beside a needlepoint rendition of the 23rd Psalm.

"Thanks, Tom," Ben said, "for being my father," and Olsen took Ben's broad, brown hand, and clapped it between his own. Then he let go.

"So—are you ready to get married?" said Olsen.

The pipe organ processional started it: a foreign and mystical transport that Olsen felt reverberating in his feet. The scent of wedding flowers on the altar dizzied him. Jasmine, on her father's arm, came down the aisle, glorious in her bridesmaids' wake, with the voluminous rustlings of fabrics and wedding programs in the background, like whispers from God. Against his will, Olsen kept looking toward Mary.

I'm staying in Indian River a few extra days. I have to talk to you about something important.

She sat, unescorted and gleaming, in the front pew, beside Abby and Abby's parents. In between the whispers of God, the heady scents, the reverent upsurges of organ music, and even in the profound silence before the wedding party turned to the altar, his eyes kept darting toward Mary. But she did not meet his gaze.

Lies, and truth that's never spoken, and things that don't matter hogging the conversation for a lifetime—is it any wonder the world is falling apart?

Last night's rehearsal had been just that—logistics, a walk-through—it hadn't prepared Olsen for today's territory, these tides of the mystical washing around him, with Pastor Burmeister the sage in his white robes and embroidered sashes, his bass voice a chant, his wisdom an invisible halo; and Ben the initiate, with Jasmine poised to his left, rustling in her white satin with blue bouquet, colors of the sky.

The pastor based his wedding message on a familiar verse from Psalm 139: *All the days ordained for me were written in your book before one of them came to be.*

Cara and I broke up for good, and now I can finally have what I want: you.

Olsen looked up at the cross; it was suspended above the altar. Then he looked higher, to the image of Jesus in the stained glass window. Jesus with arms outstretched.

Life crucifies you; sometimes you even crucify yourself; but that doesn't have to be the end of your story.

Eventually the wedding words and music merged and surged into Pastor Burmeister's pronouncement, "Introducing Mr. and Mrs. Benjamin Wendling!" and the newlyweds walked up the aisle arm in arm, and in the excitement Olsen glanced over at Mary, who smiled and cried and embraced Abby and refused to look his way.

The Calvary Church reception hall was wide and high-ceilinged and bright with summer evening light, fragrant with food, festive in white and blue linens and garlands and ribbons and flowers, and rollicking with a hundred guests. When it was time for the sparkling grape juice toast, Olsen stood up in front of his chair at the head table. Conversations ebbed, the room grew quieter, and as Olsen waited, he caught Mary's eye and smiled at her.

She was seated at one of the front tables. She wore a lavender dress, and her gold cross on the chain. Her hair swept loose and dark on her shoulders. She smiled back at Olsen, lightning, and looked away.

Then Olsen told the wedding guests how he had seen Ben and Jasmine grow close through their years at Tucson State, how he admired their devotion, how perfect they were for each other, and how their love had begun as friendship, which made all the difference.

He straightened his black bow tie and smiled. "Those of you who know me know I'm not a Bible scholar. But a Bible verse seemed only fitting for a sparkling grape juice toast at a church wedding. So I did a little research." Olsen pulled a slip of paper from his tuxedo jacket. "From the Song of Solomon," he said.

Olsen looked out at the guests. Then he turned to Ben and Jasmine. **My boy and the beautiful girl you love...if only you could teach me what you already**

know...before you go out in the world...together...in love...and so much wiser than I am

He put a hand on the table to steady himself, glanced down at the slip of paper. Then he read the verse aloud.

"This is my beloved," he said, *"and this is my friend."*

He lifted his glass to them. "Forever and ever, Amen. To Mr. and Mrs. Wendling!" Olsen said, holding his sparkling grape juice toward heaven, and the chorus of cheers and clinking glasses rose up and ran in waves around the room, and the newlyweds sealed the blessing with a kiss.

After dinner the dancing started, with all the ceremonial pairings: bride and groom, bride and her father, groom and his mother, best man and maid of honor, and all the wedding party, to the music of a five-man band. Afterward Olsen drifted along the sidelines, awaiting a moment to seize and ask Mary to dance. He watched Mary waltz with Abby's father, twist with Rakowsky, polka with Jasmine's father. Watched her from the wrong side of a three-year abyss.

Three years.

Three years of Olsen looking out for Ben in Tucson, and Ben looking out for him; three years of pushing Mary from his thoughts but chasing her in his dreams; of living with Cara in his house in the Catalina foothills, never advancing past the verge of marrying her, until Cara had had enough procrastination.

What did we really want to stand for in this life?

❦   ❦   ❦

On the edge of forty-nine, Olsen could look back and see his life story unvarnished, unedited, well-written in spots, sloppy and enigmatic in others.

As a child Olsen had imagined the father he wished for; he had shaped that wish-father with longing, drawn him in all the details a mind's eye could see. And Olsen had eventually become that father to Ben, as fate joined them in a way flesh and blood could not understand; Ben had become his friend, the son who had saved him, and the best part of his story.

The tides of Olsen's faith had ebbed and flowed across time, waters sometimes clear, sometimes muddy. His Sunday mornings in the Arizona desert were no longer a weekly ritual, but God still tapped at the door of his thoughts. That spring Olsen had told Branigan he liked the college coaching, the all basketball, all year round, but missed teaching more as the seasons rolled on. Told

Branigan he was going to get an Arizona teacher's license, and didn't know where it would lead; he would have to follow the spirit.

Before Cara left him, finally, that May, and headed for Berkeley, she pronounced her final diagnosis: that Olsen was too confused and selfish to love someone else; even worse, he did not love himself; a part of him was happy to be unhappy; and she saw that it would never end.

Olsen knew it was not worth protesting. He wanted to explain there was a hole inside him too old and too deep to repair, a hole that gaped and let the happiness fall through. But he knew Cara would tell him that was a choice, like everything else in life.

Women who were not Mary were only substitutes, anyway, imposters in his life, concessions in disguise. No matter how good, perfect, right for him the woman was, even Cara, it was all just killing time. It was that simple. He knew it did not make sense. But it was one part of the story he had not been able to rewrite.

❦   ❦   ❦

At the rehearsal dinner the night before, Mary had avoided him with aplomb and ambiguity. Her distance could have been explained away by the busy restaurant, the crowd of guests, her duties as mother of the groom. But when Olsen left, with only Mary's "Hello again" and "See you at the wedding" to show for their reunion, his feet had dragged heavy with regret.

Now at the reception, the wedding band struck up a new waltz, a moderate tempo, a muted trumpet with a modern edge. Olsen went up behind Mary, touched her shoulder and said, "Would you like to dance?" When she turned to face him, the power of her closeness shocked him. She smiled and said, "Yes," and blood careened into his heart like whitewater.

On the dance floor she slipped her hand in his, lightly, and he touched his fingertips to the small of her back, and they fell into a one-two-three, one-two-three, across the parquet. Muscles in his body tightened into high alert, new hope and old fear and the unknown colliding.

"It's been a long time, Thomas," Mary said. Her face looked happy, but did not match her voice.

"Yes," he said. "I wanted to talk to you last night at the rehearsal dinner. But it was so crowded."

Mary wore gold hoops in her ears, and her breath was warm, with a scent of mint, and the fabric of her lavender dress slipped beneath his fingers.

"So, we did the right thing, you and I," Mary said. "Was it worth it?"

Olsen must have imagined her voice, her words, the last chance dangling in her wry and solemn question—because as soon as he blinked, Mary was smiling at him, tilting her head, and saying, "Where's Cara? I haven't seen her. Is she here?"

"No," he said. The dance floor was crowding up. "It's a long story. I'll have to tell you later, when we're alone—I mean, if you want."

"All right." Her earrings glinted in the lights, her gold cross slipped back and forth over the front of her dress. One-two-three, one-two-three.

"So how's everything at Tucson State?" Mary asked. "Basketball and everything?"

"Great. Good. All's well. And how's your new job?"

"Doesn't seem so new anymore," Mary said. "It's been almost two years." She looked at Olsen, her hand resting like a feather in his. "I like helping the girls. It makes all the difference, you know, for them to find they're not alone in the world. Sometimes I have Ben stop by the center when he's in town," she said. "You should see these girls' faces when they meet him. Five minutes with Ben gives them more hope and courage to be mothers than anything I could ever tell them."

Too huge, too important, for an easy rejoinder; hesitation filled his mouth where the words should have been.

One-two-three, one-two-three.

"How's good old Romeo?" he asked.

"Ben didn't tell you? Romeo died last winter."

Shit.

"I'm sorry to hear that," Olsen said. "I always had a soft spot for that dog. He treated me just like family. How old was he?"

"Fifteen," she said. "Old for a big dog."

"Will you get another one?"

"Oh, probably. Someday."

And the dance ended.

Everyone clapped for the band, and the trumpet player announced a fifteen-minute break in the music, and Mary said, "Well, then," but Olsen could not read the look on her face.

"Can I get you something to drink?" he asked. "You can really work up a sweat waltzing." He grinned miserably.

"Yes," she said. "I'm thirsty."

Olsen carried two glasses of punch through the wedding crowd and back to Mary's table, where to his relief she was sitting all by herself, no Abby, nobody else with her. His hands trembled slightly and the punch sloshed out of the glasses onto the tablecloth. As soon as he sat down, shirt plastered to his back with sweat, Josh Reiter came up behind him and slapped his shoulder.

"Hey, Coach," said Josh, "we need some pictures of all the groomsmen together—didn't get any before the ceremony. And the photographer says we've gotta get outside quick—the sunset's fading fast and then it'll be too dark. Come on—out on the church steps."

"Right now?" Olsen looked toward the doors. He saw Ben and Matt Pender and the rest of the groomsmen gathering, and the photographer with his huge camera hanging around his neck, and all of them tossing back cans of pop, laughing.

"Yup. Right now," Josh said. "It shouldn't take too long."

"Well," said Olsen.

"Go ahead, Thomas," Mary said. "I'll be fine. Actually I could use a little breather here. I'll see you when you come back." She put the glass to her lips, tilted her head back and drank, then put the glass on the tablecloth.

And when Olsen came back inside twenty minutes later, she was gone.

She was not on the dance floor. He looked for her in the church kitchen, but found only the caterers, cleaning up. He looked outside in the little garden behind the church, where she might have gone to see the night sky, but a young couple sat together on the wooden bench by the flowers, just the two of them.

Olsen went back inside, loitered around the corridor awhile to see if she came out of the ladies' room. He said hi to Abby, asked if she had seen Mary; but the answer was no.

Then Olsen walked down the corridor, around the corner, and down the deserted hall to the sanctuary. The doors were open. Mary sat inside, alone, in the front pew on the right.

The sanctuary lights were all turned off, but eternal flames flickered in their candleholders in the tiny alcoves on both sides of the altar. And a spotlight glowed on the stained glass window of Jesus.

Olsen entered the sanctuary and started walking down the aisle, his tread silent on crimson carpet. About halfway there he called out, "Mary?" softly, so as not to scare her, but she didn't turn around.

When he reached the front pew, he said, "Mary?" again, and she answered, "Hello, Thomas," without looking at him. He sat down and slid across the smooth wood, close to her. Her hands, brown and unadorned, were folded on her lap. She was looking toward the altar, and did not turn to face him as she spoke.

"When Ben was five years old," she said, "on the most beautiful October Sunday afternoon, I took him apple picking. Drove out to one of those orchards in the country. No one else was there, and I thought the place was closed. Then the farmer came out and saw us, went and got his horse-drawn wagon, drove us out through the fields and trees to the far corner of his orchard. He said he'd be back to get us in an hour, and gave me a big canvas bag to collect our apples in, and drove away with his horse and wagon."

She looked down, tucked her hair behind her ears, looked up at the altar again.

"Ben and I started to walk through those apple trees. I'll always remember how it used to feel, to hold his little hand in mine. I keep those things here," she said, pressing her palm to her chest. "The sun was white...the wind was warm...to this day, twenty years later, when I catch the scent of apples, I'm back in that orchard, holding Ben's little hand," she said, her eyes looking beyond the altar and past the walls and back across the years.

"I watched Ben run ahead of me through the trees," Mary said, "and in that moment, I had a revelation—that God wasn't going to hold anything back from him. No matter what mistakes I had already made, or what mistakes I still had in store, I saw that Ben belonged to God—that he belonged to Life. I saw that I didn't have to worry."

For the first time since he sat down beside her, Mary looked at Olsen. "It almost felt like we were in heaven—the sky so blue, the wind so sweet and warm and quiet, just Ben and me in the apple orchard, and that perfect peace. Have you ever had a time like that?" she asked.

Almost.

"But God didn't work the way I used to think He would," Mary said. "He didn't give Ben NBA talent, or an Einstein brain, or a winning lottery ticket. He gave Ben some good people in his life who love him. His friends. Jasmine. Abby, and her parents, and Virgil—Virgil really loved Ben, you know." She looked in Olsen's eyes. "And you, Thomas. You, most of all. His third father." She turned her face toward the altar again. "In the worst of times, it's the love that carried Ben through. When you lose everything else—even your faith—love is still there."

Olsen wanted to reach for her, but he waited.

"And I did what I promised God I would do," Mary said. "I have loved Ben so much. More than anything. One child, one life—sounds small, doesn't it?

But when it's a child you love, that one life is the universe. That life—is life. I know you understand."

She looked like a child herself, sitting there in the flickering light, and a crevice began to break inside Olsen at the thought of having to leave the church and keep on trying to live without her.

"I'll never have a child of my own flesh and blood," Olsen said. "But because of you, I do have a son, a child of my heart." He reached for her hand then, and she let him hold it. "If not for you, Mary, if not for you and Ben, I would be so alone," and his voice broke.

"Whether it's flesh and blood, or something else, that brings people together," Mary said, "it's all the hand of God at work. There's only one flesh and blood that really matters, that really makes us all family."

At first Olsen didn't understand what she meant. Then he saw that she was looking up at the stained glass window. He turned and looked up to Jesus, too: outstretched arms, amber eyes.

"What happened, Thomas," Mary said, "with you and Cara?" He was still holding Mary's hand lightly; she entwined her fingers in his.

"Well," he said. He paused. "We broke up. Actually, she broke up with me."

"After all these years?"

"Yeah," said Olsen. "And she moved to California. To Berkeley. She got a great teaching position in their graduate psych program. A real honor."

"When did this happen?" asked Mary. "When did she leave?"

"Oh, right after the school year ended. A month or so ago. But it was over before that."

"Thomas, why? What happened?"

Olsen looked up at the wooden cross cut in smooth clean planes. At Ben and Jasmine's wedding flowers on the altar. At the Christian banners draped on the sanctuary walls. He looked over his shoulder at the rows of pew decorations and garlands and more flowers and wedding programs left behind, everything phosphorescent in the flickers of eternal flame and stained glass glow.

"I couldn't go through with all this. Well, with Cara's version of this," he said.

"All this what?"

"The wedding. I couldn't go through with the wedding. No matter how many times we set a date." Olsen sighed. "Cara was brilliant, beautiful, funny, talented, everything," he said. "And I did love her. But I could never take that final step and marry her." He kept his eyes on the cross as he said so.

"Why not?" Mary asked. Their hands were still entwined.

Olsen turned his face to her. **Mystery divine, dark eyes aflame, as ever, as always.**

"Because she wasn't you," he said.

Mary looked at him. Her face, her eyes, shimmering. Drew her hand out of his. Held it between them, in the silence and twilight.

Folded her hands in the lap of her lavender dress.

"Thomas," she said. She was looking toward the altar.

Olsen watched the curve of her profile; the blood hammered in his stomach. Time, the air, the flickers of eternal flame, all began to slow and harden around him.

Mary leaned back against the pew. She closed her eyes. She said,

> *Tell me about despair, yours, and I will tell you mine.*
> *Meanwhile the world goes on...*

"The world has gone on, Thomas," she said. Her eyes were still closed. "And all our old if-onlys have faded away. I still ask myself if doing the right thing was worth it. I think it was. But look at what we lost."

What we lost. He felt his blood halting, compressing, as he watched her.

Mary opened her eyes toward the vaulted ceiling. "What happens when something you once thought you'd die for," she asked, "becomes something you learn to just live without?"

"I don't know," said Olsen, "because I will never learn to live without you."

"Once you've crossed that line," said Mary, as if she hadn't heard him, "there's no going back. At least that's what I've found." She turned her face to him, smiled slightly; she twirled a strand of hair around her finger; it all seemed to be in slow motion, like the concrete in his veins.

"The dream fades away to bittersweet," Mary said, watching him, "and all that lost hope...my God..." Her voice was soft, but bold, almost swaggering; it reached him as if from a long distance. He wanted to challenge, disagree, beg, convince her otherwise; but there was no rebuttal for lost hope; he could only stare at her from the wrong side of the line she had already crossed.

"And what do you do when it's all over?" she said. "What else can you do? You move on. *Meanwhile the world goes on.*"

Mary took Olsen's hand, and leaned toward him, and kissed him: velvet hurricane, blazing fusion, spinning edge of delusion and dream.

Then she stood up, lavender silk falling around her. She said, "Forever and ever, Amen, Thomas," and walked away, slowly, up the aisle.

❦   ❦   ❦

So there he was, sitting alone in the church, his lips burning in the silence.
She has walked away from me before…Our story cannot end this way
"So, God," Olsen said, looking toward the altar. "What do I do now?" He
spoke too softly for his voice to echo under the high beamed ceiling.

He closed his eyes and fell back, back across the years, came face to face with
the boy who still lived inside him.

> Look for me, Father, on the roof
>
> of the red-brick building
>
> at the foot of Green Street—
>
> that's where we live, you know, on the top floor.
>
> I'm the boy in the white flannel gown
>
> sprawled on this coarse gravel bed
>
> searching the starry sky,
>
> waiting for the world to end.

Then Olsen opened his eyes; the heat and light of euphoria rose inside him,
lifting him up off the pew, and he stood facing the altar with a brand new
epiphany: **That is not my story anymore.**

It doesn't matter what happened before, Ben had said—long ago, rising up
from Olsen's memory—*and it doesn't matter what happens later. God gave us
free will. Whatever happens, you don't have to fight it—you can just keep writing
your own story, your own way, no matter what's going on around you. And it's
never too late; you just make your life exactly what you want it to be, starting
today. Like my mom says—Begin; the rest is easy.*

Olsen had said, *I don't think it's that simple.*

It's whatever you want it to be, Ben had told him, *and now that I know that,
everything is different.*

The euphoria numbed Olsen's feet so that he couldn't feel the floor, and it
was not the false euphoria of frostbite, with pieces of himself about to break off
and fall to the ground: it was the real thing. Despair hit him, too: despair for
the old stories that died hard, and years he let slip through his fingers, and
words he had waited too long to say; despair for the amber eyes and out-

stretched arms he still did not understand; and for Mary's declaration of independence and lost hope.

This time, though, her parting benediction was not sprinkled with the invisible dust of her footsteps, but sealed with the blazing fusion of a kiss. Forever and ever, Amen.

Forget the former things, don't dwell on the past…See, I am doing a new thing…Do not fear, only believe…Hell is when no one believes.

❦   ❦   ❦

Olsen didn't know how much time had gone by when he felt his feet again. He turned and walked up the aisle toward the sanctuary doors, saw someone standing in the shadows there.

"Tom?"

It was Ben.

Ben…My boy…Did you know that without you, I was only waiting for the world to end?

Ben stepped out of the shadows toward Olsen. "I've been looking for you. Everything okay?"

Long past too late?

Too soon to be certain

All the old if-onlys faded away?

Maybe so

But let them go

Meanwhile the world goes on.

"Hey," Olsen said, "let's go get a breath of that sweet Indian River night." Then he and Ben wrapped their arms around each other's shoulders and went outside together under the starry sky.

0-595-32917-9

Printed in the United States
30220LVS00004B/259-294